TREACHEROUS TRUTHS

SUNCREST BAY SERIES BOOK TWO

KAY RILEY

For my readers.
You are my biggest motivation to keep writing.
I appreciate you all so much!

Copyright © 2021 Kay Riley

All rights reserved. No part of this book may be reproduced in any form or by any electronic or mechanical means, including information storage and retrieval systems, without permission in writing from the publisher, except by reviewers, who may quote brief passages in a review.

Names, characters, businesses, places, events, locales, and incidents are either the products of the author's imagination or used in a fictitious manner. And any resemblance to actual persons, living or dead, businesses, companies, locales, or actual events is purely coincidental.

Designations used by companies to distinguish their products are often claimed as trademarks. All brand names and product names used in this book and on its cover are trade names, service marks, trademarks and registered trademarks of their respective owners. The publishers and the book are not associated with any product or vendor mentioned in this book. None of the companies referenced within the book have endorsed the book.

ISBN: 978-1-7375674-2-4 [ebook]
978-1-7375674-3-1 [paperback]

Cover Design by: Y'All That Graphic
Edited by: Editing by Gray
Proofread by: VB Proofreads

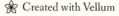 Created with Vellum

NOTE TO READERS

This is the second book in the Suncrest Bay Series and ends in a cliffhanger. Book one, Fateful Secrets, must be read first. It is an enemies-to-lovers, contemporary dark romance. Content Warnings include graphic violence, foul language, sexual scenes, and a possessive anti-hero. Suitable for readers 18+

PROLOGUE

13 Years Old.
Vanessa

"I think I should just wait here," Ky muttered as we turned the corner to my street.

"My parents are gone," I assured him, pulling his hand to keep him walking.

"Your dad's car is in the driveway. You know they don't like me."

"He took his motorcycle to work today. Don't worry, he's not home."

I opened the side garage door and stopped short when my dad looked up from his spot next to his bike.

"Uh...hi, Dad." My poorly attempted smile faltered when he saw Ky behind me.

His usually kind eyes turned cold, and a pit formed in my stomach. I didn't understand why he hated Ky so much. My parents never gave him or Zak a chance.

"Vanessa. I thought you were hanging out with Kenzi," my dad said, his eyes staying on Ky.

"We ran into Ky, and I just needed to come home and

grab my money for the movies. I forgot it," I explained in a small voice. I hated lying to my parents, but I did whenever I hung out with Ky and Zak.

"I think you can go to the movies another time. Tell your friend goodbye."

I glanced over my shoulder at Ky, who stood there rigidly. Without a word, he spun around and left the garage.

"I thought you had to work late today," I mumbled, taking a seat on the steps that led into the house.

"Is this what you do when we're at work? Hang out with the one person we forbid?" he asked, raising an eyebrow.

"Dad," I whined. "He's a good person. And a good friend. I wish you and Mom would just give him a chance. I don't understand why you don't like him."

He sighed and ran a hand through his wavy, light brown hair. His hazel eyes caught my brown ones before he turned back to his bike.

"Before I met your mother, I used to have a lot of good friends like that too."

I looked at him, confused, while he stuck his hand into the engine, trying to unscrew something.

"You're saying you don't—what? Hang out with friends you had as a kid?" I asked uncertainly.

"Some friends might seem like they are the best in the world. Until things change, and you realize they were only looking after themselves."

"Ky would never do that," I argued, immediately jumping to his defense.

He chuckled. "You think that now. Boys can't be trusted."

"You trust Mack."

"He's different."

"Why? Because you know him? If you'd give Ky a chance—"

"No," he said sharply and then gentled his tone. "Vanessa, your mom and I want what's best for you. Kyro isn't. Just trust me, okay?"

I nodded, lying once again. I didn't believe him because Ky was my best friend and was always here for me. He would never let me down.

"When I got older, I found friends that were like family," he said softly. "We were like a club. I'm still friends with them, and we have each other's backs for anything. Find friends like that, Vanessa. Like Kenzi."

"I already have friends like that," I muttered under my breath.

"Now, come on. Help me fix Stella up," he said, standing and leaning against the metal shelves. He grabbed a rag from his back pocket and wiped the grease off his hands.

"Stella?" I asked, giggling. "Why'd you name your motorcycle?"

He winked. "Don't tell your mom, but she was my first love."

CHAPTER ONE

Kyro

Opening the door to my father's study, I walked in with every muscle in my body on edge. It had only been a few hours since I failed to get Vanessa from the Crows. Well, that's what he thought. Keeping her there was better than her being here and dealing with Jensen.

Jensen sat at his desk, massaging his temples. He glanced up as the door clicked shut behind me, and I sat in the seat across from him.

"I changed my mind," he said thoughtfully, before taking a sip of bourbon.

"About what?"

"Staying away from Vanessa. I want you to get close to her after we get her back from the Crows."

My eyebrows raised in surprise. "Why?"

"Because she's going to try to find out who her dad was," he spat out with open disdain. "And I don't want that to fucking happen. I want her to stay in the dark."

I sighed. "If she stays in this town, she's going to find

out. Mack might even have told her already. And I don't see what the big deal is—"

"No one in the Crows will tell her," he cut in sharply. "I think that's one thing we actually agree on."

"Why the fuck is it so important for her not to know?" The venom in my voice was unmistakable, and I cleared my throat, trying to calm down.

He stared at me for a few moments before answering. "Because if she were to find out, then she'd be a threat to both the Crows and Kings. She's smart. And now she's vengeful. If she realizes where she comes from, she could wreck all we've been building for decades."

I almost laughed. There was no *we*. It was him. And he would do anything to stay on top.

"Before we found her in Detroit, I never questioned your loyalty." His words pierced through my thoughts. "To me or to the Kings. But ever since she's been back, I can't help but wonder if you're doing everything you can to get what we want."

"I am," I snapped. "I kept her here like you wanted. Brought her to the bank. She didn't know anything."

"Then you let her escape. She even took your truck."

"Like you said, she's smart. I can't predict every move she makes."

He stood from his chair, strolled over to the bar, and poured another drink. His calmness was putting me even more on edge. I stayed sitting while he turned to me and leaned against the bar with his fresh glass in hand.

"Get better at predicting her moves. I want you back on her good side. Make nice. Fuck until her pussy's content. I don't care. Do whatever you need so she thinks you're on her side," he ordered in a flat voice. "Let her believe you're helping her find the papers, for her. But I want you to get them first. Then bring them to me without her seeing them. It's not only the bank papers. Everyone knows her dad left her a note explaining everything."

Everyone but her. The only person who deserved to know.

"Fine. Consider it done." The lie flowed out effortlessly. I was finished hiding things from her. If she was going to be stuck in this town, at least she'd know the truth.

Jensen chuckled humorlessly and shook his head. "If only I could take your word for it."

"You can," I said, my voice rising. "I've done everything for you and the Kings. I've never given you a reason to distrust me, *Dad.*"

"She's the fucking reason," he screamed with fury, throwing his glass at the wall. "She was your teenage crush, but somehow even after all this time, she still has you by the balls. I need this done. She will not find out anything about her dad. Because if you tell her, I'll follow through on what I said I'd do years ago."

Anger flared, and I took a deep breath while flexing my fists, staring at the alcohol seeping into the carpet. He didn't have to remind me what the threat was. *Fuck.* I was going to have to do what he wanted. I was a mouse in his goddamn twisted maze called life, and there wasn't a damn thing I could do about it.

"I expect you to keep in touch while you're with her," he continued, ignoring my reaction. "If you run off with her, I'll call our new Italian friends. They'll have more than enough resources to find her."

"I'll get it done," I finally said, trying hard to keep the absolute hatred I had for him out of my voice.

"Good. Start planning. I want her away from the Crows as soon as possible."

Without another word, I stormed from his office and went directly to Zak's truck. Speeding out of the driveway, I turned down the road, not really paying attention to anything except my father's words. I'd been under his thumb my whole life, and it had only gotten worse once Knox was killed. He wanted someone to take over when he was done. But he'd never be done. He lived and breathed for the Kings and would die in this life. Hopefully without dragging us all down with him.

Pulling into the driveway, I let out a groan when I saw a white BMW. I put the truck in reverse but stopped when the door of the BMW opened. Too fucking late to leave now. I got out of the truck right as Mar stepped out of her car.

Attempting to plaster a smile on my face, I walked over to her. Like always, she was dressed like she just left a photo shoot. She smoothed out her black dress and smiled while I gave her a quick kiss on the cheek. Her sweet perfume engulfed me as she pulled me into a hug. I resisted to the urge to pull away and waited until her arms loosened around my neck before I took a step back.

"You need something, Mar?" I kept my tone light and cheerful while hoping she wasn't planning on staying.

Her smile turned into a pout as she crossed her arms. "I thought we were going to spend more time together now that I'm back. I was in New York for a month. Didn't you miss me?"

My gaze traveled from her perfectly curled hair to the red heels she was wearing. She had the body that broke up marriages. Men would fight just to get a taste of her. And she was given to me.

Except when I looked at her, I felt absolutely nothing.

There was nothing beneath the surface with her. No

fire. No fight. Her world consisted of shopping and social lunches. She might live in the criminal world, but she could never survive on her own. Thinking of having to share a life with someone like that made my skin crawl. I loved a challenge. Not someone who bowed to my every word. She might make someone else the perfect wife, but to me, she was a prison sentence.

"I didn't know you wanted to see me more," I finally answered.

She twirled a curl through her fingers. "It would be nice to get to know the man I'm supposed to spend the rest of my life with. I'd rather not marry a stranger."

I swallowed the panic her words caused. I couldn't exactly tell her to fuck off. Not after the hole Jensen dug us into. And people didn't say no to the fucking Italian mafia and live to talk about it.

"Why don't we plan something later this week?" I asked. "There's some King business I need to deal with."

"Business always comes first." She sighed. "Is Ryker's girlfriend still here?"

I stiffened. "No, why?"

"I thought I'd try to make friends with her. I don't know anyone in this city."

I let out a small laugh. "The names you called her last time might make that impossible. She doesn't make friends easily."

Her eyes narrowed a fraction and she frowned. "She seemed to like you. She couldn't stop staring at you when we were at the table."

"She doesn't like me," I muttered. "Pretty sure she hates me right now."

"I know that a marriage like this probably isn't what you had in mind," she said, changing the subject as she crossed her arms. "I've lived my whole life knowing I wasn't going to be able to choose the man I would marry. I think I got lucky with you. You're hot. You seem nice. We could have a nice life together."

I raised my eyebrows. She didn't sound like her usual shallow self. Maybe there were a few thoughts in that head after all.

"You don't even know the kind of man I am."

We'd barely spent time together. Her father had set up some dinners we were forced to attend, and we made small talk each time. The only time we'd kissed or even touched was the other night when Vanessa was here.

Her lips tipped up in a tight smile. "I only want two things from you. A credit card where I don't have to worry about the limit. And whenever you're feeling the need to fuck, you come to me. Not any other woman."

I cleared my throat, hiding the shock from hearing her cuss. It fell from her lips easily but didn't match her bubbly voice. Seeing the look on my face, she giggled and patted me on the arm.

"I grew up with three brothers, I know how to swear," she said as her smile faded. "But I was serious. I know the men in this life always have a piece on the side. But with me, you don't need one. I'll give you whatever you want, Kyro."

I nodded, not trusting myself to speak. I didn't want her. And I sure as hell couldn't promise not to touch another woman. If I had any chance of touching Vanessa, it was going to fucking happen. Shit, my mouth would be on hers before my brain even caught up.

Mar opened her car door. "Get it all out before we get married. I know I am."

A laugh escaped me as she got into her car. "I don't

think your dad would be too happy about either of us doing that."

She shrugged. "Then be sneaky about it, like I am. Because once we're married, it'll only be us."

"Bye, Mar," I said, putting my hand on the door to close it. I was ready to be done with this fucking conversation.

"I'm going to my dad's beach house for the next few days. When I get back, let's make time to talk."

I nodded before closing her door and stepping back, watching her leave the driveway. Running my hands down my face, I strode to the front door. Everything was completely fucked right now. And it was getting harder to see a way out of it. I opened the door and went inside, seeing Ryker laying on the couch, watching a game on the projector, while Zak was standing in a towel behind the couch. He was lathering lotion all over himself. He caught my eye and groaned.

"I've showered five fucking times and I can't get the smell of sewer off me," he grumbled, sticking his hand back in the tub of lotion.

"It's gone," Ryker said, with his eyes glued to the TV. "You made me smell you. Twice."

"Ugh, maybe it's stuck in my nose." Zak tossed the lotion bottle on the couch. "I'm taking another shower. What did your dad want?"

I leaned against the door, explained everything Jensen had said, and watched both their mouths drop in shock.

Zak cleared his throat before speaking. "But you told her you never wanted to see her again only six hours ago."

"I know."

"She's going to run the second she gets the chance."

"Yeah."

"I bet she fucking hates you for leaving her there."

"I know."

"You wrecked her twice now—"

"Fuck Zak," I snapped. "*I know.*"

He scratched his arm and then paused, smelling his hand before looking back at me. "I'm just pointing out that there is more of a chance of Mack helping us than her helping. You saw how she acted because of what we did seven years ago. Now, she's met Mar. And you left her with the Crows. And stomped on her heart. I know you didn't mean it, but she believed your speech."

"We'll figure it out," I replied with a confidence I didn't have. Zak was right. The next time I saw Vanessa, she'd either be broken or murderous. And she didn't break, so I expected the latter.

"How are we going to get her away from the Crows?" Ryker asked.

"She'll get away herself. Finding her after is going to be the issue. I want all the vehicles she might take chipped with a GPS tracker. Her and Kenzi's bikes and Teddy's car," I said, sitting on the couch. "Jensen already has people at the bank and her old house."

"You're that sure she's going to get away from Mack?" Ryker asked with a shake of his head. "They have her under lock and key."

"She got away from both of you," I pointed out with a ghost of a smile. "All it took was some ketchup and water."

"Man, it looked like blood," Zak defended himself.

"Because you never see blood in this life," I said sarcastically.

Ryker rubbed his neck sheepishly. "She acted it out perfectly. You would've believed her too, if you were there."

I shook my head but didn't answer. No, I wouldn't have fallen for it. Which was why she waited until I was out of the damn truck to do it. I knew her too well for that. Another reason I was wary of this plan working. She knew me just as well, and lying to her was bound to end badly. But Jensen didn't bluff, and right now, I couldn't afford to chance it.

"I'm just saying when she's back with us, we better make sure she doesn't have a phone," Zak muttered while walking toward the bathroom. "I really don't want to go to prison again."

I scoffed. She wouldn't do that. She'd think of something worse. Her desire for revenge had only intensified over the last seven years, and right now it was all aimed at me.

CHAPTER TWO

Vanessa

I didn't move an inch when the dead bolt creaked, signaling someone was opening my door. I stayed on my back on the cot and continued to stare at the white ceiling.

"Finally done fighting?" Mack asked from the doorway.

I lifted my head to glance at him. "Isn't that what you wanted?"

With his arms crossed, he leaned against the door frame and chuckled. "I thought it would take longer than three days."

"Yeah, well I want a shower."

"I want you to find the damn paperwork," he snapped.

I sat up and swung my legs over the side of the cot before putting my elbows on my knees and resting my face in my palms.

"I think you're lying about us getting married tomorrow," I stated in a bored voice.

"And why is that?"

"Because unless something changed in the past three weeks, we need to sign the marriage license, and doesn't that take a few days to get?" The smugness in my tone was undeniable.

He smirked and my heart dipped. I should have known they had something else planned.

"In Vegas, we can get married the same day. We're flying out there tomorrow evening."

Fuck that.

I kept my face in my hands while trashing the idea of trying to escape during the wedding ceremony.

"I don't know what else you want me to do," I said, with defeat clinging to every word. "You already took me to my house. I'm sure you already checked out the church—"

"Wait. What church?"

Standing up, I turned and faced him. "You know. The church we went to every Sunday morning? My parents were very good friends with the pastor. They were always meeting with him after the service."

"So?"

I threw my head back and laughed cynically. "God. For someone who wants this paperwork so bad, you really didn't do your homework."

Fingers suddenly gripped my chin and pulled until I was looking at him. "Don't fucking mess with me. Why is the church important?"

"Because my dad would leave stuff there."

"What kind of stuff?"

"Just stuff."

His fingers dug into my cheeks. "Stop talking in circles and spit it out."

"Kenzi and I were skipping the service one day and hanging out in the basement when my dad and the pastor came down the stairs." Ripping my face away, I rubbed my jaw and continued, "We hid and followed them through the basement where Dad put the papers in a cabinet."

"How long ago was this?"

"I don't know. I was either fifteen or sixteen."

He grinned and backed up to the door. "Thanks, Vanessa."

"Whatever. Was that enough to earn a shower?" I asked coldly.

"Sure."

"Actually, can I go to one of the other bathrooms where there's a jetted tub? I'm sure there has to be at least one in this house. You'll be gone long enough for me to enjoy one."

He turned back around. "Why would I be gone long?"

"That basement is filled with cabinets and files. It's going to take you forever to go through them all."

"I'll ask the pastor," he said dismissively with a wave of his hand.

"He died. Right before I left town," I informed him with a shrug.

"Fuck," Mack huffed out, rubbing his face. "Do you know where they put the paperwork?"

"I do. I could try and draw you a map or something—"

"No. You'll just come with us. We'll leave after your shower," he said. "We need to get it done fast. I have other plans tonight."

"Nope, I'm good."

"No?"

"Listen, I'm sure you can find it on your own." I sauntered over to him and patted his arm. "You're a smart guy. You don't need me. I just want to take a nice long bath—"

"You're coming."

I raised my wrists to his face. "These are still cut to shit, and I don't feel like having the cuffs back on."

He grabbed my right wrist, and a sharp breath escaped me. I locked my muscles, waiting for him to pull my arm, but he didn't move.

"It doesn't matter what you want," he said gruffly, pushing my hands out of his face. "Hurry and take a shower, then we're leaving."

He strode out of the room, leaving the door open.

"I need some clean clothes," I called after him. "I'm a medium."

Danny, who had been in the hall the whole time, led me to the bathroom. As soon as I locked the door behind me, a grin spread over my face. Mack Brooks thought he was smart, but I just played him like a fucking fiddle.

Every word of the church story was bullshit, but it was good enough for me to leave this house.

I sat in the back seat of the SUV and tugged down on the shorts that barely covered my ass. Instead of getting me some sweats like I expected, Mack got me a pair of daisy duke shorts and a tight crop top, along with a thong and a red, lace bra. The pocketknife and my license barely fit, but I managed, and the bobby pin was in my pocket.

I glanced irritably at him. "I can't believe you want me to wear this to go into a church."

"You look fucking hot," he said with a heated smirk. "And it's even better because I know just what you're wearing under the clothes."

I scowled, scooting as far away from him as possible. "Imagine all you want. You'll never see it."

"We're about to get married." He leaned closer to me. "I'm sure I'll see you in a lot less."

I shoved him away. "Fucking try and see what happens."

He chuckled as Danny parked on the side of the street. He pulled out the damn handcuffs and reached for my arm, and I jerked my hand back.

"You think no one is going to notice a girl in cuffs? Especially in these clothes?" I asked snidely. "Plus, my wrists are still fucking raw."

"Even with the threat of Kenzi, I still don't trust you," he snapped, roughly grabbing me and snapping the metal around my wrists. "You'll put this over your hands when we leave the car."

He threw a large hoodie at me and reached over, adjusting it over my arms, being careful to hide the handcuffs completely. Danny opened the door and helped me out, and I glanced around. It was Sunday, and the street was busy. He had to park almost a block away from the church, which was perfect.

With me sandwiched between Mack and Danny, we started walking down the sidewalk. Mack causally wrapped his arm around my waist, and I resisted the urge to pull away. At least not yet.

Halfway down the street, we came to a park bustling with people. Kids played on the playground, and groups of moms were on the side chatting. Men surrounded the grills, laughing with each other. The smell of cooking hot dogs filled the air, mixing with the cigarette smoke that was coming from Danny's clothes. I slowed down and Mack looked at me suspiciously.

"Let's go," he warned quietly, pushing me forward slightly.

"I am," I replied casually. "I'm just enjoying the fresh air. Seeing people do normal things. I almost forgot what that's like."

"Your life was never normal."

"You're right. Normal is boring anyway."

His arm around my waist tightened, and he tried to hurry me up. He was smarter than I gave him credit for. I hadn't done anything yet, but he sensed something.

"I hope you enjoyed the view of my ass in these shorts," I mumbled. "You won't see it again."

"Whatever the fuck you're about to do—don't. Unless you want Kenzi to pay for your mistakes," he growled under his breath, his eyes darting around the crowd surrounding us.

"Next time use a threat you can actually carry out," I sneered. "You have no idea where Kenzi is. Which means you have nothing to keep me compliant. So, Mack. Fuck you."

Panic swept over his face before he clenched his teeth. It was the look I needed to make sure he really couldn't touch her. With a smirk, I stopped dead in my tracks.

The ear-piercing scream that ripped through me made us the center of attention. Pulling away from Mack, I screamed again.

"Help me!" I shrieked, shaking the hoodie off my arms. "He's trying to take me."

"Fucking Christ," Mack muttered, trying to pull me back to him.

The women were closest, and they came down on us like vultures. They started hitting Mack and Danny with whatever was in their hands. Diaper bags, juice cups, an umbrella. All of it came down the guys' heads.

"Stop—" Mack attempted to say but was cut off when a woman swung her purse at his face.

His arm left my waist and he tried dodging the items flying at him. Danny was already retreating, trying to get back to the car. A woman grabbed my arm and pulled me away. I gritted my teeth when the cuffs pulled against my skin but kept moving. By now, the men had jumped in, and punches were getting thrown.

I ducked and twisted until I was on the outside of the frenzied crowd while Mack and Danny were still somewhere in the middle of it all.

"Are you all right?" the woman asked. Her blonde hair was a mess from trying to get through the crowd with me. She was still holding my arm and I gently pulled away.

"Yes. Thank you so much," I said in a small voice. "I thought they were going to kidnap me."

She glanced at the cuffs in sympathy. "They almost did."

Yelling pierced the air, and I looked back to see Mack fighting his way out of the grip of two men. Danny came up behind him and hit one of them in the face. It reminded me of a mosh pit at a concert. My stomach dropped, seeing them. I needed to get out of here in case they did manage to get free.

"I feel..." I waved my hands in front of my face. "Oh my god, I think I might pass out. Do you have any water?"

The woman nodded. "Right over there on the bench. Sit down, I'll be right back."

The second she turned around, I bolted. Without a backward glance, I ran through the park and behind the church. Leaning my back against the rough bricks, I reached into my pocket and pulled out the bobby pin. In record time, my wrists were free, and I tossed the cuffs on the ground. I was seriously becoming a pro at that.

Peeking around the corner, I saw the woman searching for me. Mack and Danny were nowhere to be seen. I turned back around and glanced down the street. Everyone's attention was still on the crowd. A bounce was in my step as I moved down the sidewalk. I was free.

I started running with a smile on my face. It faded slowly when Ky's last words entered my mind. He expected me to leave town. I didn't blame him for hating me, but there was no way I was leaving. My heart panged thinking about seeing him again. I would just have to make sure that didn't happen. He was a distraction. One I couldn't afford.

My running became a walk when two police cars came screeching down the street with their sirens blaring. Keeping my head down, I turned the corner and sped back up. Teddy's house was only a block away, and I needed something to drive. Kenzi's dirt bike should work. It was still in his shed, and the keys hung in the kitchen.

The house came into view and my moves became sluggish. Going into that house was the last thing I wanted. Regret ate at me while I walked to the back of the house where Kenzi's window was. It was my fault Teddy was killed. I gripped the ledge of the window frame and squeezed until my hands hurt.

Maybe it would be smarter to just leave. I looked up and stared at the clouds, knowing it wasn't possible. I needed to know what my parents were hiding. Even if they were keeping secrets, I still wanted to find out who killed them and why. If I left now, I would never be at peace.

I lifted the window and slid inside, landing on the floor. It was eerily silent. Going straight to the dresser, I pulled out a pair of yoga pants that Kenzi left me days ago. So much had changed in such a short amount of time. I tried not to think about everything while taking off the shorts and sliding on the yoga pants.

I threw on a hoodie over the small crop top and then went to the closet. Kenzi's helmet sat on the floor, and I grabbed it before pulling out a blue backpack. I stuffed the shorts in there and another T-shirt and then left the room. My footsteps seemed deafening while I walked through the hallway. I prepared myself for the living room, not knowing what I was going to walk into.

But it was empty. The broken table was gone, and only a small red stain near the door remained. Tears snuck down my cheeks before I realized it. All I could think about was how heartbroken Kenzi must be. Finding her was important, but first, I needed to get out of Suncrest for a bit.

With a deep breath, I crossed the living room and went into the kitchen. I grabbed the shed and bike keys before climbing back out the window. Glancing around to make sure no one was around, I jogged to the shed and unlocked the door.

Dust covered the dirt bike, and I put the key in and twisted before kickstarting it. The engine roared to life on the first try. I put on the helmet and snapped the visor down. After pushing the bike out of the shed, I closed the door and locked it back up.

Climbing on the bike, I took off the second my ass hit the seat. A rush filled me, and my stress melted away as I cruised down the street.

CHAPTER THREE

Vanessa

I rode all the way to Cornwell and went up and down the streets in the business area until I found what I was looking for. There was one spot left on the street to park, and I took off my helmet and shook out my hair.

Glancing at the building in front of me, relief filled me. A branch of my credit union. Good thing I didn't go with a local bank in Michigan all those years ago. I walked through the doors, taking my license out of the front pouch of the backpack while getting in line for the tellers.

"Next, please."

I walked up the older woman and smiled politely. She looked back with a small frown. Her brown hair was pulled back in a strict bun, and her black pointed glasses fit her stern attire.

"Hello. I lost my debit card and I need to withdraw some money," I said, handing her my license.

She looked at it before glancing back at me. "Ms. Becca James. Far from Michigan, aren't you?"

"Yeah. On vacation."

"Do you have your account number?"

"No, but I have my email and other information for the account. I lost my phone, so I can't exactly look it up," I answered with a hint of aggravation.

She typed in all my information as I rattled it off to her, and it must have satisfied her because she finally gave me a tiny smile. "How much would you like to withdraw?"

"One thousand, please."

She nodded and started taking money out of her drawer. She counted it all three times and counted it to me. Then handed me a receipt.

"Here you go. And your remaining balance is right there." She pointed to the top of the receipt. "Have a good day."

"Thank you. You too," I replied, turning away and glancing at the paper.

I froze for a second before whipping back around. "Excuse me, this can't be right."

She looked at me over the top of her glasses. "It's correct."

I looked back at the number and back at her, not sure what to say. This receipt showed there was over twenty grand in my account. When I left Michigan, I only had a few thousand.

"Listen, I'm sorry. But this amount isn't right." I put the receipt back on her counter. "Can you please check again?"

"Yes," she answered curtly.

Her fingers typed away on the computer for a couple of minutes before looking back at me.

"It's the correct amount. Your joint account owner has been making regular deposits—"

"My what?" I screeched so loudly my voice echoed

through the bank. I took a deep breath and tried to say the next thing more calmly. "I don't have a joint account. I have a single account with me. Just me."

She looked at her screen again. "No, another person was added a couple of weeks ago—"

"I want them off the account. Right now," I snapped. "Who is it?"

"I'm sorry. You don't have the authority to take him off the account. He's primary owner—"

"I've had this account for years," I cut her off, my voice getting higher with every word.

"Is there a problem here?"

I spun around to see a short, stout man in an ill-fitting suit. His gray hair crowned the bald top of his head.

"There sure as hell is." I grabbed the receipt from the counter and handed it to him. "My balance is wrong, and I do not have someone else on this account with me."

He looked at the receipt and his face paled. "Ms. James, please join me in my office. We can talk about it there."

I gritted my teeth as I followed him into his small office. His desk was cluttered with papers, and there were five dirty coffee cups sprawled near his computer. I sat down stiffly in the chair across from him and folded my arms.

"Why is there someone else listed on my account?"

He cleared his throat. "He's been making sizable deposits—"

"I don't care. Who is it?" I asked sharply. I was pissed. Here I was, sitting in the dark again. And this time it was with my own money.

"Mr. Banes thought it was in your best interest—"

"What?" I jumped from the chair and leaned over the desk. "Which one was it?"

"Excuse me?" he asked, his voice shaking slightly.

"Mr. Banes." I spat the name out. "Was he older with black hair? With the devil in his eyes. Or was it the younger one? The one who looks like a Greek fucking god but has the heart of a monster? He also goes by the name Dumbass."

"Uhh," the manager stammered out and reached up to wipe sweat from his brow.

Then I saw it. The Rolex on his wrist. My eyes darted around the room. Nothing else in here had anything of value besides that watch. Understanding dawned, and I slumped back in my seat.

"They either blackmailed or bribed you," I said quietly. "Or both."

His mouth dropped open and fear ran rampant on his face.

"Who was it?" My voice was stone cold. I felt bad that this guy got dragged into it, but I wanted answers.

"Mr. Kyro put himself on the account three weeks ago," he finally said.

Right after they took me from Detroit.

My nails dug into my palms while this information sank in. Why the hell did he do it? To hide his money? I had no idea.

"Can you take him off my account?" I asked tightly.

He shook his head. "No, I'm sorry. He said they'd be watching."

"Of course he did," I muttered.

"Ms. James," he said it so low, I had to lean in to hear him. "He gets emails whenever there's a withdrawal."

My body locked up. *Shit.* Who knew how long of a head start I had. I had his money. And if he thought I was using it, he'd find me. I leaped from the seat and bolted to the door. Without another word to the manager, I fled the bank and got back on the bike.

I needed to go south. To the city where I knew people could help me find my dad's motorcycle. Good thing I'd already met one of them before. I didn't know his name, but it would be easy enough to find out.

Hopefully.

It took less than two hours to get to Brown City. The last time I was here was when Skull tried attacking me and he ended up dead. Hard to believe that was only a few weeks ago. This city was decently large, about the same size as Suncrest Bay. After stopping at a local restaurant and chatting it up with the bartender, I found out where the bikers hang out.

I was parked across from Rob's Bar. The building was large with a wooden porch wrapped around the dark grayish brick building. Most of the bricks were covered with dirt, and it looked like half the wood on the porch was rotting. Windows lined the front, but the panes were painted black, making it impossible to see inside.

Around ten motorcycles were parked in front, along with a couple of cars. It would probably get busier later. I watched from across the street as two women entered the bar in clothes that made those shorts Mack bought look modest. I glanced down at my overlarge hoodie and yoga pants, letting out a groan. If I walked in there like this, I'd look out of place.

I started the bike back up and went down to the Walmart a mile away. Hurrying through the store, I threw the things I needed into the basket. Eyeliner, some chunky bracelets, a pair of black ankle boots, and whole pack of bobby pins. I paid and left, going to my next destination.

The small run-down motel I chose was only a couple of blocks from the bar. It was the closest one around where I could pay the guy at the front desk a little extra and he didn't ask for a credit card. Heaving out a sigh, I walked to my room. I wished I had pulled out more money from the bank. I didn't want to go back there now knowing Ky could see how much I was taking out.

I unlocked the door, shoved it open, and flung my backpack on the floor before locking the door behind me. The room was small and surprisingly clean for how little it cost. The dark blue carpet was worn, and the curtains were stained, but the white comforter and sheets looked clean. A long dresser held a tiny ancient box TV with bunny ear antennas.

Going to the mirror near the window, I put on the eyeliner, much thicker and darker than usual. I pulled the shorts out of the backpack and slid them on before pulling the hoodie off. Examining my reflection in the mirror, I smiled. Now I was ready to go into a biker bar.

The bra Mack bought me made sure my chest would be the focal point for any man who looked at me. The small black crop top dipped so low I was almost worried about bending over. The bracelets I got covered up the cuts on my wrists. I slid on the boots and shoved the hotel key, a couple bobby pins, and some cash into my pocket before walking out the door.

The sun was just starting to set, and a chill was in the air. I hesitated before getting on the bike. I didn't want attention on myself when I showed up to the bar, and coming on a bike would do that, especially dressed like this. Not to mention, wearing shorts was just asking to get a burn from the pipes. But I needed a quick way to escape if things went south. I hopped on and rode the two blocks back to the bar.

The place was packed. There were three long rows of motorcycles parked out front, and cars took up most of the lot on the side. Men and women were sitting on the porch railing, smoking and having a good time. Most of the men had MC leather cuts on, and for the first time all day, nerves jittered through me.

I hated going into something without a plan. But I didn't know the president's name or where their clubhouse was. Only that he was with the Dusty Devils. And he was nice to me even when I had a gun on him. All the motorcycle clubs knew each other. If anyone knew where my dad's bike was, this was the place to start.

I parked my bike far into the parking lot with the other cars and ran a hand through my hair a few times. Already, a few curious stares pointed my way. I raised my chin and sauntered to the front door as if I belonged here. Ignoring the looks I was getting, I pushed open the door and walked inside.

The music was loud, and the room was hazy from smoke. Weed, cigarettes, cigars—the smell overpowered everything else. Empty peanut shells littered the floor, and all the tables were littered with empty beer bottles. Two pool tables were off to the side, and there was a small dance floor opposite of those. Straight back was the bar, and two older women were behind it, working overtime to fill all the drink requests.

I usually liked places like this because they were always the most fun. But not tonight. Not when I was alone and didn't know another soul in here. In a city where I didn't know who was a foe or a friend. I zeroed in on a guy playing pool. His leather cut was what I was looking for. Dusty

Devils. Although I was sure he was only a prospect from the lack of anything on his vest. Still better than nothing.

I quickly went to the bar and ordered my usual cranberry vodka before heading to the pool table.

"Anyone have next game?" I asked, flashing a smile.

He turned, and his eyes lit up as he gazed from my face to my body. He looked a little younger than me, with light green eyes and brown hair that was almost as long as Mack's. Small tattoos were scattered on his arms, and he wore dark blue jeans and a black T-shirt under his cut.

"Absolutely not," he said with a wink. "Actually, we can play right now. My friend sucks at pool anyway."

The other guy grumbled and walked away while I bit my lip and giggled. "Thanks. I'm Becca."

No way I was using my real name. The Dusty Devils did deals with the Crows, and I wasn't chancing anything.

"I'm Tim." He walked around the table and started racking the balls. "I'm a regular here and never seen you before."

I took a deep breath. I was going to make nice with him, but I was tired and didn't feel like having every man in here looking down my shirt while I played a game of pool.

"Yeah, I'm looking for someone." I leaned next to him and placed my lips next to his ear. "Your president. He helped me out a couple weeks ago, and I wanted to thank him. Is he here tonight?"

Tim stiffened and pulled away from me, suspicion all over his face. "If you're here to cause trouble—"

"I'm not," I promised in a hurry. "I really just want to say thank you. In person."

He hesitated before answering. "He's not here tonight."

"Maybe you could take me to your clubhouse—"

"Hell no," he snapped. "Listen, I don't know who you

are, but you can't just come barging in here asking questions like that."

"I'm sorry—"

"I gotta go." He pretty much ran away before I could get another word out.

"Shit." I took the straw out of my drink and downed it.

I should have played the damn game of pool and let him think we were going to fuck.

I walked over to the bar and sank onto a stool while asking for another drink. No point in leaving now. I had nowhere else to go. Maybe another club member would talk to me. I slowly sipped the second drink and watched people dance before someone sat down next to me.

"I just talked to Don," Tim said, leaning his arm on the bar. "He said he doesn't know anyone named Becca."

Don? My confusion cleared instantly when I realized it was the president's name. I smiled and took another sip before answering.

"Next time you call him, tell him it's the girl whose claws are longer than his dick."

Tim's mouth dropped and his face turned beet red. "I—I don't think I want to say that to him."

I patted him on the shoulder. "Trust me. He'll know who I am."

Tim mumbled something under his breath before hopping off the stool and walking outside. I tapped my foot and finished my drink, waiting for him to come back. A few minutes later he came back inside and sat on the same stool.

"Yeah, he remembers you," Tim said. "But Becca wasn't the name you told him."

"I have my reasons."

"He's curious to see what you want. But he's busy until

later tonight. Are you staying around here? I can come pick you up later and bring you to the clubhouse."

I pursed my lips, not really wanting to tell people where I was staying. But I could always move to another motel. Meeting with Don was the whole plan, so I'd take it.

"Sure," I said, rattling off the motel name and room number.

He pulled out a joint and grinned. "You look stressed, want to join?"

My smile matched his. "After the three weeks I've had, that sounds fucking amazing."

CHAPTER FOUR

Kyro

Zak burst through the front door and then stopped, putting his hands on his knees. I set my laptop down and stood from the couch while Ryker walked out of the kitchen. We'd been trying to find a way back into Mack's house all fucking day.

"I just talked to Cam, the guy Jensen put on to follow Mack. They followed his car into town and saw Mack and another Crow get out with Vee." He stopped and took a few deep breaths.

"Any day now," I said impatiently. "Where'd they take her?"

Zak held up a finger and blew out a breath. "I just ran all the way back to tell you. Give me a second."

Flexing my hands, I silently counted to five. "Okay time's up."

Zak's lips tipped up into a gleeful grin. "Vee fucked them over. She's gone."

"Does Cam know where she went?"

He shook his head. "He lost her too."

"How long ago?" Ryker asked.

"Maybe a couple hours," Zak answered, walking to the fridge and pulling out a bottle of water. "Cam tried looking for her before facing Jensen."

Of course he did. Going back to my dad empty-handed never ended well. Smiling, I shook my head. I knew she'd get away from them. And she did it even faster than I expected. I almost wanted to just let her go. Not even try to look for her. But I couldn't. My dad would call the Italians and they'd find her within a week.

I ran a hand through my hair. "Ryker, check all the vehicles you put trackers on. I bet she took one of them."

"Don't you want to hear what she did?" Zak asked with a laugh.

I raised an eyebrow. "Probably stabbed one of them. Or both."

"She somehow convinced them to take her to Main Street right after church got out. They were walking past the park." He stopped and paused dramatically until I glared. "And then she started screaming that they were kidnapping her. Cam said it was a madhouse. Mack had baby formula all over him, and the only reason he's not in jail is because Vee disappeared."

"And because his dad has cops in his pocket," Ryker pointed out.

"Well yeah, that too."

Before I could ask Ryker if any of the trackers were moving, my phone went off. I glanced at it and chuckled.

"She was in Cornwell," I said, looking up. "She took money out of her account."

"She's not there now." Ryker stared at his tablet. "She's in Brown City. She took Kenzi's bike."

What the hell was she doing there?

It took us an hour to get to Brown City, and now we were parked next to the bike Vanessa used. An empty bike. Next to a run-down bar.

"What the fuck is she doing here?" I asked, searching for any sign of her.

"I have no idea," Zak answered. "Does she know anyone from the motorcycle clubs around here?"

"Not that I know of." *But her dad sure as hell used to.*

Ryker cleared his throat. "What exactly are we going to tell her once we see her?"

"We need to play this careful. If she finds out we're lying, she'll try to leave. And screw us just as bad as she did Mack. Probably even worse," I said with a sigh.

"No. She'd definitely fuck us over worse." Zak shoved my shoulder. "Especially you."

"Just follow along with the plan we came up with on the way here," I snapped.

"She's going to hate you even more," Ryker muttered.

"I'd rather her hate us and stay alive than find out the truth and end up dead. Or worse." I sat up straighter when the front door of the bar opened and two people walked outside.

The man let the woman walk out first before handing her something. She lit it and smiled at him. I narrowed my eyes. It looked like Vanessa, but that couldn't be her. Her eyes were surrounded by thick eyeliner. She was wearing shorts so short I could almost see her ass. Her shirt just covered her chest, and if she leaned over just a little, she'd be showing everything.

My jaw snapped shut when I saw her rib tattoo. She moved her hair over one shoulder after passing the joint to the guy she was talking to, and he leaned closer as if he couldn't hear her. She looked sexy as fuck. He was fucking dead.

"I know I don't know her as well as you two," Ryker said, and I realized neither of them had seen her yet. "But why don't we tell her about the threat from your dad?"

Zak snorted. "I love Vee like a sister. She's smart and can hold her own. Obviously. But she has a couple flaws—"

"She doesn't trust easily," I cut in gruffly. "And I ruined that even more when I left her with Mack. Anything we tell her now, she'd take it and run to do things on her own. She won't trust us even if we tell her the truth."

Zak nodded. "When she's mad, she acts before she thinks. Example number one, when she called the cops on us and sent us to prison without a second thought. And I'm pretty sure she's even angrier now."

"If she gets that paperwork before us, she'll use it. To destroy the Crows. The Kings. Probably me. She won't stop to listen to reason. And I can't take the chance to try. Word would fly around Suncrest in a heartbeat if she did that," I said darkly. "Jensen would find out I told her."

"Holy shit," Zak said with wide eyes, looking out the window before swinging his gaze at me. "You can't kill him, man. We need to talk to him. You know she came here for a reason."

"If he fucking touches her..." My words drifted off as I watched her walk off the porch and head toward the bike before turning back around and saying a few more things to the guy she was with.

"Go out behind her bike," I ordered. "Stay out of sight until she tries to run."

They both nodded and slipped out of the truck, quietly closing the doors. They were lost in the shadows after a few seconds. I watched as she walked back to her bike and pulled the keys out of her pocket. I quickly jumped out, leaving the truck door open behind me. Only a few feet separated us, and I forced myself to stop staring at her ass while she picked up her helmet.

"This is what you consider running away?" I asked casually, crossing my arms and leaning against the truck.

The helmet fell back onto the bike seat, and she straightened up before slowly turning around. The hatred I expected was there, deep in her eyes, but there was something missing. After threatening her at Mack's, I figured fear would be there like it was when we found her in Detroit. Only there was none.

She twirled the keys around her finger as she glanced around, most likely looking for Zak and Ryker. My arms fell to my sides, and I moved closer to her, my muscles tensing. She was confident, not scared.

"If I remember correctly." She tapped her chin. "You said my time in Suncrest was over." She waved her arm around before settling her piercing gaze back on me. "Does this fucking look like Suncrest to you?"

Fuck. This girl.

She could piss me off and make my dick hard in the same breath. It wasn't just her body that set me off. It was her strength and stubbornness. I would never tire of it, no matter what happened between us.

"We need to talk," I said, taking another step forward. She moved back and I smirked. She might act tough, but she was still smart enough to be wary of me.

"Where's dumb and dumber?" she asked, her eyes darting behind me to the truck.

"Back to the nicknames, huh?"

She shrugged. "Well, you're still a dumbass, so it fits."

"Come on, Vee," Zak said, coming up behind her with Ryker next to him. "Trying to hurt our feelings?"

She looked over her shoulder and gripped her keys tighter. By the time she turned back around, I was right in front of her. Her breath caught when her chest brushed against mine, and she tried moving away, only to knock into her bike. Her usual strawberry scent was masked by weed and cigarettes from being in the bar.

"Back off, Ky." She tried to shove me away, but I didn't budge. "You're the one who said you never wanted to see me again. After leaving me behind. So why the hell are you following me?"

"Things changed."

She raised an eyebrow. "That was fast."

"Get in the truck and we'll talk about it."

A sarcastic laugh left her, and she trailed her hand up my chest. "Not happening."

I grabbed her wrist but let it drop when she flinched. My eyes narrowed at her covered wrists. Grabbing her just under the elbow, I pushed the bracelets up, revealing scabbed over cuts.

"Mack did this?" I asked, anger rising with each word.

She yanked her arm back. "He's just rougher with the handcuffs than you guys are."

I gritted my teeth, watching her readjust the bracelets back over the cuts. Mack was dead before this, but now he was going to suffer first.

"Let's go, Vee," Zak spoke up. "Get in the truck. We'll explain everything."

"Fuck you," she snapped, keeping her eyes on me. "There's nothing to explain. You still want the paperwork, which is why you're here now. I'm guessing your daddy is the one still calling the shots."

I grabbed her upper arm. "It's cute you think you have choice."

Instead of pulling away, she leaned in closer and grabbed a fistful of my shirt. "And it's stupid to think I wouldn't recognize Zak's truck."

Boots kicked up gravel, and I reached behind my back for my gun, only to grab air. *Son of a bitch.* I was so fixated on her, I left it in the damn truck. Two guys came up, surrounding me, and three more appeared behind Zak and Ryker. Their hands were empty of weapons, but I was sure that would change.

"You really need to stop thinking you can get away with anything when you're not in Suncrest." She smiled smugly, and my grip tightened on her arm. "You're lucky I'm using bikers instead of cops this time."

I ignored the guys around us and focused only on her.

"Raindrop." I paused when I saw it. The sliver of pain behind the fortified front of bitterness and sarcasm. It vanished as quickly as it came, but I decided to try to tell the truth—well part of it, instead of lying. I softened my tone. "I'm not mad about what happened with Knox. I want to help you find the paperwork. For you."

I was being honest. I wanted to help her, but for her to stay safe, secrets needed to be kept until I could tell her everything. This was the best way.

Her eyes stayed cold and unreadable. "Whether that's the truth or not, I don't give a shit. You betrayed me so many times I'm losing count. I don't need your help. I'm doing it myself."

Glancing over her shoulder, I saw Zak nudge Ryker and mouth, *I told you so*. I knew this would be her response. Truth be damned. I'd hurt her too much already.

She still had a grip on my shirt, and she pulled me closer until my eyes met hers again.

"If you didn't guess already, I'm not leaving like you want me to," she said defiantly. "I'm getting the money that belongs to me. I'm finding out who the hell my parents were. And there's nothing you, your dad, or anyone else can do about it."

"You're going to start something you may not be able to handle," I warned.

"I guess we'll find out."

She pushed me away, and I took a couple of steps back with my hands raised, nodding to Zak and Ryker to do the same. I could let her think she got the upper hand. For now. Until we weren't surrounded by MC members.

"Thanks guys." She flashed the bikers a large smile before starting her bike and speeding off, sending rocks flying.

Her engine faded as she rode away, and I let out a long breath. That did not go how I wanted. Zak cleared his throat and grinned at the bikers.

"I figure none of you want to tell us why she was here?" he asked.

The guy to my left gave us a hard stare. "You can leave now."

His threat hung in the air, and I laughed coldly. "Whatever she promised you for your help, she isn't going to give you."

The guy to my right stepped up. His curly hair flew in all different directions, and his raggedy button-down shirt was nearly bursting at the seams under his leather cut.

"She didn't promise us anything. But she knows our president, and he wants to make sure she stays safe," he replied, crossing his arms.

My eyes flew to his vest. The Dusty Devils. She didn't know anyone from that MC. *That she remembered, anyway.* Then it clicked, and I let out a short groan. The only time she met their president was when Skull attacked her. I knew he said something to her before he left but didn't know what it was. He must have taken a liking to her just from that short encounter.

"Come on," I grumbled to Zak and Ryker before climbing in the truck. They followed, and once the doors were shut, Zak pulled out and parked across the street.

"Ryker, pull up the tracker and find out where she's going," I said. "We have to catch her while she's alone."

"How the hell does she know bikers?" Zak asked, perplexed.

"Remember the shit show with them the day Skull attacked Raindrop?" My hands closed into fists, remembering how she looked when she tore into that room after she got away from him. "She had a gun on their president, and he laughed. He likes her. And now he's helping her. We need to change that. He can't tell her anything about her dad. Or who she is."

"Shit," Zak replied, rubbing his eyes. "How the hell did she find them so fast?"

I shrugged. "She's determined."

"Got her," Ryker announced, looking up from his tablet. "She just stopped at a motel only a couple blocks from here."

"Drop me off there. Then you two go and talk to Don and convince him to leave Vanessa alone. I don't care what it takes. Give him a deal with the guns that he can't pass up."

They nodded, and Zak put the truck into gear. I looked out the window, thinking about what I was going to say to her. Because whether she liked it or not, she wasn't finding that paperwork without me.

CHAPTER FIVE

Kyro

I SILENTLY MOVED IN FRONT OF ROOM TEN AFTER paying the guy at the front office two hundred dollars for the information. The motel was quiet; she seemed to be one of the only guests staying here. Deciding on the nice approach before slamming through the door, I covered the peephole with one hand and knocked with the other. Light footsteps grew louder by the second until they stopped. There was a long pause before she threw the door open.

The small smile that had been on her face disappeared, and her lips parted in shock at seeing me. I frowned. *Who the hell did she think it was?* She instantly tried pushing the door closed.

"I don't think so, Raindrop." I rammed the door with my shoulder and shoved my way in. She backed away, crossing her arms and glaring while I reached back and swung the door shut. She was still wearing the clothes from the bar, except she'd taken off the boots.

"How the hell do you keep finding me?" she asked, keeping a wide distance between us.

I grinned. "I told you I loved the chase."

She huffed out a breath and brushed hair out of her face. "I don't have a phone to track, or a credit card…"

She trailed off, deep in thought, and I waited, leaning against the wall, knowing it wouldn't take her long to figure it out.

"The bike? How'd you know I'd take that one?"

"I didn't. Everything you could have taken has a GPS tracker in it. Ryker's good at those. There's one in my truck too. That's how we found you at the cemetery."

"Oh my god," she shrieked, throwing her hands up. "You're the one who told me to leave. I left Suncrest. Now leave me alone."

"I can't. And you're not planning to leave anyway."

"What do you want, Ky?"

"I want to help you find the papers."

"So you can give them to Jensen?"

I ran a hand down my face. "What if I made you a deal?"

"I don't trust you enough to do that."

My heart panged, and defeat crawled through me. I was doing all of this for her, but I was pushing her too far. Far enough she might not come back to me.

"Dad knows what you did to Knox." I watched as her face went ashen and she squeezed her left hand into a fist.

I moved closer to her. "Let's find the paperwork and split the money. Keep my dad happy so he doesn't try to kill you, and you'd still have more than enough to leave and disappear."

"No."

"Raindrop—"

"I'm done," she said coldly. "Done playing by everyone else's rules. I'm doing this my way."

"Jensen has a whole gang behind him, and then some. The Crows too. You can't go through all of them yourself."

She opened her mouth to reply but stopped when heavy footsteps trudged down the sidewalk and then stopped right outside her door.

I raised an eyebrow. "Expecting someone?"

"No," she answered, looking me straight in the eye.

"Hmm," I murmured, moving to the door. She was waiting for someone, which was why she didn't hesitate to open the door when I knocked.

"Make it up to me," she said, crossing the room until she was in front of me with a hand on my chest.

"What?"

"For leaving me with Mack. For lying to me for years." She grabbed the back of my neck and pulled until her lips were on my cheek. She whispered, "Make it up to me, and I'll show you how sorry I am for what I did."

She pressed her body flush with mine, and her hand traveled down my stomach until her fingers grazed over my cock, which was already trying to bust out of my pants from her being this close. Lust and shock intertwined, and I stood there with wide eyes until three knocks tapped on the door.

I turned my head to the sound, but she grabbed my cheek, keeping my focus on her.

"Who's that?" I asked, suspicion slamming into me.

"Don't know," she murmured. "No one knows I'm here besides you. Could be housekeeping. Or maybe they got the wrong room number."

It was the tiniest flicker toward the door. The way her voice went up just a notch. She bit the inside of her lip for a fraction of a second before catching herself. If I hadn't been staring so intently or been so close, even I would have missed it. She had always been good at lying, but I could always tell. Now, it was nearly impossible.

She was distracting me. Whoever was at the door, she didn't want me to know.

I pulled away, fully intent on ripping the door open. Until she gripped the front of my shirt, yanked me down, then slammed her lips against mine. On reflex, my hand went to her hair, wrapping my hand around it and tilting her head back.

My other arm went around her back, keeping her pressed against me. She opened her mouth, and I slipped my tongue inside. She tasted like cranberry and vodka, and I decided it was my new favorite drink.

I didn't give a single fuck about anything besides the girl in my arms. The person outside this room, my dad, the Crows, the Italians. Right now, it was only her. It would always be her. I would never stop protecting her no matter what I had to do. Even if she hated me for it.

In the distance, the footsteps retreated and faded, and she tried to pull away, but I gripped the back of her neck and pulled her closer. She bit down on my lip, almost hard enough to draw blood, and I jerked away.

Her eyes were dark with lust, and her chest heaved with every breath. She wanted me as bad as I wanted her, but her anger and distrust were rivaling against it. I understood. Except in this moment, I didn't care. I wanted her.

"You realize you just started something I'm going to finish?" I asked in a low voice, striding forward until she backed into the wall.

She bit her bottom lip and my cock jerked.

"I was only offering a kiss." She tipped up her chin defiantly, and I grabbed it in my fingers, tightening my grip when she tried pulling away.

"A kiss is all you want?" I asked while using my other hand to unbutton her shorts. I pulled the zipper down and sucked in a breath when I caught sight of a lacy red thong.

Releasing her chin, I lowered my head and ran the tip of my nose up her neck, feeling her goosebumps rise.

"Tell me no," I whispered once my lips grazed her ear.

"You're an asshole."

"Tell me to stop."

"You fucking lied."

"Tell me to leave."

"You betrayed me."

"Tell me to let you go."

"Fuck you."

It was all I needed. She wanted me and was just too stubborn to admit it. But she just did in her own way. I reached around and grabbed her ass and lifted, shoving her into the wall. Her legs wrapped around my waist as my mouth claimed hers once again. Her anger poured into the kiss, and I dissolved it with every stroke of my tongue.

She came up for air and pressed her hands into my chest. "This doesn't mean anything. I'm using you. For a release. For an orgasm. After, our problems will still be the same, and I want you gone."

Instead of answering her lies, I let her go, and she stood in front of me. I crouched down and slid the shorts off until they fell to the floor. Rising back up, I grabbed the bottom of her shirt and pulled up until it was off her and on the floor.

"Holy fuck," I breathed out.

She wore a matching red bra and looked absolutely fucking edible. I ripped my shirt off and pressed back into her, feeling her soft skin against my mine. I kissed her neck, and she threw her head back and moaned.

Hearing that diminished my last drop of self-control. I swung her up in my arms before crossing the room and tossing her on the bed as she let out cry of protest. Her eyes met mine, and the mix of defiance and lust had me pulling my boxers off and climbing on top of her before another word was said.

I slipped my hand beneath the panties, my thumb and index finger moving in small circles around her clit. Her hips rolled, trying to match the rhythm of my fingers as I moved faster.

She tensed, and I sped up as her breaths became fast and ragged before her entire body locked up. I pinched her clit and she cried out, coming in an instant. I swirled my fingers, not slowing down until her orgasm faded out.

"Fuck," she moaned in between deep breaths.

I grinned. "We aren't done."

"Hmm. I got what I wanted. You can have fun finishing yourself off."

I chuckled at her words. "Baby, the only place I'll be finishing is in your sweet pussy."

She shoved against my chest, trying to get the upper hand, and I nipped her neck while letting my hand drift to her stomach. Her fingers slid up my neck to my head, and I reached up and grabbed her arm before she could get a grip on my hair. I grabbed her other arm and pushed them both into the mattress next to her head.

I wedged myself between her thighs until my cock grazed her clit. She sucked in a breath, and her struggles to get her arms free were forgotten as she ground against me, her body already begging for another release. I groaned as she rolled her hips, and then I pulled back, realizing I couldn't do this for another second without burying myself inside her.

"Condom," I muttered, releasing her arms.

She suddenly put her weight all on one leg and pushed off, rolling us until she was on top. She gripped my wrists and slammed them down on the bed, just like I had with hers a few minutes ago. I stayed still and raised an eyebrow, wondering where she thought she was taking this.

"How many women have you fucked bare?"

My eyes widened and then narrowed at her question.

"Just you," I answered, the memory of our first time flashing through my mind.

"Same," she said thoughtfully. "I'm on birth control."

What she was implying wasn't lost on me and I grinned, attempting to move my arms, but she shook her head.

"You left me with the Crows and told me we were done." She lowered herself down until my cock rubbed against her entrance, making me release a sharp breath. "But here you are, acting like it didn't fucking happen. Why?"

Words were impossible as she moved back and forth, grinding her pussy against me. My silence had her smirking while she tightened her grip on my wrists, as if she really expected that would help her stay in control.

"Answer me. And then I'll let you fuck me," she purred in my ear before dragging her lips down my neck.

Let me. I almost laughed. She wanted me as much as I did her. I would be inside her before the night was over.

"Everything I've done has been for you. Even leaving you there."

She bit my neck hard enough to leave a mark. "Not good enough."

"How about if I didn't do it, you'd be dead right now."

Her movements stopped, and she lifted her head to look at me as she scrutinized my answer. Our stare off lasted a minute before she spoke again. "Tell me."

I yanked my arms up, easily breaking her grip on me. She gasped in surprise before trying to grab me again, but it was too late. I was already back on top of her with my legs between her thighs, spreading them apart.

"Ky," she hissed, trying unsuccessfully to push me off her.

I grabbed her hair and tilted her head back until she was looking at me.

"It's hot when you try taking control baby," I murmured, feeling her nails digging into my chest. "But it's not happening tonight."

"It's not happening again. Ever. Including tonight, since you can't be honest and give me an answer." The bite in her tone almost made me believe her, until she lifted her hips, and I could feel her arousal through her lace panties.

"We had mics on when we came to get you," I said quietly. "Ryker cut them off, but my dad heard enough to realize you had something to do with Knox's death."

Her breathing turned fast, and fear slid into her gaze. My hand stayed in her hair, but I loosened my grip, knowing she wasn't going anywhere while I spoke.

"He had eyes on us the second we left the Crows' house. If you had walked out that door with us, he would've had you in a heartbeat."

"You could have tried to sneak me out—"

"You're not understanding," I snapped. "He already suspects what I'd do to keep you safe. He might not have killed me, but I can't say the same for Zak and Ryker. They would have been right at my side, trying to keep you safe. His guys wouldn't have let me get near you."

My words thawed the anger that had been burning in her eyes, and her nails dug deeper into my chest as she listened.

"He wouldn't have just killed you. Suffering is my dad's specialty, but you know that. That's why you ran after betraying the Kings."

"Why—"

"You got your answer," I interrupted, lowering myself back on top of her. "We're done talking."

"Ky—"

"Done," I growled, watching her eyes narrow before she tried pulling out of my grip.

"I don't know how the hell you had time to go shopping, but I'm glad you did," I muttered, changing the topic as I stared at her red bra.

She chuckled. "Yeah—no. I bought the bracelets and eyeliner. That's it. You think I'd spend money on this?"

I froze before running my hand down her body until I gripped the thong and then tore it from her body.

"What the hell?" she yelled, looking at the destroyed piece of cloth on the floor.

She rolled me off her and then jumped out of bed with me right behind her. The jealousy that flared in my chest smothered any other emotion.

"Take it off," I ordered, eyeing the bra.

"What?" She crossed her arms, pushing her breasts up even more.

"If you didn't buy it, that means Mack did," I snarled. "Did he see you in this?"

"No," she replied with her eyes blazing. "He bought me clothes, and I wore them because I didn't have anything else."

I advanced on her, ready to strip her bare. "Doesn't matter. He bought it with the intent to see you in it."

"You think I'd let him? He'd be missing a body part if he tried touching me," she seethed.

"Take it off."

Her lips twisted up into a grin. "No. It's mine. And I happen to like it."

She knew what those words would do to me. Mischief danced in her eyes while she waited for me to do something. Excitement I haven't felt in years burned through me, and it all went straight to my cock.

"You want to play?" I asked huskily. "I'm not in the mood to play nice."

"I don't want you to play nice," she bit out.

I stared at her, understanding what she meant. She didn't want it to be romantic. She was angry. She wanted to let it out. On me. And I was perfectly fucking fine with that.

"Last warning. Take it off," I demanded.

"No."

In a couple of seconds, I had her turned away from me, already unclipping the bra. I reached over her and lifted the bra over her head until it was behind her back. I pushed her into the wall, and she tried pushing back, but the straps were still around her arms. She squirmed, attempting to shift it down so it would slide off her.

"Oh no, you had a chance to take it off," I murmured. "Now, it's staying on."

I pulled the bra down until the straps sat between her elbow and wrist and then started twisting it around before tying it off in a knot. It stayed above the cuts on her wrists and was secure enough that it would stay in place.

I chuckled, watching her try to struggle out of it, but the bra stayed put. I spun her around and lowered my mouth to her nipple. She went still and rested her head on the wall. I sucked gently for a second before biting down just hard enough for her to cry out. I used my fingers on her other nipple before switching my mouth to that one too.

The noises she made almost forced me to take her right there, but I needed to savor this. After tonight, I didn't know if she'd ever let me in again. With her nipple still in my mouth, my hand lightly brushed down her stomach until it was between her legs.

She was dripping wet, and I groaned. I dragged a finger through her folds, and the second I hit her clit, she jerked. She was so sensitive from already coming once.

"Touch me," she breathed out, her fight turning into desire.

"Say please."

She met my eyes, and with clenched teeth, she said, "Please."

Fuck. That one word turned me on even more. She didn't give in to anyone. Except me.

I picked her up and flipped her over my shoulder, ignoring the string of curses leaving her mouth. I walked across the room and swept the old TV off the dresser with one arm. It hit the carpet with a thud while I laid her down on her stomach where the TV used to be. I pulled until her legs hung off and her tiptoes just touched the floor.

Her thighs were pressed together, and I slipped my hands in between them, pulling them apart. Even with her arms tied behind her, she tried lifting herself off the dresser. I pressed my palm onto her back, pushing her back down.

I gripped her hip with one hand and grabbed my cock with the other as I guided it to her entrance. She was dripping wet, and I slid inside her with a groan. This was as close to heaven as I was getting. I moved slowly at first, relishing in the pleasure that only she could give me. No one could ever fucking compare to her.

She laid on the dresser as I thrust, and her moans turned into screams as she edged closer to her second orgasm. Her fingers clasped together tightly as her legs began to tremble. Her pussy convulsed, and she screamed my name as she came again, and I couldn't help but grin.

My balls started to tighten, and I slowed, not ready to let her go yet. I pressed up against her ass, staying inside her as she fought to catch her breath. After a couple of seconds, I started moving again. This time I couldn't control myself. Each time I plunged into her was harder and deeper than the last.

I reached up and gripped her hair, and she looked over her shoulder at me.

"You're going to come one more time," I demanded.

Her eyes were glazed over from pleasure, and she only nodded. Letting go of her hair, I gripped her hip again while moving my other hand over her engorged clit. I rubbed it with two fingers, and she writhed in pleasure as I felt my own building.

"Fuck. Oh fuck," she screamed out, coming for a third time.

I was right behind her. My balls tightened and all my muscles tensed as I exploded inside of her. I quickly undid the knot in the bra, letting her arms fall free before I leaned my weight on top of her. My lips grazed her back, and we laid there for a few moments, catching our breath.

She moved first, and I stood back up, letting her turn to face me. I caught her gaze and sighed. Her eyes were frosted with venom and conflicted with the after-sex flush on her cheeks.

"I just needed a release. Fighting would only fuck up

my knuckles more than the door did." She flashed me her cut up knuckles before trailing her fingertips down my chest. "I don't hate you for leaving me with Mack. Not after finding out what I did to Knox."

I gritted my teeth, knowing she was about to set me off.

"But I'm not going back with you." It came out sharp, and truth dripped from every word. "I won't help the Kings. Or the Crows. Jensen obviously wants this money just as bad as he wants me to pay for Knox."

Her hand landed on my cheek, and she gripped my jaw, meeting my gaze. "I won't help you. Because every word out of your mouth is a half-truth."

"What if I said I was doing this all for you?" I asked quietly.

She stiffened. "It wouldn't matter."

"You think I wanted to leave you with Mack?" I growled, sitting up and grabbing the hand she had on my face. "Maybe I had a reason for it."

"Maybe you did," she argued back. "But you didn't share that with me. You left me there with my heart destroyed. Now that you're already back, I believe there was a reason you did it. But like I said, it doesn't matter. I'm doing this by myself. And whatever secrets you're keeping, I'll find those out too."

"You're not going to like what you find out. And if you keep digging, you may not even make it out of Suncrest alive."

We sat there, my hand gripping hers, being the most honest we've been with each other in years.

"I'll survive until I find out why the hell my parents tried selling me into a marriage," she said bitterly.

She jerked her hand out of mine and started walking to the bathroom. Her inner thighs were soaked, and the sight of that made me want to take her again. I watched her curvy ass sway before she stopped and looked over her shoulder.

"Thanks for the fuck." She smirked. "At least if I don't survive, I can enjoy life until then. Be gone when I get out."

I put my arms behind my head and stared at the ceiling. She was going to be pissed, but I wasn't going anywhere.

Leaving was never an option.

CHAPTER SIX

Vanessa

THE WATER FROM THE SHOWERHEAD CAME DOWN AS A light drizzle, and I stood under it, trying to rinse all the shampoo out. I scrubbed my head harder than necessary, thinking about what the hell I'd just done.

It was just sex. No feelings. No attachments. That's how I'd look at it. I kissed him to distract him from Tim being at the door. I didn't want him knowing I was talking to the Dusty Devils. It was only supposed to be a kiss. Apparently, my body had other ideas.

And fuck me, he didn't disappoint.

Ever since we'd had sex in Zak's truck, my pussy had decided to be a traitorous bitch. After everything. After him lying. Or finding out about Mar. He even left me with the fucking Crows, and I was still panting after him like his dick would solve all our problems.

Stepping out of the shower, I dried off, knowing the chance of Ky actually being gone was slim. Gritting my teeth, I ran my fingers through my tangled hair. I didn't have a brush, so this would have to do for now. He needed to be gone so I could go back to the bar and talk to Tim again.

Wrapped in a towel, I opened the bathroom door and scowled when I saw Ky sitting on the bed. His jeans were back on, but he looked way too comfy there after I'd told him to leave. I walked forward, ready to start yelling. But stopped, seeing Zak and Ryker hanging out by the door.

Zak caught my eye and grinned. "Ky said you needed clothes. Good thing we packed a bag before we left Suncrest."

He tossed the duffle bag he was holding, and it landed near my feet. I glanced at Ky, who was watching me with a small grin. I flipped him off before storming back into the bathroom with the bag of clothes. I wasn't going to stay with them, but I wasn't going to turn down having fresh clothes. Slamming the door shut, I unzipped the bag, revealing a pile of my own things. They even had my toothbrush and hairbrush. I rolled my eyes while brushing my hair. If they expected me to just go back with them, the night wasn't going to end well.

I changed into a pair of yoga pants and a T-shirt before zipping the bag back up and hoisting it over my shoulder. I found the guys in the same spot as earlier. Deciding to just take the chance and try to leave without saying a word, I swiped my keys from the small table. I strode to the door, only to have Zak and Ryker step in front of me.

"Come on, Vee," Zak murmured. "At least say hello before leaving."

"No." I tried to shoulder my way past him, failing when he didn't budge.

I dropped the bag from my shoulder and let out an annoyed sigh before turning to Ky, who was watching in amusement.

"Let's skip the whole arguing part." I crossed my arms.

"No arguing from me," Ky replied with a shrug. "We just want to talk first."

"Right," I muttered warily.

"I *can't* tell you about who your dad was," Ky said as he stood up. "Not because I don't want to, but because I can't. Not without you getting hurt."

I laughed bitterly. "Spare me the speech about saving my feelings, Ky. After what I've been through in the last few weeks—"

"He doesn't mean your feelings," Ryker interrupted. "He literally means you physically getting hurt."

My gaze darted from Ryker to Ky as my curiosity heightened. Ky stayed silent, and I sighed.

"If you aren't going to explain, then I'm gone." I turned back to the door, bending down to pick the bag back up.

I didn't hear him move, but I could feel him behind me before he even opened his mouth. The bag was yanked out of my grip, and his hand was on my shoulder, spinning me around until I faced him. His eyes were clouded over with tension and nervousness, and he seemed to debate his words before he spoke.

"Keeping this from you was the hardest thing I've ever had to do," he forced out hoarsely as his hand drifted from my shoulder down to my hip. Even with the conversation turning heavy, my body jolted alive from his touch.

"We didn't have a choice," Zak spoke up from beside me. "We still don't."

"Your parents promised if we told you, they'd move and take you with them," Ky explained, his eyes going hard. "You thought you were being all secretive, sneaking around with me. But they always knew. And they let it happen as long as we kept our mouths shut."

My heart stuttered, and a cold crept through me while listening to their reasons for keeping me in the dark.

"When you found out about the Kings and started helping on jobs, that was nearly the last straw." My eyes stayed on Ky as he spoke. "You have no idea how close it came to you leaving Suncrest."

Zak shook his head. "I'm pretty sure they thought your crush on Ky would end. A teenage fling. But it never stopped. The deeper you got with the Kings, the more they tried pushing you into Mack's arms."

Ky's grip tightened on my hip, and he stepped forward, backing me into the wall. I didn't push him away as I processed their side of the story. Some of the anger melted away, thinking about what they had to go through.

"My choice was to keep it from you or never see you again. But their threat wasn't even the worst one."

"Your dad?" I guessed, knowing I was right when his eyes darkened.

He nodded. "The second he found out about the deal between the Crows and your family, he wanted you gone. I convinced him I was keeping you close to help the Kings."

"He was going to kill you." Zak looked past me as if reliving the memory. "He was only waiting to find out how to get away with it without your parents finding out it was him."

"That was the first time my dad and I fought. I nearly broke his jaw, and he almost put me in the hospital."

Memories flashed though my head, remembering when I was fifteen and Ky disappeared for a week before coming back to school with fading bruises.

Ky continued, "That was when my dad suspected I cared about you more than I'd admit. And I think he got a high knowing you were working with the Kings when it was the last thing your parents wanted. He told me and Zak that if we breathed a word of anything about the Crows or your parents, he'd kill you."

"Not just kill you." Zak's voice rose in anger. "He said he'd pass you around to his friends and make Ky watch before killing you."

I swallowed down nausea from imagining that and had no doubt Jensen would've done it. He was a vile piece of shit.

"It was my idea to send you to prison. You would have been safer there. Or so we thought," Ky muttered. "Looking back, we were young and fucking dumb."

"We almost decided to tell your parents to take you out of Suncrest to get away from Jensen—"

Ky cut Zak off. "But it was too late. We found out about the deal with the Crows and knew even if you left, you wouldn't be free. And...I was a selfish asshole who couldn't let you go. I was convinced I could keep you safe."

I bit the inside of my lip, hearing his confession. What would I have done if I was in his shoes all those years ago? I had no idea. I couldn't blame him for the past. But could I trust him now? I wasn't sure of that either.

"And now?" I asked. "What's stopping you from telling me?"

"Jensen," Zak answered. "He's letting us be the ones to stay with you. He finds out we're not doing what he wants, you won't be dealing with us."

"You'll be dealing with him," Ky scowled.

Fuck that. I wanted to stay as far from Jensen as possible, even more now after hearing his threat. I pulled away from Ky and paced the room. The money wasn't worth it. I should take my chances and leave now. Maybe the bikers would help me.

"It's too late to run now," Ky said from behind me, proving he still always knew what I was thinking. "My dad is in bed with the Italians, and they have too many resources. They'd find you in a day."

I frowned and whirled back around. "And how does your Italian *fiancée* feel about you spending so much time with another girl?"

Guilt spilled into his gaze, and his jaw ticked. "I told you, she doesn't mean anything. You think I had a choice?"

"Are you fucking her?" The question came out before I could even think.

"No," he bit out.

Damn it, his answer made me happier than I cared to admit. I shouldn't care who he had sex with.

"Why?" I crossed my arms. "What's the reason Jensen wants you to marry her?"

Ky took a deep breath. "It wasn't Jensen who wanted it. It was Mar's father, Antonio."

I couldn't contain my surprise. "Why?"

"They said they want to build alliances on the West Coast," Ky answered. "Then they offered money to Jensen, and he fucking took it, even knowing there'd be strings attached."

"Wait, wait." I held a hand up. "You're telling me you're being forced into a marriage?"

"Vee," Zak warned, obviously hearing my voice change.

I laughed. "It's ironic. The same shit you kept a secret from me is happening to you now. How does it feel?"

I kept my voice light, but my insides were pulled tight at the thought of him marrying someone else. It shouldn't bother me. Even after everything, I couldn't stomach the sight of seeing him with anyone. Especially that fucking princess.

Ryker spoke up, reminding me that Ky and I weren't alone. "If she finds out you and Ky...are more than just friends, shit will hit the fan. You might want to be more careful."

"Yeah, find somewhere else to fuck other than my truck," Zak grumbled as he leaned against the wall.

"That won't be a problem." My gaze cut to Ky. "Because it's not happening again."

My heart jumped, realizing those were the wrong words to say when Ky's eyes lit up in challenge. *Nope*. We were done. If I couldn't run, then I needed to stick with my plan to get help from the MCs who knew my dad. I couldn't do that with Ky. Because when I was with him, thinking straight was impossible.

"Now you know." Ky stared at me. "I lied to protect you. I want to help you, Raindrop. Fucking let me."

I hesitated, knowing my words wouldn't go over well. I crept closer to the door, and Ky's eyes tracked my moves, his frown deepening with every step I took.

"Vee." Zak sighed. "We just explained it all. What else do you want?"

"I want you to stop lying," I exploded, yelling louder than I intended. "You know who my dad was, and you still won't tell me. I get it. I do. Jensen is one scary motherfucker. But there are still secrets, and I can't do it anymore. I'm finding them out. On my own."

Zak and Ryker both glanced at Ky, who was staring at me. For once, I couldn't read the look on his face, and unease settled over me. But I stood my ground. I wasn't going to be in the dark anymore.

"If I tell you," Ky said quietly. "Then you can't run off with the truth to go and do it without us."

I nodded, keeping my mouth shut and my eyes on him.

Guilt wrapped my heart and squeezed. I just told him no more lies, and here I was, doing the same damn thing. Ky sighed and moved across the room, stopping only when he was close enough to graze his knuckles under my chin and tilt my head back.

His voice was low, keeping his words between just us. "I need to know you won't leave after I tell you. I'll fucking do anything for you, Raindrop. But I won't help you get yourself killed because you want to do this alone."

My lips formed the lies, and they were out before I'd even thought about it. "I won't leave."

He stared intently for a few moments before he dropped his hand from my chin. "Your dad was in an MC. One of the biggest in the state. If you find them, they're going to want to get involved with Suncrest again. My dad doesn't want that. It would be trouble for the Kings."

His answer deflated me a bit. After knowing about my dad's bike and his club friends, I guessed my dad was part of a motorcycle club. It wasn't a surprise. I expected something bigger.

"Which MC was he in?" I asked.

The seriousness in his eyes evaporated, and he backed away with a grin. I bristled at the sudden change, realizing he wasn't going to answer me.

"Ky," I warned. "You said you'd tell me."

"I did. Part of it. I'll tell you more in a week."

The smugness in his tone was pissing me off, even though I had no right to be mad. I hadn't been honest either. I was out of here the second I got the chance. I guess I could wait a week until I found out the name of the MC. Unless I talked to the Dusty Devils before then.

Ky's words rattled me, and my childhood flashed through my eyes. Raising a questioning glance to the three of them, I decided I wasn't ready to drop the subject quite yet.

"I don't consider myself stupid." I shot Zak a glare when he snorted. "Especially after working with the Kings. I think I would have noticed if my dad was in a motorcycle club doing illegal business."

"His MC..." Ky hesitated as if not sure how much to say. "They did things differently than any other club I know."

"What does that mean?"

Zak spoke up. "They didn't do the dirty stuff, Vee. They had people from other clubs and gangs do that while they sat in their cozy suburban houses. They had serious money. And a silent partner."

"Silent partner," I repeated as Ky shot Zak a glance I knew well. He didn't want Zak saying any more. "Why are you talking like the MC doesn't exist anymore?"

"Because they aren't in Suncrest anymore," Ky snapped. "We don't deal with them."

"Who is their silent partner?"

"Well, if we all knew that, then it wouldn't make them a silent partner," Zak snarked with a laugh.

Ignoring him, I focused on Ky. "Why is this MC so different?"

He shrugged. "They just are. They don't like people in their business. Everything is done out of sight, under the table. They stay on the right side of the law, while others deal with the dark side of it."

I opened my mouth to ask more, but Ky shook his head. "That's it, Raindrop. I'll tell you more in a week."

There was a twinge of guilt stabbing me repeatedly, but it wasn't enough to stop my plan. He was still under his father's thumb. He'd admitted he would do anything to keep me safe, which pulled at my heart way more than it should. But I was past the point of trying to stay safe. There was too much to uncover. I had people to find, like my parents' killer. I needed to repay the Crow who had killed Teddy. And I was going to do whatever the hell I needed to get it all done.

Even if that meant lying to Ky.

CHAPTER SEVEN

Kyro

"You still think she's going to bolt, don't you?" Ryker asked from the back seat.

She kicked us out of her motel room after promising she'd stay put. I told her I trusted her, and she was testing me to see if I'd leave her alone. So, I walked out her door. And my eyes hadn't left that damn door once in the last hour while we sat in the truck across the parking lot. Zak was already passed out, snoring in the driver seat, and Ryker was getting restless.

I rubbed my eyes. "I think she wants answers and it's clouding her judgment."

"Are you really going to tell the rest of it in a week?" he asked curiously.

I stared, watching as her light went out, plunging her room in darkness. I wasn't sure what I was going to do yet. I didn't even tell her the full truth tonight. I shared as much as I could without telling her everything. Because if I did, there was no doubt she'd take it and run.

"I need to go talk to Don before she does," I said. "I called him, and he's meeting me at the bar across the street. Can you watch her room until I get back?"

Ryker shook his head and scoffed. "Isn't the main component of a relationship trust? You and Vee seem to be lacking that."

He was joking, but it still felt like a punch in the gut. There was a time she trusted me more than anyone in the world. And I did still trust her. I trusted her with my life. Did I think she would try to leave the moment she had the chance? Yes, I fucking did. But she was still mine, and that wasn't changing. If we looked at our parents and our childhoods, I thought we had grown up better than expected.

"Go," Ryker said, bringing me back to the present. "I'll watch her."

I nodded, jumping out of the truck and sticking my gun in the back of my jeans before crossing the street. Opening the door to the sports bar, I saw Don already sitting at the bar. Flat screens filled the walls, and men were yelling and laughing at the football game playing. I sat down on the barstool next to him and got the bartender's attention so I could order a beer.

"What's this I hear about you causing trouble at my bar?" Don asked the second the bartender walked away.

"No trouble," I replied. "Just a miscommunication."

He turned slightly and I did the same. He looked pissed as he leaned his tatted arm on the bar.

"I told that girl to come to me if she needs any help. And you're stopping her. Why?" he asked.

I sighed. "We're protecting her. She came from Detroit with some nasty people chasing her. Her best friend is the daughter of the gang boss of Detroit. He's our business partner and asked us to watch her."

His green eyes pierced me as I shared my bullshit story.

"What's her name?" he asked.

"Becca James."

Let him research her. All her information would come up from Michigan and prove my story. I sipped my beer and casually watched the TV in front of us as he sent off a text. Most likely sending the name to someone to check out.

"Why's she trying to get away from you if you're helping her?"

"She wants to go back to Detroit. But if she does that, she's most likely dead. At least until those guys can be dealt with," I explained before reaching across the bar and grabbing a bowl of pretzels.

"From what I saw between you two last time, it's more than just you protecting her. You like her."

I gritted my teeth. "It's complicated."

He let out a laugh. "It always is when it comes to women."

I nodded in agreement, taking another sip of beer.

"All right, I'll stay out of it then," he promised, apparently glad the situation was over. "Get her back to Suncrest with you. I already deal with the Disciples, I don't need Kings in my city too."

"We'll leave tomorrow," I promised. "But I'm pretty sure she's going to try to talk to you again before we go."

"I'll give Tim the message that we're staying out of it. He'll be at the bar all day tomorrow."

Relief lightened my mood, and I downed the rest of my beer. One less thing I had to worry about.

"What's going on in Suncrest?" Don asked with a touch of wariness.

My fingers clenched around the beer bottle, and I forced myself to relax my shoulders. "What do you mean?"

"Teddy Hill."

He didn't need to say anything else. The Crows majorly fucked up when they killed him. I expected the MCs to get involved at some point.

"It wasn't us."

"Who was it?"

"Don't know. But we're trying to find out." The lie came out easily, and I threw another pretzel in my mouth. If they found out it was the Crows and confronted them, they would find out Vanessa was back in town.

"I can't get ahold of Bill either," Don said with more suspicion than I'd like.

"He probably left to get some space." I shrugged. "He took off after the Aces were killed too."

He ran a hand down his beard and frowned. "I can't believe it's been seven years. Vanessa would have been your age if she survived."

I hummed in answer and drank more beer, wanting to get the hell off this conversation. Most everyone in Suncrest knew that Vanessa had survived. But Teddy and Bill let the rumor spread outside of town that she had died along with her parents. Although it was a surprise that they didn't tell anyone when she came back. The Dusty Devils were close with her parents. I thought for sure they would have heard she was alive by now.

"I know you were close to her," Don murmured before letting out a short laugh, seemingly lost down memory lane. "Stone hated his daughter hanging out with a King."

"I know," I said gruffly.

"It wasn't you, kid." Don threw a hand on my shoulder, and I stiffened. "He didn't want her in the life at all."

"And that's why she was going to be married off to a Crow."

"Yeah...there's a reason for that, but it doesn't matter now," he said with a voice full of regret.

It took some serious willpower not to ask what that reason was. But asking about Crow business wouldn't go down well. Maybe there was more to the story I didn't even know.

He finished his beer and set it down with a sigh. "I know you miss her. I do too. She was my goddaughter. I regret that the last time I saw her was when she was barely out of diapers."

I jerked my head in a curt nod, acknowledging his words. I didn't want to talk about Vanessa and give him any sort of hint that she was still alive. It would cause an all-out war between the gangs and the MCs.

"I think I'm cutting myself off," he said with a shake of his head. "Look at me getting along with a King."

I forced out a chuckle and watched as he slid off the stool and started walking away before turning back around with a dangerous look in his eye.

"If we find out the Kings had anything to do with Teddy's death, things won't be peaceful. You should pass that message on to the Crows too."

With that, he turned back around and strode out of the bar. I ran my hands down my face, knowing things weren't going to be peaceful. They were about to turn bloody.

"Give me the fucking keys, Ryker."

I balanced both coffees in one arm and shoved the motel key into the lock before twisting the knob and flinging open the door.

"Just wait until Ky gets back—ow, shit. Did you just bite me?" Ryker yelled.

"I'm not waiting. Give me the keys."

I walked in to see her clinging to Ryker's back while he held the keys above his head. She was pulling his arm down just as he moved in front of the bed and fell sideways until they both crashed onto the mattress. I stayed quiet, watching with interest.

She got the leverage she needed and had Ryker's arm under her knee while trying to pry the keys out of his fist. She was quick, and every move she made was thought-out. Fighting in Detroit had taught her a lot.

Too bad her size was a disadvantage.

Ryker jutted his hips up, knocking her off balance, and she toppled off him with a cry.

"He'll be back any second—"

"I don't care." She dove back on top of him, but he grabbed her arm and pulled until her stomach was flat on the bed. Jumping on top of her, he sat on her back as she screamed in frustration at not being able to move.

"Morning," I said, finally letting my presence be known.

Ryker glanced over his shoulder, and relief flooded his face. "Thank fuck. You can deal with her."

"Get off me," she snapped, and I let out a chuckle but cut it off when she climbed off the bed and gave me an icy glare.

Her eyes were bright with anger and her face was flushed. She crossed her arms with a huff before she saw the coffee in my arms.

"Is one of those for me?" she asked, her attitude melting to sweetness in an instant.

"Yeah..." I answered. Her eyes darted to Ryker for half a second before crossing the room and holding out her hand.

"Ryker, you may want to leave before I give her this," I warned, attempting to keep a straight face. Her eyes narrowed slightly, and the annoyance was suddenly back full force.

Ryker glanced from the coffee to Vanessa before he grumbled something under his breath and strode to the door, letting it slam behind him.

"I wouldn't have thrown it on him if it was still hot. Then I would have felt bad." She shrugged before grabbing the coffee from my grasp.

"He was just doing what I asked."

She scowled. "You said you trusted me."

"And you said you wouldn't take off."

"Oh Ky, you should know by now." She trailed her fingers up my arm, not realizing the game she was starting. "If I wanted to run, you wouldn't know about it until I was already gone."

The truth of that statement hung in the air as she took a sip of her coffee. I set mine down on the table.

"Where're you trying to go?"

"None of your business."

"Raindrop, this isn't going to work if you can't be honest," I said, fully aware of what a fucking hypocrite I was being.

"Fine." She shot me an irritated glare. "I want to go back to the biker bar and say bye to Don."

"Why?"

"Because he was nice to me that day with Skull."

Now I didn't feel so bad about lying.

"I can take you." I pulled the truck keys out of my pocket. "I dropped Zak off at the gym, and he'll be there a couple hours."

"I have my bike."

I crowded her space, and she tipped her head back to look at me. "There are two ways this could work. We go in the truck together. Or I follow you. Either way, I'm going with you."

"Fuck, fine," she huffed in defeat. "We'll take the truck. I need to change first."

She grabbed her bag and stomped to the bathroom, slamming the door behind her. Drinking the rest of my coffee, I scrolled through my phone until she emerged from the bathroom. My mouth dropped open before anger rolled through me.

"We brought you clothes," I snapped, taking in her outfit. It was the same thing she had worn at the bar last night.

"I know." She smirked. "I wanted to wear this."

She bent over to zip up her boots, and I watched as the bottom of her ass almost popped out. I clenched my fists to keep from grabbing her, not wanting to play into her game. There wasn't a chance in hell she wanted to have sex. She was on a mission to talk to the bikers. No, she was doing this to get under my skin; I knew that. But it didn't stop my pulse from spiking.

"Why are you trying to piss me off?"

"Want to hear something else that might piss you off?"

I ran a hand down my face, following her outside. "What?"

She opened the door to the truck and stopped to look at me. "I'm not wearing anything under these shorts."

Without a word, I eliminated the space between us until her back hit the truck. She raised her hand to push me away, but I grabbed her arm and shook my head before giving her a small grin. I ran my knuckles down her cheek as she frowned.

"You keep talking like that," I murmured, "Zak's going to have to get his truck detailed and cleaned—again. Because you're one more word away from getting bent over in that back seat."

Her lips parted in shock, and she released a sharp breath.

"Keep pushing me, Raindrop," I warned before running my hand down her body until it rested on her hip. "We'll both enjoy it when I snap."

She cleared her throat, and I expected her to shove me away. Instead, she moved forward until my erection pressed into her stomach. Excitement shot through me, but I stayed still, knowing she was up to something.

"Who says you'll snap first?" she asked casually as she lifted her head to meet my gaze. "Maybe I will."

"Go for it."

She finally pushed me away. "When I snap, it won't be enjoyable. Stop acting like we're together. I'm not here to get back with you. Or to be your fuck friend. I have things to do. Like find out who killed my parents. And get the money. Then leave Suncrest Bay. For good."

"You think you're just going to leave—"

"I'm still here because you said you'd help me get what I want," she interrupted. "Nothing else."

My jaw snapped shut, and I took a deep breath to stay in control. She had a one-track mind right now and nothing I said was going to change that.

But she wasn't fucking leaving.

She turned on her heel and walked away from the truck, back to the motel.

"Change your mind about going to see the bikers?" I called out.

She glanced over her shoulder. "No. I'm getting my keys and taking the bike."

"I'll just follow you."

"Have a fucking blast."

I chuckled as she slammed the motel door behind her. Sure, she was pissed. But that wasn't the reason she was taking the bike. It was because every time we had been alone, our clothes disappeared.

A few minutes later, she came back out and I straightened up at the sight of her backpack on her.

"The bike still has a tracker on it. No point in trying to leave," I said, leaning against the truck.

"I'm not leaving."

"Right," I muttered as I moved to get into the truck.

I pulled out and followed her the short couple of blocks until we parked in front of Rob's Bar. Nerves weighed me down as I jumped out of the truck and waited for her take her helmet off. If she said anything about who her dad was, everything would change. And not for the better.

Without a word to me, she bounded up the steps while the wood creaked under her. I followed close behind, attempting to keep my face blank. She pulled the front door and mumbled under her breath when it didn't open.

"It's eleven in the morning," I said. "They probably don't open for another couple hours."

"Then I'll come back later."

I sighed. "We need to get back to Suncrest."

She whirled around to face me. "Why the hurry? I'm safer from the Crows here."

"This isn't our city. We're leaving. You want to find that paperwork, right? We can't find it from here."

She opened her mouth, but before she could say

anything, the bar door opened. I looked over her shoulder as a guy stepped out. The same guy she was smoking with last night. I shot him a cold glare, and he quickly glanced away from me. Vanessa turned back around, and I moved until I was right at her back, making sure this guy knew she was with me.

"Tim," she said, and I didn't have to be looking at her face to know she was giving him her deceptively innocent smile. "Hey, I'm sorry about last night, I had an uninvited visitor—"

"It's fine," Tim cut in quickly. "Listen, I'm sorry. But Don changed his mind and doesn't want to see you."

She stiffened and leaned back, brushing against my chest, but she didn't pay me any attention as she stared at Tim.

"Why?" she asked, barely masking the irritation that was radiating off her.

Tim ran a hand through his hair. "We don't want to get into gang business. We have enough shit on our plate already. Sorry."

He threw me a respectful nod before walking back inside and locking the door behind him. I inwardly groaned just as Vanessa whipped around and shoved me back.

"You," she hissed. "What did you say to him? When did you even fucking talk to him?"

"It doesn't matter. None of this is their business," I answered as I moved back toward the truck with her right on my ass.

"They could have helped me with my dad—"

"No, Don didn't know your dad," I lied.

We got to the truck, and I waited for her to keep yelling, but she stayed silent as she slipped her helmet back on.

"See you back at the motel," she said with smile before taking off.

A sinking feeling filled me as I watched her disappear down the street. I seriously fucking doubted I'd see her at the motel.

CHAPTER EIGHT

Vanessa

I TOOK THE LAST BITE OF MY STRAWBERRY ICE CREAM cone before standing from the bench. Kids played baseball in a field next to me, and a game of basketball was happening on the court across the park. A couple skated by on the sidewalk in front of me as I pulled Ryker's phone out of my back pocket. After finding it in my motel room this morning, I had turned it off and kept it in my backpack until now.

It had been a few hours since I'd left Ky at the bar, and I couldn't help but imagine how bad he was freaking the hell out at me being gone. I chuckled to myself as I walked down the street, watching people live their carefree lives. A kind of life I didn't think I'd ever have. Not that it really bothered me. I loved the excitement too much. I just needed to get out of this current predicament of being on everyone's most wanted list.

I turned the phone on, wishing I knew Ryker's password because the phone was useless without it. I didn't know him well enough to attempt to guess what it could be. A few moments later, it became a nonissue when the phone started ringing. Glancing at the name, I grinned before answering it and putting it to my ear.

"Hey, Zak."

There was silence and then a long groan before he spoke. "Vee. We seriously should have known you took it. It went missing when you did."

"Are you with Ky?"

"Not at the moment. I was digging through my truck for the hundredth fucking time in the past three hours looking for the damn phone you stole."

"Yeah, I just turned it back on," I said as I turned a corner and leaned against a newspaper stand.

"I know. We tried tracking it."

"I figured you would."

"We found your bike."

I laughed. "That's why I ditched it after I left the bar."

"You told Ky you wouldn't run," Zak said, his tone turning serious.

"I'm not running."

"Sure as hell seems like it."

"I'm not. I wanted some time to myself before we go back to Suncrest. I was going to come back later tonight."

"Come back now."

"No. When we go home, you three are going to be my shadows. I won't be able to go anywhere because of Jensen and the Crows. I need one free day before I'm caged in Suncrest again," I said sharply. I ran a hand through my hair and continued walking down the street.

"I'll tell Ky—"

"Don't," I cut in. "If you tell him, he'll come get me now. I just need some space. I swear I'll come back to the motel later. I'll even keep the phone on. Don't tell him. Please."

He sighed and mumbled something under his breath. I waited, growing more impatient by the second.

"On second thought, I'll just dump the phone and not come back at all—"

"Wait," he snapped. "Fine. I won't tell him, and you keep the phone on. And come back tonight. You know he's going fucking crazy looking for you."

"He'll be all right. See you tonight, Zak. No later than midnight."

"Yeah," he grumbled. "I don't know why the fuck I'm trusting you right now."

"We all want the same thing. To find the papers. No point trying to do it myself."

"Don't do anything stupid, Vee," he warned.

I giggled. "Never. Bye, Zak."

Hanging up before he could reply, I slid the phone in my back pocket. For once, I'd told him the truth. I didn't plan on leaving yet. I wanted to know more about my dad. I had already tried going back to the bar, and they'd kept the doors locked and ignored me, so the MCs were a dead end. For now anyway.

But I was done thinking about that for today. I planned on enjoying my freedom by day drinking and doing whatever the hell I wanted.

AFTER SPENDING THE DAY BOUNCING AROUND restaurants and drinking enough to keep a happy buzz, I ended up in a club. It was only eight at night. I had more than enough time to dance and have fun before heading back to the motel. I looked up clubs in the city on the phone before picking this one. It was clean, a place where the college kids and middle-class women went to get out of the house. I doubted gang members partied here.

I sat at the bar and sipped my drink, watching the crowd of people dance under the strobe lights. The music was good, and I tapped my foot with the beat as the alcohol burned through my veins. I'd taken three shots since being here, and I was feeling them. Leaping from my seat, I inched closer to the dance floor. The back of my neck prickled from nerves, but the liquid courage chased them away. I could dance by myself and still have fun.

I moved through the crowd and started dancing to the music as I walked. Closing my eyes, I lost myself to the music until hands found my waist. I stiffened, ready to pull away until he spoke next to my ear.

"Why is such a pretty girl like you dancing alone?" The guy spoke loud enough for me to hear him over the music.

"I didn't realize dancing required two people," I said stiffly as I debated leaving.

"Care to join me for one dance? My friends over there don't think a girl as gorgeous as you will want anything to do with me. I'd really like to prove them wrong."

I glanced up and saw a group of guys staring at us and then quickly looking away before I could catch their eyes. They were all dressed in designer clothes, and one of them laughed and shoved the other guy's shoulder before trying to sneak a glance back at me. They looked like a group of college guys trying to have a fun night. I forced myself to drop the suspicion. I was in a club on a packed dance floor. And I had my pocketknife in my bra. They couldn't do anything to me here.

"One dance," I said with a laugh and let my body relax into him as we started to move to the music.

"I owe you a drink after this. You have no idea how much shit I'd get if you turned me down," he replied, keeping his hands on my hips. "I'm Brad."

Leaning back until I was against his chest, I didn't reply. He didn't need to know my name. It wasn't like I would ever see him again. After some dancing, I'd be gone. He smelled like clean soap and ridiculously expensive cologne, and it was good combination. But he smelled wrong. Because he wasn't Ky. I pushed that thought from my head as fast as possible. I could dance with whoever the hell I wanted.

His hands disappeared for a few moments before he put them back on my waist. When the song ended, I attempted to move away, but his fingers dug into my hips, keeping me in place. My heart thudded and I swallowed the panic. It wouldn't be hard to get away from him. I'd dealt with worse.

I tried twisting around, but he grabbed my upper arm, making sure I couldn't turn. His other hand was still on my hip, and I froze for a moment, trying to think through the haze of all the alcohol I'd had. Taking a deep breath, I got ready to tell him to move his hands until his scent hit me.

Fuck me. It wasn't the college preppy guy.

"Ky," I huffed out, trying again to pull away.

He chuckled as he moved his hand from my hip and wrapped it around my stomach, yanking me until my back hit his hard chest. He kept a tight hold on my arm with his other hand as he rested his chin on my shoulder.

"You really think Zak wouldn't tell me?" he asked, his lips right next to my ear.

"I expected him to hold out until at least ten," I mumbled.

"He even told you not to do anything stupid," he said with a dangerous edge in his voice.

"I didn't."

"Dancing with some fucking frat boy is stupid."

"I can do whatever—or whoever the fuck I want." I tried again to turn around, but his hold was too tight.

A low rumble of a laugh shook his chest, but instead of being joyous, it was laced with threat. I tensed as unease overtook any of the alcohol buzz I had left.

"Do you remember what I told you when you first came back to Suncrest?"

"You said a lot of things."

"I told you what would happen if another guy touched you."

I scoffed. "You said that was payback for—"

"It was never for payback," he whispered in my ear. "When I see another guy touching you, I see fucking red."

We were still standing in the middle of the crowd as people danced around us. We weren't moving, but everyone seemed oblivious to us as they enjoyed their night.

"You don't get to decide who touches me," I sneered. "Especially when you have a fucking fiancée."

Without a word, he started walking forward, and I dug my heels in, but he just tightened his hold on my waist and lifted until my feet left the floor. I tried squirming out of his grip, and he let go of my arm, only to wrap his other arm around me, making sure I couldn't go anywhere.

"Let me go," I demanded, clawing my nails into his wrists.

He ignored me and walked until we were behind a table in a corner of the club, facing the crowd of people dancing.

"I wasn't going to leave," I said, not sure what he was doing. "I told Zak I'd come back to the motel tonight."

"This isn't about you running," he replied, putting his head back on my shoulder. "This is because you smell like the guy who was all over you."

"He wasn't all over me. We were just dancing. Let me go, and we'll leave."

"You don't want me to let you go."

"Why's that?'

"Because if my hands aren't on you,"—he reached up and grabbed my chin, forcing me to look across the dance floor— "then they'll be on him. And he'll be fucking dead."

CHAPTER NINE

Vanessa

THE GROUP OF GUYS I SAW EARLIER WERE SITTING there, drinking and talking. But a fifth guy joined them, and he was glaring daggers at Ky. It was obvious he was the one I had been dancing with. His blond hair was cut short, and he ran a hand through it as his gaze caught mine. He motioned to Ky and raised an eyebrow.

Ky laughed, and his breath tickled my neck. "Look at that, he wants to come to your rescue. You think he can take me on, Raindrop?"

My stomach plummeted, knowing he didn't have a chance against Ky.

"Leave him alone." I turned my head and looked at Ky for the first time since he grabbed me on the dance floor.

He grinned in amusement, but his eyes were dark, revealing the anger burning through him. His fingers left my face and glided down my neck to my collarbone.

"As long as my hands stay on you, then I won't touch him."

I let out a nervous laugh. "Let's just leave."

"No."

"Why? You got what you wanted," I snapped as my own anger rose, and I tried prying his arm off my waist.

"Not yet," he murmured while his hand drifted down my stomach until he tugged on the top of my shorts.

I stiffened and pushed his hand away. "What the hell are you doing?"

"Showing him and anyone else who's watching that you're mine."

"I'm not."

"Want to fight me on it?" he asked, releasing me. "Fine. I'll show him another way."

I pulled him back when he tried walking away. "Don't hurt him, Ky. He knows nothing about the Kings or who you are. He just wanted to dance."

"He wanted more than that."

"Nothing else happened."

"I know it didn't." He grabbed my hips and turned me back around until his chest pressed against my back. "I got here five minutes after you did."

"I should have turned the phone back off," I muttered, freezing when he slipped his fingers into my shorts.

I glanced back at Brad to find him still staring at us. I shot him a small smile and shook my head, silently trying to tell him I was fine. I didn't want him coming over here. His frown deepened, and he crossed his arms as he sat with his friends.

"Damn," Ky breathed out. "You were actually telling the truth this morning. You really aren't wearing anything under these shorts."

"Ky," I hissed, trying to move away, but I only ended up

bumping into the table in front of me before he pulled me back to him.

"*Mine*," he growled in a low voice as his fingers moved lower, grazing my clit.

The high-top table we were behind was cube shaped and solid wood. I was grateful no one could see below my waist. Ky's hand was hidden, but to anyone looking at us, it was obvious what he was doing. Brad was still watching, and his eyebrows raised as he leaned forward in his seat.

My body flushed with heat and my stomach clenched in pleasure even as I fought to keep a clear head. We were in public. With people watching. Yet somehow, it made it even hotter. The music drowned out everything else besides Ky's words while he brushed his lips over my ear.

"You're about to soak through these shorts," he murmured. "And I've barely even started."

He moved his fingers slowly in circles, and I gripped the edge of the table, swallowing a moan when he moved faster.

"Next time a guy touches you, I'm not going to be as nice," he warned, pinching my clit and making me cry out in pleasure.

"Ryker touched me, and he's still breathing," I forced out in between breaths. Even as turned on as I was, it was pissing me off how he was trying to control me. Not that I was going to stop him from giving me an orgasm.

"That was different. Did you enjoy his mouth on you?" he asked, with a mix of anger and lust smothering his voice.

I stayed silent, not expecting that question.

"Ryker's looking right now too. I bet he's remembering how you tasted."

My head snapped up to search the crowd until I saw Ryker sitting at the bar but turned in the seat, facing us. He met my eyes and didn't even try to hide the fact that he was watching.

"You want him to go down on you again?" He kept his fingers moving fast enough that my legs trembled, making it difficult to keep standing.

"Like you'd let that happen."

"I'm surprised too." He let out a small chuckle. "But watching you come undone was fucking hot. Except if it did happen again, it wouldn't just be him touching you. It would be both of us."

I sucked in a breath, and the image of that happening only increased how fucking turned on I was. He slid a finger in me as his thumb stayed on my clit, and I threw my head back on his shoulder.

"You'd like that, wouldn't you?"

I didn't answer as the pleasure built within me. His fingers were close to bringing me over the edge and talking was becoming harder. His dirty words were making it even more difficult to concentrate. I'd never seen this side of him, and I liked it more than I cared to admit.

"I doubt you'd let that happen," I muttered, trying to stay in control of the conversation. "You're too much of a possessive asshole."

"I'm a possessive asshole who loves seeing you scream in pleasure." His fingers moved in sync with the song that played, and my body started to lock up as I inched closer to an orgasm. "Watching Ryker eat your pussy while my cock is in your mouth is something I'd really fucking enjoy."

"Holy fuck," I whimpered, trying to close my legs as his touch and words became almost overwhelming.

He grabbed my thigh with his free hand, pulling it away from my other one without slowing the assault on my clit. I leaned against him; unable to fully support myself anymore.

I didn't even realize his hand left my leg until he gripped my chin, turning my head, making me look back at the guy I'd danced with.

"Show him, baby," he ordered as his fingers coaxed my orgasm over the edge. "I want him to watch you come, knowing he won't ever fucking touch you."

"Asshole," I breathed out, even though my eyes immediately sought out Brad's gaze. He was already staring at me, and he couldn't seem to decide how he felt. His mouth was tipped down with his lips pressed together, and he looked ready to leap from the chair. But his eyes were betraying how turned on he was as he watched me.

"He wants you," Ky murmured before kissing my neck. "But he doesn't have the balls to do anything about it. Probably a good thing. He'll go home breathing."

My eyes stayed locked on his as Ky rubbed his thumb in circles and my pussy spasmed around his fingers. My legs tensed, and my grip on the edge of the table tightened even more as the orgasm ripped through me, stealing my breath. He let go of my chin and wrapped his arm around my waist, holding me up as I leaned against him. He finally pulled his hand out of my shorts once the orgasm diminished and pulled my arm, turning me around until I faced him.

Staring across the dance floor, he licked his fingers. I rolled my eyes as I caught my breath, glancing around to see if anyone else was staring. Aside from Ryker and Brad, our little corner held no interest to anyone else.

Thank fuck.

Ky turned his attention back to me, and he leaned over and rested his hands on the table, caging me in.

"I think all that talk about a threesome turned you on as much as my fingers did," he said with a grin still on his face.

"Yeah, you've gotten better at dirty talk," I muttered, trying to push past him. "I need to go to the bathroom."

He didn't move out of my way. "It would be fucking hot. But you're right, I might be too much of a possessive asshole to let it happen."

"Good thing I'm in charge of who I sleep with, not you." I patted his cheek before ducking under his arm and darting away before he could grab me.

"Don't test me, Raindrop," he yelled after me. "The second you get out of the bathroom, we're leaving."

I raised my arm and flipped him off without looking back. Pushing open the bathroom door, I went to a stall and cleaned myself up while muttering under my breath. I was regretting not wearing panties now. My shorts were soaked, and I had nothing to change into until I got back to the motel.

I left the stall and started washing my hands as the door opened.

"Are you okay?"

I whirled around to see Brad looking at me with concern. Wiping my wet hands on my shorts, I backed away from the sink.

"You need to leave," I hissed, my eyes going to the door behind him.

"Did that guy hurt you?" he asked. "I couldn't tell if you wanted it or not. But if he forced himself on you, I'll call the cops right now—"

"You seem like a nice guy," I rushed out. "I'm fine. He didn't force me into anything. And you need to get the hell out of here before he finds you with me. Go back to your friends and forget about it."

"Come with me. I'll keep you safe—"

I cut him off with a sharp laugh. "You can't keep me safe. I'm leaving anyway."

As I stepped to the side of him to get to the door, he grabbed my wrist and pulled me back. The healing cuts on my wrist burned under his grip, and I tried wrenching away, but he was stronger than he looked.

"Don't leave with him," he tried convincing me. "He's a thug and dangerous."

I went deathly still as I met his gaze. "Get your fucking hand off me."

He had no idea what he had walked into, and if being nice wasn't going to get him to go away, I'd have to change tactics. His grip didn't loosen, and I glanced toward the door again, knowing one of the guys would be in here any minute.

"He ripped me away from you on the dance floor." He frowned. "I'm going to have bruises on my shoulder because of him."

I nearly rolled my eyes. "Be lucky that's all he did. You need to get out of here before he does worse."

"I should sue his ass. You don't need to put up with that."

"Oh my fuck," I muttered, my patience almost gone. "You know what, you stay in here and I'll leave."

"No. You need help—"

I raised my arm and slapped him across the face. Instead of letting me go like I expected, his fingers tightened around my wrist even more.

"Shit." He tugged me closer. "I was trying to help you, but you're nothing more than a ghetto slut. Maybe you deserve whatever happens to you."

Rage caused my muscles to go taut, and I threw him an icy smile. With my free hand, I reached inside my bra and pulled out my pocketknife. Flipping it open, I aimed for his arm and sliced deep enough to break skin. With a surprised yell, he released me and backed up.

"What the hell?" He glowered at me while holding his arm.

I lifted the knife and pressed it into his chest, pushing him back until he hit the wall. He raised his arms while his eyes darted from the knife to my face.

"I'm really starting to think there are no more good people in the world." I sighed, keeping the knife on him. "You're a prime example. You dress the part of a nice guy. You have the gentleman voice and smile. But the second I don't bow down with what you want, you try to control me."

"I'm sorry," he breathed out shakily.

"Now you're sorry. A minute ago, you didn't care what I said unless it was what you wanted to hear." I trailed the knife down his chest without my eyes leaving his. "I said I didn't need your help and I meant it. Just because I have a vagina doesn't mean I'm weaker than you."

"I never said you were—"

"What is it that makes you think I'm a ghetto slut?" I asked in a calm voice as my eyes narrowed. "It can't be my clothes or my tattoos. You saw those earlier, and if I remember correctly, you called me pretty and gorgeous."

"I'm sorry. I really am," he repeated in a desperate attempt to get me to back off.

"Is it because I got off in the middle of a club?" I asked, tilting my head to the side. "It seemed like you enjoyed watching though."

Beads of sweat appeared on his forehead as I pressed the knife harder. It wasn't enough to break his skin, but it kept his attention on who had the power in this room.

"Or am I just a slut when I tell you to get your hands off me?"

"You're not a slut," he stammered out. "I was mad, that's all."

"You think he's dangerous," I murmured. "I can be just as dangerous. If not more. Because no one suspects it from me."

"I get it," he said quickly. "You don't need my help."

"I already have enough guys in my life trying to control me," I snarled, dropping my calm act. "You don't come close to that list. I'm not the weak one in this room."

"No, you're not."

I looked behind my shoulder, seeing Ky leaning against the doorframe with Ryker standing behind him.

"Oh god," Brad cried out.

Ky strode into the room until he was standing at my back. I lowered the knife and looked back at Brad, who was staring at Ky.

"Why are you looking at me?" Ky asked as he slid his hand around my waist. "She's the one who has you by the balls."

He glanced between Ky and me and then at the knife that was now by my side. My heart hammered, wondering what Ky was up to.

"What now?" Brad asked, looking at Ky. His tough act was showing now that the knife was off him. "Going to beat the shit out of me because I touched something you own?"

My grip tightened, and I resisted the urge to stab him in the leg. Ky wrapped his arm around me and pulled me back, stepping into the space I had been standing in. His hand went to Brad's throat, and he squeezed until Brad was clawing at Ky's hands.

"Let's get something straight." Ky spoke calmly as

Brad's face started to turn red. "I don't own her. No one ever will."

I arched an eyebrow, staring at the back of his head. Sometimes, it sure as hell felt like he thought he owned me.

"She's strong. Smart." He glanced down at the cut on Brad's arm. "And dangerous. She wasn't born to be owned."

My heart betrayed me and flipped at his words. Brad tried to speak but didn't have the air to make a sound.

"But she is mine," Ky growled as Brad's face began turning purple. "Mine to touch. Mine to protect. Mine to kill for. She'll always be mine."

His words didn't bother me nearly as much as they should. I had always been his. From the time we were five. Even after everything, being with him felt like home. I wanted it. But I couldn't stop my plan. I wanted justice for Teddy. Revenge for my parents. I wanted the secrets to unravel around me so I could stop running. Ky would never be free of the Kings or his father. We couldn't be together.

Not while Jensen was alive.

My stomach churned as if Ky could read my mind. It wasn't the first time I'd thought of it. I wouldn't feel an ounce of guilt if Jensen was killed. But he was Ky's father. And blood was everything to their family. Ky might hate him, but could he really be okay with me wanting his dad dead?

"Please," Brad gasped out, causing me to look back at him.

Ky released his grip, and Brad sagged against the wall, holding his neck as he gulped in air.

"I better not see you again," Ky threatened. "If I do, you won't walk away."

Brad nodded frantically as he slid to the floor and stared anywhere besides me and Ky. I turned around and looked at

Ryker, who was watching the door to make sure no one came in. I met his gaze and a hot flush traveled through me. *Son of a bitch.*

Ky's dirty words rushed to my head, and Ryker looked a little unsure but grinned anyway. No doubt thinking about what he witnessed earlier. I liked Ryker but could never love him. Not like Ky. But sex could be just about pleasure. I already knew Ryker's tongue was up to the job. Sex with both of them would definitely be fucking pleasurable.

"Not a fucking word," I muttered as I moved past him, going into the hallway.

He chuckled as I walked away, and I rolled my eyes. This was not how I'd expected the night to go. Biting my lip, I searched the crowd for the person responsible for ruining my little solo vacation. I caught sight of him, chatting up a bleach-blonde girl at the bar, and I hurried my steps.

"Hey, baby," I purred, wrapping my arm around his waist.

Zak's jaw dropped in surprise. "Vee, what—"

"The babysitter called," I interrupted him. "The baby's been up all night with the stomach flu. I guess now we know why you were shitting your pants before we left tonight."

Zak spluttered, his words not making any sense, and I suppressed a laugh at the outrage on his face.

"Baby? Flu?" the blonde screeched, jumping from her seat. "You never said you were married."

"I'm not—"

She slapped him across the face and stalked away before Zak formed a word in his defense. I burst out laughing, dropping my arm from his waist.

"What the fuck, Vee?" Zak asked as he rubbed his cheek.

"You ratted me out," I stated before downing the rest of his drink.

"You know how Ky is," he complained. "And you fucking snitched and sent me to prison for four years. This comes nowhere close."

I shrugged. "We're leaving anyway. I'm sure Ky will be here any second."

"I'm here now."

An arm went around my shoulders, and I glanced up, already knowing who it would be.

"Time to go home," Ky said as he steered me to the exit.

My stomach rolled with nerves, thinking about going back to Suncrest Bay. Fun time was over, and life was about to get even more complicated.

CHAPTER TEN

Kyro

I GROANED, ROLLING OVER ON THE COUCH AND throwing the pillow over my face. Someone was in the kitchen making way too much fucking noise.

"You want some coffee?" Ryker called out, slamming a cupboard shut.

I tossed the pillow away and sat up, rubbing my eyes. "You get up way too early."

"This isn't early." He laughed. "I already went for a run."

"I slept like shit." I stood up and stretched before going into the kitchen. "The couch sucks."

"And why are you on the couch?" he asked with a raised eyebrow.

"Vanessa went into my room last night and locked the door," I muttered.

"You have a key."

I poured a cup of coffee. "I know. But she's jumpy. I can tell she wants to run, so I'm trying to give her space."

"We should have made the fourth room a guest room instead of an office." Ryker shook his head. "Because if you're staying away to keep her from running, you'll be living on the couch. What if it's just a ploy for her to leave while we're all sleeping?"

"The alarm is on," I answered. "She tries opening a door or a window, it'll go off. And unlike my dad's house, she has no idea what the code is."

"I have no idea what the code is—yet."

Vanessa sauntered into the room, stealing the coffee cup from my hand before leaning against the counter. My gaze traveled over her body, and it took everything in me not to grab her and drag her back to my room. She was wearing one of my shirts. That was it. The shirt barely covered her ass, and when she moved to put sugar in her coffee, I got a glimpse of her lace panties.

"Raindrop," I warned as I tried to stay in control. "I love seeing you in my clothes, but I'm not the only one who lives in this house."

Ryker chuckled, purposely looking anywhere but at Vanessa. I moved until I was in front of her and placed my hands on the counter on either side of her. She tilted her head up and grinned while trailing her fingers down my chest.

"You didn't seem to have a problem with people looking at me last night. I wanted to see how serious you were about that threesome with Ryker."

Ryker coughed up his coffee, and Vanessa giggled before pushing my arm away and going to sit at the table.

"Damn, Vee," Zak said, walking into the kitchen. "It's not even noon. Too early to start talking about that."

"We're not talking about it," I snapped as memories from last night flowed through my mind. That was the first time we'd done anything in such a public place. And I definitely wouldn't be opposed to doing it again.

"Fine." Vanessa took a sip of coffee. "I want to talk to Kenzi. Where is she?"

"You would know her better than us," Zak replied. "Where do you think she is?"

She frowned before glancing at me. "Just tell me."

I poured myself another cup of coffee while I answered. "We don't know where she is. We told her what happened and that she needed to get out of Suncrest for a while. She said she was going somewhere with her girlfriend."

"Give me your phone," she demanded, looking at me. "I want to call her."

"She left her phone here so it couldn't be traced," Zak explained, sitting down next to her. "And we agreed with her. After the Crows killed Teddy, we figured they'd go after her to get to you."

"You have no way to contact her?" Vanessa asked, clutching the coffee cup.

"She has all of our numbers," I assured her. "She said she'd call us."

She stayed quiet, staring at her coffee. For once, her emotions were splashed across her face. Guilt. She felt she was the reason Teddy was killed. And why Kenzi had to leave town. I gritted my teeth to keep quiet. None of this was her fault. It was her fucking parents who tried selling her to the Crows. They started all of this and left it for her to deal with.

Seeing her guilt, I decided not to mention the fact that we got Kenzi out of town to keep her away from my dad too. He would have used Kenzi to get to Vanessa, just like Mack did. The amount of money in those bank accounts could put the Kings back on top, and Jensen would do anything to get it.

"She'll be fine." I sat down next to her and Zak. "Teddy was her dad. She knows how to survive."

"Was Teddy in the MC with my dad?"

I hesitated before answering. "Yes."

She lifted her head, and her questioning gaze landed on me. "And Bill was too?"

I nodded while standing back up. I knew answering the question about Teddy was a mistake. She wasn't going to stop now.

"Who else?" she pressed.

Ignoring her, I walked down the hallway as her chair scraped against the wood floor. I opened my bedroom door and stripped off my shirt.

"Who else was in the MC with my dad?" she asked from my doorway.

I glanced over my shoulder and caught her gaze roaming my body before she looked at my face. Grinning, I slid off my shorts.

"Not yet, Raindrop. I told you I'd give you more answers in a week."

"Fine, I'll find out myself."

She spun on her heel and stalked out of the room with me right behind her. I grabbed her arm and stopped her in the hallway.

"Where do you think you're going?"

"To the bank, to talk to Bill."

I scowled. "You were going to walk out of this house and go by yourself?"

Her eyes traveled down to my boxers before she shrugged and tried tugging out of my grip. I pushed her into the wall and crowded her space, causing her smile to flatten as her eyes flashed with defiance.

"I thought we understood each other," I said quietly, resting my hands near her head. "I tell you about your dad, and you don't go running off by yourself."

"I planned on coming back after I talked to Bill."

I laughed. "That's not going to happen."

Her joking mood disappeared, and she tried pushing me away. "You can't keep me here, Ky."

"Try me."

"I came back with you because you said you'd tell me about my dad. You haven't told me all of it. I'll find out the rest myself," she said coldly.

"You walk out that door by yourself and my dad or the Crows will have you in a matter of hours." My patience was waning. "It's too late for you to leave town. They'll find you."

"I tried leaving town, only to find out you took over my fucking bank account," she said bitterly.

"You wouldn't have gotten far with a few thousand dollars anyway," I said, knowing my words were going to piss her off even more. My dad wanted me to close down her account. Instead, I'd added money in case she ever needed to leave. Then I put my own name on the account because the thought of her disappearing again was enough to drive me crazy.

"I want to go talk to Bill," she demanded.

"He left."

"What do you mean he left?" she asked, obviously not believing me.

"He took off after Teddy was killed."

"I want to go to the bank and see for myself."

I backed away, running a hand through my hair. "Wait

until I get out of the shower, and I'll take you. But he's not there."

"Hurry up," she said, pushing past me and going back into my room. "Or I'll go by myself."

I looked down the hall and saw Zak, who nodded at me. He wouldn't let Vanessa leave on her own. Mack's guys were scouring the city for her. If Jensen found out I couldn't keep her under control, he'd take her. It was too dangerous for her to go anywhere in Suncrest alone.

I walked back into my room as Vanessa was sliding on her leggings. She ignored me while I walked into the bathroom and closed the door. I shook my head and slid off my boxers before turning on the water. Going to the bank was risky. But if I didn't take her, she'd try to sneak off by herself. I'd just gotten her back and didn't plan on letting her out of my sight.

Vanessa hopped out of my truck as soon as I parked outside the bank. I quickly followed behind her as she made her way through the parking lot.

"I think they missed a spot," she said, throwing a glance at me over her shoulder. "I saw a red stain in the middle of the back seat."

I shook my head and scoffed. "They've had my truck for a week, cleaning it. There isn't one drop of ketchup left. You're gonna have to try harder next time."

A laugh escaped her as I caught up to her. "You should have seen Zak's face when he thought I got blood on him. It was fucking priceless."

"I'm sure it was." I pulled open the bank door and let

her walk in first. "But you know they're going to be even more on guard if you try something again."

Her smile disappeared as she caught my gaze. "No point in trying again. We're both working toward the same thing. Finding the money. I have no reason to leave."

Her words sounded like the truth, but after everything, there was no way I fully believed her. I didn't answer as she looked toward Bill's office. I followed her gaze and saw the lights off and the door closed.

"Ms. Ace."

The teller who had helped us last time we were here stepped in front of us and gave Vanessa a warm smile. And completely ignored me.

"Hi." Vanessa returned her smile. "I need to see Bill."

The lady frowned and looked at me for the first time. "He's not here."

"I told you," I murmured, placing my hand on Vanessa's lower back. "Let's go."

This place had always been a neutral place for the both the Kings and Crows. But only because of Bill. Now that he was gone, I didn't expect the Crows to play nice if they found us here. Vanessa held her ground as I tried turning her toward the door.

"When will he back?" Vanessa asked, ignoring my attempts to leave.

"We don't know," the lady answered. "He took an extended leave of absence. But..."

She trailed off while glaring at me. I wasn't sure how much she knew, but it was obvious Bill had said nothing nice about me. I shot her a smile, and her face flushed, even though her frown remained.

"But, what?" Vanessa pressed.

"He left you something. But only for you to read."

Vanessa glanced at me. "I understand. Don't worry, no one else will read it."

I kept my thoughts to myself while the lady walked back behind the teller line. Vanessa wasn't opening that letter until we could both read it. The lady came back with a sealed envelope and hesitated before handing it to Vanessa.

"He also said the bank isn't safe for you while he's gone," she said in a low voice. "Actually, it sounded like he wanted you to leave Suncrest if you could."

"Already tried that," Vanessa muttered, before clearing her throat. "Thank you for giving me this. I'm sure whatever he wrote will help me."

The lady nodded and went back to work while I guided Vanessa out the lobby door. The second we were out of the bank, I plucked the envelope from her hand.

"Hey," she protested as I slipped it into my back pocket.

"We'll read it when we get back to the house." I kept my hand on her back while we walked back to the truck.

"I'm more than capable of holding a letter that's addressed to me."

"I'm curious." I opened the truck door for her. "What were the odds of you reading it on the way home and then ripping it up so I wouldn't be able to see it?"

She shrugged. "About fifty-fifty. But I would have told you what it said. You know, since we're working on honesty and all."

"Right." I let out a small laugh. Honesty. If only it were that easy.

I got in the truck and pulled onto the road, glancing over to see her staring out the window.

"Kenzi will call. I'm sure she's fine."

"After all these years, how are you still always in my head?" she asked with a roll of her eyes.

"We've given each other pieces of ourselves. No matter how hard we try, there's no escaping it. And I don't want to."

"Even after everything?" she asked cautiously. "Ky...I got your brother killed."

My grip on the steering wheel tightened. "Knox was my brother. But he was also a cruel asshole who only cared about himself. And sometimes the Kings. He wouldn't have spared a second if the roles were reversed, and it was you who would have been killed."

"You still have to feel something about me being the reason he's dead," she persisted.

I sighed. "Yeah. There is a part of me—a small part—that's sad he's gone. But you know how we were, even as kids. We weren't close. We barely tolerated each other. I don't blame you. We expected shit to go down that night. Even if your call was the reason the Crows went there, there were two other gangs too. It was already planned."

"Your dad will never forgive me."

"No, he won't."

"I'm sorry, Ky," she whispered, letting her emotions out for once. "I'd take it back if I could. You might act like only a small part is sad, but I know you too. It hurt you. You two were raised in this life together. He was your blood."

I pulled to the side of the road and leaned closer to her.

"He was my blood. But you...the person I was warned about over and over. The perfect storm that would destroy me. You're the one who kept me from becoming like my father." I held her cheek as she stared at me. "There is no one on this fucking planet who will ever come before you."

She blinked rapidly before pulling away from my hand. "Besides secrets."

"There are reasons I can't tell you everything right now." I watched her eyes harden again.

"The MC my dad was a part of—is that the only secret you're keeping from me?"

My heart plummeted, and I did everything to keep my face blank. There was no way I could tell her the other secret I was keeping. Not now. She was still too on edge. If she found this out, she'd leave. I wouldn't blame her, but I wasn't going to let it happen.

"Are you going to say you're sorry for sending me to prison?" I asked, raising an eyebrow. "You've been back for nearly a month, and I don't think you feel bad about that."

Suspicion lit up her face, but she just grinned, letting the questions about secrets drop. For now, at least.

"I'm honestly not sure about that," she said, acting like she was deep in thought. "You were going to do it to me first."

"Yeah, but now you know why."

This time she changed the subject. "If I wanted to go on my own and find out everything without you, would you let me leave?"

I paused. "No."

There was no point in lying, she'd be able to tell. She narrowed her eyes and crossed her arms. I sighed and pulled back onto the road, knowing the small window of opening up to each other was gone.

"So, I'm here against my will just like when you first brought me back," she grumbled, leaning back against the seat.

"You're here because out of everyone who wants you, I'm the only one doing it to keep you safe."

"What if I don't want your protection?"

"Too bad."

"You think I won't try to leave again?"

I parked in the driveway and turned toward her while resting my arm on the steering wheel. "Baby, I'll tie you to my bed if you try to leave again. But something tells me that wouldn't be a punishment."

Pink crept up her cheeks, making me grin. Getting her to blush didn't happen often. She shook her head and jumped out of the truck, getting to the porch before I even shut off the engine. Knox's face flashed through my mind, and a memory Vanessa didn't even know about flooded my thoughts. She never knew how twisted he really was.

---

16 YEARS OLD.

"She knows now," Knox said, pulling up to the factory. "You know what that means."

"Vanessa isn't part of the Kings," I argued tensely, opening the door and getting out before he could keep talking. Knox was right behind me as I unlocked the factory door.

"She will be. Dad already mentioned her doing jobs with you," he reminded me, his voice holding too much excitement for what we were talking about.

"I'll be with her every time she does a job. There's no reason to make her do anything."

Knox grabbed my arm, halting my steps. My muscles flexed against his hold as I spun around, shoving him off me.

"Every single person who joins the Kings needs to do it." His eyes blazed triumphantly, not letting this conversation

drop. "Just because you want to fuck her doesn't mean she can be an exception."

"She's not doing it," I snarled. "I'll do it. She'll be my responsibility."

His eyes widened and he barked out a laugh. "You'll do it? Dad's been trying to get you in the basement with me for months. I would've told Vanessa ages ago if I knew that's all it took."

My stomach bubbled, making bile rise to my throat. It was never a secret who my dad was. I stayed as far away as possible until he forced me to start helping with King business a year ago. The basement was a place I wanted no part of. And a place I never wanted Vanessa to see. But if I had to do it to keep the King tattoo off her knuckles, I would. Seeing her under my father's control was the last fucking thing I wanted to happen.

"We have someone down there now." Knox nodded his head to the stairs. "He has information Dad needs."

Refusing to show my hesitation, I strode down the steps without another word. The light grew dimmer the farther down I went. The odor filling my nostrils was a warning the room was filled with death. My gaze went straight to the center of the room where a man was tied to a metal chair. A long, fluorescent light hung above him, exposing his already beaten body.

Along one of the dirty concrete walls was a long table full of tools and weapons. Dried blood stained the floor, and I stepped over fresh droplets while Knox went to the table. He picked up a long knife, and the blade glinted in the light. Eagerness lit up his face while he held the knife out to me.

Staring at it, I took a deep breath. Everyone who joined the Kings had to prove they would do dirty work if needed. Torture was at the top of the list. Knox and I never had to do anything. We were born into it, and Dad expected us to do whatever he asked.

"You want to vouch for her, then do it," Knox ordered, shoving the knife closer to me.

With a glare, I took it and turned to the man in the chair. What I wouldn't give for a normal damn childhood. Knox was only a year older than me, at seventeen. Not even a legal adult, and he was already an expert in torture. He loved it and had been wanting me to join him for the last year. Looked like he was finally getting what he wanted.

I didn't relish in others' pain like he did. But I'd do it if it meant keeping Vanessa out of the basement.

There was nothing I wouldn't do for her. Even at the expense of others.

It was only a few months later when I found out who Vanessa's dad was. A secret Knox had already known. Jensen never planned on letting Vanessa into the Kings. He couldn't. But that didn't stop Knox from using that information to get me to do what he wanted.

"Hurry up, Ky," Vanessa yelled from the porch, jolting me from the past. "I want to read *my* letter that's in your pocket."

CHAPTER ELEVEN

Vanessa

"Let me read it," I said, holding out my hand.

I was in the living room with all three guys, and Ky was still holding my letter hostage. I was itching to read what Bill had written. Maybe this would be the end of all the secrets. I was fucking tired of being in the dark.

"I'll read it out loud," Ky replied, and I bit my tongue in annoyance.

Crossing my arms, I fell back onto the couch, and Zak sat next to me. Ryker leaned against the wall near the door as Ky opened the envelope. Excitement rushed through me while he unfolded the paper. He scanned it in silence, and I cleared my throat, causing him to look up.

"We can't hear you," I said sarcastically. "Read it or give it to me."

"You really need to learn patience," Ky said with a grin.

"Ky," I warned, getting ready to leap from the couch. I'd waited long enough to get answers, and they were right there in his hands.

"Fine," Ky said. He took a deep breath and started reading.

"Vanessa,

Call this number when you're alone."

Ky looked back up. "There's a number, and that's it."

Standing up, I crossed the room and grabbed the paper from his hand. After glancing at the number Bill had written, my gaze went over Ky's shoulder to the small table behind him. Where I knew there were at least two burner phones in the drawer.

I smiled. "Can I borrow one of your phones?"

"Give me the number, I'll call." Ky moved and grabbed one of the phones from the drawer.

"Umm, do you need me to read it again? It specifically says to call him when I'm alone."

Zak snorted. "And you're smart enough to know that isn't going to happen."

"Why? Scared Bill is going to spill the secrets you guys won't tell me?"

"Go sit down, Raindrop," Ky ordered, motioning to the couch. "Or you don't call him at all."

The paper was suddenly ripped from my hand, and I whirled around to see Ryker backing up before handing the paper to Zak.

"I'll just hang on to this." Zak said the number out loud for Ky, then slid the paper into his pocket.

"Assholes," I mumbled, sitting in the middle of the couch while Zak and Ky sat down on either side of me.

"Ready?" Ky asked, his finger hovering over the call button.

Rolling my eyes, I nodded as Ky put the call on speaker phone. It rang twice before Bill answered.

"Vanessa?"

I raised an eyebrow. "How'd you know it was me?"

"You're the only person I gave this number to. Are you okay? Last I heard, you were with the Crows. I'm sorry I had to leave." He sounded rushed and was speaking quietly.

"I got away from the Crows. But maybe you can explain why my parents made a deal with them?" I held my breath while waiting for him to respond.

"Are you alone?"

I stayed silent for a moment as Ky tensed, looking at me.

"Yes," I answered, deciding I wanted the truth over anything else.

"Hmm." Bill paused. "You had to go to the bank to get this number. You're still in Suncrest."

It wasn't a question, and his tone changed as he spoke. With a sinking feeling, I sighed.

"Yeah, I'm still in Suncrest."

"Kenzi left. I wanted to make sure she was okay after Teddy was killed. There's nowhere in Suncrest you'd be safe from both gangs." His once soft voice was harsh. Nothing like the quiet banker I'd met when I first came back to town. "Are you with the Kings or Crows?"

"She's with me," Ky spoke up. "She's safe."

"I'm guessing that's Kyro." Bill let out a cold laugh. "It's impossible to keep her safe when it comes to your father. Let her leave Suncrest if you really want to help."

Ky's grip tightened on the phone. "Not possible. It would only put her in more danger."

"Not if she went down to Brown City."

All three guys stiffened as my eyes snapped from the phone to Ky's face. "What's in Brown City? The Dusty Devils? They knew my dad, didn't they?"

Instead of waiting for Ky to answer, I stared at the guy with the worst poker face in the room. When Ryker looked anywhere but at me, anger surged through me. I was right to go to the Dusty Devils. They had answers I wanted.

"Liar," I hissed, shoving Ky's shoulder. "You said Don didn't know my dad."

"You'd be safe with the Dusty Devils. Don would protect you—"

Ky interrupted Bill. "That's funny, Don doesn't know she's back. Or even alive. Why didn't you tell him when she came back to Suncrest?"

"That's none of your damn business," Bill snarled, sounding more like Teddy with each word. "I want you to bring her to Brown City. Get her out of Suncrest."

"She's staying with me for now." Ky's tone left no room for argument, and it made my blood boil.

"Vanessa," Bill's voice softened. "I know you must be furious about the deal your parents made with the Crows. But I want you to know they had a reason for it. They loved you."

"What was the reason?"

He hesitated. "Only a few people know. The Dusty Devils don't even know. Or the Crows. We've kept it a secret for decades. I can't tell you when you're with the Kings."

Noticing Ky shoot Zak a questioning glance, I realized for once, I wasn't the only one being kept in the dark.

"There are people your parents have been protecting you from your entire life. Word is spreading outside of Suncrest that you're back. If the Kings, or even the Crows, find out who and why, then you'll be in the middle of something much larger than you are now." Bill's words were a warning, and it only brought a new wave of questions to my mind.

"Can you just tell me who—"

"No," Bill said sharply. "Jensen can't find out about this. You're with his son. Once I get back, I'll tell you."

"How long will you be gone?"

"I'm not sure." Bill sighed. "I wish I could share everything with you, like your parents planned to on your eighteenth birthday. But it will have to wait a bit longer. I want you to get out of Suncrest."

"Tell that to the three assholes who won't let me leave," I muttered loud enough for them all to hear me.

"You want to start looking for answers?" Bill asked, sounding resigned. "Start at Teddy's storage place. The unit your parents had."

Ky's gaze turned suspicious. "And why would you share that with us?"

"Because what you find there will lead you out of Suncrest," Bill answered. "Even if you're with her, at least she'd be safer than where she's at right now."

"Why not just tell us so we don't have to make the trip into Crow territory?" Zak asked, sounding annoyed.

"Because I didn't put it there," Bill snapped. "Teddy did. And he changed things when Vanessa came back. I don't know what's in or not in the storage unit anymore."

Ky and Ryker didn't look convinced while Zak mumbled, "Sounds like a trap."

"You think so? Then let Vanessa go by herself."

Any tiny hope of that happening was dashed when Ky looked at me, shaking his head. "Not a chance. Mack is already searching for her. She's not going alone, especially on that side of town."

"Stay safe, Vanessa. And be careful who you trust. I'm tossing this phone once we hang up. I don't want anyone in the Kings to try and track me. I'll be back as soon as I can." Bill's voice went cold before speaking again. "And this is a warning, Kyro. Feel free to pass this on to your father. If anyone hurts her, there will be hell to pay. Don't forget who her father was."

"Wait," I nearly yelled. "Please, just tell me who my dad was. What MC was he in?"

"No one's told you yet?" Bill asked in surprise.

Ky abruptly stood up, taking the phone with him. With a cry of protest, I moved to follow him but was yanked back onto the couch. Zak refused to let go of my arm, and I fought to push him off as Bill kept talking.

"She deserves to know," he seethed. "But of course, no one will tell her. It doesn't fit into yours or the Crows agendas. Vanessa, your father was—"

Ky ended the call and put the phone in his pocket. Zak let me go, and I flew off the couch, getting in Ky's face.

"He was about to tell me," I screamed. "God. What is so fucking bad about me finding out?"

"I can't," he nearly whispered, sounding almost regretful. "Not yet. You'll find out soon though. And I'm sure whatever we find in the storage unit will help you figure it out."

I backed away, knowing it was a losing battle. He wasn't going to tell me. Instead of fighting about it, I decided to talk about the thing that could help me get answers.

"So, are we going to the storage unit now or later?"

"Not yet," Ky answered. "We need to plan it out since we don't know who's running it since Teddy is gone. And it's in Crow territory."

Leaning against the side of the couch, I debated what to do. I was going to the storage unit. But I wanted to go by myself. Ky was still keeping secrets. Maybe it was all to protect me. The decision to trust him or not had been ripping me apart for days. I wanted to; I really did. But after the last seven years, I couldn't bring myself to fully trust anyone. Including him.

"You going to share the real storage locker number with us?" Ky's voice pulled me back into the conversation.

I shook my head. "So you can go without me? I don't think so. We'll all go together, and I'll show you."

"I'm getting Déjà vu," Ryker muttered. "Last time we did this, you fucking ran."

"Things change." I shrugged. "Ky said he wants to help me find answers."

All three of their faces revealed they didn't believe me, and I realized trying to go there by myself wasn't going to be easy. But not impossible.

"We'll make the plan tomorrow," Ky said as he walked into the kitchen.

I had already started making my own plan. Doing what I'd been doing for years. Relying only on myself.

The next morning was already off to a good start. Zak was at the gym, which meant I only needed to get away from two of them. Wanting answers was making me impatient. I needed to get to that storage unit as soon as possible.

Sitting at the table, I sipped my coffee as Ky and Ryker walked in.

"Jensen wants me for something," Ryker announced, pouring himself coffee. "I should be back later today."

My eyes widened and I stared down at the table, reining in my excitement. For once, luck was actually on my fucking side. Although, I wished it was Ky leaving. Getting away from him was going to be the most difficult.

"We'll be here," Ky replied, sitting down next to me. His hand went to my thigh, and I met his eyes as he grinned. "What are we going to do with the house all to ourselves?"

My gaze traveled to his bare chest and down to his ripped abs. The thought of spending all day in bed with him was nearly too tempting to say no to. I took a deep breath and stood up as his hand fell from my leg. I needed to keep a clear head. This might be my only chance to make it to the storage locker by myself.

"I need to shower," I muttered, leaving the kitchen.

Neither Ky nor Ryker said anything, causing unease to prickle down my spine. Something was off; they were acting different. I tried shaking it off as I took a quick shower before throwing on some shorts and a tank top. Even though I couldn't stop the feeling that I was missing something, I was still going through with my plan.

It wasn't to escape and leave Suncrest. I only wanted to get to the storage unit first and find out what Bill was talking about. Because there was a big chance that if it had anything to do with my dad, Ky would stop me from finding out what it was. Also, I didn't want Jensen finding out about whatever the hell was in there.

Opening Ky's bedroom door, I peered down the hall and was met with silence. I stepped into the hallway, hearing a quiet voice coming from the office. My footsteps were light as I moved closer, fully intending on eavesdropping.

Ky suddenly came out of the room, making me nearly jump. With the phone to his ear, he frowned when he saw me standing near the door.

"Hold on," he said, pressing the phone to his chest and then focusing his attention to me. "I need to take care of this. We'll go grab food when I'm done."

"King business?" I couldn't help but ask.

He nodded. "The alarm's on. Stay in the house. I won't be long."

I rolled my eyes as he walked back into the room, but then froze when he shut the door. I wasn't expecting him to leave me alone. Wandering through the house, checking to see if Zak and Ryker were still gone, my excitement was building as I went into the empty living room.

Turning toward the hall, something shiny on the kitchen counter caught my eye, and I sucked in a breath. I stared at Ky's truck keys in disbelief. Did he really leave those there on accident or was he testing me to see if I'd run?

Fuck it. I was taking the chance.

Without wasting another second, I scooped up the keys and bolted to the front door, ripping it open. The alarm immediately began blaring, causing me to speed up even more. I was in Ky's truck and down the road in less than thirty seconds. Ky had mentioned before how his truck had a tracker on it, but it didn't worry me. They all knew where I was going.

I only hoped I could find what Bill was talking about before Ky showed up. The place was huge, with hundreds of units and multiple floors. They had no idea where my parents' unit was. If I made it to the unit before they found me, I'd be fine.

I wasn't planning on leaving. I only wanted to get to the paperwork first. Because I had absolutely no plan to give it to Jensen or the Crows. I'd rather destroy it, and no one would get the fucking money.

Forcing myself to stay under the speed limit, I reached the storage place in less than ten minutes. Parking in the back, I slipped through the closest door and made my way down the long halls. I watched the numbers on the units go up as I jogged past them, and after going down three halls and up two flights of stairs, I finally stopped.

Staring at the number above the metal door, I flexed my fingers and took a deep breath. From what Bill said, it didn't sound like all my answers would be in here. But maybe my luck would stay, and my dad's bike would be in here. Remembering I didn't have much time, I spun the combination lock and got it open on my first try.

Dad used to take me here all the time and even had me open the lock a few times. Even after all this time, I never forgot the combo. It was their anniversary date. Sadness and anger mixed together and shot through me. I'd been living a lie my whole life. What was so bad they needed to sell their own daughter? Was it really to protect me?

Shoving those thoughts away, I bent down to lift the door when everything went dark. Some type of cloth material covered my head and face, and someone grabbed my right arm, pushing me into the door. Trying to twist away, I swung my left arm as hard as I could and heard a grunt when my fist connected to flesh.

There were at least two of them because someone came and grabbed my other arm. They started dragging me down the hall, and I fought with every step, but it got me nowhere.

"Let me go," I yelled, my voice muffled from the cloth.

Their grips were tight, and after a couple of minutes, a creak of a door was my only hint we weren't in the hallway anymore. They pushed me into a chair before cuffing my hands behind me. Panic flared in my chest, and I strained against the handcuffs. They weren't tight, but I still couldn't slip out of them.

I was in Crow territory, and the thought of being stuck

with Mack again nearly made me heave. It was stupid coming here without a solid plan. Shifting in the chair, I froze when I heard a shuffling of feet.

"You going to say something or stand there like a fucking creep?" I asked loudly, knowing whoever was there could hear me even through the cloth bag.

Silence was my only answer, but I could tell I still wasn't alone in the room. They were probably waiting for Mack or his dad to get here. I pulled against the cuffs again, glad the cuts were healed. Not that it mattered. Mack would make me pay for getting away from him.

After minutes of silence, the door creaked open again and footsteps came closer. I held my breath as my body locked up. I might be scared, but I sure as hell wasn't going to show whoever it was my fear. It was silent again for a few moments before someone walked right in front of me. The steps stopped, and I tensed as someone leaned over me and brushed my shoulder.

"You fucked up, Vee."

CHAPTER TWELVE

Vanessa

The cloth was pulled off, and I blinked from the brightness of the fluorescent light. Once the people in front of me came into focus, I cursed under my breath and shot the one in the middle a death glare.

"Are you fucking serious?" I grated out, pulling at the cuffs to make a point. "Was this really necessary?"

Ky, Ryker, and Zak stood in front of me. Zak looked amused as he crossed his arms. Ryker looked annoyed. And Ky...I couldn't tell what he was feeling from his blank expression.

"I don't know," Ky answered. "Do you realize now that this was a fucking stupid idea, and you should have waited for us like we planned?"

"Not really." I smiled, knowing it would get on his nerves. "It obviously would have worked if—"

Ky cut me off by laughing. "It never would have worked. I wanted to see if you'd take the chance to leave. Or stay like you said you would. You really think I would have just left the keys on the counter or left you alone?"

I knew it was too damn easy.

"How the hell did you get here so fast? I took your truck."

"We brought Kenzi's bike back from Brown City. It was on the side of the house." Ky took a step closer. "Zak and Ryker were already here waiting to see if you showed up."

"I thought this side of the town belonged to the Crows," I said, getting irritated, even though I was glad it was Ky and not Mack who had me right now.

"It does," Zak answered. "But they have no idea there's something here they need. We paid the guy up front to give us a head's up if any Crows come, but they have no interest in this place. Unless they find out we're here."

"Yeah, we should probably hurry this up," Ryker said pointedly to Ky.

"Not yet," Ky murmured, still looking at me. "I want to know why you decided to do this alone."

I scoffed. "You really have to ask?"

"Yeah, I fucking do," he snapped, his voice finally revealing his feelings. "We agreed to do this together, and here you are trying to do it alone. Why?"

I bit my tongue as he stalked closer until he was standing right in front of me. My gaze moved behind him as Zak turned around and left the room. Ryker stayed but backed away until he was near the door. I tilted my head up and looked back at Ky, who was staring at me like he could read my mind if he tried hard enough.

"I don't trust you." The truth spilled from my mouth as soon as I thought the words.

His eyes widened, and hurt flashed through them. He

didn't say a word as he stared at me, and I squirmed in the chair under his gaze.

"I told you why I lied," he finally said, speaking slowly as if he needed to control himself. "I didn't have a fucking choice. I was keeping you safe—"

"Keeping me safe by me staying in the dark," I cut him off. "Imagine if you were in my place, Ky. For seven fucking years, I had it in my head that you lied and used me. And here we are. You expect me to be okay with everything now that I'm back. I haven't trusted anyone since I was sixteen. I can't just flip a switch and act like none of this ever happened."

He stayed quiet and leaned over me, resting his hands on the arms of the chair. His scent engulfed me, and I stiffened as his eyes traveled down my body.

"You trust me enough let me touch you," he said in a low voice. "I'd say that's a good start."

"Like I'm going to turn down great sex," I bit out, not caring if I pissed him off. He wasn't the one handcuffed to a damn chair. "That has nothing to do with trusting you."

His arms flexed as his grip on the chair tightened. I glanced behind him at Ryker, who was checking his watch and tapping his foot. He didn't like that we were still here. I wondered if there was a problem, and that's why Zak left.

"I tried being nice." Ky pulled my attention back to him. "I told you why I did what I did all those years ago. I was honest. I've given you space at the house."

"You call that being nice?" I let out a short laugh.

"Oh, Raindrop." He dragged his knuckles down my cheek. "You're the only person who has ever seen my nice side. You think I'm a possessive asshole now? No baby. I held back. But not anymore."

I straightened my spine as anger tore through me. Anger

at him or myself, I wasn't sure. Because his words should make me want to fight. Instead, the dark promise in his voice was making heat pool in my stomach.

"Are you trying to make me hate you?" I asked, refusing to give in to what my body wanted.

His mouth twisted into a wicked grin as if he had been expecting those words. My pulse raced when he rested his fingers under my chin, tilting my face up a bit more. His eyes lit up in challenge, and I clasped my hands together behind me.

"Let's clear something up while I have your undivided attention." He brushed his thumb over my lips. "Hate me or love me. Run from me or stay with me. Lie to me or trust me. Fight me or fuck me. Betray me or help me. Keep secrets or tell truths. It doesn't matter, because it all comes back to one thing. That you're mine. And nothing will ever fucking change that."

His eyes didn't leave mine even after he stopped talking. To anyone else, it made him sound like a controlling, possessive asshole. And he was. But right now, with those words, he was telling me something else.

That his love for me overpowered everything I'd done in the past. Or might do in the future. It was his promise that no matter what, he would never give up on me. On us.

My heart pounded as we stared at each other. His words and actions were beginning to chip away at the numbness I had tried so hard to perfect in the last seven years.

And it scared the fucking shit out of me.

He didn't wait for me to answer and stood back up before moving behind me and unlocking the handcuffs. I jumped from the chair only for Ky to grab my arm and pull me to his chest.

"Don't try to leave again." His words came out sharp, but his eyes pleaded with me in a way that made my heart ache.

"I can't promise that," I said just above a whisper. "But... I'll try."

It was as honest as I could be, and his eyes flashed in anger. He wanted me to be all in. I couldn't do it. Not yet.

"If I'm not enough to keep you here." He nodded at Ryker, who moved to open the door. "Then maybe she is."

My head snapped to the open doorway, fully expecting to see Kenzi. But the person who walked in didn't belong here, and my mouth dropped in shock. Happiness snuck through the haze of surprise before fear took its place. She shouldn't be here.

"Are you always so handsy with people you just met?" she asked, swatting Zak's hand off her back. He raised his arms and backed away right as she caught sight of me.

"Becca," she squealed. "I mean, Vanessa. I told myself on the entire flight here, I had to call you by the right name."

Her arms squeezed around my neck, and I returned her embrace as the scent of my double life surrounded me. Her once black hair was now blonde with bright blue tips. She never could keep her hair the same color longer than a few months.

"Cassie, what are you doing here?" I asked, still not over the sight of seeing her here in Suncrest Bay. She belonged in Detroit. Where I was Becca and when life was a whole lot simpler.

She didn't let me go as she talked into my ear. "I couldn't stay there anymore. Not after what my dad did to you. It took me a while, but I finally decided to leave. You're the only person I know who doesn't live in Detroit. God, I missed you. It hasn't been the same since you left."

"I missed you too, Cass," I mumbled. I did miss her. But she didn't belong in this life. People I cared about were in danger in this city. From the Crows, from Jensen, and I wasn't sure I could keep her safe.

I met Ky's gaze as I hugged Cass and saw a spark of triumph. I wouldn't try to run now that she was here. I couldn't even escape when I was by myself. No way I'd be able to bring Cassie with me. I had no doubts about Ky keeping her safe. He'd do that for me. I couldn't leave her here, and he knew it.

"How did you find me?" I asked, pulling away from her.

Ryker spoke up. "She convinced Zak to give her our address before we left Detroit."

"She told me she wanted to mail you some of your things." Zak rubbed the back of his neck. "I never expected her to show up instead."

I looked at her. "Does your dad know you're here?"

"Umm, not exactly." She smiled sheepishly. "He thinks I went down south for vacation."

"That's just great," Zak grumbled. "Now we have to keep you alive, or your dad will come for all of us. Like we don't have enough shit to deal with."

"She's not a burden," I argued, even though part of me agreed with him. I was happy to see Cass, but I didn't want her involved in my fucked-up problems.

"She'll stay with us. And for now, we won't tell my dad. He finds out, then he'll send you back to Detroit," Ky said, stepping next to me. "But first, let's go back to that storage unit and see what's in there."

My stomach dropped. Seeing Cass had made me completely forget what I was doing here in the first place.

"I know what you're looking for, Raindrop," Ky murmured from behind me as I walked out of the office.

"Yeah, whatever Bill said was in here."

He grabbed my arm, stopping me. "It took me a while to remember, but after dealing with the bikers in Brown City, it clicked."

"Remember what?" I asked.

"I was there the day your dad mentioned his bike when we were kids," Ky said. "I left the garage but stayed outside the door because I wanted to know what he had to say about me. Stella. His bike, his first love. That's why you were in Brown City trying to talk to the Dusty Devils."

"Congratulations, you figured it out," I snarked. "It doesn't change anything, unless you know where the bike is?"

I took his silence as a no and pulled out of his grip. With Ky next to me and everyone else following us, we made our way through the halls until, once again, I was standing in front of my parents' storage unit.

"Ready?" Ky asked quietly, picking up the combo lock from the floor.

I nodded, and he lifted the metal door. I watched it roll up as my nerves heightened. Everyone was quiet, and I was surprised Cass wasn't asking a million questions. She had to be curious. I'd have to fill her in once we left.

Even though I was expecting it, disappointment crashed into me as I looked inside the unit. The motorcycle wasn't here.

CHAPTER THIRTEEN

Kyro

Vanessa's shoulders slumped as she stared into the storage unit. Even though the chance was low, she was hoping the bike was here. I looked past her and glanced inside the unit. There were a few filing cabinets, an old dresser, and a shit ton of stacked boxes.

"We really need to do this fast," Ryker muttered. "If the Crows realize we're here, we'll be outnumbered."

I nodded, knowing he was right. I hadn't told Jensen we were coming here. We didn't have any backup. I'd been trying to keep the Kings out of anything that had to do with Vanessa, but Jensen was getting impatient. He wanted the paperwork, and I only gave it days before he came looking for answers.

Vanessa went straight for a filing cabinet, and I followed her and opened the other one. Ryker and Zak started unstacking the boxes to go through them.

"I can help if someone tells me what we're looking for," Cassie said from the hall.

"You can help by going home," Zak said, shooting her an annoyed glance.

Cassie crossed her arms. "I'm not going back."

I sighed and spoke up before Zak could start arguing. "Just keep watch. Let us know if someone comes."

Cassie nodded and leaned against the doorway as she peered down the hall. The rest of us worked in silence. Most of the papers in my filing cabinet were old taxes and things about their house. I had half a mind to just take everything with us instead of staying here longer. After about twenty more minutes, I stopped when I noticed Vanessa staring at a piece of paper.

"You find something?" I asked, scooting closer to her.

Her grip on the paper tightened. "Maybe."

"Let me see it."

She hesitated, and I ran a hand down my face. "We really don't have time to fight about it. The faster we leave, the better. Give it to me, Raindrop."

She rolled her eyes and handed it over. The first word I read had my heart jumping. *Stella*. I continued to read and knew this was what we were looking for.

Stella isn't safe here. Stone and Tessa wanted me to have her if anything ever happened to them. I moved her somewhere angels can watch over her. If Vanessa ever comes home, I will bring her to Stella and explain what her parents never got a chance to. I'm writing this in case anything ever happens to me. The people who know will understand this note. If you're reading this and don't understand, then put it back down. It would be a grave mistake to think you can use Stella. This is your only warning.

Teddy.

. . .

Well, fuck. That was about as vague as he could get, and the way Vanessa was staring into space made me think she had no idea where he moved to the bike to either.

"This is fucking stupid," Zak said, shaking his head. "I feel like we're playing a damn game of treasure hunt. And we've been a step behind the whole time."

"Pretty sure that's the whole point," Ryker said, stepping away from the boxes. "We aren't supposed to be the ones to find it."

"How much money is it?" Vanessa asked.

I sighed. "No one except your parents knows the exact amount. But we know it's a lot."

"It's just the account numbers, or is there more?" Vanessa stood up and took the paper from my hands.

"Account numbers, their will, all their businesses, most likely a note to you," I rattled off everything I had heard Jensen say. The only reason he knew was because of the Crow he'd tortured years ago trying to get the information. But who even knew if the Crows had all answers? Because it seemed there was even more from what Bill said during the phone call.

"And the only person who could help us is dead," Zak muttered, and I shot him a glare. Vanessa didn't need any more guilt about Teddy dying. It wasn't her fault.

"We'll find it," I said, walking out of the storage unit. "We need to find Kenzi, she might know."

"I'll try to track her down," Ryker said. "Maybe her girlfriend's phone is on. We know they went somewhere together."

We got back to my truck, and Vanessa got into the back

with Cassie. Ryker went to drive Kenzi's bike, and Zak got into the passenger seat.

"You going to tell Jensen?" Zak asked quietly.

Vanessa didn't hear him. She was too busy explaining the last month to Cassie.

"Not yet," I answered, pulling out of the parking lot.

I wanted to keep this from Jensen for as long as possible. As soon as he had that paperwork, Vanessa was useless to him. He wanted her to suffer for Knox. That money was the only reason he hadn't touched her yet.

Zak rubbed his temples. "If Jensen finds out you're lying, we're all going to be in deep shit."

"I know."

Whether we found the money or not, none of this was going to end well.

"Where am I sleeping?" Cassie asked, standing in the living room.

We had just gotten back from the storage place, and Vanessa was digging in the kitchen, looking for something to make for lunch. I wasn't sure why; we all knew she couldn't cook. Ryker would be the one to make food.

Zak came up behind her, dragging her suitcase. "The couch. Enjoy."

"You'll get Zak's room," I answered as he stared at me in shock. "You're the one who gave her our address. So, she gets your room."

Cassie grinned and patted Zak on the shoulder. "Enjoy the couch."

"Come on," Zak said grudgingly. "I'll show you my room."

I followed Ryker into the kitchen and saw Vanessa eating a cold piece of pizza.

"Aren't you going to warm it up?" Ryker asked, taking a piece for himself.

"Nope," she replied, finishing her last bite. "Where's Cassie?"

"Zak's giving her a tour."

"What now?" she asked. "How are we going to find Kenzi? And the Crows? They're going to come after me again."

"There are Kings watching the house. We'll have help if they try coming here." I wasn't worried in the slightest. Mack wasn't stupid enough to come to my doorstep. "But you don't go anywhere alone."

She frowned. "I know, you don't have to remind me."

"What you did today proves that's not true," Ryker interjected.

"Stay out of it, Ryker," she snapped before storming out of the kitchen.

"Where are you going?" I trailed behind her to my room, and she tried shutting the door in my face.

Wedging my foot in the doorway, I pushed it back open, ignoring the glare she was giving me. I shut the door behind me and leaned against it.

"What do you want, Ky? It's been a long morning."

"I need a reason to come into my own room?"

"The last few days, it's been my room." She glanced around. "I'm actually thinking of redecorating."

"Did you already forget what I said earlier?" She stiffened as her guard went up from my words.

"What? About you becoming an even bigger asshole?" She forced out a laugh, keeping her eyes on me. "I'm not sure that's possible."

"I guess you'll find out. I'm sleeping in here again. I'm tired of the couch."

"Fine, I'll stay on the couch."

"Can't. Zak's sleeping there and Cassie is taking his room."

She bit her lip, and her gaze went to the bed beside her. "Then I'll stay in Zak's room with Cassie."

"No, baby. You're staying in here with me," I said quietly, moving closer to her. "You aren't leaving my sight after today."

"I already agreed I wouldn't go anywhere by myself."

"I know, and I'll make sure it stays that way," I promised, watching her eyes flash in anger.

"If this is your way of getting me to open up more, you're doing a shit job." She was trying to get me to back off.

I took her by surprise by crossing the room. For every step I moved forward, she backed away until she hit the wall.

"What's wrong, Raindrop?" I caught her arm when she tried darting around me. "Don't trust yourself around me?"

She lifted her head to meet my eyes, and the look she gave me made my dick swell against my jeans. The wall she'd built to keep me out was crashing down, and I was done waiting. Giving her space wasn't happening anymore.

"Like I said earlier, the only person I trust is myself."

"You're right," I murmured. "I need to prove you can trust me. And I'll start by making sure I keep word. About everything."

Suspicion flittered across her face as she stared at me. "Your word about what?"

"What did I say would happen if you tried to run again?"

Her face flushed as she remembered my words from

yesterday. She pulled away, but I kept my grip on her arm and pushed her back into the wall.

"Now, are you going to get on the bed like a good girl, or do you want to play? Either way, we're not leaving this room for a while."

"Yeah, because sex will solve all our problems," she said sarcastically while at the same time her gaze darted to the bed.

"We weren't very vanilla, even as teenagers." I ignored her comment. "Then I found those toys in your bag. And how hot you got when I talked about a threesome in the club."

Her cheeks grew pink. "I just know what I like. Nothing wrong with that."

"And that's fucking hot." Letting go of her arm, I dragged my fingers to her shoulder until they grazed her neck. "I love that you're open about it."

"Okay..." she said with a touch of uncertainty.

I ran my thumb over her lips as she sucked in a breath. "We only got a year to explore each other before our lives went to shit. And that's not nearly enough time. I want to act out every dirty fantasy you've dreamed up. What do you want to try first?"

Her eyes widened before she got defensive. "You can't keep me here and then expect me to say thank you with my pussy."

I chuckled. "Hearing you scream my name will be all the thanks I need. And I can promise that's going to happen while you're here."

She was so damn stubborn. She would never just agree with me, even if it was what she wanted too. And I knew she was aching for it as much as I was. So, I decided to say the thing her competitive nature wouldn't be able to turn down.

"I'll play you for the bed," I said casually, dropping my hand from her face. "I pick the game."

She couldn't hide her interest as she crossed her arms. "Going to choose poker again?"

I shook my head. "No, not another game of chance."

"What game?"

"Whoever gets the other to come first gets the bed. If I win, you sleep in here with me. If you win, then you can have the bed to yourself."

Her eyes widened and darted down to my jeans before meeting my eyes again. "Seriously?"

"Yup." I reached up, grabbed the back of my shirt, and pulled it over my head. "You going to play, Raindrop? Or are you going to make room in the bed for me tonight?"

Lust and determination swam in her eyes as she grinned and slipped off her own shirt. My dick jerked to life when she unhooked her bra and let it fall to the ground. *Fucking hell.* She was perfect. For the last seven years, I'd had it in my head that she'd never be back. I was going to let her go and give her a chance to leave this world and me behind.

But she was back, and I wasn't letting her go again. I didn't give a shit if that made me an asshole.

She ran her hands down her breasts before gripping the waistband of her shorts. I shot forward and pulled her hands away, replacing them with my own. Sliding the shorts off, I kept my eyes on the black lace panties she was wearing. She'd always had a thing for lace, and I fucking loved it.

I took her hand and pulled her toward the bed, stopping once we were in front of it. "On your knees, baby."

CHAPTER FOURTEEN

Kyro

She sank to her knees with a look of confusion. Shocked she actually listened to me, I moved forward with what I wanted to do before she changed her mind. Going to the dresser, I pulled out a pair of leather cuffs I took out of her bag. I'd been obsessing over using these more ever since I'd found her stash of toys.

Her eyes narrowed when she caught sight of the cuffs, but she didn't move. "What are you doing, Ky?"

"Keeping my word. You ran. Now you get tied to my bed."

"This wasn't part of the deal." Her eyes were glued to me as I walked back over to her.

Grinning, I grabbed her arm before pulling it behind her back. "You should've specified rules before you agreed."

She tensed as I fastened the cuffs around her wrists but didn't pull away. I clipped the cuffs together and then lifted her arms. She rose a bit but still stayed on her knees as I raised her arms over the short wooden post on the footboard of my bed.

Stepping back, I trailed my fingers through her hair before gripping it and tilting her head back. Her arms were stretched out behind her, and seeing her on her knees for me was almost too much. I wanted to bury myself inside her and never leave. But I had to control myself long enough to win this little game.

With my hand still in her hair, I met her gaze. She might be on her knees for me, but the fire brightening her brown eyes promised she'd never submit to anyone in this life. After the shit she'd been through, I didn't expect any different. It wasn't the reason I was doing this anyway. I had something else to prove.

I just needed to fucking contain myself long enough to do that.

"All your toys, including those cuffs, are brand new." Her lips tipped down in confusion as I spoke. "Well, except for the toys that vibrate. Those have definitely gotten some use."

"So?"

Releasing her hair, my fingers grazed her neck until I gripped her chin. "Who else?"

"Who else what?"

"How many other guys have you let use these cuffs on you?"

"Why the fuck does that matter?"

"I bet the answer is zero."

She licked her lips, and her body went rigid before she offered me a smug smile. "You really want to know what I've done with guys in the past?"

Rage scorched through my veins and my jaw tightened. I wanted to go and murder every fucker who'd touched her while she was in Michigan. Shoving those thoughts aside, I shot her a grin.

"The fact that you haven't let anyone else do this to you tells me something." Moving away from her, I went back to her bag of toys and waited for her curiosity to win out.

"Tells you what?" she asked with more than a little annoyance.

After grabbing what I wanted, I turned back to her. "Even if you refuse to admit it to yourself, you trust me."

Like I expected, her eyes lit up in defiance. "No, I don't."

"You do. Maybe not enough to trust my words. But this is a good fucking start."

She fidgeted and didn't answer. A frown appeared on her face when the truth of what I said dawned on her.

"Ready to play?" I asked, pulling my sweatpants off.

"How do you expect me to play like this?" Shaking her arms, she sat higher on her knees.

"Don't worry," I murmured, showing her what was in my hand. "You can use your mouth because, *fuck*, I've been waiting to feel your lips on me again. And me...I'll use this."

"That's cheating," she hissed, staring at little vibrating bullet in my hand. The same one I used on her last time.

"I told you I'm done being nice." I dropped the toy inside her panties, feeling how wet she already was. "If I have to play dirty to get what I want, I will."

Sliding a finger over her pussy before making sure the toy was snug against her clit, I leaned forward, brushing my lips over hers. Her breaths were already coming faster as her eyes begged me to keep going.

"I think you're underestimating my mouth." Her tone was sultry, and she stared at my boxers.

"I guess we'll find out." Unable to hold back any longer,

I pulled off my boxers. Her eyes immediately went to my cock.

With a grin, she licked her lips before meeting my gaze. "This is going to be fun."

Yes, it fucking was. I'd dreamed about being in her mouth for the last seven years. I stepped in front of her and reached for the remote to the vibrator. The second her lips touched the tip of my cock, I turned the bullet on, knowing if I waited any longer, I'd forget.

I groaned as she slowly took as much as me as she could fit, until I hit the back of her throat. Jesus Christ. It was better than I remembered. As she pulled back, her teeth grazed my shaft, making my balls tighten. Fuck, she knew exactly what I liked.

I couldn't tear my eyes from her as she began moving faster, getting in a rhythm as her hips rolled, chasing the friction she wanted. She looked up at me through her lashes as her cheeks hollowed out before she took me as deep as she could down her throat.

Not able to control myself any longer, I fisted her hair. She moaned, her body beginning to stiffen as the toy did its job. She slowed down, letting me take control while she climbed to the edge.

Her arms strained against the cuffs, her eyelids sliding closed as her orgasm came. Her entire body went rigid, and she screamed around my cock as she came. Her hips continuously rocking as her orgasm seemed never ending from the vibrator still being on her clit.

Her mouth clamped down on my cock and I threw my head back as she flicked her tongue on my tip before deep throating as far as she could go. Thank fuck she came first because that move made me lose it.

My grip in her hair tightened as I exploded in her

mouth. Pleasure tore through me as she swallowed everything I gave her. Her body jerked as the vibrator buzzed, her eyes rolling up while she got lost in a sea of lust.

With a grin, I pulled my cock from her mouth before reaching down and trapping her left nipple between my fingers. Her chest heaved as her body worked to control the sensations ripping through her.

"The game's over," she breathed out, not able to even focus on me as she spoke.

"You're already halfway there, baby," I murmured, dropping to my knees. "It would be rude to turn it off now."

Capturing her nipple between my teeth, I bit down and tugged until a moan shuddered through her chest. Her legs quivered uncontrollably as she tugged at the cuffs, her body unable to stay still.

"Oh my fuck." The curse fell from her lips as her second orgasm flooded through her.

My dick decided we weren't finished as her moans reached my ears. We were far from fucking done. Her panties were soaked when I slid out the vibrator, and she nearly jumped as I grazed her clit.

"Sensitive?"

"After two rounds with a toy, who wouldn't be?" She tugged at the cuffs. "It's bullshit, you know. Winning with a toy."

"There were no rules."

She looked entirely too sexy. Naked. On her knees. Cuffed to my bed. Exhausted from playing, but her eyes still dancing with excitement about the prospect of more. And I'd give her all she could handle.

"You knew I'd be able to get you off first." She shrugged as much as she could with her arms pulled behind her. "I understand, you needed to cheat to win."

"Raindrop." I traced her tattoo down her ribs. "I always make sure you come first. There is no better foreplay than watching you come undone in front of me. But if you don't think I can get you off with my mouth just as well as your toy does...then it looks like I have something else to prove tonight."

"Ky—"

"Will you admit you trust me?" I asked, sliding my fingers into her panties.

Her breath caught as I slid a finger in her. Fuck, she was dripping. I added a second finger and she raised back up on her knees, giving me better access.

"Can you say you trust me?" I repeated, knowing her answer when she froze.

Quiet voices from the hall paused our conversation and I glanced at the door. *This house better be on fire if someone interrupted us right now.* The noises disappeared and I focused back on Vanessa.

"We're too loud," she insisted, shaking her head. "I don't want everyone to hear what we're doing in here."

"That's an easy fix," I muttered before clearing my throat. "You didn't answer me."

"I don't want to answer you."

"Last chance."

Her eyes flashed. "Or what?"

"Are your arms sore yet?" I glanced at her wrists as she shifted on her knees.

Her head tilted curiously. "No."

"Good."

In one swift move, I ripped her lace panties off her. She let out an annoyed cry as she stared at her destroyed panties in my hand.

"That's two pairs you owe me now," she mumbled. "What is with you destroying my clothes?"

"Have you ever tasted yourself?"

Her eyes widened and she glanced down at the soaked panties. "No."

"Your taste is a high I can never stop chasing." I balled up the panties. "You are literally the best thing that's ever touched my tongue."

Anticipation darkened her eyes as I crouched in front of her. Her nipples were hard, begging me to touch them again. With my free hand, I grasped her chin, pulling her mouth open.

"This taste makes me crazy." I pushed the panties into her mouth. "If I could, I'd be your throne and let you reign over me every goddamn day. You own me, Raindrop. In every fucking way."

A shiver ran through her, goosebumps skating across her skin. Dropping lower, I laid on my back, scooting up until my head was between her legs. Her thighs were slick from her arousal, and I wrapped my arms around them, pulling her pussy to my mouth.

Her clit was swollen from the toy, and one hard suck had her body bucking above me. Keeping my grip on her thighs, I licked and played until her legs trembled around me. I paused for a moment and she ground her pussy on my face, trying to get the release she wanted.

"Is it too much?" I teased, loud enough for her to hear. "I can stop."

Her whimpers made my dick harden even more than I thought possible. Giving her what she wanted, my tongue explored every inch as her moans turned into screams of pleasure.

"Scream, baby." I nipped at her clit. "There's a reason I put those panties in your mouth."

I didn't give a fuck if the entire neighborhood heard us. And from the way her screams echoed through the room, they just might. Letting my insatiable hunger for her take over, I lured her orgasm to the edge as she tensed around me.

Her entire body shook as she came. The panties barely did anything to cover her screaming my name. I didn't let go of her legs until her body stopped rolling from pleasure. She was trying to catch her breath as I slid out from under her. Pulling the panties from her mouth, I grinned at the absolute satisfied look on her face. After unhooking the cuffs, I lifted her onto the bed and laid her down. She took me by surprise when she grabbed my arm, meeting my eyes.

"I do trust you," she admitted softly. "At least with my body. I know you wouldn't hurt me."

"Good."

She pulled me on top of her. "I want you, Ky. Fuck me. Right now."

Not even stopping to ask how the hell she wasn't exhausted, I slammed my lips onto hers, still tasting her from the panties. Her legs clamped down around my waist, and I rested a hand on the bed as I guided my cock over her entrance. She was so wet, I slid in with no resistance, filling her completely.

With each thrust, her moans became louder, and I went faster until I felt her pussy pulsating around my cock. Jesus, she was going to come again. Readjusting a bit, I thrust deeper, hitting her G-spot.

With an almost strangled cry, she quivered beneath me as she came again. Her nails clawed down my back as I raced to my own release. With a groan, I came, feeling my seed fill her. Even if I didn't want to get her pregnant, coming inside her made my primal side roar.

She was mine.

We laid there, with me on top of her and still inside her for a minute, catching our breath. I finally rolled off her to the other side of the bed. She didn't move a fucking muscle. Chuckling, I gazed over to her, seeing she was nearly half asleep.

A knock on the door had me sitting up with a scowl. We couldn't go one time without getting interrupted.

"What?" I griped out loud enough for whoever was there to hear.

"Vanessa?" Cassie's unsure voice floated through the door. "I waited until I didn't hear any more screaming. But we have a problem."

Vanessa lifted her head from the pillow, staring at the door.

"There's no problem," Zak yelled. "Go back to whatever you were doing. I'll deal with it."

"Let go of me," Cassie screeched. "I don't know if you think it's normal, but I'm not staying in a room where anything I touch is going to give me a STD."

I could hear Zak spluttering even through the door. "I've never had a fucking STD."

"You have a drawer overflowing with condoms and... and other stuff," Cassie argued back. "I'm scared to touch the door handle, let alone the bed."

I groaned, throwing an arm over my eyes while Vanessa laughed.

"Condoms prevent STDs," Zak explained slowly. "Obviously if I use them, I'm being safe. You should brush up on your sexual education."

Cassie let out a frustrated scream. "I'm not staying in there when god knows what's on those sheets."

"You realize they're going to stand there and argue until someone breaks them up, right?" Vanessa asked, raising an eyebrow.

"Fine," I grumbled. "I'll deal with it."

I had no issues dealing with it. I was happy. She admitted it. She trusted me. She was letting me back in. Slowly. But it was happening.

CHAPTER FIFTEEN

Vanessa

Rolling off the bed, I leaned against the wall for a few moments until my legs stopped shaking. Good thing Cass interrupted us. I wasn't sure I could have handled a fifth fucking orgasm.

"I swear to fuck," Ky muttered, pulling his boxers on. "Next time, we're going somewhere no one can find us."

"Maybe it's a sign we should stop doing this," I replied as I pushed off the wall.

"Say that again," he dared me in a low voice, sending a rush through me even though my body was spent.

The doorbell rang louder than the arguing voices echoing down the hall, and I slipped my clothes back on. With his shorts on, he crossed the room and slammed open the door.

"Mar," Zak practically screamed from the living room. "Hi, uh—was Ky expecting you?"

My stomach twisted hearing her name, and Ky froze with his hand still on the doorknob. He swung his head around to glance at me, and apology darkened his eyes. Shaking my head, I grabbed the cuffs and shoved them into the dresser drawer. As much as I wanted to piss off the mafia princess, I'd rather not end up in a shallow grave.

By the time I turned around, Ky was already gone. I ran my hands through my hair a couple of times to try and tame it before walking into the hall. Cassie was introducing herself as I stepped into the living room. Two large men were standing near the front door. They were dressed in plain clothes, but their stiff posture and frowns implied they were here for work.

I guess Mar and I did have one thing in common. Both of us couldn't fucking go anywhere alone.

Ryker was making drinks at the bar while Zak and Ky stood rigidly behind Cass. Mar's gaze left Cass and landed on me. Even though she was smiling, her eyes spewed a cold hate the second we locked eyes.

"Vanessa." The sweetness in her voice contradicted the bitterness on her face. "I've been wanting to talk to you. I think we got off on the wrong foot when we first met."

I barely managed to hold in a laugh, knowing she was full of shit. Ky watched her curiously as Ryker handed him a glass of whiskey.

"Do you boys mind stepping outside while Vanessa and I chat for a minute?" she asked with a look directed at Ky. "And Cassie, too, please."

The tension that had been coating the room thickened in a heartbeat. Glancing between Mar and me, Ky didn't move from his spot. Zak and Ryker stayed quiet while Cass stared at all of us in confusion, not knowing who Mar was.

"For what?" Ky asked, trying hard to sound casual.

Mar giggled. "It's girl talk, Kyro. You'd be bored. It'll only take a couple minutes."

She placed her hand on his arm, and I bit my tongue. *Fuck.* I couldn't control myself about anything when it came to him. Seven damn years I'd been gone. There had been death, betrayal, and everything in between during that time. Yet, I couldn't get it through my head that us together wasn't fucking possible.

She pushed Ky toward the back door, and he reluctantly moved with a nod of his head. Zak and Ryker followed while Cassie shot me a questioning glance.

"I'm fine, Cass," I assured her. And I would be. I might hate her, but I wasn't afraid of her. I decided to play nice, though, because her father was a different story.

Ky hesitated and looked at me before opening the door and stepping out, with everyone following behind him.

"Both of you too," Mar sang out to her two men.

The slightly larger man crossed his arms and his frown deepened. "We're supposed to stay with you at all times—"

"You'll be right outside." Her sweetness faded to annoyance when they didn't move. "Do I need to remind you of the little tidbit of information I have? Do I need to talk to my dad?"

The man's face paled, and his gaze darted to his partner, who messed with his watch. Raising an eyebrow, I moved to the side when both men passed me to get to the door. Once we were alone, Mar's grin reappeared. Her fake smile was nearly impeccable. But after meeting the personality behind the mask, it was easy to tell the difference. Especially since I had spent years perfecting my own.

"What do you want?" The words left my mouth as soon as the door was closed. I wanted to get this over with as soon as fucking possible.

"I wanted to apologize for what I said the night we met."

"Apology accepted. Is that all?"

"No..." she trailed off and sat on the arm of the couch. "I'm curious about you."

I blinked in surprise. "Why?"

"You know more about my fiancé than I do."

This conversation just turned on a road I never wanted to travel down. I forced myself to relax the tension in my muscles. She stared at me, waiting for an answer, and I shrugged.

"Yeah, I guess. We grew up here and went to school together, like Ky told you. We're not close and never really hung out."

"Until you started dating Ryker."

"Right, until then."

Her eyes narrowed, and my nails dug into my palm when I realized I'd fucked up. I knew what she was going to say before she even opened her mouth.

"You seem to know him well enough to call him by a nickname."

"It's what everyone calls him." My lie flowed as easily as the truth, but suspicion still lit up her eyes.

"I think if we're going to see each other more, it would be nice to be friends." Her lips tipped up in a smirk, and it was a hint this conversation wasn't over.

"No offense, but I don't see us being friends. I don't enjoy shopping." I lingered a stare at her sundress. "Or dressing up. Give me jeans and a shirt and I'm set."

"*Ky* seems to enjoy the way I dress." Her use of his nickname wasn't lost on me, and my neck prickled with heat. "Easy access. If you know what I mean."

My irritation with her became full-fledged anger, and keeping my face blank was becoming difficult. Ky had told me they'd never had sex. *Was that another lie?* I understood why he had done it in the past. But if he was lying about this, it had nothing to do with keeping me safe. And everything to do with keeping me from punching him in the face.

"I'm surprised a princess like you isn't waiting for her wedding night."

Fuck me.

The words were out before I could stop them. I crossed the room and poured myself a drink, attempting to keep my mouth shut. Unlike the Crows and Kings, the mafia had no reason to keep me alive. Mar could snap her fingers and one of the men she came with would put a bullet in me without another thought.

"Oh, it's way too late for that." She laughed at herself, and her heels clicked on the floor until she was behind me.

Turning around to face her, I cursed silently for being so damn short. Towering over me, she leaned closer as if trying to be intimidating. Going rigid, my hands closed into fists while my body automatically went into defense mode.

"Strawberry," I said with a snide smile, refusing to be on edge because she was in my personal space.

"What?"

"The shampoo I use. If you wanted to know, you could have just asked instead of trying to smell me."

Her face went red as she jolted back a step. "I wasn't smelling you."

"Trying to kiss me then? Because I can't think of one other fucking reason why you're in my face." My confidence grew as indecision darted across her face.

The ceiling fan was the only thing breaking the silence as we stared at each other. After a few moments, she regained her composure, and the smile was back on her face.

"Jensen doesn't seem to like you much," she stated, watching me closely.

"The feeling is mutual."

"Do your parents know your boyfriend is in a gang?"

Sucking in a deep breath, I couldn't stop the stab of anguish that sliced through me. Even after the last few weeks, the mention of them brought my childhood memories rushing to the surface. Curiosity lit up her face, reminding me to lock my emotions away.

"What the hell do you want?" My impatience was nearing its breaking point.

"What do you mean?" she asked, her eyes going wide with innocence. "I told you I wanted to be friends. I'm only trying to get to know you."

"Cut the shit," I snapped, growing tired of her game. She wasn't the ditzy airhead I had first thought, and unease gathered inside me as I tried figuring her out.

"Does your mother not approve of the men you sleep with?"

My teeth slammed together as I forced myself to stay still. She saw my moment of weakness when asking about my parents, and she was trying to draw it out. Her eyes shone in triumph from my reaction, and she reclaimed the space between us until she was close enough for me to see the glitter in her lip gloss.

"Do they not know the life you're in?" she pressed, oblivious to the fact that I was about to lose it. "That you spend your time with three guys who are career criminals?"

"You better stop talking about shit you know nothing about," I threatened as I stepped forward, closing the last few inches separating us.

"I know you act like you have some sort of ownership

over not just Ryker, but the other two guys in this house. One of whom is soon to be *mine*."

My chest suddenly burned while a sharp pain shot through my stomach. Anger was an emotion I was used to. This was something else. I swallowed thickly, realizing what it was.

Jealousy.

No. I shouldn't be feeling this. *But how could I not?* In the past, there had never been a reason to be jealous. He had always been mine. I snapped out of it when Mar poked me in the shoulder. Stiffening, I glared at her, ready to tell her to back off when she spoke first.

"I saw it at dinner when I first met you. The way Kyro looked at you," she said bitterly. "My father was too busy staring at your tits to notice."

"I don't know what—"

"I might play the part of spoiled brat, but I'm not stupid," she cut me off, still only inches away from me. "In my life, the men make the decisions. The women are supposed to look pretty and stay quiet. I learn a lot from being silent and watching. Picking up on things others overlook. You and Kyro are both good at hiding feelings. But not when it comes to each other."

Damn, she was perceptive. She just became another fucking person I'd have to watch out for because I was pretty sure I would never be on her friend list.

"I'm here...to help the Kings with something." Her eyebrows raised at my words.

I wasn't going to lie and try to convince her I was with Ryker. She already knew that wasn't the truth. I had no intention of admitting the history Ky and I had. Or what I was doing with the Kings. I had a feeling she was the type of person to use any information to her advantage. Just like I did.

"To help with what?"

"Since you seem to be such good friends with Jensen, you can ask him." My eyes darted from her face to her body before meeting her gaze again. "Now, back the fuck off."

With a smirk, she poked me in the shoulder again. "Or what?"

My muscles were begging for release, but I stayed frozen, giving her one last chance.

"Listen, little miss priss bitch," I said in an icy tone. "This is your last warning. You don't back the hell up, you'll be on the floor with a new makeover. Unless red is your favorite color, move your ass."

Shock swept across her face before her eyes flashed in anger. "My guys are right outside—"

"I'd be out the front door and long gone before they could touch me," I cut in. "Want to take the chance and see?"

She looked over her shoulder at the large window covering the back wall while I waited, expecting her to step back. Her men were standing at the sliding door, but even if they wanted to look, they couldn't. I'd learned fast that the window was tinted, and it was impossible to see inside. They'd have no idea what was going on in here unless one of us started screaming. I wasn't planning on touching her, but she didn't have to know that.

"You really want to piss off my family?" she asked, looking back at me.

"Probably about as much as you want a broken nose." Squaring my shoulders, I ignored the raging voice in my head telling me to stop while I was ahead. "Like I said, I don't like shopping much. But fighting? I'm fucking known for it. Your family is the only reason I'm giving you this warning. Now. Back. The. Fuck. Up."

My demand came out as harsh as I intended. Keeping my lethal stare on her, I jerked forward, and she immediately flinched away. A cold smile played on my lips, proving I was enjoying this far too much. She backed up a step, fussing with her hair as if there was a piece out of place.

"Smart choice." As I reached for my drink, her hand appeared in my vision before it collided with my face.

Surprise hit me more than her weak slap did. I didn't think she had it in her. If her father wasn't a fucking mob boss, I'd be laying her out by now. I wasn't dumb enough to get killed over a slap that didn't even sting, even if every instinct was screaming to punch her back. Touching my cheek and staring at her, I wondered if she was stupid or actually had a bit of spunk in her.

"I bet your parents wouldn't even miss you if you disappeared," she spat out. "Your mom is probably a bigger bitch than you."

Stupid. She was fucking stupid.

"You shouldn't talk about things you don't know about," I warned, keeping my voice eerily calm as my insides churned with anger. "It could get you hurt."

My threat was ignored when she started talking again. "I don't know what's going on between you and Kyro, but I know there's something there. Soon, he'll be with me. And in our world, my daddy tops his. Which means his life is mine to do with as I choose. I'll *own* him."

The burning in my veins became a scorching fire, and I took a step forward before realizing it. Her words shouldn't have gotten me this pissed. My brain decided they fucking did. I took a deep breath, attempting to calm myself down. She was baiting me.

Choosing to leave to keep from attacking her, I backed away, but she had other ideas. In two quick steps, she was within hitting distance, already gearing up to slap me again. Jerking to the side with my arm already raised, I backhanded her across the mouth before shoving her back. Stumbling, she managed to stay on her feet.

"Remember, you started this." She wiped her mouth and looked at the blood on her hand as I spoke. "I was going to walk away. But that's fucked now."

With a high-pitched screech, she lunged at me. It was simple to dodge out of reach. She tried hard but was sloppy, and her movements were obvious before she made them. This wasn't even close to a fair fight. Didn't mean I was going to stop. I fucking warned her.

Grabbing her arm, I swung her around, letting go when her back slammed into the wall. Her heels became my advantage when she lost her balance and fell to the floor. This was my chance to leave. I should have been out the front door by now. Before her two goons came back in. Glancing over my shoulder, I made sure they were still outside. They were chatting with each other, not looking impatient in the slightest.

Crouching down, I grabbed her chin, keeping my grip tight enough so it was impossible for her to pull away. Her eyes glistened with tears, and from the absolute death glare I was receiving, it wasn't from pain.

"This is an invaluable lesson I'm giving you," I said coldly. "It doesn't matter who your family is. If you piss off the wrong person, you're going to end up dead before your muscle men can help you. You underestimated me and lost. Be lucky I don't want to kill you."

"Bitch," she hissed, attempting to jerk away.

I breathed out a laugh. "Your words do nothing to me.

They're as weak as your manicured hands. Another lesson—take some self-defense classes. You need them in this life."

As if trying to prove me wrong, she slammed her fist into my gut. I gave her credit, if she practiced, she could probably do some damage. I wouldn't be here to find out. Letting go of her face, I straightened up and turned to leave, only to get yanked back. With her hand in my hair, she tried pulling me even more, and I braced my legs, refusing to move an inch. Reaching my arm around, I grabbed her wrist near my head, easing the pressure on my scalp.

"That was a mistake," I snarled through clenched teeth.

"You're not leaving—"

I tightened my grip on her and pulled her closer to me. Grabbing her arm with my free hand, I bent over and flipped her over my body. Some strands of my hair went with her as she landed on her back with a yelp of surprise before she went silent. Her eyes bulged while her hands flew to her chest.

"You got the wind knocked out of you," I informed her, rubbing the sore spot on my head. "You should have let me walk away."

Movement caught my eye, and my attention went to the back of the house. One of her men had slid open the door, his murderous gaze set straight at me. He was built like a linebacker with a mustache.

"Oh fuck," I muttered.

Spinning around, I bolted for the front door and got within a couple feet of it before getting smashed into the wall. A hand pressed between my shoulder blades, making it impossible for me to move.

"No one hurts a member of the Ambrosi family and lives," he said gruffly from behind me.

Fear trailed through me, knowing I seriously fucking

messed up. I let her get to me and was going to pay with my life if I couldn't get out of this. Shouting rang through the house and must have distracted the man, because his hand on my back loosened. Only a bit, but it was enough.

Pushing off the wall, I shoved him back to allow me to drop to the floor. I grabbed his ankle and used all my strength to twist it enough to make him off balance. When he swayed, I kicked my foot out at his free leg while still holding his other leg. He went down in heap, and I began crawling away.

Before making it to safety, his hand closed around my upper arm, and he pulled me along with him as he stood back up. I screamed, punching anywhere I could. My hits didn't do shit. This guy was all muscle and easily got the upper hand again. He tugged me against his chest while wrapping his arm around my neck, getting me in a choke hold.

I clawed at his arm hard enough to draw blood, but panic overtook any ability to think rationally. His grip tightened, cutting off my air. Black spots began to dot my vision as my attempts to get free grew weaker by the second.

Mar was the only person in the line of my fading vision. She stood there watching with a sinister smile on her face. One word from her and the man would stop. But she wasn't about to do that. Suddenly, my head shattered with pain from what felt like a roaring explosion before I crumpled to the floor.

With my ears ringing, I sucked in air until my lungs were ready to burst. In a daze and too shaken to stand, I scooted to the wall and leaned against it. Setting my hand down next to me, I yanked it back up when warmth coated my fingers. I looked to see a puddle of blood slowly creeping toward me.

My gaze followed the blood trail, and I saw the man who'd had me on the floor with the side of his head gone.

"Raindrop."

Ky stood in front of me, a gun gripped in his hand. He bent down, brushing hair out of my face. "You're all right. I've got you. I'll always have you."

"No, you won't." Mar's voice sounded far away, but I could still hear every word. "You just did the one thing assuring that."

CHAPTER SIXTEEN

Kyro

With my heart pounding out of my chest, I stood back up to face Mar once I made sure Vanessa was okay. I was seconds away from losing her, and my throat was still constricted from seeing the life fade from her eyes. If the other Italian man hadn't had us at gunpoint, I would've been able to get to her sooner.

The gun in my hand belonged to the guy who was dead on the floor. He'd had it under his shirt, and it was easy to grab when his arms were around Vanessa's neck. My grip tightened on it when I met Mar's stare. Her eyes danced in amusement as if she were enjoying this.

"She's coming back with us," the other man spat out.

I glanced over at him, where Zak and Ryker had him pinned against the wall. His nose was busted, and I was almost certain Zak had broken his arm.

"No, she's not." My voice was calm, but there was no mistaking the absolute certainty behind my words.

"Daddy is going to want to hold someone accountable," Mar said with a shrug. "She's the reason all this happened."

"I'm the reason." Vanessa let out a raspy laugh, and I looked over my shoulder, seeing her stand up with her legs wobbling. "You threw the first fucking punch. Don't be mad because you're weak as shit."

She came within inches of death, and she was already back at the sarcasm. Her moves were sluggish when she tried darting past me, and I snagged her around the waist with one arm, pulling her into my chest.

"Take a minute," I murmured in her ear, tightening my hold when she attempted to shove me away.

"I don't need a fucking minute," she hissed with pure rage. "I was about to die, and the last thing burned in my mind was her smug ass face. A face I'm about to fucking rearrange."

Mar slid her phone from her pocket, tapped a couple times and looked up. "One touch and my dad will be on the phone. You already gave me a bloody lip. You really want to make it worse on yourself?"

"If your dad is going to kill me, it's sure as hell going to be for more than a busted lip," Vanessa snarled, trying to rush at her again.

Her energy was all but gone, and keeping her in my arms was easier than expected. But when she turned to glare at me, I saw it. Her eyes were full of the strength she refused to let die. Seeing that made my stomach slowly unknot.

I almost fucking lost her.

"Raindrop," Mar said with a death grip still on her phone. "Kyro, I feel you haven't been honest with me. She's not Ryker's girl, is she? She's yours."

I tensed, feeling Vanessa do the same. Explaining how I

felt about Vanessa wasn't going to happen, even though I was sure she had a decent idea of it now. I didn't even realize I had said it out loud.

"The question is, where has she been in the last six months I've known you?" Mar kept talking, trying to figure everything out. "You went to Detroit and came back, and suddenly, here she is. Did you go there to get her?"

No one spoke, and Mar's eyes flashed with interest when realizing she was on the right track. The feeling I'd had last time we spoke amplified as I stared at her. She was much fucking smarter than she let on.

"But why was she gone in the first place?" Mar asked, her gaze swinging from me to Vanessa. "It's obvious Kyro cares about you. Why leave?"

"Call your father, Mariana," the man demanded, holding his broken arm while Zak kept a gun on him.

"Not yet, Benito," Mar replied as her attention turned to Cassie. "And which one of them do you belong to?"

"No one. She's a friend," Zak grated out while keeping the gun on Benito.

Cassie fidgeted uneasily, standing near the couch, her eyes darting between Mar and Vanessa. Losing interest, Mar looked back at me. I stared back, keeping Vanessa locked against my chest.

"Were you two childhood sweethearts?" she asked with a devilishly sweet smile, as she held up her phone. "And this time I don't want silence as an answer or the next voice you hear will be my father's."

"Yes," I replied stiffly.

Answering her questions was better than dealing with her father at the moment. Or at least until I could figure out a way to smooth this all over. Jensen had no leverage with Antonio or the mafia.

"But then you left." Her eyes traveled to Vanessa. "Why?"

"Why does is fucking matter?" Vanessa shot back.

"I told you, I'm curious."

"Curiosity gets you killed," Vanessa muttered under breath.

"She left because of something I did," I spoke loudly, covering up her grumbling.

Mar's face lit up and she glanced at Zak. "I overheard my dad talking to Jensen. About why you two got sent to prison. That it was because of a girl."

Again, the room was silent. *Shit*. She knew more than I would have ever guessed. Vanessa shifted in my arms but didn't try to pull away.

"I mean, it would explain why Jensen hates you so much," Mar said, looking back at Vanessa while clearly enjoying her tidbit of information. "You got his only living son locked up for four years. Prison couldn't have been pleasant. I'm surprised you didn't hold a grudge, Kyro."

"You have no idea what you're talking about," I forced out, feeling Vanessa go rigid.

"I'm right, aren't I?" Mar asked mockingly. "But you still care for her. Enough to kill for. You don't hold any resentment?"

"No, I don't." There was no hesitation when I spoke. No pause. And it was the honest fucking truth. There wasn't any part of me that was angry with her because of our past. I wasn't going to hide it. Mar knew she meant something to me the second I'd pulled the trigger.

A small frown appeared on Mar's face at my words until she shook her head and painted a smile back on.

"Daddy isn't going to be happy when I tell him I was attacked. Even you can't save her from that."

"What do you want?" Vanessa spat out, grabbing my wrist and attempting to free herself while lowering her voice. "I'm not going to touch her, Ky."

I wasn't sure about that, but I loosened my hold enough for her to pull away. She stood in front me, still within arm's reach. Mar kept her eyes on Vanessa as a hint of fear traveled over her face.

Vanessa kept talking. "You want something. That's why you haven't called your *daddy* yet."

"Hmm, now that you mention it." Mar tapped her chin, acting like she was deep in thought. "I could make this all go away."

Anger slid through me, knowing she held all the damn cards. Her family was one of the top mafia families on the East Coast. The Kings were large in California but were nothing compared to the fucking mafia.

"What do you want?" Vanessa repeated, crossing her arms.

"Benito," Mar called out loudly while keeping her eyes on me. "What will you do once I call my father?"

All eyes went to Benito, who was standing against the wall with blood dripping down his face. Zak still had the gun on him and tightened his grip as Benito held his useless arm and stared at Mar in confusion.

"Go ahead, tell them," Mar encouraged. "They might have a gun on you, but they can't do anything. Daddy knows I'm here. They'd all be dead if they did something to me. Kyro knows that."

Clenching my jaw, I glared at Benito while he peeked a glance at me. I didn't say anything because she was fucking right. She was untouchable because of her last name.

As his confidence grew, Benito's back straightened and he gave Vanessa a leering smile. "Once you call your father,

I'll tell him what that bitch did to you. She'll be dead by morning. Even though her death won't be quick. No one touches the Ambrosi family."

Squeezing the gun still in my hand, I resisted the urge to raise it and shoot him in the head. I didn't give a fuck what I had to do; he wasn't taking Vanessa.

"And what if I asked you not to say anything to my dad?" Mar asked quietly. "What if I told you I didn't want anyone finding out about this?"

Looking flustered, Benito whispered the next words as if the rest of us wouldn't be able to hear him. "Mariana, you know I couldn't do that. I answer to Mr. Ambrosi. I have to tell him."

"You're right, Benito. You're a good soldier." Mar flashed him an understanding smile.

Narrowing my eyes, my gut twisted when I realized what she was implying. Ryker glanced at me, confused, as he stood next to Cassie. Zak's posture shifted, showing me he understood like I did.

"See, Kyro. There's no possible way for me to keep this quiet." Mar feigned a sigh. "You know what you have to do."

I took a step toward Zak, knowing exactly what I had to do. Vanessa spun around, latched on to my arm, and pulled me back.

"Don't do this," she hissed. "It's what she wants. There's a reason for it."

"I know," I told her in a low voice as I caught Ryker's eye and nodded. "But I also know we don't have another fucking way out of this."

Jerking out of her grip, I raised the gun over her head when she tried reaching for it. She let out a shriek when Ryker came up behind her, pulling her back. He dragged her away from me while she fought against his hold.

Cassie's face was pale while her eyes stayed glued to Vanessa.

As I stepped up next to Zak, he leaned closer to keep his words between us. "I'll do it."

I shook my head. No, he wouldn't. The blood spilled tonight would only be on me. If Antonio ever found out about it, I didn't want anyone else sharing the blame. Benito's gaze slid from my gun to my face, and his eyes bulged when he realized what I was about to do. Vanessa was still yelling, but Ryker held her back, and I focused on the man in front of me.

"You can't hurt me." His courageous façade broke, and he looked past me. "Tell him, Mariana. It won't just be the girl that dies, it will be all of you. Put the gun down."

"You're wrong," I murmured, keeping my gaze stone cold. "I can't hurt her. Because she's an Ambrosi. But you? Your last name doesn't mean shit in this world. You were going to make my girl suffer and then kill her. You should be fucking grateful your death will be quick."

Panic engulfed his features, and sweat dripped from his forehead. He put his hands up in surrender while speaking in Italian to Mar. I didn't turn to look at her for confirmation. Her silence was enough.

Raising the gun, I pulled the trigger, shooting him straight in the heart before he could say another word. Vanessa went quiet and no one else spoke as Benito fell to the floor, unmoving. I didn't spare him another glance as I turned around to face everyone else.

"*Now*, I can make this all go away." Mar clapped her hands together. "Thank you, Kyro. Those two didn't let me do anything without reporting it to my father."

"You fucking bitch," Vanessa snarled, trying to pull

away from Ryker. "You planned all this. Starting a fight with me. Killing them. It's what you wanted."

From the pleased look on Mar's face, Vanessa's accusation was spot on.

Mar set her phone on the couch. "I judged you wrong, Vanessa. It took a lot more than I thought it would to get you to snap. But when I mentioned Ky and I slept together, the look on your face told me he was your weak spot."

My mouth fell open at her words, and my eyes went to Vanessa. "We never slept together—"

"No, we haven't. Not yet, anyway," Mar interrupted with her gaze drifting over me. "I have someone else fulfilling those needs right now. But I must say...you two look similar. I have a type, and you fit it perfectly. I have to admit, I wasn't disappointed at all when I first met you and found out you were the one I was going to marry."

"Why is your family here?" I asked the question that had been simmering ever since we met the Ambrosi family. "What do the Kings have that your father wants?"

"Sexy and smart." Mar laughed. "It's all about business, of course."

"The Italian families always stayed on the East Coast," I said, not fully believing her. "What changed?"

"We aren't the first." She tilted her head. "You probably don't remember. It was years ago. But we're not the only Italian family to conduct business in Suncrest Bay. And we won't be the last."

The new information made me pause as I stared at her. I had no idea what the hell she was talking about. Jensen had never mentioned other Italians doing business in Suncrest.

"We're getting off topic," Mar continued. "I have a couple of people who will help me cover this up without my dad finding out. No one will know that Vanessa attacked me. Or that you killed two of his men. As long as you agree to my little deal."

"What do you want?" I asked, preparing myself for what she was about to say.

She shrugged. "Nothing huge. I like having people in my corner if I need them. And if I ever need you, now you won't be able to say no. If I ever call you asking for a favor, then you drop everything to help me. That's it. One favor in exchange to make this go away."

"A favor? That's it?" I asked skeptically, raising an eyebrow.

"Yes."

"Bullshit," Vanessa snapped. "You planned all this. And then you just say it's for one little favor? Like you don't know what that favor will be."

Mar grinned slyly. "I don't know yet. But when I do, Kyro will be the first to know."

"Fine," I agreed before Vanessa could argue again. "One favor."

There wasn't a doubt in my mind that Mar already had that favor planned, but right now I didn't care. This wasn't going to get back to Antonio, and Vanessa was safe. Well, as safe as she fucking could be in this damn city.

"Perfect." Mar started texting furiously on her phone. "Someone will be here soon to clean up. Don't worry about anything, it'll all be taken care of. And Daddy won't ever find out. As long as you answer when I call."

I nodded while Zak muttered under his breath, "She's taking care of everything, so she'll know where the bodies are buried."

He was right. She had the leverage she needed. Rage coursed through me while staring at Mar. I was used to being under my father's thumb. I hated it, but it's what my entire life consisted of. Knowing someone outside the Kings had a hold on me pissed me the fuck off.

But whatever the favor was, I'd do it.

Vanessa was worth it.

CHAPTER SEVENTEEN

Vanessa

"You know, you talk in your sleep."

Picking up my pillow, I smacked Ky with it. "I do not."

He ripped the pillow from my hand and jumped on top of me. He grinned and his eyes danced with amusement. He looked way too happy after the shit that had gone down yesterday. Mar was someone I didn't see coming.

"I'm glad I won that bet," he murmured, grazing his lips down my cheek. "Being in bed with you beats the hell out of the couch."

"You cheated."

"Don't be sore loser."

"I wouldn't be. If you didn't cheat."

"Want a rematch?"

"You didn't get your fill yesterday?"

His hand gripped my thigh. "Baby, you could be my breakfast, lunch, and dinner, and I'd still spend all night licking my dessert."

My body flushed with heat just as his gaze grew somber

and he rolled off me. Leaning up on my elbows, I stared at his back while he slid on sweatpants.

"What's wrong? Scared you'll lose this time?" I asked with a sarcastic laugh.

Glancing over his shoulder, he cocked an eyebrow. "I wouldn't lose. I decided to wait. You must be sore from what happened yesterday."

"Are you talking about having four orgasms all in a row or when I was slammed into a wall and almost choked out?" I kept my voice humorous and light while brushing my fingers along my neck.

His eyes darkened as they followed my hand. "You almost died."

"But I didn't. That's how life works."

"Don't talk like your life isn't important," he growled.

"What was I saying in my sleep?" I changed topics, refusing to think about how close I was to hell less than twenty-four hours ago.

With one last look at my neck, he met my gaze again and grinned. "You said my name. 'Ky is...' and then you rolled over before I could hear the rest."

"A dumbass," I stated loudly. "That's how the sentence ended."

He chuckled. "Sure, Raindrop."

"I don't talk in my sleep anyway," I muttered, falling back onto the pillows.

The bed sank beside me, and I felt his warmth before turning my head to look at him. He had his serious face on, and I groaned. I was not in the mood to talk about life right now. My attempt to get out of bed failed when he grabbed my wrist, pulling me back.

"After yesterday, I'd really just like to relax." I sighed, leaning my head against his chest. "A day without talk about my dad. Or your dad. Or your fiancée. Or my arranged fiancé. And let's not forget the money I'm worth. Fuck. I don't think life could get more twisted."

"Don't jinx it."

Letting out a dry laugh, I shook my head. "Not sure that's possible."

"Things can always get worse." He ran his hand down my arm as he spoke. "But I'll always be here to make sure you survive whatever the fuck life throws at you."

Swallowing hard, I remembered how easily he had killed Benito yesterday. I wasn't saddened by his or the other Italian man's death. In this world, it's kill or be killed. It was them or me. And Ky didn't hesitate. He didn't care that the men were part of the Italian mafia. He was only thinking of one thing.

Protecting me.

My body tensed before I even realized it, and Ky gripped my arm, feeling my sudden change. Here I was, lying in bed with him like we didn't have a care in the world. I was comfortable with him. Because whether I admitted it or not, I was starting to trust him. *No, not starting*. I was halfway there.

Fuck. For seven years I kept my heart sealed up tight, and it only took a month of being back for him to crack it wide open.

"Don't fight it," he murmured. "You already trust me with your body. It's time to start trusting what I say too."

Annoyance flared inside my chest. He was so infuriating when he was in my head. Especially when he was fucking right. Mar's words from yesterday repeated in my head, helping the doubt set in.

Deciding to try the communication approach, I asked,

"What you said to Mar yesterday. About not having any resentment for me sending you to prison. Is that true?"

He was silent for a moment and then flipped me over until I was on top of him. Straddling his waist, I placed one of my hands on the tattoo over his heart. It was impossible not to stare at it. His fingers dug into my hips, reminding me of the question I'd just asked him.

"Look at me, Raindrop." His voice was soft but demanding. "I want there to be no mistaking what I'm going to say."

My eyes raised and met his. There wasn't a speck of humor anywhere on his face, and he kept his hands on my hips when he began talking.

"I am not mad about what you did. There's no resentment. No anger. Nothing."

"You told me you were mad when I first did it."

"Yeah, I was. But then I thought about it. I mean, I had nothing else to do but sit there and think about it." A hint of a smile appeared on his lips. "If you hadn't snitched, then you would have been the one in prison. And honestly, I'm glad it was me and not you."

Scoffing, I shook my head, causing him to tighten his grip.

"I'm serious." A hard edge replaced the soft tone he had started with. "You got out. Away from the Kings. And the Crows. You escaped the life you never had a choice in. It's what I wanted for you."

My heart ached at the truth in his voice. This was why he told me to look at him. He wanted me to be absolutely sure his words were honest. And I had no doubt they were.

"Still, four years of your life wasted," I muttered. All those years ago, I didn't have an ounce of guilt over my decision. But now...I knew why he did it, and regret was setting in.

"Not a waste. I got away from my dad."

"Ky—"

"It was the first time in my life he couldn't control me. Yeah, I was behind bars. Yet, I felt more free than I had in my entire life. It was boring. Some parts sucked. And we still dealt with some business while we were in there. But the Kings were known there, like every other prison in the area. No one messed with me and Zak. We had it easy."

"Easy," I repeated. "Not what I was expecting you to say."

He shrugged. "It was. Don't get me wrong, I was glad we got out after four years—"

"Yeah, how did you get out early?" I asked, interrupting him. "Your sentence was way longer."

"Dad pulled some strings and had us transferred to a prison in a county where he had people on payroll. I'm pretty sure a judge got early retirement from how much Jensen paid him." He let out a short laugh. "Zak was fucking ecstatic. I think he went on a binge of a new woman every night for a month straight."

"I bet Zak held a grudge longer than you," I mumbled.

He sighed. "You know he did. But he calmed down. And never stopped caring for you. That's been obvious since you've been back."

"I know." I shifted a bit, but he didn't loosen his grip on my hips. Meaning this conversation wasn't over.

"I like this." He grinned playfully, tugging the hem of his shirt I was wearing. "You in my bed. Us having a conversation without you trying to get away from me. I could get used to this."

"Too bad reality will probably bust down the door any second," I murmured, regretting opening my mouth when his smile faded.

This used to be my fucking dream.

To spend lazy mornings in bed with him. I wanted to wake up bathed in his scent from wearing his clothes. I longed to hear his carefree laugh when we played the games our competitive sides craved. I wanted every night to end with the soft touch of his hands exploring every inch of my body.

But life dealt its cruel hand before we even had a chance.

Brushing my fingers across his tattoo, I exposed my vulnerable thoughts for only a moment.

"I think I spent so long refusing to let anyone in and relying only on myself," I whispered, not meeting his gaze, "I don't know if I'll ever be able to entirely trust someone again. Even if I wanted to."

"Don't worry, Raindrop. You will. Your trust is something I'll never stop chasing."

CHAPTER EIGHTEEN

Kyro

SITTING ON THE PATIO, WATCHING VANESSA AND Cassie hit the volleyball back and forth, I realized how little I'd laughed in the last seven years. Vanessa's high-pitched giggles rang through the air, causing a warmth to spread through my chest. A feeling I hadn't felt in a long damn time.

Fuck, I missed that sound.

"She sounds like a damn banshee," Zak grumbled, plopping into the chair beside me. "She hasn't laughed like that since she's been back."

I nodded, watching Vanessa dive for the ball and nearly faceplant in the sand. Her smile was carefree, and it was bothering me that I couldn't tell if it was real or not.

"You two seemed pretty cozy this morning," Zak said, giving me a pointed look. "And she's not trying to run off for once. Did you two actually talk instead of fuck last night?"

"She's not trying to leave because Cassie's here," I

answered, turning to look at him. "And because I still haven't told her everything about her dad."

"I'm guessing you still haven't told her the other thing. About Jensen?" Ryker asked from behind me as he flipped burgers on the grill.

"Fuck no, he hasn't told her." Zak twisted around in his chair to glare at Ryker. "No one is going to tell her. We'll go to our damn graves before we tell her."

Ryker raised his hands in the air with the spatula still in his hand. "Calm the hell down. I wasn't going to tell her. I was only asking if Ky has."

"She's going to find out," I muttered. "It's only a matter of time now that she's back."

"If she does, you can kiss your chance of ever having her trust you goodbye," Zak stated harshly. "I'm not trying to be a dick, but I honestly don't know if she would forgive you for this."

"It's not like Ky did anything." Ryker came to my defense. "It was Jensen—"

"Doesn't matter," Zak interrupted. "It matters that she's been back for a month and we haven't told her. She's warmed up again because now she knows why we did what we did seven years ago. This...she's going to flip her shit if she finds out we knew this entire time and said nothing."

I swallowed my next words as Vanessa and Cassie joined us at the table. Vanessa came up behind me, stealing the beer from my hand before sitting across from me. Sand was stuck to her skin, and she absentmindedly brushed some off her bikini top, freezing when she noticed me staring.

With a devilish grin, she ran her fingers down her breast as my eyes stayed glued to her hand. That's all it took. My dick sprang to life, and I was ready to haul her back into the bedroom.

"Can you guys at least wait until after we eat?" Zak grumbled.

Vanessa giggled. "Sure, Zak. I'm starving anyway."

With one last look at me, she moved her hand away and leaned back in her chair. "Are we any closer to finding Kenzi?"

"No," Ryker answered, setting the plate of burgers on the table. "She took us seriously when we told her to disappear."

"You don't think Mack could have found her?" Vanessa asked, fear slipping into her eyes.

"No. We would have heard if the Crows had her," I reassured her.

"We should be out looking for my dad's bike instead of staying here." Her gaze landed on the food. "Acting like life is normal."

"Do you have a lead on where the bike could be?" Zak raised an eyebrow. "Because if you have information, please share."

"We're not leaving until we know where the hell we need to go," I spoke up before they started arguing.

"I'm working on finding her," Ryker grumbled. "She went completely offline. No phone. No computer. No way for me to track her."

"Is that how you guys found Vanessa? You tracked her electronics?" Cassie asked curiously.

I stiffened, opening my mouth to steer off this subject, but Zak fucking beat me to it.

"We can thank Kenzi for finding her," he answered with a chuckle.

Shock passed over Vanessa's face as she went rigid. "Kenzi never would have told you where I was—"

"I mean, she technically didn't tell us—"

"Zak," I snapped, running a hand down my face. "Shut up."

Getting defensive, the humor disappeared from Zak's voice. "It was years ago. It doesn't change anything now."

"Good, then tell me," she demanded.

Ryker glanced at me, keeping his mouth shut. I sighed, jerking a nod to Ryker while reaching in the cooler to grab another beer.

"I didn't find you," Ryker said, looking back at Vanessa. "Ky did."

Her gaze swung to me. "How?"

"I knew Teddy was the one to help you disappear. The Kings were aware he had a guy who forged papers. Teddy hated me, so there was no chance of him talking to me." I paused. "But Kenzi...we grew up with her. And I figured since her dad helped you, she had a good idea of where you were."

"No way she told you." Vanessa crossed her arms. "And I know you wouldn't hurt her. What did you do?"

"Hey, Ryker and I knew nothing about this." Zak shrugged. "Ky did it all on his own. We had no idea you were in Detroit until we went there to meet with Cassie's father."

Vanessa's eyes widened in surprise, and I could practically hear her thoughts. There were never any secrets between me and Zak. We told each other everything. When I found her, it was the first time I had done something completely on my own.

I hadn't trusted myself to tell anyone else. Even Zak and Ryker. For those two years after I'd found her, it was a daily struggle to stay away and not approach her. All it would have taken was one word from either of them and my self-control would have snapped.

"Spit it out, Ky. How'd you find me?"

"Why do you want to know so bad?" I countered, taking a sip of beer. "To make sure it doesn't happen again?"

"Is that why you don't want to tell me?" she argued back. "So you can do it again if I leave?"

That was exactly what I was going to fucking do. She'd have two gangs and the mafia on her ass. Teddy wasn't here to help her again. She wouldn't get far.

"I staged a run in with Kenzi at a bar when she was out with friends," I explained, knowing she wasn't going to drop it until I told her. "She left her phone unlocked on the table and I grabbed it without her noticing."

Vanessa slumped back in her chair, realizing Kenzi hadn't purposely sold her out.

"I scrolled through all her texts. It didn't take long. There were only a couple names I didn't recognize, one being Becca James." Feeling a little bad for calling Kenzi out, I added, "That text chain was the only one where the history had been deleted. I had her phone back on the table before she even realized it was missing."

"I should have figured it had something to do with you when Ky kept disappearing for a few days every couple of weeks," Zak said while reaching for a burger.

"We thought he had a gambling problem." Ryker let out a laugh. "He kept saying he was going to Las Vegas."

"Jensen didn't catch on?" Vanessa asked skeptically.

"He didn't know," I replied. "Ryker and Zak covered for me. He had no idea I was out of town."

"You came every few weeks? To what? Check up on me?" Vanessa looked torn between being surprised and pissed the hell off that I'd known where she was for two years.

I nodded. "Once I knew your alias, finding you was simple. I usually only stayed a day or two, made sure you were good, and then came home."

Vanessa chewed on her burger, her gaze not leaving mine. She might have been opening up more, but there wasn't a doubt in my mind she was already coming up with a backup plan in case she needed to leave town again.

"Anyway..." Zak grabbed the volleyball and tossed it in the air. "Who wants to play?"

Cassie jumped up and stole the ball from his hands. "I do. Vanessa, you're on my team."

Vanessa's eyes lit up as she grinned before slowly standing up and leaning her hands on the table. My gut churned with excitement, knowing exactly what she was going to say when she opened her mouth.

"Me and Cass against you and Zak," she told me. "But it's my turn to pick a game."

"Uhh, Vanessa," Cassie questioned, holding the ball up. "We are playing a game."

Zak rubbed his temples. "You'll learn fast that Ky and Vee have their own games. It's how they compromise."

"So, they both win?" Cassie's confusion increased as she looked at Vanessa, whose attention was fully on me.

"No. Only one wins—"

"But the loser usually gets something too," Ryker piped up.

"What do you want, Raindrop?" My curiosity was burning. Usually, I was the one to play first.

She didn't hesitate for a second. "If Cass and I win, I get one free pass. To walk away. Without you stopping me. Better yet, you can't even touch me."

A smile played on my lips, remembering how our last no touching deal went.

She scowled. "I mean absolutely no touching this time Ky. Not even a damn finger."

"You were begging for my fingers last time."

Zak groaned as Cassie's mouth dropped open at my words. Laughing, Ryker finished eating his burger as he watched our exchange. Leaning back in my chair, I rested my hands on the back of my head, waiting for her to finish.

"One time," Vanessa repeated. "I tell you I'm leaving, and you let me go."

Dread pushed out the relaxed daze I'd been in all day. I should have known that's what she'd want. Even if she was starting to trust me, she needed a way out. She'd been relying on herself too long not to do this.

After a minute of silence, I finally made a decision. "Okay."

My one-word answer made suspicion swim in her eyes. "Are you going to tell me what you want if you win?"

"That's the thing," I murmured. "I can't think of anything I want."

Indecision crossed her face. I was changing our game and she wasn't liking it at all. I swept my arm in the air.

"See this? My girl. My best friends. One of your best friends. All of us together. Having a good time. I have what I want today."

"This isn't real life, Ky," she reminded me in a quiet voice. "It's a reprieve. And probably a very small one."

"You're right." I rubbed my chin as if deep in thought. "Which is why I'm just going to add on to what you want."

"Excuse me?"

"If I win, then you can still leave. But you only get twenty minutes before the no touching rule expires."

Both Zak and Ryker's eyes snapped to me, but I didn't look away from Vanessa.

"And..." I trailed off, knowing she wasn't going to keep quiet after this. "You have to get yourself off within those twenty minutes. Or you don't leave."

Zak busted out laughing while Vanessa's jaw clenched. Cassie cleared her throat as a blush coated her cheeks.

"There it is," Ryker muttered with a chuckle.

Zak slung an arm around Cassie's shoulders. "This is what we meant by compromise. Now, if Vanessa wins, she gets to leave like she wants. And she gets an orgasm out of it. And Ky gets to watch his girl touch herself. A win-win."

Cassie pushed Zak away, looking between me and Vanessa. "I think he did it so Vanessa doesn't try to leave when they're in public. She'd have to do it when they're alone."

Damn. She hit it dead on.

"You can't just add things to my side of the deal," Vanessa scowled.

"Says who?" I shot back. "There are no rules, baby. Unless we make them. This is mine. Agree or not, I don't care. But I'm not changing my mind. If you say no, the deal doesn't happen, and you won't even get a chance to try to leave."

She bit her lip. "Fine. Deal."

I smirked. "Good, then let's play."

Zak looked at me gleefully while stripping off his shirt. He loved volleyball and was a better player than me. Vanessa was good, too, but she was out of practice. Standing up, I slid my phone out of my pocket and stiffened as I read a text.

Jensen- Meet me for dinner at the restaurant. Bring Vanessa.

My good mood vanished with a weight landing back on my chest. I had no idea what he wanted, but I'd planned on keeping Vanessa away from him for as long as possible. At least the restaurant was a public place. Better than him showing up here if I didn't bring her.

"You good?" Zak asked when he realized I wasn't behind him.

"Yeah," I muttered, choosing to keep this to myself until after the game.

Following Zak, I went to the opposite side of the net from Cassie and Vanessa. Cassie was holding the ball, waiting to serve.

"Ready?" she called out.

Seconds after we nodded, she leaped in the air, jump serving a wicked fast hit. The ball bounced in the sand before Zak or I even moved a muscle. We looked at each before staring across the net. Vanessa's grin was smug as hell.

Zak glanced at Cassie before shaking his head. "Well. Fuck."

CHAPTER NINETEEN

Vanessa

"That game was bullshit," Zak grumbled from the back seat where Ryker sat next to him. "You could have mentioned Cassie plays volleyball like she was in the Olympics."

Twisting around to look at him, I couldn't help but gloat. "That would have completely defeated the purpose. You never would have agreed to play."

"Hell no, we wouldn't," Zak replied, shooting a glance to Ky, who was driving. "Not sure Ky would have agreed to your deal if he knew."

Seeing how Ky's grip tightened on the steering wheel, I knew Zak was right. They'd both been confident about winning. Instead, they got fucking owned, thanks to Cass. She'd been playing volleyball since she was ten.

Now, I had a card to play, and it took off a bit of the pressure that had been building in the past few days. I hated not having a way out if I needed one. Even though this wasn't much, it was something.

I didn't plan to leave anytime soon. At the moment, I was perfectly content staying with Ky and the guys until we found my dad's bike. But in this life, things could change in an instant. If I wanted to leave, at least Ky had to give me a chance.

We pulled into a parking lot, and the restaurant gave me an eerily familiar feeling I couldn't place. I'd been here before. It was a high-end steak place, and I glanced at my tank top, suddenly feeling underdressed.

"They aren't going to let me in dressed like this." I glanced at Ky's jeans. "None of us are dressed for this kind of place. What the hell are we doing going out to eat anyway? What if there are Crows here?"

"How do you not recognize this place, Vee?" Zak opened the door, jumping out of the truck. "This is where your adventure with the Kings started."

Climbing out of the truck, I read the street signs before spinning around to look at the restaurant again. My heart rate sped up as memories and emotions flooded through me. The night I found out about the Blood Kings.

The first time I experienced sheer terror and when my dark craving for excitement began.

"It used to be a diner," I muttered, running a finger over the scar on my chin.

"Jensen owns it now," Ryker explained while we walked to the entrance. "He fixed it up."

"At least this time you can use the front door instead of the bathroom window." Zak chuckled.

"Why are we here?" I asked, noticing the parking lot was nearly empty. "I thought we were staying close to the house because of the Crows."

No one answered me as Ky placed his hand on my waist, pushing me toward the restaurant. We were nearly at the door, and apprehension had me stopping in my tracks. I pulled his hand away from me, taking a step back.

"What are we doing here, Ky?"

He sighed. "Jensen wants to talk."

"You're not fucking serious." The frown on his face told me he was dead serious. I backed out of his reach only to slam into Zak and Ryker. No wonder they had made Cassie stay back at the house.

"He wants to kill me. Why else would he want to see me? Which do you think he wants more? Money or revenge?" I couldn't hide the panic and betrayal as I shoved Zak away when he attempted to grab my arm. "You guys are serving me up on a damn silver platter."

"Calm down," Ky snapped in a hushed voice, his eyes darting to the front door.

"Easy for you to say—"

I was cut off when Ky grabbed me, spinning me around until my back hit the smooth bricks of the building. Anger ripped through me as I tried pushing him off. One hand went around my throat while his other gripped my hip, keeping me pressed into the wall. Glancing over his shoulder, he nodded to Zak.

"Go in and tell Jensen I'll be there in a minute."

Zak and Ryker disappeared through the door without another word as Ky pressed his body into mine.

"You think this is easy for me?" His lips grazed my cheek as he whispered in my ear. "He has no idea what I've done for you. When we go in there, I have to act like you're not the most important person in my life. I told you to trust me. I wouldn't have brought you here if I thought he was going to hurt you."

"You can't keep that promise. Jensen does what the fuck he wants. This just shows you do whatever the hell he says."

"I've done everything to keep you safe," he growled. "You think I want to keep secrets from you? You think I haven't thought about killing my own father because of the fucked-up shit he's made me do? You have no damn idea, Vanessa. You're not the only one born into a life without choice."

I stiffened in shock from the harshness in his voice. His grip on me tightened as his deep, barely controlled breaths hit my cheek. He was pissed. Not at me. It was all aimed at Jensen.

"I know he won't hurt you." He paused for a moment, pulling his head away until we locked eyes. "He needs that money from your account more than anything."

"That house he's sitting in says otherwise."

"That house is because of his new alliance with the Italians. The night your parents were killed, when our factory was raided, the Kings took a huge hit. Everything we had in the factory—the guns, the drugs, were all stolen. Which meant we lost the buyers of all those things."

I stayed silent while he glanced at the door before returning his attention to me.

"He couldn't stop the Crows from expanding. He nearly lost everything. But the Kings had a lot of allies in California, and that kept him afloat until he could get back into selling guns. He owes more favors than even I know. And debts. Now, he's back on top. Because of the Italians. I don't want to know how much money he owes them."

"He's broke," I whispered, incapable of imagining Jensen Banes under the thumb of anyone.

"Pretty close to it," Ky answered. "He needs your money to get out from under the Ambrosi family. He doesn't trust them. They could wreck him and the Kings in a heartbeat if they wanted. But with that money...he could pay off the debts and regain everything he had seven years ago."

"I didn't realize we were making that public knowledge."

My face paled at the calm anger in his voice. Ky loosened his grip on my neck, letting me turn to see Jensen holding the door open. His jaw was clenched, and for once he wasn't looking at me with narrowed eyes. He was focused on his son.

CHAPTER TWENTY

Vanessa

Ky's entire demeanor shifted as he kept his grip on my arm, pulling me from the wall. His face became a cold mask, and the vulnerability he had just shared evaporated in a split second.

"She thinks you're going to kill her the second you have the chance. She refused to go into the restaurant. I needed to calm her down." Ky glanced at the few people walking by on the sidewalk. "Unless you wanted her to make a scene and possibly attract the wrong kind of attention. Don't want to make the same mistake the Crows did when they brought her into public. You're the one who told me to bring her here."

Jensen's gaze slid down my body, and I couldn't stop the fear from building. He fucking terrified me. More than anyone else. Mack. The Italians. He topped them all. Probably because I'd witnessed firsthand how he tortures people.

"Let's finish this conversation inside." Jensen opened the door wider, waiting for us to go in first.

My feet felt cemented in place. Even my subconscious knew nothing good was going to come out of spending time with Jensen Banes. Ky didn't hesitate and pulled me through the door. The click of the lock sent a frigid cold shooting through my veins. So much for public. Only Kings were in here.

Everything in the restaurant was black or a rich, dark brown. Lavish wooden tables covered the floor in front of the wide bar. The largest table sat in the middle of the room where Zak and Ryker were already seated. A few guys were leaning against the long bar, sipping their drinks, looking bored. I recognized a couple from when I had first gotten here and stayed at Jensen's.

The restaurant looked fancier inside than it did from the outside. I wondered if the Italians gave Jensen the money to open this place too. Or if it was just a front to wash the money from the gang's illegal businesses.

Not that I was going to ask. I planned on keeping my mouth shut the entire time.

Jensen strode past us, taking a seat at the table. A few Kings sat on the opposite side along with Zak and Ryker. There were only two open seats left. I moved next to Ryker until Jensen's voice made me pause.

"Vanessa, sit next to me. We need to talk."

Fuck me. So much for staying quiet. Rounding the table, I sat down stiffly, not liking the fact of being within Jensen's reach. He had made it clear in the past he wasn't against putting his hands on me.

Ky looked about as happy as I did when he took the seat next to Ryker. He kept his gaze on his dad from across the table as Zak shot me an apologetic look. At least they felt bad for bringing me here.

"Kyro, what else have you told her?" Jensen asked,

keeping his eyes on me. I stared back, not allowing myself to shrink into my fear. If what Ky said was true, he wouldn't hurt me—or at least not kill me.

His answer was instant. "Nothing."

"You remember what I said would happen if you did?"

Confused, I broke the stare-down with Jensen to look across the table. All three guys were on edge. Ky's hands were on the table, balled into fists. Zak stared blankly behind me, but the vein above his eye twitched. Ryker shifted in his seat, not looking at anyone.

"I haven't told her anything," Ky repeated gruffly.

"Vanessa." I turned back to look at Jensen, becoming immediately wary when he said my name. "Do you know who your dad was?"

"No." My voice was raspy, and I reached for the glass of water in front of me. Fuck, he made me nervous. I hated it.

Jensen didn't look convinced. He signaled to the bartender, who brought a full bottle of top shelf whiskey to the table. I shook my head to decline a drink; everyone was silent as the guy poured everyone else a glass.

With the fresh drink in his hand, Jensen started the conservation back up. "I think you and I have a mutual acquaintance, Vanessa."

"I mean, I've lived here my whole life. Helped with your gang. And dated your son. I'm sure we have a couple mutual acquaintances."

The words didn't sound as bad in my head, but from the glares all three guys were giving me, I should have kept my mouth shut. They were right. I shouldn't try to piss off Jensen. Trying to control my sarcasm was still a work in progress.

Jensen chuckled, only furthering my thought that I should have stayed silent.

"This person...you only met once. On accident."

Glancing at Ky, he looked as confused as I felt. It was obvious this was important, but I had no idea who Jensen was talking about.

Jensen leaned over the table, keeping his words between us. "Think Vanessa. Who have you met on accident?"

"I don't know who you're—"

"Let me help. His head is shaved and half covered in tattoos." Jensen spoke so quietly I had to move closer to hear him. "You broke his nose. Pissed him off pretty good that a seventeen-year-old girl bested him."

My body went numb. Even my heart seemed to stop beating. A lump formed in my throat just like that night seven years ago, and I felt trapped in the nightmare of my childhood living room. Each shallow breath caused my mouth to become so dry, I couldn't swallow.

My brain scrambled to reject the image of the man Jensen was describing. I rested a hand on the table to steady myself just as fingers grasped my chin and jerked my head up until all I saw was Jensen's satisfied smirk.

"I guess Kyro didn't tell you anything else. I had to be sure." He let go of my face before taking another sip of whiskey.

"You," I breathed out shakily. "No. NO!"

"Rain—Vanessa, what did he say?" Ky was halfway out of his seat.

"You son of a bitch," I screamed, leaping from my chair. "You killed my parents. The Kings killed my parents."

The shock melted into pure rage as I stared into Jensen's uncaring eyes. His lack of response only edged on my anger. Forcing myself to look across the table, I felt my chest constrict when guilt covered all three of their faces.

They fucking knew.

"The Kings killed them," I mumbled under my breath, unable to stop saying it. It was right in front of me, but my mind was still in denial.

"Sit down, Vanessa," Jensen ordered, apparently bored with my reaction. "I'll give you a minute to calm yourself before we continue."

A laugh escaped me. "Calm myself? You just told me you killed my parents, and you think I'm going to fucking calm down?"

Blood rushed to my ears, and all I could hear was my racing heart. Ky was trying to talk to me, but I was blocking him out. I was done listening.

Jensen stood up, towering over me. "This changes nothing—"

"It changes everything," I hissed.

"You will still find the bank paperwork—"

"If you think for one second that I'm still going to help." I shoved Jensen away from me. "You're crazier than I thought. Fuck you."

Jensen's nostril's flared and a speck of uncertainty passed through his eyes. "You *will* get me that money."

With a roar, I charged at Jensen, unable to stay still any longer. Hands grabbed my shoulders, jolting me back, just like I'd been expecting. Sparing a quick glance at the face of the guy who was holding me, I grinned before shoving my knee into his balls.

His hold on me faltered as I brought my fist up and smashed his face. Knowing I had seconds before the other Kings grabbed me, I reached under the guy's jacket and grabbed his gun from the holster, clicking the safety off as I pulled it out.

I aimed for the guy's knee, and the shot rang out through the restaurant as he went down screaming. Shuffling a few steps away, I turned to keep my back on a wall, making sure no one could come up behind me. I lifted the gun, pointing it straight at Jensen. Shock creased his features as he stared at the gun and then at me in disbelief.

"If anyone tries to fucking touch me, you're dead," I told him coldly. "If someone shoots me, they better shoot to kill. But wait—if they do that, you have no chance of getting the cash you so desperately need."

With his face flushed, Jensen nodded to his guys to back off. I planted my feet, keeping the gun leveled with his chest.

"I've agonized for the last seven years over who killed my parents. You were always on that list. I think my past with Ky kept me from ever fully believing the Kings had anything to do with it. But I can't deny it now." My finger was on the trigger. With only a bit of pressure, I could avenge my parents.

"I didn't kill them," Jensen spat out. "You were there that night. I wasn't."

"You ordered the hit," I screamed. "You're the reason they're dead."

"Vanessa." Ky's voice was soft as he stepped into my peripheral vision as my eyes stayed glued to Jensen. "You'll regret it if you do this."

Would I?

Would I care if Ky hated me if I killed his father? From what he said earlier, I thought he hated Jensen as much as I did. Did I care what Ky would think? I wasn't sure. All I could focus on in this moment was the murdering asshole in front of me. I couldn't let him walk away.

"Fuck you, Ky. You knew. I've been back for a month, and you didn't tell me." I sucked in a breath. "You knew that night too. That's why we left Suncrest for the day. You just brought me back too early."

"No." Both Jensen and Ky spoke at once.

Raising an eyebrow, my gaze didn't leave Jensen. "No?"

Jensen shifted, his eyes darting to the gun in my hand. "Kyro didn't know that night. I told him to leave the city because shit was going down that I didn't want him a part of."

"I don't believe you."

"Vee, we didn't know." Zak spoke up. "Not until we got out of prison."

"Jensen knew we never would have helped kill your parents," Ky rushed out. "Knox knew. I didn't."

"Well, even if that's true, it doesn't help you." Jensen stiffened at my words, realizing I wasn't going to lower the gun.

"I didn't kill them."

I laughed. "Seriously?"

"I didn't," he snapped. "The guy you met, the one who did it, was contracted by someone else. I just made a deal with them that I could have some men there to look for the paperwork when it happened. That's why the cops were there."

"So, you knew they were going to be murdered that night?"

He gritted his teeth. "Yes."

"Who ordered it?"

"I only spoke to the guy who was contracted to kill them. He's a professional and wouldn't give up a name."

"Then you're useless." I raised the gun a bit higher.

God, this feeling fed into my craving. Having control over Jensen, even if just for a couple of minutes. I had the power. I didn't want to let it go. He was a piece of shit. Ky hated him. He either had my parents killed or knew it was going to happen and did nothing to stop it. He would kill me in an instant if he had the chance.

He began laughing, and I scowled. "You think this is funny?"

"All talk. You're not going to shoot me." He took a small step forward. "Don't you want to know why Kyro said you'd regret killing me? You still need answers."

"I don't have to get them from you."

"You know, you look just like your mother." His eyes gleamed cruelly. "I heard she begged for them to spare you before she was killed."

Anguish tore through my chest. "You shouldn't talk shit when you have a gun aimed at you."

"You won't shoot me. You're weak." Jensen was trying to piss me off enough for me to make a mistake. It wasn't happening.

"Not another step, Ky," I ordered, seeing him inching closer out of the corner of my eye. "Your daddy and I aren't done talking yet."

"What did I say before?" Jensen rubbed his chin. "Oh, right. You're not a fighter. You run. This conversation was interesting. But there's nothing else I care to share. Put down the gun, Vanessa."

"I'm done running."

I pulled the trigger.

CHAPTER TWENTY-ONE

Kyro

She pulled the trigger right as I lunged, pushing her arm up. Jensen ducked as the bullet hit the front door window, shattering the glass. Tugging the pistol from her grip, I handed it off to Zak, preparing myself for the hell I knew she was going to give me for stopping her.

"What did you do?" she hissed, trying to tear away from me. "Fuck, if I wasn't dead before, I am now."

"No, you're not." I pulled her close, speaking in a low voice. "He still needs you."

Jensen's bellowing laugh made her freeze. Jesus, she was shaking. I wasn't sure if it was from fear or rage. Probably both. Someone would have to be stupid to not be afraid after attempting to kill Jensen Banes. But I couldn't let her go through with it.

"That was a surprise." Jensen glanced at the glass pieces covering the floor. "I didn't think you had it in you."

"You know nothing about me." Cold fury saturated her voice as she tried tugging out of my hold.

"Get him patched up," Jensen ordered as two Kings carried the man Vanessa shot to the back of the restaurant. "Vanessa, you're coming back to the house with me. Consider your freedom gone after that stunt."

"Stunt?" She snorted. "I fully intended on putting a bullet in your chest."

"Hey, Vee." Zak stood in front of us, blocking out Jensen. "And I mean this in the nicest possible way—shut the fuck up before you make this worse."

"Worse? It can't get worse. Whether I help or not, he's going to make my life a living hell before trying to kill me. I'm not wasting my fear on him anymore." Her face revealed nothing but hate. My stomach twisted, knowing her feelings weren't only directed at my father.

The small amount of trust that had been slowly growing over the last month was wrecked. Because of the secret I'd been dreading her finding out about. A secret I had no fucking choice about keeping from her. She needed to understand why.

"Tell her," I demanded, pulling Vanessa behind me and Zak as I spoke to Jensen. "Tell her why she would have regretted killing you."

Jensen raised his eyebrows at my words. "And why would I do that?"

I hesitated as my stomach fell. *Why?* I couldn't tell him she was the love of my fucking life and losing her because of his lies would destroy me. He might have a hint that I cared for her. But if he knew my real feelings, he'd try to take her away in a heartbeat.

Zak cleared his throat. "I, for one, really don't want her being that pissed at me again. Last time I ended up in prison. Pretty sure this time, she'd stab us in our sleep. At least if she knows Ky and I aren't the ones to blame, then I'm safe."

Leave it to Zak to use his sarcasm to save me from having to answer. He always had my back, no matter what situation we were in. I relaxed a bit, knowing his words would make Vanessa need to find out what he was talking about.

"What do you mean?" She grabbed Zak's arm, turning him toward her. "Blame you for what?"

"Nothing," Jensen snapped. "We're leaving."

I laughed, knowing I was about to push the limits. "What's wrong, Dad? You're not worried about all of Vanessa's anger falling on you, are you? Even if she knows the truth, it's not like she can do anything about it."

I was baiting him, and from the way his lips pressed together, he was not happy. I never talked back to him. Especially in front of his men. His eyes darted around the room before landing back on me.

"Everyone out," he commanded sharply, and his men hightailed it to the employee door before he finished speaking.

"It seems important to Zak and Kyro for you to know why my son saved me from death," Jensen murmured, his voice deadly. He eyed me with intense interest as he spoke. "Obviously wanting to keep his father alive isn't enough."

Ryker stood next to Zak as Vanessa stepped up beside me. Her spine was rigid while she stared at Jensen.

"I love Kyro," Jensen stated, keeping his cold gaze on me. "But unlike his late brother, he lets feelings get in the way of making the hard decisions. He just needs a little push to make the right choices. I needed insurance to make sure he stayed on track."

"Insurance," Vanessa repeated, tilting her head to glance at me.

My fingers curled into fists, hearing his way of explaining the screwed-up shit he'd done in the past. He was always a boss before he was a father. My family consisted of the people standing beside me, not the blood who looked at me as weak.

"Yes. That mutual friend we have." Jensen strode to the table and grabbed his whiskey, downing it in one swallow. "He's my insurance."

Vanessa peeked at me before looking at Ryker and Zak, waiting for someone to clear up the confusion.

"He's a professional contract killer, Vee," Ryker said in a low voice. "What do you think Jensen would have him do?"

Her eyes widened, and she looked back at Jensen. "You'd kill Ky if he didn't listen to you? No, that's not right. He's your blood. Family before anything..."

She trailed off, trying to piece everything together on her own. Zak and Ryker didn't move a muscle as I leaned down, speaking in her ear.

"He wouldn't kill me," I said gruffly. "He'd kill the people I care about."

"Zak and Ryker?" she whispered in shock.

I nodded, looking back at Jensen. His jaw twitched as he watched Vanessa take in the information. No one else in the Kings knew their boss threatened his son to keep him in line. And Jensen planned to keep it that way.

"So, if Ky doesn't bow to your every whim, you kill his two best friends?" Vanessa asked, with a mix of anger and disbelief vibrating her voice.

"Contrary to what you think, I'm not a monster," Jensen replied coolly. "It's only for important matters."

"Like what?" she asked, crossing her arms.

Jensen rubbed his chin. "Let's look at what just happened. You tried killing me. Kyro stopped you. If he hadn't, our mutual friend would come investigating. And he's one of the fucking best. Let's just say my life is tied to Zak and Ryker's."

Jensen stopped talking to pick up another glass of whiskey as Vanessa processed what he'd said. Gritting my teeth, I stayed quiet, knowing she'd figure it out quickly.

"You got yourself a hitman to make sure your own son doesn't kill you? Or let you die?" She breathed out a shaky laugh. "Holy fuck. Blood doesn't mean shit to you. You don't even trust your only family."

Zak stifled a groan, and I barely managed to keep from pulling her behind me. Her words were going to enrage Jensen. To him, family was still everything, no matter how fucked up it got.

"I blame you for having to do this," Jensen hissed, taking a step forward. "You made him soft. There's no place for women in this life, unless it's for a quick fuck. Whatever the hell you did as kids made him grow up differently. He would have been just like Knox—"

"Probably a good thing he didn't grow up like Knox," Vanessa cut in, only fueling the fire. "Because if he did, he'd most likely be where Knox is now—in the ground."

"You little bitch," Jensen seethed, charging forward. "You got one of my son's killed and somehow got into the head of the other one."

Gripping Vanessa's arm, I stepped in front of her. "There's no way to get the money if she's dead. You need her alive for now."

My words cut through his rage, and he froze mid-step. If he could, he'd kill her right then. But paying the debt off to the Italians was just as important to him as getting revenge for Knox was. The accounts were in Vanessa's name. No one would ever get the money if she was dead.

"I don't give a fuck what you do to me," Vanessa said quietly. "Torture me. Hurt me. It doesn't matter. I'm not giving you the money. You're right, I'm a bitch and I'm stubborn as fuck. I've learned secret after secret since being back, but this...knowing you had a hand in my parents' deaths, I won't fucking help you."

"Okay," I muttered, pulling her toward the front door. "Let's go outside for a minute so you can calm down."

Jensen kept silent as we walked past him, his loathing stare focused straight on Vanessa. I half expected him to stop us and breathed a small sigh of relief once we were outside. We stopped near my truck as I glanced back, seeing two Kings standing near the entrance, watching us. Jensen didn't fucking trust me with her anymore.

"Nothing you say is going to make me change my mind, Ky. I won't help him. I'm going to end up dead either way." She leaned against the truck, trying to create distance between us.

"No, you won't," I snapped.

"Is that the reason you kept everything from me?" she asked, with pain filtering through her gaze. "Because he's holding the lives of your friends over your head?"

"Yes."

"You think he'd really kill Zak or Ryker if you told me the secrets he didn't want me to know?"

"There's no thinking about it, Raindrop. He would have, without any fucking hesitation."

"So fucked up," she breathed out. "Did you try finding him? The hitman?"

"We couldn't find him." That was an understatement.

The guy was a fucking ghost. Ryker had tried tracking him. We didn't have shit to go on. Not even a name.

She bit her lip before asking, "You really didn't know about anything the night my parents were killed?"

"No," I answered, making sure she was looking at me. "Zak and I didn't find out until after we got out of prison. We knew shit was going down that night, but we had no idea he had anything to do with that."

Her posture relaxed slightly at my words, and she ran a hand through her hair as she stared past me at the men watching us.

"I can't go back in there," she whispered. "I can't be around him. One of us will end up dead."

"I know."

"I won't make you choose between saving me or keeping your best friends alive." Her voice grew stronger. She was blocking everything out. The hurt, the sadness, the small amount of trust she had for me. I could see it all disappearing under the cold exterior she'd survived with for the last seven years.

"You really think Zak and Ryker wouldn't do anything to help me protect you?" I asked in an attempt to keep her from shutting me out. "You're their family. Zak's been your best friend for as long as I've been in love with you. You might not know Ryker very well, but he heard your whole life story. He knows how much you mean to me. They would both lay down their lives for you."

"And what would be the point?" she snapped, her eyes blazing. "Because once Jensen gets what he wants, I'm dead anyway."

"No—"

"I understand why you did it. The secrets to keep Zak and

Ryker safe. I get it. And I'm glad you did it." Instead of feeling relief from her words, they filled me with dread. Because I knew her well enough to figure out what she was doing. "Jensen has such a strong hold on you, and he won't ever fucking give it up. Because you're his son. He's already proven he'll do whatever he needs to keep you in his life. Willingly or not."

"You think I don't know that?" I growled, closing the inches between us.

There wasn't a damn day in the past seven years when I felt at peace. But the night I confronted her in Detroit? Staring into her deep brown eyes? Even when she looked at me with hate, fuck if that didn't calm the constant raging storm in my soul.

"You'll always be his puppet," she snarled, shoving me back. "Our lives were fucked the second we were born. There's no getting away from it."

"Don't," I warned her.

"We'll never be together." The weight of her words crushed my chest, even if I knew she didn't mean it. "I'll be caged or dead if I stay in this city. And you can't leave."

She shoved me again as her hand brushed my pocket. Understanding hit me and I chuckled, grabbing her wrists before pushing her against the truck.

"Get mad, make a scene." I shook my head as she glared at me. "Then steal my keys from my pocket. Trying to take my truck for another joyride?"

Her silence proved I was right. With a sigh, I let go of one of her wrists and pulled my keys from my pocket. Glancing back to make sure my dad's guys weren't watching too closely, I slid them into her hand, closing her fingers around them.

Her lips parted in shock as she glanced at her hand

before meeting my eyes again. Running my knuckles down her cheek, I leaned closer.

"I don't want to keep you caged," I murmured. "I want to keep you safe."

"You're going to let me go?" she asked, her eyes narrowing in doubt.

"Yes." My hand was still on hers. "But I'm asking you to stay. I've been protecting you my whole life. Trust me to keep doing it."

The answer was obvious before she even spoke. Her body stiffened as the she clenched the keys tighter.

"No."

Letting go of her hand, I backed up a step. "Fine. But remember what I said, Raindrop. Run from me or stay—either way, you're still mine. You always will be."

"Let's stop kidding ourselves, Ky," she muttered before her blank gaze landed on me again. "There is no way our story ever would have gotten a happy ending. We're done. Too much shit has happened. And it's only going to get worse."

"Keep denying it. You know we aren't done."

"We are. If you're really letting me go, I'm gone."

"What about Cassie?"

The blank look disappeared, and she frowned. "I know you'll keep her safe until she decides she wants to leave Suncrest. I'll get in touch with her."

One of the guys cleared his throat, tapping his watch when I looked at him. Apparently, Jensen was running out of patience.

"One last thing." Grabbing her hips, I pressed my body against hers, and she tilted her head to meet my gaze. "If you come back, that tells me we aren't finished. You can come back angry. Revengeful. I don't give a fuck. It only means one thing. That you still love me. Because baby, we both know you still do."

Stretching on her tiptoes, she brushed her lips across my cheek before breathing out her words. "If I ever come back, it won't be for you. It'll be because I have what I need to pay back the Crows for what they did to Teddy. Or to repay Mack for his hospitality when he had me. But I plan to get the hell away from here."

She moved to back away, and I grabbed a fistful of her hair, tugging it back until my eyes met her heated gaze. Her hand flew to my chest in a useless effort to push me away.

"You're not planning on leaving," I stated in disbelief.

"Yes, I am—"

"You wouldn't even have brought up Teddy or Mack if you were going to leave for good. You just need to get away from Jensen first. From me."

"This isn't about you," she snapped, not even trying to deny what I said.

"It's about revenge," I murmured, studying her face intently. "You're craving it. Needing it. It's going to get you hurt. Or killed."

"Let me go, Ky."

"Stay with me." My grip in her hair tightened as her nails dug into my chest. "You want revenge? I'll fucking help you."

"I don't want your help."

My patience all but disappeared. I never would've handed her my keys if I'd had the slightest idea she still wanted to go after the Crows.

"You need me," I growled. "You can't do this alone."

"Who says I'm doing it alone?"

Frowning, I stayed quiet for a moment until I realized who she was talking about.

"The Dusty Devils?"

She nodded. "They knew my dad, Ky. They'll help me."

"I don't like it."

"It's not fucking up to you," she snarled. "Now let go of my hair."

"What if I told you who your dad was? Would you stay?"

"No."

I wanted to rip those keys from her hand. She'd only been back a month, and we had spent half that time at each other's throats. It wasn't enough time. Then again, it was never enough time when it came to her. Loosening my hold on her hair, I shot a glance over my shoulder. The two Kings were still waiting impatiently by the door.

If I took her back into the restaurant, Jensen would bring her to his house. That wasn't fucking happening. If I tried leaving with her, not only would he get the Italians to track us down, Zak and Ryker were still in there. At least if she was with the MC, they could protect her.

It was fucking killing me that the Kings were the ones she had to be protected from. It wasn't going to be this way forever. Even as teenagers, Zak and I were making plans to get out from under Jensen. The damn hitman and Italian mafia screwed that to hell.

Before I could change my mind, I slid my hand from her hair to the back of her neck.

"Then go," I forced out gruffly. "Go back to the house first. I'm sure by now you know where we keep the spare cash. Take Kenzi's bike. You'll get farther with it than you would with my truck."

"I have to make it believable."

"What?"

She grinned, but it lacked its usual intensity and didn't reach her eyes. "Jensen can't know you're letting me leave."

I pulled her closer. "Hmm, sounds like you care."

"I don't hate you," she whispered. "Not after knowing why you did it all..."

I sighed. "But?"

"My heart can't take any more back and forth. I can't do any more secrets. No more lies. Even if it was to protect me. I'm done." Her eyes hardened as if she was already preparing to shut me out. "It's better for everyone that I leave."

"You don't know that—"

Gripping my shirt, she crushed her lips onto mine. Before I could even taste her, she pulled away.

"One for the road," she muttered. "Bye, Ky."

Without giving me a chance to say a word, she gripped the arm that was still holding the back of her neck. Gritting my teeth, I relaxed my body, knowing what she was about to do. She twisted my arm to nearly the point of pain, and I turned away from her to relieve the pressure. I wondered if she would be strong enough to do this if I actually fought back.

"Hey," one of the guys yelled.

She was running out of time. More guys would be here any minute. Her grip on my arm loosened as she kicked me right behind my knees, sending me to the ground. Seconds later the truck door slammed shut and the guy's shouting was muffled by the engine's roar.

I spun around right as she turned down another street, disappearing. My heart raced as despair dug a pit in my stomach. It was the right thing to let her leave. The safest.

But if that were true, why did it feel so wrong letting her go?

CHAPTER TWENTY-TWO

Vanessa

"I'll be fine," Cass assured me as I dug through the desk, grabbing the cash I'd found a couple of days ago. "Go. I'll stay here until I decide where I want to go."

"I really don't want to leave you here with everything going down," I muttered, stuffing the money into my backpack.

"Do you trust Ky and his friends?"

I paused and looked at her. "Yes. Mostly anyway."

"Then I trust them too." She threw me my hoodie. "I'll be fine."

I wanted to take her with me. But if something happened, Ky could protect her more than I could. Especially if I crossed paths with Mack again.

Slinging the backpack over my shoulder, I slid the bike key off Ky's keyring. The only issue was the tracker still on the bike. Not sure it mattered; Ky knew where I was going. And after letting me leave, I doubted he'd tell Jensen.

"Stay safe, okay, Cass?" I wrapped my arms around her,

giving her a tight hug. My throat got tight as I said goodbye. With everything going on, I had no idea when or even if I'd see her again.

"Don't worry about me." She pushed me away gently. "Go."

Without another word, I rushed out the back door to the motorcycle. I needed to get out of Suncrest before the city was crawling with Kings and Italians looking for me. Nerves kept my stomach clenched as I rode through the streets. The second I was on the highway, my grip on the throttle relaxed a bit.

The things I had learned at the restaurant filtered through my mind as I cruised down the highway. It all made sense now. Why Ky and Zak had lied to me all these years. I would have done the same thing. Thinking about the guilt Ky had to go through made me hurt.

Having to choose between me and his two best friends must have torn him apart every damn day. He'd been balancing both, keeping me safe and them alive. It was time to take myself out of the equation.

I couldn't stay in Suncrest. Jensen would never release his hold over Ky. I wasn't going to make Ky choose between me and his best friends. For seven years, I had become an expert in keeping my heart locked down. Ky had cracked it open since I'd been back.

And I was going to force it all away. Even if I saw Ky again, I wouldn't let him in. Our story was over, like it should have been all those years ago.

He would never let me go, so I'd do it for him. It was better this way. I wouldn't be able to live with myself if Zak or Ryker were killed protecting me. They'd do it without hesitation. But what would be the point? Too many people wanted me. For money. For revenge. I wasn't ever getting out of this life alive, and I refused to drag anyone down with me.

Except those who deserved it. Mack and the Crows were going to their graves with me.

Excitement filtered through me as I focused on where I was going. The Dusty Devils had known my dad. They'd have the answers everyone in Suncrest refused to tell me.

I was more than ready to finally find out.

Pushing the door open to Rob's Bar, I took a deep breath. My tank top and leggings had people staring. They weren't the clothes women wore to biker bars. I didn't give a shit this time. I wasn't leaving until I talked to Don.

It looked exactly the same as the last time I was in here. Bikers and their women crowded the smoke-filled room as more than a few people watched me walk to the back of the bar. Before I even made it halfway, a hand grabbed my arm. Spinning me around, Tim looked pissed to see me again.

"I thought I made it clear the Devils aren't helping you," he hissed, his eyes darting around. "Don gave me one job. To make sure I told you to stay away. You know what happens to prospects who don't do their jobs?"

"Believe me, your president will want to see me." I ripped my arm away from him. "I need to talk to Don. Now. Is he here?"

"You're leaving," Tim ground out, grabbing my shoulders, trying to push me to the door. "Before you get me in trouble."

"Stone Ace," I screamed, digging my feet in an attempt to slow him down. "And Tessa. They were my parents. You don't fucking understand. I need to see Don."

Tim's grip loosened, and he halted his steps, realizing the entire bar had gone deathly quiet. Breathing hard, I shoved him away, searching the crowd for the one person who could give me answers.

"Don knew my parents. And the MC my dad was in," I explained loudly as everyone's attention was on me. "I need to talk to him."

My eyes went to the group of bikers who were all moving to the side. Don strode forward, his eyes gleaming dangerously as he stared at me. I straightened up, standing my ground and refusing to be intimidated.

"How do you know who Stone and Tessa are?" Don asked quietly.

"I just told you, they're my parents—"

"They only had one daughter," he snarled. "And she died when they did."

"No." I matched his stare. "I didn't. My name is Vanessa Ace. I ran from Suncrest when I came home to find my parents murdered seven years ago."

"Not possible," he muttered, studying me in a new light. "Teddy would have told me."

"My dad had a motorcycle he named Stella, and he used to say it was his first love. My mom had a tattoo on the inside of her wrist of a black rose that she hated, but never got removed." I blurted out facts, hoping to convince him as fast as I could. "Teddy Hill was like family. Recently, I found out there was a contract to marry me off to the Crows. And even all these years later, it's still valid. Which is why the fuck I've been being pulled between the gangs in Suncrest since being back."

He studied me, processing my words. "Who killed Teddy?"

"The Crows," I spat out, anger filling me as his death

flashed through my mind. "I was there but couldn't stop it."

He crossed the room, stopping in front of me. His gaze traveled down my face as I stood still. His mouth parted slightly as his green eyes explored my brown ones. Anguish took over his features, and he scrubbed a hand down his face and through his beard.

"Jesus Christ," he breathed out. "How did I not see it before? You look just like your mother did when she was younger. All this time we thought you were dead."

I relaxed for the first time since I'd stepped foot in the bar. He believed me. Letting out a breath, I leaned against the table behind me.

"What MC was my dad in?" The question I'd been obsessing over flew from my mouth as Don's eyes widened in surprise.

"You don't know?"

I shook my head. "No. The Kings and Crows seem adamant about not wanting me to know."

Don's eyes lit up with excitement. "I'll tell you everything about your parents. Well, more about Stone. I grew up with him. And about your dad's MC."

"Can it help me take down the Crows?"

"No." His answer made me frown, until he spoke again. "It will help destroy the Crows. And everyone else who has hurt you. And there's no doing anything by yourself. We'll help with whatever you need. You're family."

Bikers around the bar nodded in agreement as they watched our exchange. I bit my lip, not sure what was going to happen next. I almost wanted to run again and forget about it all. But staring at Don, I realized that wasn't an option anymore.

"Come on, Vanessa. Let's go back to the clubhouse and talk."

CHAPTER TWENTY-THREE

Kyro

Four fucking days.

She'd been gone four days, and no one had seen her. Jensen was on the fucking warpath. He had half the Kings and a few of Antonio's guys looking for her day and night.

Ever since she'd left, there had been a pit of dread in my stomach, and each day it only got larger. For now, she was safe in Brown City with the bikers. I just wasn't sure how long that would last. The tracker on the bike was disabled hours after I let Vanessa leave. She didn't want me finding her.

I poured a glass of whiskey and stared out the front window, watching the headlights of Zak's truck turn into the driveway. Doors slammed shut a few seconds before the front door opened and Zak and Ryker walked in. They went straight to the bar and poured glasses from the same bottle I had taken out.

"She's definitely still there." Zak shook his head. "They have bikers watching the road coming from Suncrest. They knew we were in Brown City the second we passed the welcome sign."

"I thought they'd be out looking for her dad's bike," Ryker muttered. "I doubt it's in Brown City."

Zak strolled into the kitchen and opened the freezer to grab ice for his drink while I finished mine in one swallow before setting the empty glass on the bar.

"Maybe Don already knows where it is," I replied.

"Is Cassie outside?" Zak's voice was curious as he looked out the back glass door.

"No, she's in your room." I moved until I was standing next to him and saw what he was staring at. Someone was having a bonfire on our beach, about halfway to the water.

"Who the fuck has the balls to do that?" Zak asked. "Everyone knows this is the Kings' beach. And the Kings know it's ours."

"Only one person," I murmured with my heart thudding a bit faster. "It's her."

Zak squinted, leaning closer to the glass. "After leaving, you think she'd just come back alone?"

I bumped my shoulder into his. "You said she was in Brown City."

"Man, we had two bikes follow us the entire time we were there," Zak explained defensively. "Just like when we went two days ago. We figured she was at their clubhouse."

Ryker stood on the other side of me, and we all scanned the beach, trying to see anything through the darkness. There was no movement besides the flickering flames.

"Before we go out there," Zak said, raising a hand. "Let it be known that I think it's a fucking bad idea and a trap."

"Let's go." I slid open the door but stopped when Zak grabbed my arm.

Holding up one finger, he jogged away from us and

disappeared into his room. As we waited, I grabbed my gun while Ryker did the same. Screaming poured out of Zak's room when he stepped back into the hall and shut the door behind him. Loud thudding accompanied the screaming that Zak was purposely ignoring as he came back into the kitchen.

"What the hell did you do to her?" Ryker asked, staring in the direction of the bedrooms.

"Locked her in my bathroom," Zak mumbled, pushing past me and opening the door.

"Why?" I followed him outside with Ryker right behind me. On the beach, the fire was still going with only one person sitting there. I was positive it was her.

Zak groaned, and I looked back at him as he ran a hand down his face. "Because we don't know what the hell we're walking into. I don't want to have to worry about her too."

Both mine and Ryker's mouths dropped in surprise.

"Don't tell me you like her," Ryker cautioned. "You know, at some point her dad is going to take her back—"

"That's why I did it," Zak interrupted. "If she gets killed, then her dad will go after us. I'm making sure that doesn't happen. We have enough fucking problems."

"Sure, you are." Ryker patted him on the shoulder, causing him to scowl.

"I am," Zak snapped. "I don't like her. I haven't even tried to fuck her. I'm not stupid enough to mess around with the daughter of a Detroit gang boss."

The fact that he hadn't tried sleeping with her told me he didn't look at Cassie like all the other girls. I didn't say it out loud because he wouldn't admit to it anyway. And my impatience hit its breaking point knowing Vanessa was just on the beach.

"Come on." Leaving the patio, I stepped onto the sand.

"I'm with Zak. This is a bad idea," Ryker grumbled, following me.

I silently agreed. She wouldn't just come back. She either needed our help or...I honestly didn't know. I brought my gun, but not because I was worried she'd do something. She might not be alone. Nerves kept my senses heightened as we got closer. She was sitting with her back to us, leaning back on her hands, while she faced the fire.

Sand weighed down my shoes with each step, but I didn't take the time slip them off. Clouds covered the moon and stars, making the fire the only source of light. A breeze blew her hair off her back as I stopped a few feet behind her. Waves crashed onto the beach, drowning out the sound of Zak complaining behind me. All three of us were on edge. I glanced behind my shoulder to see them both scouring the beach.

"You were right."

Her voice carried through the waves and breeze, strong, yet there was a touch of sadness.

"Right about what?" I asked, cautiously taking a step closer while Zak and Ryker stayed behind me.

"I can't do it alone."

Doubt wormed its way through everything else. Her coming back was the last thing I expected. She'd been adamant about not wanting my help. Or even being around me. This was something else.

"I want to find out who killed my parents. I want to know why the fuck they tried marrying me off." Her voice rose and became bitter, but she still sat there facing the flames. "There's enough secrets to drown in, and I'm tired of trying to stay above water. Time to build my own damn boat."

She jumped up and brushed the sand off her jeans as

my breath caught and my cock stirred. Her jeans showed every curve of her ass. The thin black shirt she was wearing clung to her back like a second skin. She turned around, and my eyes widened. Her shirt dipped almost to her belly button before it tucked into her jeans. Her breasts were almost halfway out, and it took everything in me to stay where I was. She looked sexy in anything, but this was a far cry from the leggings and tank tops she loved to wear.

My gaze finally made it to her face, and I tensed, feeling Zak and Ryker do the same as they stepped up on either side of me. The black eye makeup and bright red lipstick only furthered the ferocity in her eyes. They didn't show an ounce of humor even when she let out a short laugh.

"You told me I couldn't do it alone," she said, her eyes not leaving mine. "That I needed you."

My hands closed into fists and my heart hammered against my ribs. By now, she had to know who her dad was. The confidence she had made me wonder if they had already found the paperwork.

Her hair whipped around, and the flames danced behind her from the wind. Lightning lit up the sky above the ocean, but my gaze stayed on her. She raised her arms up and smirked.

"You're not the only one with power in this town. Either are the Crows," she said loudly.

Movement out of the corner of my eye had me twisting my head to the side as I pulled out my gun. Zak and Ryker did the same, all three of us pointing in different directions.

"Motherfucker," Zak muttered under his breath.

Men surrounded us. At least thirty. All had leather cuts on. Some from the Dusty Devils and the rest from two other MCs. A few had their weapons raised at us, but most seemed content with just staring.

Don stepped forward; his glare pointed at me. "When we talked, you purposely didn't tell us who she was."

I matched his stare, saying nothing. We both knew why I'd done it.

He glanced at the gun in my hand before nodding to one of his guys. The same curly haired guy we saw outside the bar in Brown City. He and two other men closed in on us with their guns raised.

"Put yours down, Ky," Vanessa demanded from behind me. "I still have something to say, but my new friends here don't trust you."

I turned back around, facing the triumph that glowed on her face. She had us and knew it. We weren't going anywhere until she gave the order. My grip tightened on the pistol before I bent down, dropping it in the sand. Zak and Ryker hesitated before doing the same.

"I get it," she said with a small shake of her head. "Why Jensen didn't want me to find out."

There it was. She finally figured it out. A wave of relief trickled through me. The one secret I'd been keeping from her since we were teenagers was finally free. The relief was short-lived, knowing Suncrest was about to turn bloody once the Kings and Crows found out she wasn't in the dark anymore.

"Now what, Raindrop?" I asked. "Going to keep your promise of taking down the Kings?"

Uncertainty flashed through her eyes for a split second before she locked it away. I stepped toward her, only for someone behind me to grab my shoulder tightly, jerking me back. Reflex had me swinging my fist before a thought went through my mind. My knuckles smashed against the guy's cheek, and two other bikers shot forward at me. Ryker and

Zak turned, ready to fight, even knowing full well we were outnumbered.

"Enough," Don roared, stepping out of the crowd.

Anger burned through my veins, and I steeled my spine, letting my face morph into the cruel mask I was known for.

"This isn't Brown City. You're in Suncrest Bay." I thundered, loud enough for everyone to hear. "The Kings' city. My fucking city. Your MCs have no power here."

"They don't." The fury in her voice overrode mine.

I gave Don one last warning glance before focusing my attention back on her. Confidence and anger radiated from every part of her body. I might tower over her, but she now knew the power she possessed, and there was no taking it away from her. Even knowing the fallout from this was going to be disastrous, my lips tipped up, threatening to expose my real feelings.

She fucking came back.

"They don't own this city." Her eyes danced in excitement. "But my dad did."

"He used to," I said in a low voice that only she could hear.

She ignored me. "I thought being with you and the Kings was what I was destined to do. I was good at it. I always remembered thinking how lucky I was to be with the guy I love and living life with a never-ending rush."

She moved until she was right in front me. Ryker, Zak, and the bikers were forgotten while we stared at each other.

"What everyone knew, besides me, was that I was born into this life. My dad wasn't just in an MC, he was the president of one. The largest in California. They had more ties, allies, and money than the Kings ever had. I thought the Kings ruled Suncrest. But they didn't. He did."

While the truth spilled from her lips, her eyes hardened

to a degree of coldness I'd never witnessed before. I kept my mouth shut, knowing she wasn't done.

"Angel's Aces." Pride shone through the anger when she said it. "My dad's MC. Even now, years after he died, all the other MCs came together to protect me."

"We would have done it sooner if we weren't told that she died with her parents," Don spat out, walking into my line of sight. He stopped a few feet away from Vanessa and gave me a glare of death like I was the one who told him. "She never would have had to run. She always had a home with us."

If her dad trusted them so much, why the hell did Teddy and Bill keep her return a secret from them? It didn't make any sense.

"The Kings or Crows aren't going to stop, even if you get involved." I spoke to Don, knowing he was the reason for the other two MCs being here.

He let out a deep laugh before running a hand down his beard. "The Crows are fucking done. They dug their grave by killing Teddy and threatening an Ace. As for the Kings... that's up to Vanessa."

Don was talking as if his MC had the power to deal with the Crows and Kings. They never did anything in Suncrest Bay. It was only the Aces. The Angel's Aces used to be bigger than us. Half the shit we did went through them. They controlled almost everything in Suncrest Bay. But that was then. They'd been gone seven years.

"I can see your wheels turnin', kid." Don's lips tipped up in a knowing grin.

"You better remember who you're talking to," I snarled, taking a step closer to him and Vanessa. "You might have the guns now, but if you think you can run this fucking city, think again."

"Oh, it won't just be me." All traces of humor were gone from his face. "You really think the Aces are gone? Let me tell you a little secret—they aren't."

Rain began to fall, and the cold drops hit my face, but I didn't blink while trying to gauge if he was lying or not. I kept my expression blank, not giving away the fact that, as far as my dad knew, the Aces fell apart after her parents were murdered. Teddy and Bill were the only ones we knew of who stayed in town. A weight fell on my chest with this new information, and my gaze swung to Vanessa, who was already staring at me.

"How does it feel?" Her voice was quiet, but lethal. "To not know everything?"

Apparently, I didn't curb my shock quick enough because she saw right through me. She had always been the only one who could. Rain soaked her hair and dripped down her lashes as the fire behind her grew smaller. I flexed my fingers, resisting the urge to wrap them in her hair and kiss her until the anger in her eyes turned into need. She could act like she hated me all she wanted. Whether it was a show for the MCs or if she was even trying to convince herself, we both knew she didn't.

I chuckled, remembering we weren't alone on the beach. Showing her how I felt was one thing. Showing weakness to others was something I refused to ever do. The MCs came here tonight trying to claim what wasn't theirs. Actually, two things. This city and Vanessa. They weren't going to have either.

I moved forward a couple more steps until I was close enough to see the water sliding down her chest and disappearing under her shirt. Her breath hitched before she tipped her chin up and scowled. The fire in her eyes burned even brighter than the one she stood in front of.

"I know enough to still be in the game," I said quietly, keeping my words between us.

"It's not a fucking game," she snapped.

I tore my eyes from her for a quick moment, taking note of the gun in Don's hands. He didn't like me being this close to her, but he wasn't stopping me. An urge to test a crazy-ass theory popped into my head, and before thinking logically, I brought my hand up and brushed a wet strand of hair out of her face. Her body stiffened, and she narrowed her eyes, but she didn't push me away.

"Life's a game, Raindrop." I ran my fingers down her cheek. "And now you finally have all the pieces to play in the big leagues. You think the Crows will just roll over because you have people backing you? You think my dad will?"

She clenched her teeth and tried jerking away from my hand, but I caught her chin, keeping her eyes on mine.

"Let her go," Don warned.

I grinned, looking only at her. "You brought all these guys here to show that you're untouchable. But that's not true. Not for me."

She didn't answer as her fingers curled into fists. Thunder rumbled before lightning lit up the beach, and we were both soaked. But none of that mattered. We stared each other down, neither of us willing to look away or even blink.

"Here's a little game," I murmured, bringing my face closer to hers. "I bet you told them not to hurt us. You want to hate me. Forget about me. Because it would be easier. But you can't. My name is tattooed over your heart just as permanently as Raindrop is over mine."

I half expected a gun to my head. These bikers played by their own rules, and I wasn't sure how far they'd go to listen to what one girl wanted. But I needed to prove two things. One was that she still cared. If she stopped them from putting a bullet in me, then I knew there was a part of her that would forgive me for our fucked-up past. If she didn't stop them...that was fine too. Only she held the lit match that kept the shadows from completely blackening my heart. Without her in my life, I'd turn out as cruel as my father, and that was something I didn't want.

The other was specifically for the MCs. They came into my town acting like they owned it. Walked onto my fucking beach with *my* girl as their bargaining chip to try to take Suncrest. This had never been their city. If the Aces were really still alive and kicking, then let them try and reclaim their territory. These MCs had nothing here, and they needed to remember that.

Her gaze didn't leave mine, both of us refusing to lose in the mini battle of wills. My hand still gripped her chin, and I reached out and grabbed her hip with my other, wanting to see how far I could push until she shoved back. Fury clouded her brown eyes, but she still didn't move. This was supposed to be her night to prove she didn't need me. I was messing it up and gave it only moments before her rage boiled over.

Out of the corner of my eye, I saw Don move forward with his arm raised. Vanessa's eyes widened, and a sliver of panic slid through for a split second before she covered it. I kept my hands on her even when cold metal touched my temple.

"Let her go," Don ordered gruffly.

"No."

"Your funeral," he muttered.

"Stop," Vanessa ground out.

Her eyes finally left mine and focused on Don, with

danger lurking in their depths. I grinned in victory and opened my mouth to say something but didn't get the chance. The hand that had been holding her jaw was now in her grip and being wrenched backward. Grunting in surprise, I tried pulling away when she hit a pressure point in my palm near my thumb, sending a jolt of pain through my hand.

She pulled me closer and shoved her knee straight into my stomach. My gut twisted and I nearly doubled over. My other hand was still gripping her hip, and I leaned into her while trying to get a breath. She stepped back, and I would have faceplanted if she hadn't pushed my shoulder, keeping me upright. My knees hit the wet sand as her fingers yanked my hair until my neck was bent back and I was looking into her eyes again.

Fuck.

Only she could set off such conflicting emotions.

Blood rushed through my ears and anger shot through me faster than a bolt of lightning. Being in a position of weakness was something I'd vowed never to let happen again after I got out of prison. But as I stared at her through the rain hitting my face, I didn't make one move to get up.

Because at the same time, seeing this side of her caused my heart to beat faster and swell with pride. She was strong. Confident. No matter what she went through, giving up was never an option. I had spent my life doing whatever was needed to keep her safe. I'd let my soul burn to let her keep hers, and I'd do it until my last breath. Knowing she would always fight for herself if I wasn't here to do it gave me a feeling I couldn't describe.

My dick strained against my jeans while her grip tightened in my hair. My girl could hold her own, and it was fucking hot.

Her eyes glowed with taunting confidence, and she was fighting a grin. I flashed one of my own and her smile turned cold.

"We can keep playing games, Ky," she hissed as I watched water drip down her lips. "You might be a King, but I'm a fucking Ace. And I'll trump you every time."

CHAPTER TWENTY-FOUR

Vanessa

My words sent his jaw locking in fury while his hands clenched. There was an unreadable look in his eyes which shot unease through me. I expected him to be angry and act on it. But he stayed on his knees, making no attempt to get up. This was supposed to be it. The end of our story. I wasn't his, and the secrets were out. Now, I had what I needed to repay the Crows for what they did to Teddy. The connections were growing, and I knew I was close to finding out what my parents had kept from me.

This needed to be the last time I had to be around him because my self-control was close to nonexistent when I breathed the same air as him. I needed a clear head to plan the vengeance I craved.

"Doesn't mean I'll stop trying," he said with a cocky grin and challenge brimming in his eyes. "You thought this show you put on would scare me away?"

I hesitated, not sure what he was thinking. That was exactly what I'd hoped would happen. He shook his head and let out a laugh. Zak and Ryker were staring at us, both rigid with tension as a few bikers kept their guns on them.

Ky was right. I told Don I didn't want them hurt. My reason for doing this was purely selfish. I could have just disappeared and left Ky wondering where I'd gone. But no, I needed to prove that I could overpower the Kings. That Jensen Banes wasn't a threat to me anymore.

"This brings back memories, doesn't it?" Ky asked, breaking into my thoughts.

My gaze dropped to his mouth, and I swallowed, refusing to give him the satisfaction of an answer. The rain, the storm, the beach. It was identical to the night he first kissed me. Whenever it rained, I always thought of him, even when I was in Detroit.

"Full circle," I forced out. "Ending our story just like it began."

If I thought he was mad a minute ago, it was nothing compared to how he looked when I said that. He jerked his head, and my fingers slipped through his wet hair until he was free of my grasp. Shooting to his feet, he invaded my personal space like he owned it.

Grabbing my face with both hands, he pulled me until our noses were nearly touching.

"Does this feel like the end, Raindrop?" he growled. "Because to me, it's a new beginning. A way to start over with truths instead of secrets."

My heart ricocheted through my chest at the promise steeped in his words. Before I could respond, his lips crashed onto mine. Cold and wet, the same as when we'd first kissed. His taste was just as addicting. And his claim on me even stronger now than all those years ago.

He was ripped away when Don pulled his arm, tearing us apart. Ky's eyes darkened as he looked away from me. He pulled a knife from his pocket, flicked it open and pressed it to Don's throat, all in the time it took me to catch a breath.

"You don't fucking touch me," he snarled with such venom, a shiver ran down my spine. The man he was for me disappeared in a heartbeat, and he easily switched to the gangster everyone else knew him to be.

Don slowly released Ky's arm while glowering and grinding his teeth. His gun was still in his other hand, but he kept his arms down at his sides. The rain had slowed to a drizzle and the wind was gone. Silence stretched along the entire beach.

Ky kept the blade to Don's throat as he spoke. "Get the fuck off my beach and take your friends with you. I want you out of my city. You want to take down the Crows? Be my fucking guest. You want the Kings? Go ahead and try. Suncrest is ours. You aren't taking it. You kill me tonight, my father will have all the Kings on your doorstep by morning. You think I came out here without calling backup first?"

"The Aces—"

"I don't see them here, do you?" Ky spat out, making my pulse rise in anger. This wasn't how the night was supposed to go.

"We'll leave," Don said, his face going red. He glanced at me, not hiding how pissed he was. He came out here to make a stand against the Kings and got beat at his own game. In front of two other MCs. *Fuck.* I didn't want the people who were helping me to back out. I needed them.

Ky pulled the knife from Don's throat, but kept it raised while waiting for the bikers to retreat. Don jerked his chin at me, and I bristled at his silent demand, but moved to follow him. I needed to smooth this over so the Dusty Devils would still help me. A hand grabbed my elbow, spinning me back around.

"Not so fast," Ky said, his tone still dangerous, though not as chilling as it had been when he threatened Don. "We need to talk. Now that you know, this changes everything."

I attempted to pull back, but he wasn't about to let me walk away that easily. Nerves swarmed me. Jensen already wanted me dead because of who I was. He wanted me to suffer because of what I'd done to Knox. If I was here when he found out I brought three MCs into Suncrest to threaten his gang, he'd go through whoever he needed to get to me.

"Let me go," I demanded. "If I'm around when the Kings get here, even you won't be able to stop your dad from hurting me."

A vein above his eye twitched, and he shot a glance to Don before looking back at me. I arched an eyebrow. *Interesting*. Maybe he lied about calling backup. There was probably no one coming. He only said it to get the bikers to leave. I opened my mouth to call him out on it, but he released me and backed up.

"Come back to the house tomorrow so we can talk," he ordered as Ryker and Zak stepped up next to him.

"Sure, Ky. I'll check my schedule," I snarked.

"I'm serious," he said softly. "This changes everything."

"No, it doesn't," I muttered before turning and following Don off the beach and back to their bikes. Nothing had changed. Jensen Banes was alive, and everyone under the sun wanted me for my money.

"That's not how it was supposed to go," Don said from behind me as I wiped water from the seat of my bike. Annoyance filled his voice, and I didn't blame him.

I sighed. "I know. I'm sorry—"

"We should've just taken them by surprise. Now they know. And the Crows will most likely hear what went down too." He shook his head. "And now everyone knows that you can't hurt him. A fucking King."

"He's my entire past. Believe me. I wish it wasn't like that, but I couldn't do it."

"Once the Aces come back, only one will come out on top. And it won't be the Kings or Crows. Kyro better choose his side now. You or the Kings," he warned. "But even if he does choose you, the Aces will never trust him."

"How do we even know the Aces are still a thing?" I asked quietly. "Bill disappeared weeks ago and hasn't been heard from since I called him."

"Don't worry, kid. He'll be back, and I can promise you he won't be alone."

Keeping my doubts to myself, I climbed on my bike. "I need to clear my head. I'll be back at the clubhouse in a couple hours."

"Don't stay in Suncrest, it's not safe."

"I won't," I promised. "I'm just going to ride along the coast for a while."

Don nodded and waited for me to take off before getting on his own bike. The roar of dozens of motorcycles filled the air, making their presence known to anyone within hearing distance. On the way into town, they had all come separately. I guess they didn't care who knew now.

Goosebumps covered my exposed arms as the wind hit me. Standing in a storm and having no change of clothes hadn't been the best idea. But I didn't want to go back to the clubhouse yet. The conversation with Ky replayed in my head as I reached the outskirts of Suncrest, and I gunned the engine, shooting onto the open road.

I got lost in my head as I rode, inhaling the fresh air and enjoying the hum from my engine. The night was pitch black, with clouds still hiding the moon and stars. Headlights came from behind me, and I slowed down and veered toward the side, waiting for the car to pass. But it matched my speed and stayed behind me. Unease prickled the back of my neck, and I glanced in my mirror. All I could see were headlights. And they were close.

Revving the throttle, I sped up, only for the car to do the same. My unease became full-fledged panic. I was too close to Suncrest for this to be random.

"Shit," I muttered, glancing around me. A cliff was on one side of me, and a mountain blocked the other side. There were no other roads to turn on for a few miles at least. I pushed the bike faster as my stomach coiled with nerves. The car stayed on my ass, easily matching my pace.

Headlights suddenly lit up the road ahead of me and I squeezed my brakes. The bike skidded along the wet pavement to a stop. My pulse raced at how close I'd come to smashing into the black SUV that sat sideways, blocking both lanes. The car behind me rolled slowly into my back tire, forcing my bike forward and nearly tipping it at same time. I leaped off before it fell and heard a car door open. Without even turning around, I knew who it was.

Knowing running was a waste of time, I pulled off my helmet and turned to fix an icy glare to the guy who stood in front of me.

"Mack. How the fuck do you keep finding me?"

CHAPTER TWENTY-FIVE

Vanessa

He stood just outside the SUV and grinned as his gaze traveled to my feet and back up to my face. His hair was pulled back and hidden by the hoodie he had on. Footsteps came from behind me until I felt someone at my back.

"You really thought a pack of bikers coming into our city wasn't going to get our attention?" Mack asked with a mocking lilt in his tone. "We watched them at the beach behind Ky's house. And then followed you. I'm surprised you went off by yourself."

A chill ran through me as he spoke, but I refused to show him my fear. I doubted I'd get a second chance at escaping him again. Eyeing my bike on the ground, I took a deep breath. The back tire was under the car, and it wasn't drivable anymore.

"Tell me," Mack said quietly. "How the hell you convinced three different MCs to come into a city that isn't theirs and threaten a gang as powerful as the Kings?"

"I think you know how," I said, keeping my voice strong.

His eyebrows rose in shock, and he didn't answer.

"We have to move the car," the guy behind me said. "They've been holding up traffic for fifteen minutes."

I glanced over my shoulder at Danny. He met my gaze and smirked. Rolling my eyes, I looked back at Mack, who was staring at me with a frown.

"Get in the car, Vanessa." He opened the door to the SUV and waited like he actually expected me to listen.

Warm breath covered the back of my neck as Danny tried pushing me forward.

"Don't fucking touch me," I snarled, turning and throwing a punch to his jaw. He cursed and staggered back before raising his hand to me.

"Danny," Mack warned. "Stop."

Danny lowered his arm but stayed close while glaring and rubbing his cheek.

"I'm not here to take you again," Mack said, raising his arms like he wasn't a threat. "I want to make a deal."

"Right," I scoffed, stepping away from Danny. Maybe I should just try to make a run for it. Or try to get one of their keys. I had no intention of going back with them again.

"I need to show you something," Mack said. "That's it. I show you and you'll want to take this deal."

"Fuck you."

"Vanessa." His voice went from friendly to frigid in an instant, and he stepped forward. "Get in the damn car."

"Just tell me what you want, and I'll go home and think about it. I'll call you in a few days with my answer." My voice dripped in sarcasm because we all knew he wasn't about to let me walk away.

He sighed before nodding to Danny, who grabbed my arms, yanking them behind my back. I flung my head back, catching his chin. With a grunt, he tightened his grip and dragged me to the open door next to where Mack stood. He slammed me down onto the back seat, and I hissed in pain as the seatbelt buckle dug into my hip.

"Get off," I screeched as Danny climbed on top of me, practically sitting on my back.

"I gave you a chance to come on your own," Mack said from outside the car. "Stop fighting and we'll get there faster. Then you can leave."

I didn't stop struggling, not believing a word he said. Danny had my wrists in one hand and was tying some sort of rope around them with the other. Once it was tight enough that I couldn't pull out of it, he let go of my wrists and tied it.

He gripped my arm and pulled me up until I was sitting in the middle of the seat. I tried scooting away, but as soon as Danny left the car, Mack slid in and pulled me back next to his side.

"This is a piss poor way of trying to make a deal with me." My chest heaved while trying to catch my breath as I glared at the side of Mack's face. He turned to look at me before speaking.

"You know, for someone who's supposed to be a badass fighter, you always seem to be someone's prisoner." Mack's leering smirk had me gritting my teeth.

"Hmm, I wonder why no one comes after me alone." I pretended to ponder. "There's always two or three assholes surrounding me. Not a very fair fight."

His grin faded as my eyes went to his neck. Letting my body relax, I let out a short laugh.

"Oh, that's right. The one time you were alone with me, I had a piece of glass cutting your neck." My gaze turned deadly. "I am a fucking fighter. I don't care how many try to keep me prisoner, I won't ever bow down to anyone. Including you."

"How long have you known about the Aces?" he asked gruffly, changing the subject abruptly.

The driver turned and started driving down the road, away from Suncrest Bay. I glanced at the back window and back at Mack in confusion.

"Why does it matter?" I bit out the question, having no intention of telling him shit.

"Ky tell you?"

He chuckled when I didn't answer. "I figured it wasn't him. One of the MCs then?"

"It doesn't matter how. I know. And now you can't force me to marry you. You try anything; they're all going to come after you. You're not getting me or my money. Nothing you show me is going to change my mind."

"We'll see," he murmured, grabbing something from his pocket and leaning toward me.

I pulled away, but he reached for my hair and dragged me back. In his hand was a red bandana, and he covered my eyes before letting go of my hair and tying it behind my head.

"What the hell is this for?" I tried to keep the panic out of my voice about having one of my senses cut off.

"You can't know where we're going."

"Why?"

"You'll find out."

I slumped against the seat, only able to see my lap through the makeshift blindfold.

"I thought the secrets were fucking done," I mumbled.

Hot breath hit my cheek, and I flinched in surprise while he whispered next to my ear.

"This town was born in secrets, Vanessa. No one will ever know them all."

I didn't respond and turned my head away from him. Leaning back against the seat, I slid down an inch and the bandana slipped a bit. My heart raced, and I stilled for a moment before moving a little more. Suddenly, fingers gripped my chin tight enough to bruise, and I cried out.

"Move again, and you'll spend the rest of the ride with your head in my lap," Mack threatened without letting go of my face. "Got it?"

"You do that, and I'll make sure my new friends make you suffer before I kill you," I growled.

My jaw ached when he gripped my chin harder, and I tried to pull away, only for him to yank me back. I felt the bandana get adjusted back to how it was before, then he let me go, and I tore away from him.

He laughed, but it was cruel. "You're lucky it's not me in charge of this plan."

I swallowed at his threat and kept my face blank. I couldn't imagine his father being so heartless. Kannon Brooks had always been kind to me. But then again, so had Mack.

"I'm surprised I haven't seen your dad yet," I said, purposely sounding bored, as if I didn't care where I was. "Do I get to see him tonight?"

"No."

Even though I hated being in another situation where I wasn't in control, I couldn't help but be curious. For once, Mack was leading me to a secret instead of me staying in the dark. A pit of dread formed in my stomach because I was sure it still meant nothing good for me.

My clothes started to dry while we drove for what felt like

hours. Whoever was driving turned on music, and I kept my mouth shut the entire time. Mack didn't attempt conversation at all, he only paid attention when I tried moving away from him, and he then would just pull me back to his side. My arms were tingling from the rope and lack of moving. I shifted every few minutes trying to get comfortable, but it did nothing.

Finally, the car slowed, and my ears perked up at rocks crunching under the tires. We stopped, and Mack took the blindfold off. I blinked until my eyes adjusted and then glanced around. It was pitch black out, and all I saw in the headlights was a small cabin surrounded by trees. I couldn't even begin to guess where we were.

"If I untie you, promise to behave?" Mack asked skeptically with a raised eyebrow.

I bit my tongue and kept the sarcastic remark to myself. My arms were killing me. I only nodded, and he gave me a warning look before grabbing my arm to turn me away from him. He worked on the knot while I looked out the windshield at the tiny cabin.

There was a small porch with one rocking chair on it and a *no trespassing* sign in the one window next to the front door. It looked like a hunting cabin, but I doubted that's what the Crows used it for.

My arms fell free, and I groaned when the blood rushed back, making it feel like they were filled with pins that were stabbing me under the skin. I shook them and then stretched them out as Mack opened the door.

"There's nothing around here for miles," Mack informed me, grabbing my arm above the elbow and pulling me out of the car with him.

"Don't run, got it." I rolled my eyes as he walked toward the cabin with an iron grip on me. The car Danny had driven pulled up behind the SUV and parked, but no one got out.

"How about you drop the fucking attitude?" he snapped, reaching into his pocket and pulling out the key. "You'll be thanking me when we go in here."

"Doubtful," I muttered.

He twisted the key and opened the door. Darkness greeted us, and Mack used the flashlight on his phone until he found the light switch and flipped it on. I squinted from the sudden brightness, and my muscles tensed. I didn't know what was in this cabin, and I wanted to be ready for anything. Mack stood in front of me, blocking my view. I stepped to the side and took in the small space.

The whole cabin was one room. There was a kitchen area to my left, with a single sink and a mini-fridge and microwave on the short counter. The right side was the bathroom, but it was completely open with no walls. A toilet and stand-up glass shower were on each side of an old porcelain sink. An old plaid couch sat in the middle of the room, and in front of it was a box TV and radio.

My gaze moved behind the couch, and my heart began to beat faster. There was a bed with a large form under the blankets. I took a step forward, but Mack grabbed me and pulled me back.

"Who is that?" I hissed quietly, not sure I wanted to know.

Rattling caught my attention, and I shifted my focus to the floor. A cold fear gripped me, and I stood there frozen, realizing what I was staring at. In the middle of the room, drilled into the floor, was a thick metal hooked circle, and attached to it was a heavy chain. I followed the chain to where it ended, and my heart stopped when my eyes landed back on the bed.

Without meaning to, I moved backward to the door, only stopping when Mack tightened his grip on my arm. Like I guessed, this wasn't a hunting cabin, it was a fucking prison. Terror flowed through my veins as I watched the person climb out of the bed. I had just found out the secret about my dad's MC, and I had a feeling that might pale in comparison to what I was about to be exposed to.

The figure stood up and stretched before walking closer to us. The chain was fastened around his ankle and shook with every step he made. My gaze slowly trailed up, and when I finally made eye contact, I reared back and gasped.

The only reason I didn't fall to my knees was because Mack still had a hold on me. My mouth fell open, and I tried forming words, but my brain was void of anything other than who was standing in front of me. My breathing became fast, and my nails dug into my palm.

"Look at you. The angel I never thought I'd see again."

CHAPTER TWENTY-SIX

Vanessa

My mouth went dry as I stared at the ghost in front of me. He seemed so small, his clothes were huge and baggy and nearly hanging off him. One of his eyes was purple and blue, and he had a busted lip. My head swung to Mack, and he was watching my reaction with interest.

"After seven years, you have nothing to say to an old friend?"

I looked back at him, my eyes still disbelieving what was right in front of me. His voice was the same but lacked the power he used to have.

"Knox?"

My voice came out shaky, and I nearly leaned into Mack before I realized what I was doing. Knox's black hair was longer than it used to be and fell into his eyes before he pushed it out of the way while he inspected me. His eyes were hard and lacked emotion, and his once straight nose had a small kink in it like it had been broken once or twice. He looked even more like Jensen now than he did as a teenager. My eyes fell to his hand; the skin where his King tattoo used to be was blemished and scarred.

"Vanessa...you grew up," he said, surprise coloring his voice.

"Knox—how—I can't believe..." My voice trailed off when I realized why he was here. Mack. The Crows. They did this. Red clouded my vision, and I turned to Mack, ready to land my hits anywhere possible. But he was prepared and grabbed both of my wrists before I even lifted my arms.

"You fucking twisted piece of shit," I shrieked, trying to pull free. "God, this is so fucked. You've had him here all this time?"

He grunted, trying to keep me in his grasp. "Calm the hell down. Or I swear I'll call Danny in here and have him beat Knox until he's near death and make you watch."

I stilled, wishing I could kill him with my glare alone. Mack didn't let go, and he backed me into the wall.

"We have a lot to talk about, and I need you to stay fucking calm. Got it?" he demanded, getting too close to my face.

I nodded stiffly and pushed away from him before moving closer to Knox. My eyes warmed in sympathy when I looked at him again. And a crashing weight of guilt landed on my chest at the same time. Fuck, this was all my fault, and I was guessing this fate had been worse than death. I needed to get him out of here.

"Why'd he bring you here, Vee?" Knox asked, his eyes narrowing as he glanced at Mack. "Hope he doesn't expect to keep you captive too. My brother would never rest if you disappeared."

"Knox," I whispered, regret filling my voice. "Everyone thinks you're dead."

After a brief pause, he let out a calloused laugh. "Of course they do. I mean, it's been years."

I swallowed through the lump in my throat and just stood there. I didn't know why the hell Mack had brought me here, but I needed to find out. If only I could tear my eyes from the man in front of me. I'd never liked him. But seeing him like this, and knowing it was my fault, made my stomach clench with what felt like a hundred knives.

"Have you been here the whole time?" I asked hesitantly.

He shook his head, glancing at Mack again. "No. They move me around."

"Why?" My question was for Mack. "What the fuck did you gain from keeping him captive for years?"

"For a moment like this," he answered coldly. "Anything you say isn't going to make me feel bad, so save your words."

"Shit," I breathed out, running my hands up my face and then through my hair. "I thought Jensen was the worst person I'd ever met. You just changed my mind."

"And how is dear old Dad?" Knox asked quickly. "It's been forever since someone's been here who wanted to talk to me."

Another twist of guilt wrenched through my heart. "He's the same old asshole."

"And how's my little brother? You two married yet?"

Mack stepped forward. "Enough. We have more important things to discuss."

I leaned against the wall and crossed my arms, steeling myself for this conversation. My gaze kept going back to Knox, as if he'd disappear if I looked away. Mack seemed almost nervous, which meant what he was about to say was going to piss me off. Knox moved, and the chain dragging along the floor broke the silence until he sat down on the ratty couch and looked between Mack and me.

Mack cleared his throat. "I want the money from the accounts. All of it."

"No more talk of marriage?"

Knox's face morphed into confusion as he listened with rapt attention.

"No. The MCs know you're back. If I was forcing you, they'd make it their mission to take us down."

"Too late for that one," I muttered. "You already threatened me. Your guy killed Teddy. The MCs already plan on dragging you down."

"That's why you're going to stop it," he said before purposely lingering his stare on Knox before looking back at me.

I should have seen it coming. Maybe it was the shock of finding out he was alive. But it just clicked. He was going to use Knox as leverage. I pushed off the wall and rose to my full height before looking him dead in the eye.

"If I don't go back to the Dusty Devils, they'll go after the Crows," I said coldly. "You don't have a threat to keep me here even if I tell you no."

Mack looked at me thoughtfully before answering. "I'm not going to keep you here."

His words did nothing to soothe me.

"But if you don't agree right now, I'll deliver you, along with Knox's head, to Jensen Banes personally. Ky wouldn't even get a chance to see you before Jensen kills you." His voice was much too calm to match the words he was saying.

"And what's stopping me from saying I'll do it and then leaving and telling Ky?" It might be stupid to just come out and say it, but we were going to talk about it anyway. There was no point in waiting around.

"I'll kill Knox myself and then go after your precious King and his two friends. Then I'll go after Kenzi. Maybe after that, your friend Cassie. I've done my homework since you left, Vanessa. I know every person you care about. And you can't keep them all safe."

He grinned, and it sent ice dripping down my spine. My shoulders moved with each breath I took as I tried to stay in control. I kept my clenched fists at my sides and forced myself to stay quiet. I would do anything to keep them safe. And he fucking knew it.

"And don't think you can tell Ky and I won't find out about it. The Kings, especially Jensen, aren't quiet when they're after something. And if they find out Knox is alive, they'll come after him with guns blazing."

He was right. I wasn't sure I'd be able to calm Ky down enough to listen to reason if I told him. Jensen wouldn't stop to hear me out. He'd do whatever it took to get Knox. Except listen to me. The person who had betrayed his blood and his gang.

"Now," he continued as he kept his eyes on mine, "if you do what I say, I'll leave them all alone. And...I'll let Knox go."

Knox inhaled sharply and looked at me with eyes begging me to agree. I shook my head skeptically before turning back at Mack.

"You wouldn't let him go. The Kings would torture and kill all the Crows if Jenson found out you kept him a prisoner this whole time." I glanced back at the couch. "Knox would kill you if he was ever free."

A snarl grew in Knox's throat at my words, but I was speaking the truth.

"Knox and I have an understanding if I let him go." Mack put his hand up when I opened my mouth. "And no, you're not going to find that out. It doesn't concern what I'm asking you to do."

I begged to differ, but one look at Mack's face told me he wasn't going to share it with me. I was burning with suspicion. He was putting a lot of trust in me to leave this place and keep his secret.

I stayed silent, processing his words.

"All you want is the money?" I finally asked.

Mack nodded. "I want all of it. You give it to me, and Knox is free. And we'll leave the Kings alone."

I wasn't sure I believed that last part. Or any of it. There was still a piece missing, but I couldn't see it. I wasn't sure I could say no either. It wasn't just my life on the line. It was everyone I knew and cared about.

"Fine. When I get the paper—"

"You don't have it yet?"

"No. The one person who could have brought me to my dad's bike was killed. By your people," I seethed out, letting my anger bleed through my words.

"Teddy?"

"Yeah, Teddy. Maybe if your guy hadn't killed him—"

Mack stalked toward me. "Do you have any leads?"

"No."

"You're lying."

"Why would I lie when I just agreed to give it all to you?"

He scrubbed a hand down his face and scowled. The reason for his anger dawned on me, and I laughed cynically, making his eyes shoot to mine.

"All that talk, but you really weren't going to let me go until I gave you that paperwork, were you?"

It was his turn to stay quiet, and I sauntered over to him. "It's okay, you can *trust* me to keep this secret, Mack."

I was antagonizing him but couldn't help myself. Everyone in my life thought they knew more than me. I was fucking sick of it.

"You think it's a joke?" he growled, grabbing the back of my neck, bringing me close to him. I stiffened but didn't push him away. He pulled his phone from his pocket as his fingers dug into my neck, and my eyes darted between him and the phone. After a minute of scrolling, he shoved the phone in my face.

My breath caught as I looked at the live feed of a camera. Of Ky's house. And Zak and Ryker's. Where Cassie was staying. Mack messed with the phone for a few moments before showing me again. My stomach dropped as I watched Kenzi's mom walk into a house.

"We can't find Kenzi. Yet. But we know where her mom is," Mack said as I stared at the phone. "Can you imagine her grief if you're the reason her other parent is killed too?"

"You fucking asshole." I raised my eyes and glared while he slipped his phone back in his pocket.

"You breathe a word of Knox being alive to anyone, and they're all dead," he hissed in my ear before letting go of my neck and shoving me away. "You don't give me the money; they're all dead."

After seeing what he had done to Knox for seven years, I believed him. Defeat sank through me, and I glanced at Knox.

"Fine. I'll give you the money. Once I get it. I won't tell a fucking soul," I said shortly. "But you won't get anything until Knox is free. Can I go now?"

Mack's lips tilted up. "And here I thought you'd want to catch up. Tell him all about your last seven years."

Guilt ripped me apart as Knox looked at me, tilting his head. I gave him a silent apology, knowing Mack was about to spill my own secret. To the person I fucked over even worse than Ky.

"Knox, did you know that the night we raided the factory, Vanessa sent Ky and Zak to prison?" Mack asked causally.

Knox's eyes flew to mine in disbelief.

"Wait—" I tried to say, but Mack kept going.

"The same night we got a tip from a girl on a payphone, telling us about you moving shit from the factory. And that she wanted the Kings ruined. It was the only reason we went that night."

"Is that true?" Knox asked, his voice deathly quiet. The building rage on his face reminded me of the boy I knew all those years ago.

"I'll get the paperwork and get you out of here, Knox. I promise," I choked out hoarsely. "I'm so sorry."

"You're the reason I've been here for seven fucking years?" he roared, leaping from the couch and rushing toward me.

I pressed myself against the wall. I deserved his anger. It was my fault. The chain dragged on the floor and then pulled taunt when Knox was a couple of feet away. He growled in frustration at not being able to reach me.

"Calm down. She's going to do what I want, and then you'll be free." Mack stepped up behind Knox and grabbed his shoulder, yanking him back. "Right, Vanessa?"

I nodded as an idea popped into my head. I wouldn't have to go through all of that if I could get Knox out now. I wouldn't have to lie or keep another damn secret. Or be under someone's thumb like I'd been since being back in this town.

Mack stepped between Knox and me, turning his back to me. It only took a moment to decide my next move. I stayed on my tiptoes to keep the old floor from creaking under me as I moved forward. Knox watched, and his eyes widened before darting to Mack and then back at me. Squaring up, I turned sideways before lifting my right leg and smashing my foot into Mack's back.

He flew forward and landed on his hands with a groan. Leaping onto his back, I wrapped my arm around his neck and squeezed. I just needed to hold my grip long enough for him to pass out. With a roar, he grabbed my arm, then rolled until I was under him. His spine pressed into my stomach, pushing me into the floor while he tried prying my arm off him.

"Knox," I yelled, and that seemed to jolt him out of the daze he was in.

He crouched down and punched Mack in the face. It was a weak hit, and Mack's grip on my arm only tightened. Knox hit him again and then reared back, grabbing his fist as his face scrunched in pain. Mack grunted before ripping my arm from his neck. His grip on my wrist was impossible to get out of, and his body was crushing mine. The front door crashed open, and Danny ran in with his gun in hand. He pointed it at Knox before glancing at Mack and me on the floor.

"Back the fuck up, Knox," Danny ordered, keeping the gun trained on him.

Knox clenched his jaw but sat down on the couch. Mack twisted, staying on top of me, and moved until we were face to face. He slammed my wrist onto the floor before reaching for my other one, and I barely fought back. There was no point. Not with Danny standing above us with a gun.

With my wrists pinned near my head, Mack took a couple of seconds to catch his breath as he glared at me.

"Fuck," he spat out. "Do I need to show you how serious I am?"

Panic clawed in my chest, and I shook my head. "I shouldn't have done that. I didn't think—"

"Danny." Mack cut me off before glancing up and jerking his head toward Knox.

"No, don't," I cried out. "I'll get you the money—"

"You remember Knox being the big bad gangster, don't you, Vanessa?"

Mack's words rang in my ears as Danny grabbed the chain and pulled, sending Knox sliding to the floor. I struggled against Mack's grip while Danny kicked Knox in the stomach a few times before punching him, no doubt giving him another black eye.

"Mack, stop. Please," I screamed in his face, hearing Knox's grunts of pain as Danny wailed on him.

"Knox isn't the guy he used to be. He's weak. Broken." He moved both of my wrists to one hand and grabbed my jaw with the other, turning my head until Knox filled my vision. "Because of you. I'm giving you a chance to fix it. Are you going to do what I want, or fuck it up?"

Emotions clashed as I stared at Knox. He curled up in a ball while Danny threw fists relentlessly all over his body. Mack was right, he wasn't the cruel, heartless person I once knew. Knox was a shell of nothing. All because of me. So much for no more secrets. Looked like I was keeping another one. I couldn't just leave him here to die. Fuck me for having a conscience.

Mack kept his grip on my chin and turned my head until I was looking into his eyes. His ruthless stare bore into me, and I hardened my gaze without meaning to. Why was I the one everyone looked at as weak? Someone who did their bidding, bending my will, and waiting for me to break. I refused to fucking break. I'd survived too long for that.

He brought his head down until his lips grazed my cheek. "And if Knox's death isn't enough to convince you, let me up the stakes."

"I already said I'd do it," I hissed, failing to pull my face from his mouth.

"I know you will. Because if you don't, I'll replace Knox with the other Banes brother. And what I've done to Knox will look like child's play compared to what Ky will endure."

Dread crawled down my limbs while his breath hit my cheek as he chuckled. I flinched hearing Knox cry out from another hit. Not that I could see him. Mack was holding my jaw hard enough to leave marks.

"The Kings own half this city," Mack said in a low voice. "But Jensen is obsessed with finding Knox's killer. And Ky...he's obsessed with you. Ever since you came back to town, it's been easy to do things they never would've let slide if you weren't distracting them. Like surveillance on Ky's house. They're off their game, and I have you to thank for that."

"I won't say anything," I pushed out through clenched teeth.

He lifted his head to look at me. "Call the MCs off us too. I don't want them fucking with us or our business."

"Fine."

"When you find out where the papers are, you better come find me before you get them."

"Got it." I was done fighting. Here I was being used as a pawn, *again,* and there was nothing I could fucking do.

"We'll drive you back to Suncrest—"

"I'm staying with the MC," I interrupted sharply. "In Brown City."

"Not anymore. You're going back to the Kings." He moved and pulled me off the floor. "Call the MC president and tell him whatever the fuck you need to, so he'll back off. That you love Ky so much, you can't be away from him. I don't care what you say as long as it works."

I swallowed my words; they wouldn't do anything to change his mind. Knowing Knox was alive and a prisoner, because of me, was bad enough. Having to face Ky and not tell him the truth was going to be torture.

"Why?" I asked, as he tugged me toward the front door. "Why don't you just keep me with you?"

"Because if the MCs and Ky knew I had you, they'd both come after the Crows."

I glanced back before I walked out the door. Danny was sitting on the edge of the couch while Knox stayed curled up on the floor. I opened my mouth to tell him I would get him out of there, but Mack yanked me onto the porch and shut the door.

"And what's stopping the MCs from coming to get me if I'm with the Kings?" I asked. "They made it pretty clear they would protect me until..."

I purposely trailed my words off and kept walking back to the SUV, until Mack's grip tightened and he pulled me back to him. This was my one last shot of keeping him from taking me back to the Kings.

"Until what?" he asked with a frown.

"Didn't you hear? The Aces aren't gone like everyone thought," I revealed, watching his eyes widen.

"You're lying." A trace of fear entered his gaze.

I shrugged. "Fine, don't believe me. You'll find out soon enough when they come back to the city."

He stared at me for a few moments before opening the car door and pushing me in. "The MCs won't chance coming back into the city again. Not after tonight. And I know once Ky has you, he's not going to let you out of his sight. Which for now, is what I want."

"You should really make up your mind." I shook my head. "You took me from the Kings, and now you're forcing me to go back to them. I'm getting fucking whiplash."

"You bringing the Dusty Devils into it changed everything. The Kings want to find the paperwork as much as I do. The MCs don't. They'll try to keep you out of it."

"I'll find it myself—"

"No." He picked up the red bandana off the seat and looked at me. "You'll stay with Ky. Find where the damn paperwork is. Soon."

"And how am I supposed to get ahold of you when I find out? Should we swap numbers?"

He scowled at my sarcasm before answering. "You already know we're watching Ky's house. Just go out front and give a signal. We'll see it and come get you."

"What signal?" I asked through clenched teeth, hating the fact I was doing this.

He pondered that for a moment. "Just stretch your arms or something. Make it obvious enough for us to know."

"How do you expect me to get away from the Kings?"

"Don't worry about that, I'll come get you."

"You said you wouldn't hurt anyone—"

"And I won't," he interrupted. "As long as you behave and do what you're told."

"Fuck you," I muttered under my breath, unable to stay quiet.

He ignored me. "If the Aces really are coming back, then you better hurry the fuck up and find it before they do.

Or you can say goodbye to everyone you love. I don't make empty threats."

"I'll find it." I turned away from him, leaning back against the seat.

"You better hold up your end," he warned. "We'll be watching, Vanessa."

CHAPTER TWENTY-SEVEN

Kyro

Steam filled the bathroom as I stepped out of the shower, wrapping a towel around my waist. I leaned my hands on the counter and stared into the fogged mirror. Tonight was a shitshow. Those motorcycles weren't quiet when they left, there was no hiding it from the Kings now. After they left, I drove around for hours. The chance of finding Vanessa was small, but I couldn't stop myself. I even went all the way to Brown City and cruised around trying to find the Dusty Devils' clubhouse.

Probably a good thing I didn't find it, because I wasn't thinking straight.

With a sigh, I walked into my room and slid on some shorts before heading into the living room. I needed a fucking drink. I stopped in my tracks seeing Jensen sitting on the couch. His piercing gaze slid to me as my muscles stiffened. Zak and Ryker were already in the living room, both with drinks in their hands. Cassie must still be in the bedroom because she was nowhere to be seen. Zak stood near the bar while Ryker sat on the opposite end of the couch from my father.

"Dad," I greeted him, going to the bar and pouring a glass of whiskey. I turned and faced him while standing next to Zak.

"A shower was more important than picking up your phone and calling to tell me that MCs rode into our fucking city?" His voice was soft but full of venom. "It's been hours since my guys saw the bikers riding out of our city."

"I was going to come see you," I replied. "I figured this wasn't the kind of conversation to have over the phone."

"Was Vanessa with them?"

"Yes."

"Where is she now?" He stood from the couch and looked around. "You let her go back with them?"

"*Let* isn't exactly the word I'd use," Zak mumbled under his breath.

"Does she know about her dad?" Jensen asked.

I nodded. "I told you she'd find out. The MCs are backing her. All the ones who were tied to her dad's MC. And they're pissed. About keeping Vanessa. And Teddy—"

"That wasn't us. It was the Crows," he cut in with his voice rising.

"You think they care?" Zak spoke up. "They want to take back everything we built after the Aces disappeared."

"Not happening," Jensen spat out as his eyes flashed in rage. "Did she find the bank papers?"

"We don't think so." Ryker stood from the couch, moving next to me as he poured another drink.

Jensen stayed silent, and I downed my whiskey. The burn settling in my chest helped bear the tension coating the room. Finally, he cleared his throat, and my eyes narrowed at the look on his face.

"She's too much of a fucking risk." He kept his voice calm as heated fury seized me. "I knew it years ago, and I was right when she sent you to prison."

It took fucking everything in me to stay quiet. I didn't move a muscle because if I did, I wouldn't be able to stop myself. He might be in here alone, but he always had men with him. I hurt him; he'd kill Zak and Ryker. After taking several deep breaths, I relaxed my fists and met my dad's gaze. Then I said the only thing that would stop him from going after Vanessa.

"The Aces aren't gone."

His eyebrows shot up in surprise before he schooled his expression. "You'll say anything to save that fucking girl."

"It's true," Ryker interjected from beside me. "The MC president told us the Aces were coming back."

"Angel's Aces disbanded after Stone was killed," Jensen muttered as if he were convincing himself. "They disappeared seven years ago. No one's heard from them since."

"There had to be a part of you that thought they'd come back." I paused to take another drink. "Why else would you still be cautious of Bill and Teddy?"

"They still had protection from the other MCs," Jenson snapped.

"You try to hurt Vanessa; they won't stop until the Kings are done." I kept my voice quiet, but my rage wasn't hidden, and Jensen tensed as I spoke.

"All right," he finally said after a minute of silence. "I won't hurt her. We'll welcome her into the family. Just like the Crows wanted to do."

"What?" I asked as Zak and Ryker both straightened up.

"Seeing as you already have a *lovely* fiancée." He looked from me to Zak. "She has to marry someone else."

"You're fucking insane," I snarled, shooting forward.

Ryker grabbed my arm and pulled me back as Jensen smirked. I shook Ryker off and walked behind the bar, trying to put anything in between myself and my father.

"I was going to let you choose one of your two friends," Jensen said with a shake of his head. "But I can't trust any of you enough for that right now."

"You're not going to touch her—"

He cut me off. "Seven days. You find the paperwork and get me her money in one week. Or I'll marry her and make sure I get that money."

Rage. Pure, unfiltered rage was all I fucking felt when I shoved the bar away from me. The clatter of bottles rang in my ears as I flew toward him. My fist connected with his jaw, and he went to the floor. I gripped his collar, pulled him to his knees, and hit him in the face again. A car horn blared from outside, but I didn't stop. I threw a third punch before getting pulled away.

"Ky, calm the fuck down," Zak hissed. "His men are outside."

"He won't touch her." I let Zak drag me to the couch while my dad stood back up, holding his face. Ryker stepped in between us, keeping an eye on Jensen.

"I failed you, son," Jensen said before grabbing one of the fallen bottles and twisting open the cap. "I tried teaching you that women destroy you. For you, it's only one. I don't understand it. Why the hell is she so important? Why can't you just forget about her?"

I didn't answer while I sat on the couch, running my fingers over my knuckles.

"I'm your father," Jensen roared, throwing the bottle at the wall. "Your fucking blood. The only blood you have left. And you choose her over me?"

"You threaten my best friends' lives to make sure I follow your rules," I forced out through clenched teeth. "You're not a fucking father."

"Because of her," he screamed, raising his arms. "All of it. If you could just see past her, I never would have had to do any of that."

I leaped from the couch. "There is no seeing past her. There's only her."

It was the first time I admitted to him how I truly felt about her. But there wasn't a trace of surprise on his face. There was only anger. He wanted a relationship with me like he had with Knox. It would never happen.

"Seven days, Kyro. I don't have those papers in my hands, I'll have her instead. You want to try to kill me? Go ahead. I'll make good on every fucking threat," he promised as his gaze hardened.

The door flew open before I could reply, and Greg walked in, looking pleased.

"Look who we found," he announced, peering through the open doorway.

Two Kings walked in, and I sucked in a breath. In between them was Vanessa. She looked pissed and was struggling as they held her. Zak moved in front of me before I took a step near her.

"Stay calm," Zak muttered, looking back at Jensen.

"Get off me," Vanessa snarled, pulling against their grip.

I glanced at Jensen, and he nodded at his guys. They released her, and she shot forward, away from them. My heart was racing, and ice slid through my veins. I'd been looking for her all night. But I didn't want her anywhere near my dad. Especially now.

I locked eyes with her, and her gaze was guarded. It was obvious she didn't want to be here.

"Vanessa." Jensen looked beyond pleased she was here. "Already tired of your new friends?"

She glanced behind me to look at him, and a wave of emotions swept through her face. Surprise came first before guilt darkened her eyes. As quick as it came, it was gone, and she stared coldly at Jensen.

"She was practically pushed out of a car." Greg closed the front door. "Didn't seem like she wanted to get out. Looked like it was the Crows."

My jaw clenched, wondering how the hell the Crows had found her. I let my gaze drift down her body, and I took another step forward when I realized her cheeks had red marks on them.

Fucking Mack.

"The Crows?" Jensen watched Vanessa thoughtfully as she stayed in the middle of the room. She was rigid, and even though she wasn't moving, I could tell she was trying to find a way out of here.

"Yes," she forced out stiffly.

"They brought you here?" I asked in surprise.

She looked at me. "Yes."

"Why?" Jensen asked before I could.

She hesitated while glancing back at Jensen.

"Might as well just say it," he said, sitting back down on the couch. "I'm not leaving until you explain."

"The Crows don't want me with the MCs," she said slowly, as if choosing her words carefully.

"And the reason they brought you here?" Jensen pressed, losing his patience.

Again, she looked at me. "Because Mack knew the Kings and MCs would come after them if they had me."

Not the Kings. *Me.* I guess Mack wasn't completely stupid. It only took me a day to find her the last time they had her. If I had to do it again, I wouldn't leave until Mack was fucking dead. He knew that. He must also have realized the MCs and Kings would have made temporary peace to get her back.

"Smart," Jensen muttered, before standing up. "The Crows know the MCs won't come back into the city right now. The tension is too high."

"What do they want?" I asked, knowing there had to be a motive behind them doing this.

"Nothing," she answered quickly.

I raised my eyebrow. She thought out everything before she spoke. Her lies were usually as smooth as her truths. Not this time. Something had her shaken up. Jensen stayed silent as he stared at her, showing even he knew she wasn't telling the truth. He narrowed his eyes and stalked toward her. I bolted forward, planting myself in front of her before he got close.

"Kyro," he bit out. "Move."

"No."

Ryker and Zak were next to me in seconds. Betrayal passed over Jensen's face before he shook his head. His eye was starting to swell from where I'd hit him, and the corner of his mouth still had blood on it. I wished I could have done worse. I couldn't decide who I hated more. My own father or Mack.

"I only want to hear what she has to say." Jensen looked past me, to his men. "If we can't have a civil conversation... I'll take her back with me."

Vanessa pushed past me and Zak until she was standing in front of us. I grabbed her arm, but she whipped around and shoved me back.

"I'm fine, Ky."

I gritted my teeth and moved right behind her. She had

her mind set on something, and there was no stopping her. Sometimes I forgot she wasn't the same girl I grew up with. She used to follow. Follow Zak and me when we did King business. She'd listen to what my dad said. She followed her parents' rules. Most of them anyway. She wanted to please everyone.

I saw the change happening when she was sixteen. She had still done what others asked but was fighting it. She loved what she did with the Kings, but it wasn't enough. She wanted more. The night she sent me to prison was when she found herself.

She had gotten a peek at the dark secrets in our world, and it shattered her ability to trust. Instead of doing what others wanted, she protected herself. And didn't look back. She would never follow again. But she would trust again. Like I was right now, I'd always be behind her, waiting until she needed me.

"I know you aren't going to let me go." Her words pulled me from my thoughts. "And I'll stay, willingly. But not with you. I want to stay with Ky."

Jensen pressed his lips together, and his face turned a shade darker. People didn't talk to him like that. He was the boss. Apparently, Vanessa didn't give a shit anymore.

"You think you have a choice?" he asked after a few moments.

"The Crows are trying to save their asses." Vanessa shrugged. "Mack knows they fucked up when his guy killed Teddy. They didn't want to risk the MCs coming after them if they had me. But they wanted me to stay in Suncrest. So here I am."

"You'll stay with—"

"I stay with Ky, and I'll call the MCs right now and tell them I'm deciding to stay in Suncrest," Vanessa interrupted.

Jensen flexed his fists as his eyes went murderous. I moved forward even more until my chest brushed Vanessa's back. He wasn't going to touch her. I didn't know what she was trying to accomplish other than to piss him off.

"Fucking women," Jensen muttered before forcing out a laugh. "You think you can hide behind my son and get away with whatever the hell you want?"

"Does it look like I'm hiding?" she shot back with anger filling her voice.

"Maybe I need to use the same threat with you as I do with my son," Jensen said quietly.

CHAPTER TWENTY-EIGHT

Kyro

Vanessa stiffened against me at Jensen's words. I narrowed my eyes at him and clenched my jaw to keep from saying anything, knowing it would only make it worse.

"You may not be in love with Zak, but you love him like family, don't you Vanessa?" Jensen asked before nodding to his men behind me.

"Get the fuck off me," Zak snarled.

I looked over my shoulder to see two men grabbing Zak's arms and dragging him forward. They pushed him until he was in the middle of the room, between Vanessa and Jensen. Every cell in my body screamed to move, but I stayed still. If I tried to intervene, it would only be worse for Zak.

Vanessa froze as she watched Zak try to rip away from their grip. Greg stepped in front of Zak and threw a punch to his cheek. She tried bolting forward, but I wrapped my arm around her waist and pulled her back until she slammed into my chest.

"Don't," I said in her ear as she struggled against me. "It's not you or me that's going to get hurt. It'll be him.'"

"Shit," she whispered. Worry saturated her voice and she stopped moving.

"Two more hits, Greg," Jensen ordered while he stared at me as if waiting for me to argue.

Anger caused my muscles to tense while guilt weighed me down. This was because I'd attacked him. He would never take it out on me. No. He saved that for my best friends. Greg swung again, and Zak's head snapped to the side from the blow. Vanessa flinched in my arms but made no attempt to move. Ryker was beside me and stayed silent as he watched Zak.

The men pushed down on Zak's shoulders until he was on his knees. Zak didn't make a sound when Greg hit him a third time. His nose started trickling blood, and he wiped it away with his hand. He was almost shaking from rage but kept quiet while Greg backed away.

"Let's try this again, Vanessa," Jensen said as one of his men pulled out a gun and placed the barrel of it on the back of Zak's head. "I'm fucking sick of your mouth. You have no power here. You'll do what I say, or you can say goodbye to your friend."

"Fuck this night," Vanessa muttered under her breath before speaking loud enough for everyone else to hear. "Then what, Jensen?"

I stared at the back of her head, wishing I could see her face. *What the hell was she playing at?* Jensen's eyes widened slightly before he took a step forward.

"Excuse me?" he asked, his gaze not leaving Vanessa.

"You kill Zak, then what?" she asked, her voice strong. Whatever was bothering her earlier had disappeared.

Jensen opened his mouth and then closed it again,

trying to search for words. His eyes were steeped with murder, and fear for my best friend intensified.

"You kill him, then what will you have to hold over your son's head?" Vanessa asked.

"You really want to test that?" Jensen snarled, losing control.

"Then I guess you'd go after Ryker next." Vanessa kept talking as she ripped away from my grip. I let her go and stayed where I was. For once, I had no idea what the fuck she was trying to do.

"Vee." Zak twisted his neck just enough to look at her. The gun stayed on the back of his head, and he looked at her questioningly.

She ignored him and didn't look away from Jensen. "After you kill Zak and Ryker, then what? You'd have no more leverage to control Ky. Then what's stopping him from going after you?"

Jensen stared at her before shaking his head. "Fucking ruthless. You only care about yourself. You could live with yourself if you're the reason they're killed? That's the difference between you and my son. He's proven he'd do anything for the people he loves."

"Fuck you," she hissed. "You have no idea what I'd do for the people I care about."

"You'd let them die?" he asked raising an eyebrow.

"Would you?" She crossed her arms. "Because if they die, so do you. Ky would come after you with everything he fucking has if you kill them. You might consider blood to be above everything else. But to Ky...Zak and Ryker are family."

Jensen's gaze cut to mine, and I lifted my chin, silently showing him Vanessa was right. Tides were shifting, and I didn't know what the fuck was going to happen after tonight. But now, Jensen knew where I stood. And it wasn't beside him.

"There's still one person Kyro cares about," Jensen said quietly, looking back at Vanessa. "And he's already proven he'd do anything to keep you safe. Including betraying his own blood."

"But that's the thing." I could hear her grin in her words. "You can't kill me."

Jensen pulled his gun out and aimed it at Vanessa. "What's stopping me? The money? Honestly, I don't think it's worth dealing with you anymore. And you still owe a debt for getting my other son killed."

He was lying. He needed that fucking money. But I still shot forward, trying to get in between the gun and Vanessa. She moved faster and crossed the room until she was standing right in front of Jensen. He faltered for a split second, but kept the gun aimed at her.

"Do it," she demanded, leaning forward until the gun hit her chest. "Fucking do it and see what happens. Because it won't just be Ky who comes after you."

"You think I'm scared of the MCs?"

"You couldn't kill me years ago because you were scared of one MC. And now they're back. Tell me, what do you think Angel's Aces will do to you if they find out you killed me?"

I almost didn't recognize the look that crossed Jensen's face. *Fear*. I'd never seen it before. He never showed weakness. He got over his surprise after a moment, and his anger returned. Silence saturated the room as they stared at each other.

"They're gone," he finally said, though he didn't look convinced.

"You wanted to know why Mack brought me here?" she

asked. "Because he knows they're coming back. And whoever the fuck is keeping me prisoner when they get back to town is going to regret it."

Her threat pierced the air, and my heart thundered as I stared at Jensen. His grip on the gun was so tight, his knuckles were white. He slowly lowered it to his side as he kept his gaze on Vanessa. I didn't need to see her face to know she was grinning. Confidence emitted from every pore in her body.

"The second I find out you're lying about the Aces, you're done."

His words didn't faze her as she leaned toward him. "Your threats don't mean shit to me anymore. But here's one of my own. If you kill Zak or Ryker. If you hurt me. If you hurt Ky. I will fucking kill you. I have the MCs backing me. And the Aces. You and the Kings will be done if I say the word."

Holy shit.

No one threatened Jensen Banes and lived to talk about it. And she hadn't just threatened him. She'd done it in front of his men. Pride mixed with fear as I waited for Jensen's reaction. He stood there, his body rigid, while hate spewed from his eyes. Greg looked unsure as he stood in front of Zak.

"You think your new Italian friends have more power than all the MCs?" Vanessa asked, obviously not finished. "Or will they even think you're worth it once they realize how many enemies you have?"

"You have no idea what the fuck you're starting." Jensen stepped closer to her.

She held her ground. "I didn't start any of this. But I'm ready to finish it."

Jensen looked at her in disbelief. "Damn. It's too bad

you were born into the wrong family. You really were made for this life."

His words made me step forward, and he glanced at me in warning. Hot rage rippled through me as I stilled. He wasn't about to let her get away with threatening him.

"I won't kill you," Jensen murmured. "Don't want the MCs trying anything right now. But you'll stay with me to make sure they stay away."

Jensen nodded to one of the men who was standing near Zak. He moved behind Vanessa and grabbed her arms. She cried out in surprise and tried jerking away, but Jensen gripped her hair, holding her still. A snarl ripped from my throat, and I lunged forward, only to stop when Greg swung his gun toward me. Then he pointed it at Ryker while the other King kept his gun on Zak.

"I won't shoot to kill," Greg said. "But I'll make sure he's in a wheelchair the rest of his life if you take another fucking step."

I forced myself to stay where I was. Glancing away from Greg, I focused back on Vanessa.

"It seems we're at an impasse." She chuckled.

My mouth dropped open. She was playing with the devil, and I had no idea what was making her think she'd win.

"An impasse?" Jensen let out a short laugh and pulled her closer. "You think you have power here? You've been pulled like a puppet your entire life. Used. The only reason you're important is because of the money you're tied to."

"Money controls this world. If it's money that makes me important, I'll take that any fucking day. Because men like you will do anything for it. And you're in luck. I'm willing to share the money with you. As long as I get to stay with Ky, we'll find it and I'll give you half."

"You're trying to make a deal with me?" he asked as his face grew red in anger.

"Yes. Let me stay here, and once I find it, we'll split it," she said calmly. "And I'll make sure the Aces and MCs leave you alone."

He kept silent while considering her words. After glancing at Greg, he let go of her hair and backed up a step.

"Fine," he said slowly. "You have seven days."

I took a deep breath. He was going to keep to his word about taking her. It wasn't fucking happening. Greg lowered his gun, and the King backed away from Zak. Jensen made his way to the door and looked back at me.

"One week, Kyro. And if you need anything, my men will be outside." His open warning of being watched wasn't missed by any of us. "I hope you enjoy the choice you made. Choosing a girl over me. And your gang. She's going to get you killed."

I didn't answer as they all left and shut the door behind them. I might still be a King, but Jensen didn't trust me at all anymore. I'd be cut out of everything. I wasn't upset about that. But now I wouldn't know anything about what the Kings were planning.

"I need a phone so I can call Don and tell him I'm staying here." She turned to face me. She was composed, as if what just happened didn't faze her. But her left hand was closed in a fist, and her chest was heaving as she controlled her breathing.

"What the fuck was that, Vee?" Zak snapped, getting in her face. "You almost got us all killed."

"Jensen wouldn't have killed any of us." She defended herself and pushed him back. "He needs you to keep Ky in line. He never would have done it."

"You don't know that," Ryker spoke up as he went to grab a bottle of whiskey.

"I was right," she yelled. "He backed down. He needs us all for different reasons. I called his fucking bluff and he backed down."

"This isn't a game of poker," Zak exploded, backing her up until the back of her legs hit the couch. I watched, letting Zak say the things we were all thinking. He was right. She was lucky one of them wasn't killed tonight.

"No, it's a game of life." Her gaze cut to me. "Right, Ky? Life's a game. And I'm tired of being the one everyone threatens. I won tonight."

"What did the Crows threaten you with?" I stepped up beside her and Zak.

Pain flashed through her eyes before her face went blank, and she shrugged. "I already told you. They didn't want the MCs or you coming after them."

"Bullshit. Jensen's not here anymore. Tell the truth."

"That is the truth."

"Did you promise them the money when you find it?" I asked, refusing to back down.

She didn't answer, and I grabbed her arm and pulled her in front of me. She didn't fight back or even look at me.

"Did they threaten to kill me?" I pried, trying to get her to respond. "Kenzi? Cassie? What deal did you make for them to let you go?"

She snorted, finally looking at me. "Let me go? You think I wanted to come back? They shoved me from the car, forcing me back here. I was trying to go back to Brown City."

I let go of her arm. "Fine, don't tell me. I'll find out at some point. You should know by now secrets don't stay covered for long in this town."

"You kept secrets from me for years," she argued back while sitting on the couch. "Can I see your phone or not? If I don't call Don soon, he's going to come looking for me."

Sighing, I walked to the desk and grabbed a phone that couldn't be traced. I tossed it to her, and she caught it while jumping from the couch. I followed her to the kitchen, but she turned and shoved me away with a frown. She nearly jogged down the hall and tried slamming my bedroom door while putting the phone to her ear.

My palm slapped the door before it clicked shut, and I pushed it back open.

"Go away," she demanded.

"Make me."

I crowded her space, and she scowled while attempting to back away. I followed until she hit the bed.

"Is there a reason you don't want me listening?" I asked in a low voice.

"Hey, Don," she spoke into the phone while glowering at me. "No, I'm fine. Listen, I changed plans. I think it will work better if I stay in Suncrest for a while."

Don's voice got loud enough for me to hear as he protested. She took a deep breath and tried to turn away, but I had her pinned between me and the bed.

"No, this isn't because of Ky," she nearly whispered, as if I wouldn't be able to hear her. "I know I couldn't hurt him. But he's not the reason I'm doing this."

I tilted my head to the side, curious to hear what she'd tell him. I doubted she'd spill the real reason. The Crows were holding something over her head, and I'd find out eventually.

"Ky's a part of my history. Not my future." She met my eyes. "I'm not doing this to be with him. I'm doing it to find the paperwork."

"Liar," I murmured, not letting her words get to me. They weren't the truth.

"No, I'm not with him," she said loudly, trying again to move.

I chuckled, grabbed her thighs, and lifted until her back hit the mattress. She let out gasp as she landed, and I straddled her hips before she could get up. Her eyes frosted over in a silent warning, which I ignored. My finger slid over her jeans, and I undid the button. She grabbed my wrist with one hand while holding the phone with the other.

"Am I your dirty secret, Raindrop?" I asked quietly enough to keep Don from hearing.

She ignored me and tried to push my arm away from her. "No, don't come here. I'm fine. The Kings and Crows won't hurt me. They still want the money."

I moved off her and started sliding her jeans down, and she sat up to shove me back. Grabbing her wrist, I pulled her close and ripped the phone from her ear. Her mouth snapped shut to keep from protesting out loud and she reached for the phone. Putting the call on speaker, I muted it so Don couldn't hear me.

"Why don't you want him to know you're with me?" I asked as Don rambled on in the background about coming back to Suncrest.

Her eyes darted from the phone to me. "Because he's going to think I'm choosing you over him and my dad's MC. He'll think I'm some lovestruck girl who chooses a guy. A guy who betrayed me over and over."

"I didn't betray you," I growled. "I did everything to keep you safe."

"He doesn't see it that way." She reached for the phone again and I lifted it higher, keeping it out of her reach.

"Vanessa?" Don asked. "Hello?"

"Give me the phone," she snapped.

"If you don't want him to know, better be quiet," I warned with a grin, unmuting the call.

She glared at me as she spoke. "Sorry, bad connection. I'm fine. Really. I'll keep in contact with you and let you know what I find out about the paperwork."

I set the phone down and grabbed her jeans, sliding them down to her ankles. She silently tried pulling away, but I pushed her until her back hit the mattress again.

"Don't do this Vanessa," Don implored. "Come back to Brown City."

My fingers slid inside her panties, causing her to still. With my eyes staying on hers, my fingers slowly started moving in slow circles around her clit. Her attempts to get the phone halted and she threw a hand over her mouth.

"No," she finally forced out through her fingers. "I need to find the paperwork. I have to go. I'll call back later."

"I didn't bring my guys to Suncrest just for you to back out," Don grated out, sounding pissed. "Where are you staying? I want to come talk to you."

I slid a finger inside her while my thumb went over her clit. She barley suppressed a moan when I started moving again. With my free hand, I muted the call.

"Tell me," I demanded. "You really think I'm only a part of your history?"

"Screw you."

I laughed, moving my fingers faster, and her back arched off the bed. "Why not just tell Don the truth? I'm helping you find the money."

"No," she bit out, trying to stay in control.

"So stubborn," I murmured, reaching for the phone. "You think you can stay quiet? Let's see."

I unmuted the call again before pulling her panties

down and replacing my hand with my mouth. She sucked in a breath as I slid my tongue over her pussy. I trapped her thighs in my grip and pulled her closer to the edge of the bed. *Fuck.* She tasted like the sweetest dessert. Something I would never tire of.

"Where are you?" Don repeated. "I don't like this. Someone is forcing you to do this. Or you're choosing a fucking King over your own family."

"I'm fine," she answered, her voice higher than normal. "I'm not choosing Ky over anyone. I haven't been his for years. It's not changing now."

I nipped at her clit and her thighs tightened around my head.

"I'm coming to get you—"

"No," she said quickly. "You can't come into Suncrest now. Both gangs are on edge because of what happened tonight. They all know what went down on the beach."

"Vanessa—"

"Fuck," she cried out. I grinned and doubled my efforts as her legs started to tremble. "Trust me. I'm a big girl, and I've been able to take care of myself for years. I can handle myself—"

"You're the one who came for my help," he cut in sharply.

"Yeah, your help." Anger and lust mixed together as she spoke. "I didn't come to you to be ordered around. This is my life. I can choose what I want. I have to go. I'll call back later."

Impatiently, I let go of one of her legs and blindly felt around until my hand closed over the phone. Ending the call, I tossed it to the floor before wrapping my arm back around her thigh. I twirled my tongue around her clit until her body started to tense.

"Oh my god," she nearly screamed as her orgasm crashed over the edge.

I didn't stop until her body relaxed on the bed. Her breaths came out ragged as she lay there. I lifted my head to see her leaning back on her elbows, already watching me. Her face was flushed, and she dropped her legs from my shoulders.

"Welcome back, Raindrop." I grinned before licking my lips, still tasting her. "Mmm, I could spend all fucking night showing you just how much I missed you."

"How can you be in such a good mood after the shit that just went down with Jensen?" She scooted higher up on the bed.

I grabbed her legs before she could move out of my reach. "There's always shit happening. I can't fix any of that right now. But I can enjoy the night in my favorite spot."

Her head tilted to the side as she raised an eyebrow.

"Right here," I murmured, putting my head back between her thighs.

"Ky—"

"With your legs squeezing the life out of me." I paused, slowly dragging my tongue up her thigh, feeling her goosebumps rise.

She moaned, spreading her legs wider, giving me a perfect view.

"We shouldn't be doing this," she murmured without moving. "We need to find Kenzi. I'm guessing when Jensen said seven days, it didn't mean anything good."

"We can do that tomorrow. Tonight, we're celebrating."

"Celebrating what?"

"You came back."

I realized that was the wrong fucking thing to say when her legs tensed around me.

"Ky," she breathed out with regret filling her eyes. "Nothing changed. I didn't come back for you. I didn't have a fucking choice."

My anger simmered silently as she rolled off the bed. Standing up, I watched while she slid one of my hoodies on and it fell almost to her knees.

"I'm not talking about you coming to the house." I forced myself to stay calm. "I'm talking about the beach."

Her eyes flashed in defiance, meeting my gaze. "I wanted the Kings and the Crows to know I was with the MCs."

"And you did it where you knew you'd be safe." I let out a humorless chuckle. "In my backyard. Because you *trust* me."

"Yes, Ky," she snapped. "I trust you. But we can't—"

"Can't what?" I strode across the room, backing her into the wall. "Can't be happy? Can't take one day at a time and enjoy each other? I know why you're pushing me away. You don't want to see Zak and Ryker get hurt. Believe me, either do I. I live with that shit daily. I do something that pisses Jensen off, they pay the fucking price."

She stayed silent, lifting her chin to look at me. I rested my forearm on the wall next to her head, leaning close.

"There's no more secrets. It's done." I shook my head. "You have no idea how it feels not to have to keep things from you."

"Yup. No idea," she muttered, her voice laced with sarcasm.

"Knox being killed wasn't your fault," I said gently as her eyes fill with guilt.

"We're not talking about this," she warned.

She tried pushing off the wall, and I lifted my other arm, pressing it against the wall near her head, caging her in.

Huffing out a breath, she stared over my shoulder, refusing to look at me.

"Let me in," I murmured softly. "Give me your burdens. Share your pain. Steal my strength. Drown your sorrows. Use me in whatever way you need to."

She still stared past me without saying a word. Pressing my body to hers, I could feel her heart beating out of her chest. Her body might not be showing it, but my words were causing a reaction.

"Let me in, Raindrop," I repeated. "Or I'm going to fucking destroy the wall you've built to keep me out."

Her eyes snapped to mine, and I rested my forehead on hers.

"I don't care how long it takes. Or what I have to do. You're going to let me in again. Because this bullshit charade of pushing me away has nothing to do with how you feel about me."

She suddenly turned her head away from me, and I caught her wrist when she tried bringing her hand to her face. With my free hand, I gripped her chin, forcing her to turn back toward me. My heart stuttered at what I saw.

This girl.

She was so damn strong. Even as kids, she'd never let anything get her down. The times I had seen her cry were few and far between.

And that meant the lone tear trailing down her cheek spoke more than any of her words could have.

CHAPTER TWENTY-NINE

Vanessa

I WAS FINE. FAN-FUCKING-TASTIC.

I had promised Mack the money when I found it. I'd also promised Jensen the money. Kenzi was still in the wind, and I didn't have a clue how I'd find that money.

I had to play nice so I didn't piss Jensen off enough to take it out on Zak and Ryker. We had to hide Cassie every time Jensen showed up at the house the last two days, so he didn't know she was there.

And let's not forget the whole threat Mack used about killing everyone I cared about if I spilled his secret. Every time I stared out the front window, I wondered where the Crows were hiding.

Then there was Knox. The man who'd been captive for seven years. Because of me. The brother of the person I loved most in this world. But Knox was also a man who used to torture people for fun. I gave it an eighty-twenty chance he would try to kill me if he got free because of what I did to him. Even with how broken he looked at the cabin, he still had rage in him. And if he got free, he'd want to let it out on someone.

Sitting at the table, I let out a groan and buried my head in my arms.

I was so fucked.

"Vee, just tell him so he'll stop asking," Zak begged, pulling me back to the current conversation going around the breakfast table. "It's been two days of you guys arguing back and forth."

"For once, I agree with Zak." Cassie chewed on a bite of toast as she shrugged.

"I already told him." Rubbing my temples, I glared at Ky. "Mack brought me back here because he knew Ky and the MCs would go after the Crows if they had me."

"And I know you're lying," Ky shot back. "There has to be more to it. Mack wouldn't drop you off on my doorstep because of something that could happen."

"I think we should finally call Kenzi and see if she can help." Ryker continued to flip the bacon on the stove as if what he'd just said was public knowledge.

Ky's jaw ticked and Zak's mouth dropped open as I bolted from my chair. Ryker froze as the bacon grease jumped from the pan. His gaze slid from me to Ky, and his eyes widened when he realized he'd just let something slip.

"Do not fucking tell me that you found Kenzi and decided not to let me know." My rage focused solely on Ky because it would have been his call to make.

Zak let out a nervous laugh. "We were going to tell you—"

"When?" I snapped. "I've been here nearly two days."

"There was no point." Ky stood up, stepping closer to me. "Jensen has men outside day and night. If we call Kenzi and she tells us where the money is, you'd want to go right away. Without a plan. Without a second thought. You wouldn't wait to come up with the best way to go."

"You don't know if that's what I would have done—"

Ky cut me off. "What did you do when you found out we needed to go to the storage locker? You didn't think. You only acted."

"This isn't your call to make," I hissed. "It's my money. My friend. You should have told me."

"I was waiting until we could get out from under Jensen first." His eyes clouded over as he began to get annoyed. "You want to lead him straight to the money? Because that's what will happen unless we have a plan."

He had a point. Only it didn't matter. Jensen wasn't getting the money. I was choosing Mack. He was the bigger threat at the moment. He had eyes on everyone in this house. And Kenzi's mom. I couldn't chance it.

I glanced at Ryker, who was focusing on not burning the food. "How'd you find her?"

"Ryker found out that Allie, Kenzi's girlfriend, was still taking college classes online. He hacked into the school website and got an email," Zak explained.

Cassie continued to eat as she watched our conversation unfold. My stomach twisted, and I didn't know if it was terror or excitement. It was a step closer to getting the paperwork I wanted. And the money everyone else wanted.

"How long ago did you find her?" I asked.

"Not long," Zak answered quickly. "Two nights ago. Ryker literally found her a couple hours before you brought an entire biker gang to our beach to threaten us."

I scowled. "It wasn't to threaten you—"

"We know, Vee. It was for the Kings. For Jensen." He

shot me a grin to show he was joking with his next words. "But their guns were pointed on us that night, not Jensen."

"Email Allie," I demanded, getting back on topic. "Tell her it's me and I want to talk to Kenzi."

Ryker glanced at Ky, who hesitated for a moment before nodding. Ryker pulled out his phone and began typing as I sat back down.

Now we just had to wait.

"She sent us a Zoom link," Ryker announced, with his phone in his hand as he came into the living room.

I raised an eyebrow. "Zoom?"

"She probably still isn't using a phone." Ky took the phone from Ryker. "Ready to call her?"

"Can I at least hold the phone?" I reached my hand out impatiently. "If we're video chatting, I want to see my friend. It's not like you won't be able to hear everything we say anyway."

"Fine."

I blinked in surprise when he dropped the phone in my hand. Usually, it was more of a fight. The call stopped ringing and I glanced down at the screen, a smile tipping up my lips as I saw Kenzi.

"Vee, how are you?" she rushed out. "Are you okay?"

"I'm all right." She frowned at my words, knowing I hadn't called her just to say hi. "How are you? I'm sorry you had to go into hiding because of me."

Kenzi giggled, glancing away from the camera. "It's completely okay. Allie and I are holed up, nice and cozy. It's actually pretty nice to get some uninterrupted time to relax together."

It made me happy to see her so happy, even though a small stab of envy sliced my chest. It would be fucking amazing to run from my life right now. She must have noticed the change in my look because she turned serious.

"I'm guessing the guys are with you, seeing as Ryker is the one who emailed Allie?"

All three mumbled hellos, and I nodded. "Yeah, and my friend, Cass, from Detroit."

"It's been a full house," Zak grumbled, obviously still upset he didn't have his room back yet.

"Kenzi." Ky spoke up. "We need to know if your dad ever mentioned anything about where he took stuff from the storage place."

She frowned. "What kind of stuff?"

"My dad's bike," I nearly whispered, scared for her answer. "I have to find his motorcycle."

"I didn't know Dad moved it from the storage unit." Kenzi studied me as she spoke. "You want to find it, Vee?"

She was asking me for a reason, and my heart jumped. She knew where it was. Raising an eyebrow questioningly, she silently asked if I wanted her to say it out loud or not. My eyes darted to Ky who was watching me intently.

Clearing my throat, I shook my head. "I need to find it."

"I'm sorry, I don't know where it's at if it's not at the storage unit."

"It's okay, Kenzi."

She suddenly laughed. "Where I'm at right now. It reminds me of where we went camping as kids. You remember, Vee?"

She nodded into the screen, her way of telling me this was the hint about where my dad's bike was. I smiled gratefully. She was giving me a chance to keep the information to myself if I wanted. Which I did.

"I remember." I used to love going camping. My family and Kenzi's would go all the time. They were some of the few happy childhood memories I had that didn't involve Zak and Ky. "We used to ride our dirt bikes for hours on the trails."

"Where is it?" Ky asked, suspicion flitting across his face.

"A few hours north of LA," Kenzi replied. "God, I haven't been up there since we were kids. I wonder how much it's changed."

"Neither have I," I murmured, my thoughts going back to my past.

"When I come back, we need to go." She tilted her head to the side and gave me a knowing look.

That was it. The bike was either at the camping site or something there would lead us to the bike. My heart pounded at my new secret as all three guys stared at me. Even though Kenzi was acting completely normal, they could sense something.

"What's the name of campground?" Zak asked casually as his sharp gaze stayed on me.

My answer was the truth. "I don't remember. It's been so long since we went."

I honestly didn't remember the name of where we camped. But I knew exactly how to get there. It was less than an hour out of Suncrest.

"I'm going to go. Good luck with everything. Be careful, Vee," Kenzi said softly. "Let me know when it's safe to come home. But hey, no rush. We're enjoying it."

With a small laugh, we said our goodbyes, and I stared at the blank screen. The urge to tell the guys was nearly overwhelming. More than anything, I wished it was them I was working with instead of keeping Mack's secret.

My mind went back to the cabin. It was too much risk to tell Ky. Even with the Kings watching this house, too, I couldn't chance it. If Mack even had a guess that I'd spilled everything to Ky, the first person he'd go after was Kenzi's mom. Kenzi had been through enough.

No, actually the first thing Mack would do is kill Knox and be sure to tell Jensen it was my fault. And if Jensen found out, I wouldn't be with Ky anymore. He'd make sure of that. Disgust skated over my skin at that thought.

Fuck, no matter which way I turned, there was no right answer. No easy way out. Did I know if the choice I was making was the right one? Hell no. But I was doing the best I fucking could and hoped what I'd chosen would save the people I cared about.

Nearly jumping when Ky pulled the phone from my hand, I looked up to see him watching me curiously. Letting my face go blank, I met his stare.

"What's wrong?" he asked, moving in front of me, making it impossible for me to stand from the couch.

"Nothing," I muttered, reminding myself I needed to keep my emotions in check or Ky would see right through me. "Seeing Kenzi just brought up some feelings I'd rather not think about."

"You heard her, she's fine," Zak spoke up. "All this won't last forever, Vee."

Running my hands through my hair, I stood up. "I need to get the hell out of this house. I'm going crazy. Can we go out to eat or do something?"

The guys all exchanged a glance, making me roll my eyes. I hated how they thought they were in charge of what I did. Glancing out the front window, I realized I needed to figure out how to let Mack know I'd gotten the information. I would love to hide out in this house for as long as possible, but Jensen was getting antsy already. And his threat of seven days wasn't lost on me. I needed to be gone by then.

"Not many places we can go," Ky muttered, still watching me suspiciously.

"I don't give a fuck. As long as the place has food, and it's not in this house."

Ryker shrugged. "Jensen's going to make sure you're being followed if we leave."

"Fine. Let him. We can even go to his restaurant." They all looked at me in surprise. "I didn't even get to try the steak last time we were there."

"Seriously?" Ryker asked. "You want to go there?"

I shrugged. "Sure."

"You guys go." Zak plopped down on the couch next to Cassie. "I'll stay and watch our uninvited houseguest. I'm not in the mood for steak anyway."

Cass rolled her eyes but nodded. "Bring some food back for me, seeing as I can't leave this house."

Ky and Ryker followed me out of the house, both on edge as they stared at two cars across the street. Jensen had men watching our every damn move. He wasn't even trying to hide the fact that he didn't trust his son anymore.

As the guys got into Ky's truck, I paused and stared across the street. I had no idea where the Crows were, but I knew they were here somewhere. I raised both hands and threw my middle fingers in the air. If Mack wanted me to give him a signal, he wouldn't miss this one.

"What the hell are you doing?" Ryker had his head out the window.

Keeping my hands in the air, I answered. "Fuck this city. I'm done with it all."

"Get in the truck, Raindrop," Ky called out. "Or we go back in the house."

I jumped into the back seat with my stomach tumbling with nerves. I did it. I almost wished I could take it back. Going back to Mack was the last thing I fucking wanted. But I'd do it to keep everyone safe.

Glancing back at the house, I wondered if I'd be back.

I should have said goodbye to Cass and Zak.

CHAPTER THIRTY

Vanessa

The restaurant was slow for a Friday night. Only a few cars were in the parking lot. I guess Jensen really didn't care how busy it was since it was most likely used for laundering his money. I closed the truck door and turned, freezing when I caught sight of someone staring at me.

Danny. He was across the street and shot me a leering smirk when I met his gaze. He glanced at the restaurant before looking back at me and tapping his ear. My face paled. What the fuck did that mean? They had ways to listen, even in the restaurant? He suddenly frowned before rushing down the sidewalk.

"Don't let him shake you," Ky murmured in my ear, making my heart spike. "We figured the Crows would be keeping tabs. He's not going to touch you."

"Can we just go eat?" I spun around and made my way to the entrance, with food being the last thing on my mind.

We got a table near the window, and I stared at the table

in the middle, remembering the last time I was here. I had been so close to killing Jensen. He and Mack were on the top of my shit list. I wanted them gone.

Ky's hand landed on my thigh under the table, and I raised an eyebrow at him. Even with everything going on, his touch sent heat shooting through my stomach.

"You've been back two days, and I haven't touched you since you were on the phone with Don." His hand traveled higher up my thigh, and I squeezed my legs together.

"Ky," I hissed, looking at Ryker who was across the table, scrolling on his phone. "You waited until we were out of the house to start this?"

"Every time we're in the house, we get interrupted. I think we might have better luck in public."

Flashbacks to the club in Brown City filled my mind. That was fucking hot. Apparently, Ky thought so, too, seeing as he wanted to do it again. After a couple of seconds, I spread my legs apart. I had leggings on, but even through the fabric, his touch was setting me off.

Might as well enjoy one last orgasm before my life went deeper into hell.

His fingers reached the waistband of my pants just as Ryker cleared his throat. My face flushed as I met his eyes. He raised an eyebrow before looking at Ky.

"If I had known you wanted private time, I would have stayed home with Zak," he muttered.

Ky chuckled. "You don't want to watch again?"

My mouth dropped open. "Ky. Stop. We are not doing this."

"No, you guys go ahead." Ryker stood up. "I'm going to walk down the street and grab some tacos from that food truck. Text when you're done...eating."

Ky's hand didn't leave my stomach as Ryker walked

away. Shaking my head, I glanced at Ky, who had a shit-eating grin on his face.

"Ryker has a point. I don't want to just touch." He looked up, getting the server's attention. "I want to eat."

"Yes, Mr. Banes?" the server asked with a mix of fear and respect in his voice.

"The restaurant is closed. Tell everyone to leave. No need to pay their bills."

My eyes widened at his words as the server stood there, not sure what to do.

"Did I not make myself clear?" Ky asked, his eyes darkening as his voice went cold. "I want everyone the fuck out. Now."

"But Mr. Banes, there are still people eating," the server stuttered out, looking around as if wishing he could be anywhere else.

"I don't give a shit." Ky stood up as I hid my face in my hands. "Can I have everyone's attention please?"

Peeking through my fingers, I watched as the few people who were eating turned their attention to our table. The server stood next to Ky, visibly shaking as his face grew red.

"Sorry for the interruption, but the restaurant has to close early. Consider your food on the house." Ky smiled before glancing toward the door.

Following Ky's lead, the other two servers began ushering people out, apologizing as people walked out the door, even before their meals were done. In only a few minutes, it was only us and the restaurant crew.

"I want everyone out. Even in the kitchen," Ky demanded, staring at our poor server. "You'll all get paid for the entire day."

With a quick nod, the server disappeared into the kitchen as I stared at Ky.

"I can't believe you just did that," I muttered. "Jensen is going to flip his shit when he finds out."

"I don't give a fuck." He pulled me from my chair, wrapping his arm around my waist. "Getting you alone seems to be impossible, so I decided to make it happen."

His lips grazed my neck, sending tingles down my spine. A second later, my stomach dropped when I realized something. *We were alone.* For the first time in weeks. The deal we made crossed my mind. The one I won. My one chance where I could tell him to let me walk away, and he couldn't stop me.

If I could leave, then I wouldn't have to worry about anyone getting hurt when Mack came to get me. It was the best way.

"Stop thinking," Ky murmured, feeling my body tense. "Relax. And fucking enjoy what I'm about to do to you."

Before I could say a word, he kissed me. His tongue clashed with mine as I melted into the kiss. I could enjoy it for a second before leaving. His hand traveled under my leggings, brushing my pussy over my panties.

"Ky," I breathed out, realizing if I didn't say it now, I wouldn't be able to stop.

"No more talking."

He reached behind me, knocking everything off the table. The silverware and glasses crashed to the floor, the breaking of glass echoed through the empty dining room. A gasp left me as he lifted me up and laid me on the table.

"Ky," I tried again as he started sliding my leggings off. "Wait."

He paused with my pants halfway down my thighs. Meeting my gaze, his eyes darkened when he saw my face.

"Whatever you're about to say—don't," he growled.

"I'm sorry," I choked out. "I'm playing my card. I want to leave."

"Why?" He snapped, not moving a muscle. "Where do you need to go?"

"Let me go, Ky," I whispered as his grip tightened on my legs.

"Fuck," he snarled, stepping back. "Who's keeping secrets now, Raindrop?"

My heart sank. He was trying to cover his hurt up with anger. His gaze drifted down my body, and he forced out a small grin as he pulled out his phone.

"Twenty minutes to get yourself off before the no touching expires." He messed with his phone. "Timer's about to start, baby."

Well, shit. I forgot about the damn strings he attached when we made the deal. My eyes darted to the door, wondering if I could make it before he caught up to me. From the way he tensed, I seriously doubted it.

Clatter from the kitchen had me shooting off the table. Pulling up my leggings, I shot Ky a glance. He didn't seem fazed by the noise, making my heart hammer.

"I thought everyone left." I crept back, surprised when Ky stayed where he was.

"You really should have waited to play your card until we were actually alone," Ky murmured, his eyes dancing between anger and arrogance from knowing my chance to leave was gone.

"Fuck," I muttered, bolting for the front door. Now that Ky knew I wanted to leave, he would literally lock me in his room until I told him why. That couldn't happen. Mack would do anything to get to me and that money. I didn't want anyone getting hurt. My only chance to leave without that happening was now.

Halfway to the door, an arm snaked around my stomach, pulling me into a hard chest. He spun me around, and my eyes widened when I saw Ky standing near the table still. I glanced down at the arm on my stomach before looking over my shoulder.

"Ryker," I mumbled. "I thought you went to get tacos."

"It's a good thing he decided to stay in the kitchen to eat instead of leaving, don't you think, Raindrop?" Ky's voice dripped with sarcasm and danger. He was pissed I tried leaving.

"Ky, please. Just let me go. You don't understand. I'm doing this for you. For everyone I care about—"

"Tell me why."

"No."

Ryker's grip tightened as I shifted in his arms. Ky stared at me for a moment before his eyes lit up, making me stiffen.

"Hmm," he hummed out, glancing at Ryker. "If it's so important to you, then you can still leave."

I didn't say a word, knowing it wouldn't be that easy.

"But my part of the deal still stands. You need to get yourself off within..." he checked his phone, "eighteen minutes. And then you can walk out those doors."

Apprehension tore through me, not knowing what the hell he was doing. He was playing a game. A game I didn't have time for.

"You'll let me go?" I asked, knowing there was more to it.

"Sure, baby. I won't lay a finger on you for eighteen minutes, just like I agreed. But I'm sure you could use some help." Lust swarmed his eyes as we stared at each other.

My pussy pulsed as my body heated up, knowing what

he was going to say next. At the same time, dread slid through me, knowing there was no way they were letting me leave this restaurant.

I might as well enjoy what was going to happen next.

"Ryker." Ky looked at his friend. "Do you want another taste of the sweetest dessert?"

CHAPTER THIRTY-ONE

Vanessa

Ryker sucked in a breath at Ky's words. His body betraying his thoughts when his erection pressed into my back.

"Ky, really—"

"This is me proving I can be a nice possessive asshole." His eyes stayed on Ryker as he spoke to me. "I agreed not to touch you. So, I won't. I'll watch Ryker touch you instead."

I glared, even as my body burned with excitement. I was hot. Everywhere. Mack disappeared from my mind as I decided to enjoy whatever was coming next. They weren't going to let me leave anyway.

I was curious to see if Ky could actually stand to watch me as another guy touched me. Saying it was one thing... watching it happen was something else. He had never liked sharing. Grabbing Ryker's wrist, I pushed his hand down my stomach.

"Vee," he forced out, his voice husky. "Are you sure—"

"Touch me, Ryker," I murmured. "Make me yell your name while your fingers are in my pussy."

Ryker let out a strangled groan as his fingers slipped into my panties. I was already slick from arousal, and I let out a moan as he circled my clit. My eyes didn't leave Ky's. It looked like he couldn't decide whether he wanted to stop Ryker or keep watching. One thing was for sure, he was as turned on as I was. His erection pressed against his jeans as he stared.

"Lay her down," Ky ordered. "I want her clothes off. With her legs spread. If I'm going to only watch, I want the whole show."

Ryker's nervousness was nowhere to be seen as he removed his hand from my panties and swept me up in his arms. Crossing the room, he set me on top of the bar. Without a word, he slid my leggings and panties off in one move. I raised my arms, and he pulled my shirt off before unclipping my bra and letting it fall to the floor.

"Lay down, Vee." Raw desire controlled his voice, and I squirmed as his eyes grazed my naked body. He'd seen it all before, but this time was different. He wasn't nervous. Or in a rush. He knew what he wanted to do with me and was going to enjoy it.

My back hit the cold, glossy wood of the bar as I laid down. Chills raced through me as his hands grabbed my thighs, pulling me to the end of bar. Ky appeared in my vision before he pushed open the door to the kitchen and left the room.

I frowned in confusion, wondering where he was going until Ryker demanded my attention. I only saw the top of his blond hair after he lifted my legs onto his shoulders with his face disappearing between my thighs.

His lips dragged up my thigh as I shivered in anticipation. I felt his hot breath before his mouth covered my clit, and he began swirling his tongue slowly.

"Does she taste as good as you remember?" My eyes snapped open to see Ky back in the room. He stood next to the bar, watching Ryker feast on me.

"Hmmm," Ryker hummed, sending vibrations through my pussy. "Better than I remember."

My body burned hotter as I met Ky's eyes. This was something I never thought I'd be doing. But fuck, it was fun. Ky reached his arm over my body, holding something in his hand. He lowered his hand over my stomach and I jolted when something cold touched me.

Glancing down, I watched as Ky trailed the ice cube up my stomach until gliding it over my nipple. The cold sensations spreading through me were contradicting the heat Ryker's tongue was causing.

I whimpered, unable to handle both sensations at once. My hips rocked, my body begging Ryker to go faster. Ky slid the ice cube to my other nipple, moving it in slow circles.

"She likes it hard and fast, Ryker," Ky murmured. "A little bit of pain with her pleasure."

I let out a cry as Ryker switched from his slow assault to crushing his mouth to me and sucking as his tongue continuously lashed against my clit. His grip on my thighs tightened as I bucked from his tongue and the chill of the ice cube that Ky was trailing down my body.

My breathing sped up as waves of pleasure hit me over and over. My hands gripped the edges of the bar as my orgasm drew closer. Ky leaned down next to my ear, his breath tickling my neck.

"You think he can make you scream as loud as I do?" he asked, his voice smothered with need. Not touching me must be killing him. "I guess we'll find out."

My body was on fire as I got to the brink of pleasure. Squeezing my eyes shut, I let pleasure overtake everything else. My legs tightened around Ryker's head as I arched my back.

"Stop."

One word and everything was gone. Ryker's tongue disappeared, along with the cold of the ice cube.

"Ky, what the hell?" I snapped, pissed that I was so close to an orgasm and didn't fucking get it.

"You thought it would be that easy?" He chuckled. "You'll get your orgasm. Most likely more than one. But first I want you to tell me why you're trying to leave."

My heart stuttered, and I glared as I realized his game. Ryker kept his grip on my thighs but lifted his head to look at us. My pussy throbbed, needing his touch again. The silence was broken when the alarm went off on Ky's phone. I swallowed, completely forgetting about that.

He broke out in a grin as he turned it off. "Time's up. It's my turn to touch. But don't worry, Ryker can still join in too."

"If you're not going to let me come, I'm not playing—"

"Oh, you'll come," Ky promised in a low voice. "By the time we're finished, the truth will be falling from your lips as you beg to come."

Before I could say another word, Ky nodded to Ryker who immediately attacked my pussy with his tongue again. Ky grabbed my arms, pulling them over my head. Holding my wrists with one hand, he moved his free hand to my chest. His fingers were still ice cold as he rolled my nipple between his thumb and index finger.

My words were lost as Ryker's tongue and his fingers worked me up to the edge again. Ky replaced his fingers with his mouth as he pulled and teased my nipples. My arms strained against his hold as everything became overwhelming.

Until they both slowed down again. I let out a scream of frustration of being left on the edge again. My body was begging for it. I needed the release.

"Tell me, baby," Ky coaxed, tracing my collarbone. "Why do you want to leave?"

"Please," I whimpered. "Fuck. Just let me come."

"Answer him, Vee." Ryker slipped a finger inside me as he spoke.

"You don't understand—"

They didn't even let me finish until they began torturing my body again. I squirmed in Ky's hold as he trailed kisses down my neck. Ryker's teeth grazed my clit before he flicked it with his tongue, making my body grind against him, needing more than he was giving me.

My senses were overloaded as I responded to their mouths even as I fought against it. I knew they were going to stop again, but I couldn't help but let my body try to come like it so desperately wanted. I lost track of time as they brought me to the edge again and again to stop and then start all over.

"I can't," I breathed out. "I need to come. Please. This is fucking torture."

"Tell us to stop," Ky dared me, knowing what my answer would be. I didn't want them to stop. I wanted a fucking orgasm. "Or tell me the truth."

I stared at him with my chest heaving. Reality seeping through my haze. I couldn't tell him the truth. Especially not after seeing Danny outside. If they were really listening, they were getting a fucking show. But if they found out I said anything about Knox, they might hear that too.

"I made a deal with Mack," I whispered as they both

froze. "That I'd...marry him if he didn't hurt anyone I cared about."

Ky's eyes flashed in rage, and I flinched from the anger seeping off him. I had to make the lie believable. This was the best one.

"That's not fucking happening," Ky snarled. "You really thought I'd let that happen?"

I stayed silent, knowing nothing I said would make it better. My body was buzzing from nerves, especially since Ryker was still dragging his finger up and down my pussy as Ky processed my words.

"We'll talk about it later." Just like that, he let his anger go. I stared at him in surprise. "Right now, I have other things on my mind. Like giving you what you want. Let's get resituated."

At his words, Ryker stood up and I sat up in protest. I wanted his tongue to finish the damn job. Ky stepped in between my legs where Ryker had been. Gripping me tightly, he turned my body until I was diagonal across the bar. My head hung off the edge and I lifted my neck to look at Ky.

"Ryker spent so much time using his tongue, it's your turn to repay the favor, don't you think?" Ky unzipped his jeans, pulling his cock free of his boxers before brushing it against my pussy.

I licked my lips as Ryker moved in front of my face. He met my eyes, making sure I was okay with this before he slid down his pants and boxers. His cock sprang to attention as he grabbed it, running a hand down his length as he stared at my mouth.

"I liked watching him tease you," Ky murmured, pulling my eyes back to him. "Seeing you writhing with pleasure does something I can't even describe. I'm sure Ryker enjoyed it too."

Ryker made a noise of approval as Ky placed his hand over my pussy. I jumped from his touch, knowing the next time I got to the edge I was going to finally crash over.

"But this." The tip of his cock pressed against my entrance. "Is mine. No one fucks you. Except me. Understand?"

I nodded, knowing he needed to hear it. Deciding not to think about what would happen after we left this room, I gave him what he wanted.

"Yours," I whispered as his eyes gleamed with satisfaction.

Without another word, he slammed into me. My breath caught from the sudden fullness as my pussy pulsed around his cock.

"Show Ryker how good you are with your mouth," Ky ordered, as he thrust again.

Lowering my head back down until it was hanging over the edge of the bar again, I opened up, letting Ryker guide his cock into my mouth. He groaned as he filled me completely. I began to suck as Ky's fingers began rubbing my clit.

In no time at all, I was moaning around Ryker's cock as Ky brought me to the brink again. This time he didn't stop. I exploded with a muffled scream as my body convulsed from one of the strongest orgasms I'd ever experienced. Ky didn't slow down, causing another orgasm to build before the first one even ebbed away.

Ryker took control of my mouth, moving faster as he chased his own release. Ky rammed into my pussy, making sure to hit my G-spot as his fingers continued to play with my clit. My legs shook as another orgasm ripped through me before I felt Ryker tense up.

He came down my throat, still pumping his cock until he completely emptied himself in my mouth. Every single nerve in my body was on fire with pleasure as Ky kept moving even as Ryker pulled out of my mouth. Without stopping to catch his breath, he leaned over me and pulled my nipple into his mouth while his fingers gave the other one attention.

I panted, unable to form words. I couldn't even think straight between all the sensations. So many hands, everywhere. Pleasure coming from everywhere at once.

"One more, baby." Ky pinched my clit, making me cry out.

My orgasm tore through me as I screamed, not able to handle it anymore. Was it possible to die from too much pleasure? Because holy fuck, that's where I was right that moment. Ky grunted as he came, making sure his cock was buried in me.

The only sound through the restaurant was our heavy breathing. Ky pulled my body toward him until my head was resting on the bar again. I couldn't fucking move, even if I wanted to. My body was spent.

I wasn't sure how long I lay there until someone nudged my shoulder. My eyelids fluttered open to see Ky holding a glass of water. With a sigh, I sat up and downed the glass.

"That was fun." I let out a giggle and saw both of them relax. Ryker chuckled, shaking his head.

"It was," Ky agreed before meeting my eyes. "As long as you know you're still mine."

I forced out a smile. "I know, Ky."

I didn't know. But I wasn't about to ruin the night with

that. Ky's phone rang, and he looked at the screen with a frown.

"Who is it?"

He glanced at me. "Mar."

Her name brought reality crashing back. Our happy sex fun bubble burst as he answered the call. She was screaming loud enough for me to hear her, and Ky pulled the phone from his ear before putting her on speaker.

"...need you to come here now," she shrieked. "I'm calling in my favor. I need all three of you."

"Now?" Ky asked through clenched teeth.

"Yes, now. I've been trying to call you for an hour." Mar sounded crazed, and I wondered what the hell she needed.

"Can it wait—"

"No, it can't," she hissed. "This was the deal, Kyro. You owe me a favor. Get over here now before I start finding the bodies I buried."

"Jesus," Ryker muttered, handing me my clothes. "It's going to be a long night."

I nodded in agreement while slipping my clothes back on. A ball of dread weighed me down as I hopped off the bar. What were the odds of her calling the same day I signaled to Mack about knowing where the paperwork was?

It was going to be a horrible fucking night.

CHAPTER THIRTY-TWO

Vanessa

"Did she say what she wanted?" Zak asked as we drove through largest estate I'd ever seen in my life. I couldn't even see the house until we were halfway up the driveway.

"No," Ky answered, staring at the white mansion. "Just that she was calling in that favor."

Nerves had been gathering in my stomach ever since Ky had gotten the phone call from Mar. No way it was a coincidence she called in this favor the day I signaled to Mack that I knew where the bike was. Were the Crows working with the Ambrosi family? Or was Mack the guy Mar was fucking?

"Let's fucking get this over with," Ky muttered, pulling me out of my thoughts.

We walked up to the stained-glass front door, and Zak rang the doorbell before turning back around.

"Where were you guys—Ryker, is your shirt on backward?" Zak squinted through the darkness, trying to get a better look.

"What?" Ryker mumbled, looking down. "Uhh, yeah. I guess it is."

My face was burning, and I stared at my shoes, not taking the chance of Zak seeing my face. I had no regrets about what we did. It was fucking hot. But Zak would make jokes about it until the end of time.

"Where did you say you were again?" Zak asked, not hiding his suspicion.

"We went out for dinner," Ky answered casually, wrapping an arm around my waist. "It was delicious. Don't you think Ryker?"

"Yeah, delicious," Ryker choked out before clearing his throat.

I dug my elbow into Ky's stomach, and he let out a chuckle. Zak was going to find out about this at some point, and he was going to have a field day with it.

The chuckle died in Ky's throat when a man opened the front door. Our good moods disappeared as Mar's face poked over the man's shoulder.

"Thank god," she exclaimed. "It's been like a half-hour since I called you."

"You live clear across town," Ryker grumbled as we followed her into the house.

Mar's heels echoed inside the huge foyer while she moved to the back of the house. The floor was a dark gray wood, and the walls were painted a deep shade of red. It was dark and gothic, not what I expected with Mar's bubbly personality. Then again, this was her father's house, not hers.

"Vanessa can wait in there." She pointed to the door on our left. "It's a sitting area."

"She stays with me." Ky stepped in front of me with his guard up. I wasn't the only one who had a bad feeling about this.

Mar scowled. "No. This is the favor you owe me. And I don't want her there. Don't worry your sexy head, Ky. We aren't leaving the house."

"She's not staying alone—"

"I'll stay with her." Zak volunteered, grabbing my arm. "Come on, Vee."

"No, I need all three of you," Mar screeched, losing her patience. "There's a guy upstairs and he stole from me. He won't tell me what he did with it, and I need it back before my father finds out it's gone. It's a family heirloom. You need to make him talk."

I shot her a look of disgust. Holy shit, she wanted Ky to torture someone for her. Ky stood rigidly in front of me as Zak pulled me toward the door.

"Come on, Vee. We can talk while we wait."

"I think your little sidepiece will be fine for a little while by herself." Mar tried one last time to separate me from them.

I stayed rooted in my spot, her words not getting under my skin like I knew she wanted. The shit filling my head was much more daunting. If Mack was in there waiting for me, I didn't want Zak in there with me.

"It's fine, Zak." Tugging my arm out of his grip, I backed away. "You guys do what she needs, and I'll be here when you're done."

Ky's eyes bore into me while his frown deepened. Keeping my face as neutral as I could, I kept his stare until he glanced at Zak.

"Do not let her out of your sight," he murmured before

turning back toward Mar. "Zak stays with her, or she goes with us. Those are your two options."

Mar huffed out a breath, glaring at me like I was the one making the damn decisions. With a tight nod, she opened the door to the sitting area, motioning for us to go inside. My heart hammered against my ribs, half expecting to see Mack. But the room was empty.

There were two white leather sofas with a small black table between them. A pale yellow carpet stretched over the entire floor, and a standing light stood in the corner of the room. Eyeing the door on the back wall, I stepped into the room.

Zak gave me a small push forward. "You're blocking the door, Vee. We going to stand here all night?"

"Sorry," I mumbled, moving near the couches. Crossing my arms, I sat on the edge of the couch arm.

I caught Ky staring at me before Mar shut the door, and I swallowed through the lump in my throat. That was probably the last time I was going to see him for a while. If ever. I remembered vividly what Mack agreed to do if I gave him the money. He'd leave the Kings alone. Kenzi and her family. And Cassie. He'd let Knox go. But he'd never said anything about leaving me alone.

The second he got that money, I was dead.

"What's wrong?" Zak's question pulled me from my thoughts. "You've been acting strange all day."

"It's been a long week," I said lamely, my brain too wired to think of anything else.

"We haven't really had a chance to talk since you came back." He sat on the couch, relaxing his feet on the coffee table.

"I've only been back two days."

"I know why you're still pushing Ky away." He just

jumped right into it. "Ever since you found out about the threat Jensen has over us, you've been pulling away. Not just from Ky. From all three of us."

I sighed. "Zak, it's not—"

"You don't get it," he snapped, his relaxed state forgotten as he grabbed my hips, pulling me backward until I landed on the couch next to him. "You're worried for me. And Ryker. And I love you for it. But fucking stop."

I bristled. "Don't be an asshole."

"I'm not. I'm telling you what you need to hear." He yanked me back next to him when I tried standing up.

Panic crept through me at not being able to see the door behind us. I couldn't shake the feeling that something was off.

"Let me go," I pushed out through clenched teeth.

"Not until you listen."

Oh my fuck. He always was more stubborn than me. Giving up, I leaned back, keeping my eyes on the only door I could see.

"Fine."

"Stop trying to push us away because you think it's the safest thing." His grip eased up a bit as he spoke. "Do you really think I wouldn't do anything to keep you safe?"

"This isn't about me staying safe—"

"But it is," he insisted. "If I had to kill Jensen to protect you, I would. Ryker too. Even if that meant some crazy hitman would come to murder us for it."

"Stop making jokes." I scowled.

"Does it sound like I'm joking? Vee, you're family. Even after everything. I will always have your back. No matter what. And you trying to push us away? It only shows you care just as much." He slung an arm over my shoulders and pulled me close. "We'll figure it all out. Have some faith.

We've been dealing with it for years. We know how to handle it."

"Yeah," I murmured, leaning into his embrace. "But I would never forgive myself if—"

"Stop," he cut me off. "You were right the other night. If Jensen had us killed, he would lose leverage over Ky. He might hurt us, but he won't kill us. I can take a punch."

"I'm dead as long as Jensen is alive."

Zak shook his head. "Jensen knows how much Ky loves you. He knows he can't touch a hair on your head anymore."

The shocking thing was, Jensen wasn't the one who worried me anymore. At least not now, when I was keeping Mack's secrets. That little reminder made my muscles tense, and I slid away from Zak.

"What's going through that head of yours?" He gauged my reaction with a frown. "Something's holding you back."

"Nothing—"

"Or someone..." He trailed off, still scrutinizing my every move. "You're hiding something. What is it?"

"I already told Ky," I snapped. "I'm sure you'll know soon enough."

"Why don't you just tell me?"

Why? When I told Ky, I had been a trembling mess. He couldn't tell I'd been lying. If I told Zak right now, there was a huge chance he'd realize I wasn't being honest.

A knock at the door had me shooting to my feet.

"I'll get it," I rushed out, moving to the door.

He grabbed my wrist, pulling me back on the couch. "Don't fucking move, Vee. I don't know what the hell has you so jumpy, but you're not leaving this couch until you tell me what you're hiding."

His playful mood was gone, and in its place was the face

reminding me he wasn't the carefree guy he loved to act as. He could be as ruthless as Ky, if not more. He strode across the room while my heart leaped in my throat.

"Zak, wait." The words were out of my mouth before I even thought about it. Fear that a bullet was waiting for him was too much for me to just let him open the door.

My face must have shown my worry because he pulled his gun out, moving slowly as he twisted the door handle. The next second, the door slammed open, knocking Zak back. Flying to my feet, I shot forward, freezing when Zak shot me quick glare. He didn't want me in the way. Gritting my teeth, I stayed where I was.

A man flew into the room, a gun in his hand. His Crow tattoo sprawled down his arm was the first thing I saw, making my blood run cold.

I fucking knew it.

His gaze roamed over me for a moment before he turned his attention to Zak. With his gun raised, it was obvious he wasn't stopping to talk.

"No," I screamed, seeing his finger on the trigger. I lunged forward, only for Zak to shove me back on the couch.

A shot rang out, and my stomach clenched, waiting to see Zak fall to the ground. Instead, the Crow went down as blood began to stain his white shirt. Zak strode across the room, kicking the gun away from the guy bleeding out all over the carpet.

"What the hell were you trying to do, Vee?" he snapped, his back still turned to me. "Jumping in the middle of two guys with guns without a weapon? You could have gotten fucking shot."

"He wouldn't have shot me," I mumbled, standing from the couch.

"No, he wouldn't have," a quiet voice murmured from behind me as fingers wrapped tightly around my upper arm. "You were supposed to be in this room alone."

"Mack," I choked out, looking over my shoulder.

His eyes were trained on Zak, and I noticed the once closed back door was wide open, revealing the back patio. He must have been waiting out there this whole time. Turning back around, I realized in Mack's other hand was a pistol, and it was aimed across the room at my best friend.

Zak had his gun raised toward us with his face stone-cold. Mack pulled me against his chest as his fingers dug into my arm.

"Put down the gun, Zak," Mack ordered tightly.

"Let her go," he shot back, not lowering his weapon.

Zak's gaze darted from my face to Mack's gun, silently telling me what to do. He was right. I could probably disarm Mack easily enough. He only had a hold on one of my arms. But I couldn't. There was no telling how many other Crows were in the house. I already knew I was leaving with Mack.

At least I knew the three of them would stay alive if I cooperated.

My eyes widened as Danny came through the door behind Zak and shoved a gun into his back.

"Not a word, if you don't want to see him hurt." Mack kept his voice low as he spoke right next to my ear.

Zak dropped his gun, his body shaking with silent rage. He glared at Mack with pure hatred. The pain from Mack's grip was relieved when he let me go. I stood there rigidly, not moving a muscle, wondering what the hell he was going to do now.

"Time to go, Vanessa." Mack lowered his gun since Danny was here.

"She's not leaving with you," Zak spat out. "That gunshot wasn't quiet."

Mack laughed. "Ky is on the other side of the house. He didn't hear shit. By the time he realizes I was here, we'll be long gone."

Understanding filtered into Zak's gaze. "You're working with the Ambrosi family."

"Actually, Antonio has no idea. This is all Mar."

"Why the fuck would you let Vee go, just to come back for her two days later?" Zak's glare didn't leave Mack as he tried to make sense of it all.

Mack gently brushed my hair off my shoulder before grazing his fingers down my neck to my collarbone. I bit my tongue to keep from screaming my disgust, feeling like absolute shit when Zak's eyes narrowed in disbelief. I wasn't fighting back. I always fucking fought back.

But not this time. Not when Mack was holding the lives of everyone I loved.

"She needed to find out where the paperwork was. It was easier to do that when she was with you guys."

"We haven't found the paperwork..." He stopped talking, staring at my face when he realized that wasn't the truth. His gaze hardened, and for once, his inner monster was directed straight at me. And I didn't blame him one bit.

"She told you at some point during the call, didn't she?" Zak shook his head, being careful not to say Kenzi's name. "She said something only you would understand."

"We need to hurry up," Danny spoke up. "Mar can only distract them for so long."

"Keep fighting, Vee," Zak pleaded, registering the fact that I was going with Mack one way or another. "He can't kill you. Don't give him what he wants. Don't live to protect everyone else. We can take care of ourselves."

"Says the guy with a gun to his back." Danny scoffed.

Zak eyed Mack, speaking directly to him. "I pity whoever thinks they can own her. Because Ky will unleash hell on anyone and anything to make sure she's safe. When he fucking gets ahold of you, he's going to be merciless. And I can't wait to be a part of that."

Mack tensed against me but forced out a chuckle. "Good luck finding us."

He nodded to Danny, who pulled something out of his pocket with his free hand while keeping his gun trained on Zak. Panic seized me, and I attempted to shoot forward as Danny jabbed the needle in Zak's neck.

Mack wrapped his arm around my waist, holding me back. Zak's hand shot to his neck and a second later, his eyelids drooped as he crumpled to the floor.

"What did you do?" I shrieked, trying to rip his arm off me. "I fucking did what you said—"

"Calm down," Mack snapped. "It's a sedative. It's probably not even enough to keep him knocked out for an hour. I wasn't expecting to use it on him. No one else was supposed to be in here with you. The amount wasn't meant for a guy his size—"

"Me?" My stomach rolled with nausea. "You were going to drug me?"

He shrugged. "I didn't know if you were going to be... compliant. I brought it just in case."

"You didn't have to do that. I was going to come with you—"

"I could have just had Danny knock him out. But I agreed not to hurt them. See, I'm holding up my end."

Staring at Zak, I blew out the breath I'd been holding when his chest moved up and down. I thought they'd killed him.

"Let's go, Vanessa." Mack grabbed my arm again, pulling me through the back door he had come through earlier. "You know where the paperwork is?"

"Yeah," I muttered. "It's about forty minutes out of Suncrest."

"Don't sound so down." He opened the door to the SUV, waiting for me to climb in. "We're both getting what we want."

"Fuck you, Mack," I hissed. "I don't have a fucking choice."

"You always have a choice." He pushed me across the seat before sitting next to me. "You're choosing to protect the ones you love over money. I guess it's good for me that you have a conscience."

Resting my head back, I stared out the window without answering. We passed Ky's truck as we drove down the winding driveway. My heart ached, not knowing what the hell was going to happen once we finally got the paperwork everyone had been dying to get their hands on.

I wasn't sure I was ready to find out.

CHAPTER THIRTY-THREE

Vanessa

Thanks to construction, it took almost an hour to get to the campground. Mack's impatience was at its boiling point by the time we parked. My feet landed on the dirt trail as Mack got out of the SUV behind me.

"Where in the hell are we?" Danny asked, shining his flashlight on me. "There's nothing here."

I nodded to a smaller trail. "My dad used to take me camping here. He and Teddy would always disappear on that trail for hours. Someone told me the bike is most likely here."

"You don't know?" Mack sounded pissed. "I swear if you're stalling—"

"I'm not," I snapped, crossing my arms. "This is the best lead I could get. If it's not here, I have no idea."

"Then let's go." Mack motioned for me to go first.

Flashbacks of my childhood crept forward with each step I took. These camping trips were some of my favorite memories. Bonfires with s'mores. Fishing in the lake.

Endless laughing. Shaking my head, I pushed it all away. Those thoughts would only distract me.

It didn't help that my favorite memories were now tainted with the everything I'd learned since coming back home.

The trail narrowed as I stepped over the overgrown bushes. A car couldn't fit back here, only off-road vehicles. *And bikes.* I couldn't believe Kenzi and I had never come back here to check it out. My mom always made it sound boring. A place where dads went to have their man time. It never held an interest to us. Maybe that's why they said it. To keep us away.

We walked in silence, with my sense of time nonexistent. I was getting really fucking tired of not having a phone. I'd even take a watch at this point. Mack and Danny were using their phone flashlights to light up the trail in front of us.

My feet hit cement and I stopped in surprise. Mack and Danny raised their lights and moved in front of me. Following them, my tiredness ebbed away as I thought about what we were going to find. This was what everyone was after. It was going to change the balance in Suncrest.

Over the past few days, I'd slowly been losing hope that Bill would come back. Now, if I gave Mack the money, it might not matter anyway. I was so tired. Of everything. The running. The fighting. The threats. The secrets. The truths. All of it had only dug my grave. It felt like I couldn't win, no matter what I did.

And I was nearly too exhausted to keep trying. I wanted it done.

"Over there." Danny pointed to his left, and they both sped up.

Not wanting to be without a light, I hurried up, staying

right behind them. Danny raised his light over his head, revealing a gray cement wall. It went as far as his light could reach, and we began to walk around the building, trying to find the door.

Whatever this place was, it was huge. Small windows were spaced every few feet and had bars on them. We halted in front of the first door we came across. The reflection of a shiny new padlock caught my attention.

Mack noticed it too and grumbled under his breath. Danny pulled out his gun, aiming it at the lock, and I shuffled back. Mack grabbed his arm, jerking him away.

"Are you trying to get one of us killed?" Mack snapped. "That shit could ricochet."

Danny rubbed the back of his neck. "I was just trying to get this done faster—"

"Go back to the car and get the bolt cutters."

"That was like a ten-minute walk—"

"Then you better fucking run," Mack cut him off, losing patience.

Danny didn't say a word as he jogged back to the trail. Leaning against the wall, I stared at the clear sky. The stars were so bright, and I took in this tiny joy, not thinking about the asshole standing next to me. In the city, the stars were barely ever visible.

"Who told you about this place?" Mack asked, interrupting the peaceful silence.

"My fairy godmother."

He chuckled. "You're a lot bitchier than you used to be when we were younger."

My eyes snapped to him. "Probably has to do with the company I'm with. Assholes usually bring the worst out in me."

"A lot mouthier too," he murmured. "You should have

agreed to my terms the night I took you back to my house. All of this could have been avoided."

"Where's the fun in that?" My words dripped with sarcasm. "It would have been a lot easier if my life hadn't been sold before I could even legally drive. Do you know how fucked that is?"

My thoughts tumbled from my lips before I could stop them. I apparently had more resentment built up than I realized.

"It didn't have to be this way. If you would have been with me instead of Ky, life would have gone how it was supposed to—"

"Oh my god." I laughed cynically. "Do you hear yourself? How it was supposed to go? What about what I want? No one should choose my fucking life for me. Even if I had never met Ky, I never would have been with you."

"You don't know that." He stepped in my personal space. "You would have been happy with me."

"I can tell you right now, it never would have or will fucking happen," I hissed, anger brewing inside me. "Sorry, Mack, I have to be attracted to the dick to be happy. And your small one just doesn't do it for me."

His hand closed around my throat before he slammed me against the wall. Darkness blanketed his features, making it impossible to see his reaction. But his bruising grip easily portrayed his feelings. I grabbed his wrist, digging my nails into his flesh in a wasted effort for him to let go.

"Do you like making things harder for yourself?" His grip tightened, making it difficult to breathe. Flashbacks from Mar's guy choking me out bubbled to the surface, inflating my panic. Taking shallow breaths, I tried calming myself down. He still needed me. We didn't have the paperwork yet.

Choking out a small laugh, I let go of his wrist, relaxing as much as I could. "Careful, your small dick energy is showing. Did my words hit too close to home?"

"Jesus Christ," he muttered, loosening his grip. "Do you ever stop trying to piss people off?"

"When it comes to you? Never."

"You want to see the paperwork when we find it?" he asked softly before his voice filled with venom. "Then keep your fucking mouth shut and do what the hell I tell you."

Fury claimed me. A scorching heat rushed through my veins as I clenched my teeth. There was only enough light to see his shadow, but his satisfaction with my silence was obvious. The urge to knee him in the balls was almost too hard to resist. I wanted him to *hurt*.

Right now, though, I wanted to read whatever paperwork my parents had left me even more. And Mack was power hungry at the moment, which meant he really would hold it over my head. After everything, I needed to know if the papers were really worth all of this.

"Work with me and make this easier on both of us." Releasing my neck, he turned and leaned on the wall next to me while pulling out his phone.

My eyebrows raised at the wariness in his voice. "All this blackmailing becoming too much for you?"

The phone screen lit up his face, making the warning glare he gave me undeniable. "It'll all be worth it once we get the money."

"Mmmm," I hummed out, trying my best not to say what was really on mind until I had the paperwork in my damn hands. "Yup, I'm sure everything will be just peachy after that. Ky's going to come after you for taking me. You do know that, right? And let's not forget the MCs. And the Aces. They're going to be pissed."

"You really shouldn't be so worried about me," he murmured dangerously. "It's not my life being threatened."

"Not yet." I shrugged when he turned toward me. I'd learn to control my mouth someday. Today was not that day.

"These things better fucking work," Danny huffed through the darkness, his flashlight blinding me as he got closer.

He handed the bolt cutters to Mack, still breathing hard from his run to the SUV. Mack didn't waste a moment as he turned and worked on breaking the lock while Danny held the flashlight.

The snapping of metal shot a rush of adrenaline through me, and I crept closer to the door. This was it. The papers had to fucking be here. Mack threw the broken lock into the dirt before twisting the door handle. He pushed the door open slowly as Danny shined the light into the doorway from behind him.

Not able to wait any longer, I shoved past Danny, making him grunt his annoyance. Mack grabbed my arm, stopping me from entering the building.

"I swear if you try anything in there—"

"Like what?" I tore myself from his grip. "I want to find out the secrets that have been kept from me my entire life. Those papers have the answers. I'm done waiting."

"You aren't touching any papers until I see them first."

"Then what the hell are you waiting for?" I swept my arm forward. "You want to go first, then go."

With Danny right behind me, I followed Mack inside where it was it was pitch-black. Even with the flashlights, we couldn't see much. There were shelves along one wall, and my gaze halted on a light switch. Deciding it was worth a try, I walked over and flipped it on.

About six fluorescent lights flickered on, revealing the room. Cobwebs hung in the corners and layers of dust covered everything. There was a pool table in the corner with a few tables and chairs scattered around. The other wall had a large bar with full bottles of alcohol on the shelves behind it.

"Is this...the Aces clubhouse?" I asked, voicing my thought out loud.

"Probably." I looked at Mack in surprise. I wasn't expecting him to actually answer.

"Why would they have their clubhouse in the middle of nowhere?"

Mack hesitated, as if debating his words. "They liked their privacy."

Ky's words drifted through my mind about how the MC was different than any other club. The way they did everything was steeped in secrets.

"Start looking," Mack muttered to Danny as he moved behind the bar.

My gaze went to the two doors on the back wall. The motorcycle clearly wasn't in here, but it might be behind one of those doors. Staying quiet, I moved near the closest door to me.

"Where are you going?" Mack's stare was zeroed in on me as my hand rested on the doorknob.

"Helping look for the paperwork. You know, the whole reason we're here."

"You're not going anywhere by yourself."

I scoffed. "What do you think I'm going to do? We're in the middle of nowhere, I can't exactly leave."

He abandoned the crate he was looking through and

crossed the room. "Danny, keep looking out here. Vanessa and I will be in the back."

I bit my lip in annoyance as he pushed my hand away from the door. He wouldn't even let me go in the room first. If the paperwork was in there, I wanted a chance to read it before him.

"It's just a garage," he stated, stepping forward after flipping on another light.

My heart leaped from my chest, and I forced myself not to react. Peeking around Mack, my eyes drifted over the garage. Unlike the other room, this one was pristine. There was no dust. No dirt. Everything was in its place and organized.

Someone had been here recently. Mack must have had the same thought because he stiffened as he glanced around. The tools hanging from the walls held none of my interest. I couldn't see half of the garage with Mack standing in front of me.

Sliding to side of him, I froze when my eyes landed on them. Three motorcycles. All in a line near the side wall. Excitement and dread twisted my gut when I recognized the one on the left. The shiny black Harley Davidson with two metal saddle bags. The white painted A on the side proved what I already knew.

It was my dad's. He always said the A was for our last name. Ace. Now I realized it wasn't just our name. It was for the club too.

"...nothing in here." I couldn't tear my gaze from the bike even as I heard Mack's voice. I was so fucking close.

Mack snapped his fingers in front of my face. Blinking, I looked at him, only to find him staring at my dad's bike. My stomach dropped, knowing I screwed up. I let my emotions out and he caught on quick.

"Why are you so interested in your dad's bike?"

"Memories," I pushed out, which was half true. Seeing his motorcycle was strumming up thoughts about my dad that I hadn't let myself think about in years.

"Danny," Mack called out before striding over to the bike. "Keep an eye on her."

Bristling from his words, I moved away from the door as Danny ran in, glaring at me like I was doing something wrong. I ignored him, focusing on Mack.

"Is the paperwork connected to the bike?" Mack asked without turning around.

I didn't answer, knowing he'd already caught on. If the paperwork was here, he was going to find it. Danny came up behind me, grabbing my elbow.

"He asked you a question. Answer it," he demanded, shaking my arm.

"He's your owner, not mine," I hissed as his hold on me became painful.

"Her silence was enough," Mack cut in, giving me a smirk. "It's in the saddlebags, isn't it?"

"I don't know."

"We're about to find out." Mack opened one saddlebag and then frowned. "It's empty."

He switched to the other one and lifted, but the lid didn't move. With Danny still leeched to my arm, I stayed still as Mack grabbed a crowbar that hung on the wall. He went back to the bike and began trying to pry the lid off. He grunted, putting all his weight behind it, and the lid snapped open.

I bolted forward, catching Danny by surprise as my arm slipped from his grip. Mack grinned as he pulled out a large manilla envelope. That was it. The answers to everything.

Reaching out, I tried swiping it from his hand, but he raised it above his head.

"You don't touch this until I read it." His eyes glistened with excitement as he inspected the envelope.

"You should wait until we get back to the car." Danny glanced at his phone. "We've been here too long."

"Did you tell Ky about this place?" Mack asked, studying me.

"No."

"Could they figure it out?" Danny snapped, putting his phone back in his pocket.

I shrugged. "Probably not."

"Fucking Christ," Mack muttered, tucking the envelope under his arm. "Let's go."

CHAPTER THIRTY-FOUR

Kyro

"She's gone." I stared into the empty saddlebags of the motorcycle. "And so are the papers."

"We can't be that far behind them." Ryker tried to stay positive, realizing how close I was to going off. "We'll find her."

After finding Zak knocked out in the sitting area, we'd called Kenzi. She had sent us the pin to the clubhouse the second we'd told her that Mack had taken Vanessa. Ryker and I were only with Mar a half-hour, but it was a long enough head start for the Crows.

Zak leaned against the wall, rubbing his temples. "Whatever the hell they shot me up with gives a hell of a migraine. Fucking assholes."

"We'll add it to the list," I muttered, picking up the crowbar from the floor. Mack was going to pay for everything he'd done. I wasn't much for torture, but I would make an exception for him. He was going to suffer. And I was going to enjoy every fucking second of it.

"Man, I know you want to destroy this room right now." Zak glanced at the crowbar in my hand. "But can you wait until my head doesn't have its own heartbeat?"

"Can you take me home now?"

We all looked at Mar, who was standing stiffly near the door. Letting the crowbar clatter to the floor, I crossed the room, stopping inches from her. She backed into the wall as her eyes widened, filling with panic.

"You can't hurt me," she sputtered out, trying to sound strong.

"It's too bad for you that you gave your guards the night off." My voice was soft, but the threat was clear. Worry clouded her face as she threw up her hands.

"I'm sorry," she yelled, her voice shrill. "Please, take me home."

We brought her because we'd rushed out of her house so quick, I hadn't had time to question her. Thanks to her trying to distract me, she'd kicked her men out of the house for the night, which helped me out. She was working with the Crows, or at least Mack. She'd be able to tell us where they went.

"Call him," I ordered, holding out a burner phone. "Now."

Her eyes darted from the phone to me. "I can't—"

My fingers closed around her throat, and she let out a yelp of surprise. She tried pulling my arm away, but she had no strength behind her. Keeping my grip loose enough to allow her to still breathe, I leaned closer.

"You think you're untouchable because of your name," I murmured. "And in nearly every situation, you'd be right. But not right now. Not with me."

"Please, don't," she begged, with tears trailing down her cheeks.

"For your family's name to strike fear in someone, they'd have to be afraid to die." I caught her gaze so she could see how serious I was. "The only thing that scares me is losing her. I will do whatever the fuck I have to do to keep her alive. I'm not afraid to die. Especially if my death saves her. If killing you helps with that, I will fucking do it. With no hesitation."

Her body shook beneath my grip. "It wasn't Mack who I talked to. I met him for the first time tonight."

"Then who told you to set me up?"

"You can't hurt him," she forced out with her lips quivering. "Promise me you won't hurt him, and I'll tell you—"

I cut her off with a cruel laugh. "Holy fuck. Whoever this guy is, you're in love with him."

"Is it so hard to believe that someone loves me?" A spark of anger curbed her panic for a moment, surprising me.

"He's not in love with you," I stated, watching hurt slide through her eyes. "He's using you. To get to Vanessa. To get to me. Tell me what the fuck his name is. Is he a Crow?"

"I don't know," she pushed out through clenched teeth. "We don't talk business."

"Give me a name," I snarled, losing my patience. Every second we spent here was a second longer that Vanessa was stuck with the Mack.

"I only know his nickname." She took a deep breath. "King."

"King," I repeated, raising an eyebrow.

"Interesting to have a nickname like that when you're hanging out with Crows," Ryker pointed out what we were all thinking. "You think Jensen has a mole somewhere?"

"I don't know," I muttered, deciding we'd figure it out later. Right now, we needed to find Vanessa.

"I'll text him," Mar promised. "Let me text him and find out where they're taking Vanessa."

Slowly, I pulled my hand from her neck. "You aren't going home until we find out."

"Why's she so important to everyone?" she mumbled before clearing her throat. "Listen, my dad can't find out about this. That I was helping the Crows. He really wants the Kings to be allies with our family."

"We'll talk about it later." I nodded to her phone she was holding. "Text him."

I stood next to her, watching as she texted the guy she called King. Once the text sent, I took the phone and put it in my pocket, making sure the ringer was on loud. Running a hand through my hair, I glanced at Stone's motorcycle again.

I wondered what the paperwork consisted of. We knew there were account numbers for the money. Hopefully, for Vanessa's sake, there was a letter or something for her, telling her everything her parents couldn't before they were killed.

Zak came up and stood next to me. "We'll find her. We always do."

This time was different. They had the paperwork. The information everyone in Suncrest had been searching for over the last seven years. If the Crows got the money, Vanessa wouldn't be useful to them anymore.

I needed to find her before that happened.

CHAPTER THIRTY-FIVE

Vanessa

"I've been fucking patient," I snarled, trying to rip the envelope from his hands. "You read it already like you wanted. Now give it to me."

We'd been in the car for at least a half-hour, according to the radio clock. Mack had gone through all the papers and put them back in the damn envelope without a single word. After leaning forward to whisper something Danny, he went straight to his phone, and my patience hit its boiling point.

Mack's gaze darted from the envelope to me as my eyes narrowed in suspicion. There was something in there he didn't want me to see. The car slowed down; the sign out the window made me freeze, and the papers were momentarily forgotten.

"Why are we here?" I asked, masking the panic brewing inside me. The engine of a plane shook the windows of the SUV as Danny parked.

"We got the account numbers," Mack answered,

watching me closely. "Now we have to fly somewhere to get the money."

I stared at the small airfield. "Where?"

"Get on the plane and I'll give you the envelope."

"Where are we going, Mack?"

"Either walk yourself or Danny will help you get on the plane."

Blowing out a breath, I steeled my face before looking at Mack. "Am I coming back to Suncrest?"

He sighed. "We're not getting on a plane to kill you, Vanessa. I still need you to get the money."

"You really know how to make a woman feel warm and fuzzy," I muttered, opening my door.

Danny followed close behind us as Mack led the way to the small plane. Apprehension made me pause before climbing up the steps. I had no fucking idea where they were taking me. Not that it mattered. They were making me get on this plane whether I fought or complied. It was too late to back out now.

Glancing over his shoulder to see I stopped following him, he reached down and yanked me up the last two steps. Danny brushed up against my back, using his body to push me forward until we were all inside the plane.

"My turn." I held out my hand, keeping my eyes on the envelope in Mack's grip.

After a couple of seconds, he tossed it to me before sitting down. His tension eased as soon as the plane began moving down the runway. Falling into the chair across from him, I stared at the envelope. I had been so ready to read it, and now that I had the chance, I was fucking terrified.

What if it proved my parents were horrible people? What if they never cared about me and my whole childhood was a lie? I had mourned them for the last seven years. Guilt had swallowed me that entire time, thinking I was the reason they were murdered.

With a trembling hand, I pulled the papers out and set them on my lap. The first page was account numbers. The bank was on the East Coast. Somewhere in New York City. I frowned. From what I knew, neither my mom nor dad had ever been to the East Coast. But after everything, I obviously didn't know shit about the truths, so they could have at some point.

"Like we agreed, I'm not signing off on the money until you let Knox go," I mumbled, realizing how close we were to ending this. "And you agreed to leave everyone alone when you get the money."

"Don't worry, you'll see Knox soon. My guys are bringing him to where we're going."

"In New York?" Flipping to the second page, my interest spiked. They had clauses that had to be met for me to get the money. I read the second sentence and my mouth went dry. That couldn't be right. My parents wouldn't fucking do that.

Sitting there in shock, I let the papers fall to the floor as the plane tilted upward. I sucked in breath after breath, forcing myself to calm down. My ears popped, drowning out everything as panic overtook everything else.

The higher the plane climbed, the deeper terror sank into my bones. Mack wasn't taking me to New York. He was getting what he wanted in the first place. My eyes fell back to the words that were about to lock me into a lifelong prison sentence.

Vanessa Ace must produce a marriage certificate and be in wedlock to access money in account.

"No, Vanessa. Not New York," Mack murmured as I looked up, meeting his cold stare. "We're going to Vegas."

CHAPTER THIRTY-SIX

Kyro

"Las Vegas," I announced, staring at the text and wondering who the fuck *King* was, if it wasn't Mack. "They're going to Vegas."

"Good, can I go home now?" Mar stood up from the couch, only for Cassie to push her back down.

"No. You're staying here until my best friend is home," Cassie hissed as we all stared at her in shock.

"Damn," Zak muttered. "I didn't think it was possible for you to get mad. You're always so happy."

"I like seeing the bright side of things." Cassie shrugged. "There's no bright side to Vanessa being taken."

We had taken Mar back to our house as we waited for her friend to text back. And he finally had. Vanessa had told me she'd agreed to marry Mack. Now they were going to Vegas. Fuck, the thought of her marrying him made me want to put my fist through the wall.

"We need to go," I bit out, tossing the phone on the table

and looking at Mar. "Do you know where in Vegas they'd stay."

She shook her head. "No."

Headlights splashed through the front window, and Ryker shot forward to look outside. Panic widened his eyes as he looked back at me.

"It's Jensen."

Zak bolted forward, grabbing Cassie's arm. "Get in my room. Now."

"No, I want to help find Vanessa—"

"If Jensen finds out you're here, you'll be on a plane to Detroit by morning. Or he'll want to use you to threaten Vanessa," Zak snapped, pulling her into the hall. "Stay in my room and don't make a sound."

I heard his door click shut just as the front door opened and Jensen strode in with three Kings. He glanced at Mar in mild surprise before looking around the room. I stiffened, knowing what his next words were going to be.

"Where's Vanessa?"

Zak walked back into the living as no one spoke. Mar continued to sit on the couch, not meeting anyone's eyes, her leg shaking uncontrollably. She really didn't want her dad to find out she worked with the Crows.

"Where the fuck is she?" Jensen screamed, losing his patience. "She was at the restaurant with you, and then my guys lost you. Where did you take her?"

"Mar needed help with something," I answered. "I know how important your alliance is with her family, so we went to help."

Mar stared at me in terror, waiting for me to snitch on her. But that wasn't the plan. I might need her again in the future, and holding this over her head might come in handy. Meeting Jensen's eyes, I told part of the truth.

"Mack and the Crows took her." His eyes narrowed at my words. "We couldn't stop them."

"Bullshit," he spat out. "You got her out of town—"

"No, it's true." Mar stood from the couch, coming to my defense. "There was nothing they could do. They even stabbed a needle into Zak's neck."

Everyone looked at Zak, who rolled his eyes. "Yeah, they knocked me out. If I could show you the fucking headache it gave me, I would."

Jensen's gaze moved between the three of us until it landed back on me. "You're trying to figure out where they took her? When were you going to call me?"

"I didn't realize we were sharing things again," I shot back. "You haven't told me shit for the last couple days."

"You're still a King," he snapped, his eyes blazing in rage. "And you're still my son."

"Vegas," Mar spluttered out, eyeing the gun in Jensen's hand. "They took her to Vegas."

"Motherfucker," Zak muttered under his breath, glaring at Mar.

I wanted to kill her. I had no intention of telling Jensen. Mar's eyes met mine, and fear covered her face as she took in my reaction.

"I'm sorry," she whispered, trying to explain herself. "You're a damn King. How was I supposed to know you weren't going to tell him?"

"Vegas," Jensen muttered. "Mack and his father visit there frequently. They own a penthouse there."

My heart raced as I stared at him. "You know where it's at?"

He nodded, watching me thoughtfully. "You three can come. We'll need the backup. And you'll do whatever it takes to get her back. But know this, Kyro. When we get her back, she's coming with me. Your time with her is done."

Grinding my teeth, I swallowed the response I wanted to say. It wouldn't do any good. Getting Vanessa away from Mack was priority. Ryker glanced at me before I looked at Zak, and then they subtly nodded.

We'd make our own plan to keep Vanessa away from Jensen.

CHAPTER THIRTY-SEVEN

Vanessa

STARING OUT THE WINDOW, MY EYES BURNED FROM getting no sleep last night. Sipping on my third cup of coffee, I watched the people on the Vegas strip begin their fun-filled day. For once, I longed to be one of them. Someone on vacation where their only worry was blowing their money in the casinos.

Instead, I was trapped in the penthouse of a hotel with a man who would do anything to get my money. My gaze slid to Mack as he walked out of the bathroom. His wet hair hung past his shoulders, and he pulled a hoodie on before glancing at me.

"You should have gotten some sleep last night." He shook his head. "It's going to be a long day."

"Having you snore in my ear left me too nauseated to sleep." I looked at Danny. "And then I had some creeper watching me the whole time too."

Mack chuckled. "There's no way you thought we were

going to leave you in a room by yourself. Sorry, Vanessa, you won't be alone until this over. Not when we're this close."

I glared at him. "That bedroom doesn't have a way out of the penthouse. Even if I was in there alone, I'd have nowhere to go."

"The fact that you noticed that is why someone will be with you every second," Mack muttered, leaning against the black granite counter. My eyes roamed to the only other door that led out of the penthouse. It was an emergency exit and was fucking locked.

"Can I read the rest of the paperwork now?" I asked, keeping my voice calm. After reading the whole marriage clause on the plane, I freaked out. I had a full-blown meltdown, my panic and rage couldn't be calmed, and Mack took the papers away. I hadn't seen them since.

"No," Mack answered simply. "I'd rather you not destroy the penthouse."

"Why? Could it get any worse than a forced marriage?"

My question was ignored as the door opened and two men walked in. I straightened up, anger immediately setting in when I met the eyes of one of them.

"You," I hissed, stepping toward him.

"Calm down," Mack snapped before turning to the two men. "Why'd you come in here, Ethan? I told you to stay out of her sight."

I glared daggers at the man who was smirking at me. His nose was still swollen and crooked from when I kicked my foot into his face. His eyes were still purple and bruised. The guy who had killed Teddy. I hadn't seen him since that night.

"We've been in the hall all night, I needed to—"

Suddenly the door swung back open before it clicked shut. Silenced gunshots rang out, and the man standing next to Ethan went down with three bullets in his chest. Mack bolted around the counter, reaching for his weapon.

I was closest to Danny, who was leaping from the couch, already pulling out his gun. Jumping on his back, I wrapped my legs tightly around his hips as my hands went to his face. He let out a grunt as his free hand grabbed my arm. He held on to his gun with his other hand, but it was useless while my hands covered his eyes.

"Fucking asshole," I muttered in his ear as I dug my nails into his eye sockets.

He started screaming, dropping the gun before attempting to rip my fingers from his eyeballs. I held on with everything I had, refusing to stop. Gritting my teeth, I could feel the damage my nails were doing. It was disgusting, but I didn't let go.

He backed up, slamming me into a wall, loosening the hold my legs had around him. He gripped my wrists, twisting them until he was finally able to pull my hands away. I let my feet drop to the floor, pulling my arms out of his grip. It wasn't hard, his hands went straight to his face, covering his injured eyes.

Taking a moment to finally see who had barged in, my heart skipped a beat. Ky was fighting with Mack. Neither had weapons; they were in an all-out fist fight. Turning my head, I saw Zak standing about ten feet in front of Ethan. Both had their guns raised at each other and were standing stiffly without saying anything.

Reaching for the gun Danny had dropped, I crept up behind Ethan, not making a sound. Zak continued to stare at Ethan, not giving my position away. Touching the gun to the back of Ethan's head, I grinned.

"Put it down," I ordered, watching as he hesitated before lowering his gun.

"Vee, I'll do it—"

My glare shut Zak up, and he sighed before turning his attention to Mack and Ky, who were both fighting. My gaze followed his, and it looked like Ky had the upper hand. Danny was sitting on the floor, unable to open his injured eyes. I focused back on Ethan.

"I told you I would kill you," I stated coldly. "It's poetic that I get to put a bullet in your skull just like you did to Teddy."

Ethan didn't say a word, his hands shaking as he dropped his gun. Zak yelled in surprise as two more Crows ran into the room from the emergency exit door. He shot one of them and ducked behind the couch to avoid the other guy's bullets.

Without wasting another second, I pulled the trigger, feeling the splatter of blood hit my face. Ethan collapsed, dead before his head even hit the floor. Satisfaction filled me as I backed away, hitting the wall. I'd done it. At least Kenzi could now have the small peace of mind that her dad's killer was dead.

"Go, Vee," Zak shouted, looking to the door beside me that the two men had just come through. "Ryker is in the stairwell, go meet him."

My eyes found Ky's as he threw Mack to the floor. He nodded, silently telling me to go. Frowning, I shook my head. I didn't want to leave. Ky wasn't leaving this room while Mack was still breathing, and I wanted to be here for that. My grip on the gun tightened as one of the Crows zeroed in his sights on me.

Before I could raise the gun, an arm snaked out of the doorway, taking hold of my wrist. With a cry of surprise, I was yanked through the door as the gun tumbled from my hand. The stairwell was silent, none of the noises from the penthouse seeping through the closed door. Ripping my arm free, I raised my fist, ready to attack, only to lower it with a gasp of shock.

Knox stood in front of me, his bruised face inspecting me. "Come on, Vee. Let's get you out of here."

CHAPTER THIRTY-EIGHT

Kyro

With one more punch, Mack fell to his knees. He was done, but that didn't stop him from trying to get back up. I pressed down on his shoulder, and he let out a grunt as he landed on broken glass.

"Even as kids you couldn't beat me in a fight." Keeping my hand on his shoulder, I grabbed the knife Zak was holding out. "What made you think you'd be able to now?"

He glared through his one eye that wasn't swollen shut. "Fuck you, Ky."

I let out a cold laugh. "Amazing last words. If you have anything else to say, spit it out now. I really wanted to draw this out, but it looks like we're running short on time. Still...I can make it fucking hurt."

I plunged the blade into his stomach, being sure not to hit anything serious. All the torture Jensen had forced me to do was coming in handy now. I knew exactly where I could stab him without it being fatal. Even if I couldn't do what I wanted to him, he was still going to suffer first.

Wiping the trickle of blood coming from my lip, I took a step back as he doubled over, clutching his stomach. I scanned the room, seeing all the Crows dead or dying. Besides Danny, who was knocked out, but he wouldn't survive the day either.

"Where is she?" I glanced at Zak.

"She went out to the stairwell. I'm sure she's met up with Ryker by now."

"There's things you don't know," Mack coughed out, blood dripping from his mouth. "I have leverage. You can't kill me."

"Leverage? You don't have Vanessa anymore," I snarled. "You'll never touch her again."

Mack laughed feebly. "Not Vanessa."

"Too bad for you, she's all I care about." I crouched down, ready to slice him again, and he threw out his hand, trying to block me.

"Knox!" he screamed. "Knox is alive."

I froze with the blade inches from him. My heart galloped as ice raced through my veins until I realized how desperate he was. With a shake of my head, I stood back up.

"Of all people, you choose to say someone who died years ago?" I couldn't hide the anger. He thought he could use my dead brother to get under my skin. And it was fucking working.

"He's not dead," Mack admitted, his voice laced with pain. "We—we've had him ever since that night at the factory. We took him and staged his death so no one would come looking."

"You're lying," I snapped, my mind going crazy with the possibility that Knox could actually be alive.

"How the hell do you think we knew all about your operations?" He stared up at me. "Your deals? Where you kept everything? The secrets? How do you think we were able to grow as large as you? Because he told us everything."

My grip on the knife became painful as his words sank in. It wasn't fucking possible. With a yell of rage, I punched him across the jaw. His head snapped to the side, and he fell to the ground. I might have hated Knox, but he was still my brother. The thought of him being a prisoner to the Crows for years was snapping my control.

"Even if he is telling the truth," Zak spoke up, trying to calm me down. "We don't need him. We can talk to Kannon."

Mack's sad laugh had us both looking at him. "My dad is on his deathbed. He's sick. I run the Crows now. He knows nothing anymore."

Running a hand down my face, I bent down, getting eye level with him. Resting the knife on his chest, I made a decision. It must have shown on my face because his eyes dilated from pure fear.

"If Knox is really alive, I'll find him," I promised. "You being alive or dead won't change that."

"Wait—"

"See you in hell, Mack."

Lifting the knife to his neck, I froze when the barrel of a gun was jammed into the back of my head. *Fuck.* Clenching my jaw, I kept the knife where it was.

"Put it down, Kyro."

My mouth dropped in surprise. "Dad?"

Jensen's voice shook with uncontrolled fury. "If Knox really is alive, then we need him. I will not let you kill the one chance I have to make my family whole again."

"If he is telling the truth, we can find Knox ourselves." I tried turning around, but he shoved the gun deeper into my skull. "We can't get him out of this hotel with us. His men are everywhere downstairs."

"We'll figure it out."

"I'm not letting him leave this room alive," I snarled. He wasn't going to get another chance to get near Vanessa again.

"You will," Jensen ordered in a deadly soft voice. "Because if you kill him, I'll kill you. I love you, Kyro. But let's not pretend we both don't know who my favorite was. I thought it would land on you to take over the Kings. But if Knox is alive, then the legacy is his. He fucking deserves it."

I waited for his words to stir up any emotion. Nothing hit me. There was no pain. No disbelief. No heartache. Because I didn't see him as a father. I hadn't in years.

Jensen kept on with his threat. "And if you die, then who will be here to protect Vanessa?"

Anger poured through every nerve in my body. Mack stayed silent, being smart enough to know Jensen was his way to survive this.

"I'll kill you, Zak, and Ryker," Jensen murmured as if he was discussing dinner. "Leaving no one to protect the girl who helped ruin my life. And I fully intend to repay her for that."

"You'd kill me? Your own blood?" I tried guilting him, knowing it wouldn't work. Not on Jensen Banes.

His voice filled with venom. "You chose her over your own blood. And you were about to do it again. I'll make her life so miserable, she'll wish she was dead. But you know how I like to play with my prey. I'll keep her for years, letting my men use her however they want."

"The Aces and MCs will still protect her if I'm dead." My voice trembled from the rage I was suppressing. Mack wasn't even the one I wanted to murder now. It was my own father.

"You're right." He paused for a moment. "I'll just do what the Crows did with Knox. Let the world think she's dead. She wouldn't even get a chance to leave this hotel."

My hand loosened around the knife in defeat. He would do it. I couldn't take the chance he'd actually get his hands on Vanessa. He always carried through on his threats. And his anger at Vanessa was the worst I'd ever seen. Everything he just said, he would do.

The knife fell to the floor, and Mack blew out a long breath. I glared at him, silently telling him this wasn't even close to being over. He was dead the second we were away from Jensen.

Shooting to my feet the moment the gun was off my head, I spun around. Zak stood between two other Kings. Their questioning looks at Jensen surprised me. They were loyal to him. But seeing their boss threaten his son was probably something they thought they'd never see.

"I need a hospital. Before I bleed out," Mack spoke through gritted teeth as blood seeped through the fingers that were covering his wound.

"Call the doctor," Jensen snapped to one of his men. "Ours will come up here and get you stitched up."

Even if they were unsure of what they had just seen, they didn't hesitate to follow orders. Zak's gaze met mine as two more Kings came into the room. The men who were once my family overlooked us as if we meant nothing. One guy gave me a quick sympathetic look before helping try to slow Mack's bleeding.

The Blood Kings had always been my family. But not anymore. Not since the night I stood up to Jensen in my living room to keep Vanessa safe. And what just happened now sealed my fate. The crown tattooed on my back wasn't anything more than a memory now.

I had no idea what was going to happen next.

"Where's Knox?" Jensen asked Mack, pulling me from my thoughts. "You play with me; I'll put a bullet in you myself."

CHAPTER THIRTY-NINE

Vanessa

"I think we should go back." Worry saturated my voice as I stared at the steps we had just come down. We'd only gone down one flight of stairs, and Knox nearly dragged me the whole way. It felt wrong leaving Ky and Zak up there.

"I heard Zak." Knox gave me a push to keep going. "He wanted you out of there. We need to get out of here before Crows show up. I got away for the first time in years. I'm not fucking going back."

Guilt seized my heart as we descended another flight of stairs. "How'd you get away?"

"I don't think they expected the Kings to come." He readjusted the hoodie he was swimming in. "They left me alone in the hotel room, and the guy watching the door was shot. I took my chance and ran. I knew you were all in the penthouse, so I went up the stairs."

"I'm sorry," I choked out, stopping to look at him. "I had no idea the call I made would—"

"Stop," he grated out, his eyes flashing in anger. "Let's not go down memory lane."

I bit my lip at his reaction. I knew he'd still be angry. Not that I could fucking blame him. He hadn't tried to kill me yet, and I just needed to keep it that way. Maybe he had changed in the last seven years.

"Vanessa?" Ryker's voice echoed through the stairwell. It sounded like he was still a few floors lower than us. I grinned, glad he was here. When he wasn't in the stairwell like Zak said, I was worried something had happened to him.

"I'm up—" Knox's hand flew over my mouth, silencing my words. Coming up behind me, he wrapped an arm around my waist, dragging me the couple of feet to a door. Pushing it open, he pulled me through before shoving me against the wall, keeping his hand over my mouth. All of that only took a few seconds, and the stairwell door shut before I got over my shock.

"What the fuck are you doing?" My words were nearly incoherent because of his hand.

He wasn't looking at me. He was watching the door, probably to see if Ryker would come through. I wasn't waiting to find out. Grabbing his wrist, I twisted until his hand fell from my face.

His eyes widened in surprise as I reached out, slinging my arm around the back of his neck, getting him into the crook of my arm. Before he had a chance to tense, I swung my body to the side, putting all my weight into it until his head slammed into the metal door.

Dropping my arm, I booked it down the hall. I had no idea what floor I was on, and there was no one in the hall. Running past the numbered doors, I considered screaming, but didn't want to alert any Crows to where I was.

His heavy footsteps were all I heard over my pounding heart. Fuck, was he working with the Crows? Or did he want to kill me because of what I had done to him?

I shrieked when I was suddenly ripped backward by my hair. The pain made my eyes water as I slammed into his chest. He grabbed my arm, twisting it behind my back and pulling it up until I couldn't move without searing pain in my shoulder.

Brute fucking strength. That's all he was. The broken man I'd witnessed at the cabin was nonexistent as he overpowered me.

"What the hell are you doing, Knox?" I panted, trying to keep my fear hidden.

He didn't say a word as he pushed me forward. Planting my feet did nothing but make him pull my arm higher. My shoulder burned as I fought against his hold. Let him fucking break my arm. Wherever he was taking me would be far worse than this.

He opened the door to a storage closet and shoved me in, locking the door behind him. Stacked shelves of towels and cleaning supplies were piled high on both sides of me. After he flipped the light on, he released my arm. Spinning around, I smacked him across the face as he leaned against the door. His relaxed posture added even more to my unease.

Chuckling, he rubbed his jaw. "You've got even more spunk than you did as a kid. I gotta say, you surprised the hell out of me. I always thought you'd be one to follow the Kings the rest of your life. But you don't take orders anymore, do you?"

Ignoring his question, I refused to show him how shaken I was. "Everything that happened at the cabin. What was that? Some kind of show? Because you're not the weak pussy you portrayed yourself to be when you tried punching Mack. You didn't want to get away that night."

His eyes lit up, and I swallowed through the lump forming in my throat. There was the Knox I remembered. The cruel, callous man who never showed mercy. The lifeless look I had seen at the cabin was long gone.

"It was all a set up," I whispered as a chill swept through me.

He smirked, tilting his head. "You always were smart. That's why I told Mack we needed to make it believable. You needed to *see it*. Feel the guilt, thinking it was your fault I was with the Crows. You wouldn't have just agreed."

"You fucking asshole," I hissed, taking a step toward him, pausing when he slid an arm out of his hoodie.

"I'm so glad I can take this damn thing off," he muttered, acting casual.

He pulled his hoodie over his head, and I jolted forward, kneeing him in groin. He hissed out a breath while reaching for my hair. Ducking away, I shoved my shoulder into his ribs, trying to back him away from the door.

The hoodie fell to the floor. His black T-shirt revealing the ripped muscles I already knew he had. His hands gripped my hips, and I braced my arms, letting my palms get the brunt of the pain as he slammed me into the wall.

Placing his hand on the back of my neck, he kept the side of my face pressed to the wall. I reached my hands behind me, trying to hurt him any way I could until he let go of my neck, catching both my wrists and bringing them above my head.

His laugh sent ice sliding down my spine. I flinched from his breath hitting the back of my ear as he leaned close to me. Gritting my teeth, I didn't say a word. He was trying to intimidate me. It's what he used to do when we were younger. I wasn't going to give him what he wanted.

"Mack told me how you were a fighter. I wanted to see for myself. He was right."

"What do you want, Knox? Why do all this?"

"You know, I think I deserve an Oscar for my acting that night." His grip tightened around my wrists. "Don't you agree, Vee?"

"I guess," I ground out as his body pressed into mine. "I mean, you really had to get the shit beat out of you for it to look real. I'm sure that was fun. So yeah, good job."

"That wasn't part of the plan," he snarled. "I never thought you'd try to attack Mack. I had to make it seem like I wanted to escape. Or you would have caught on."

"You're working with the Crows," I stated, knowing at least that was true. "Why? For my money?"

He sighed. "Aren't you going to ask what happened that night? When you betrayed the Kings? You never should have made that call."

"Obviously," I muttered. "But good news, we can tell Jensen I didn't get you killed. That'll get one gang off my back for a while."

"He'll know soon enough." His words caused my heart to beat faster. There was a plan I wasn't seeing. "I enjoyed my time away from Suncrest, but it's time for me to come home."

"What happened that night?" My curiosity had me asking the question out loud.

"Funny thing. I had a whole plan for that night." His hand wrapped in my hair when I attempted to move. "I already had a deal with the Crows. Then come to find out you called to give them information. It all worked out perfectly. Even though I couldn't believe it when I heard that you snitched on Ky. I never thought I'd see you turn on him."

"A lot has happened that I never expected," I muttered. "You rising from the dead is one of them."

A cry escaped me when he yanked on my hair until my neck tilted back. His other hand still held my wrists, and I clenched my teeth to keep from making another sound.

"What do you think my little brother would do if he saw me touching you like this?" he murmured, his lips nearly grazing my neck.

I tensed, his touch shooting revulsion through me. His sudden switch in topics threw me into the past. It was his way to keep people on the edge, not knowing what he was going to say next. Not playing into his games, I relaxed against his hold.

"I don't need Ky to fight my battles. I've learned how to deal with monsters on my own."

He pulled my hair even more, twisting my neck until I met his heartless stare. "Don't make the mistake of thinking you can win against me, Vee. I'm not the kid you remember. I'm much fucking worse. You're scared of Jensen. You should be terrified of me."

I stayed silent, keeping my glare filled with as much hate as I could. His grip was bruising my wrists, and he kept his body against mine; he leaned his head against the wall as his gaze moved upward.

"You wanted the King tattoo across your knuckles so badly when you found out about the gang." He dragged a finger over my hand as he flipped topics once again. "Is that still what you want?"

"You know I'll never be a King," I hissed. "I'm an Ace—"

"I forgot you know about your dad now." He shook his head. "We'll have to deal with the MCs later."

"What does that mean?"

He let go of my hair, ignoring my question as I straightened my neck. "Right now, we have an appointment."

Fear lit through me, and I pulled against his grip. "What the fuck are you talking about?"

"Don't worry, Vee. You'll find out soon."

CHAPTER FORTY

Kyro

"Where the fuck is she?"

Ryker frowned, running a hand down his face. "I told you. She wasn't in the stairwell. I thought I heard her, but I went up and down two damn times, and she wasn't anywhere."

It had been two hours since I had last seen her before she disappeared through the stairwell door. The plan to get her out of Vegas without Jensen finding out was shot to hell. She was most likely still with the Crows. Glaring down at Mack, who was lying on the couch, my hands balled into fists. We were still in the same hotel, just in a different suite on the fourth floor. Jensen and a few of his men stood near the window, far enough for them not to hear me.

Police got called after what happened at the penthouse, but there was a reason Mack had chosen this hotel. The hotel was under Crow management. And even some of the cops. They swept it under the rug as a noise complaint and left us alone after Mack called them.

"Tell me every single place she could be," I demanded, making sure Mack heard every word. "Or I swear, I'll rip those fucking stitches out and finish what I started."

"I don't know," Mack forced out through the pain.

"Who else would have her?"

"I don't know."

"Where's Knox?"

Mack didn't answer, knowing it was his leverage to leave this hotel alive. Looking over my shoulder, I noticed Jensen watching me. Zak stepped in front of me, blocking Jensen out.

"We've been all over this hotel," he said quietly. "She's not here, man. We'll find her."

My body was jittery with a heavy feeling that had been getting worse ever since Vanessa had left my sight. In this life, I had no idea whether she was even still alive. We had ransacked the penthouse looking for the paperwork but came up empty.

Mack refused to tell us where it was, and for the first time ever, Jensen wasn't using torture to get the information out of him. Because he wanted Knox. My jaw snapped closed as my anger got the best of me. We didn't know if Knox was alive. Jensen was taking the word of a man who was trying to save his own ass.

The ringing of a phone caught my attention, and I pulled Mack's phone from my pocket. It was a text, and I stared at the name. *King*. The same name Mar gave us. Not able to read the text until the phone was unlocked, I crouched next to Mack, holding the phone out.

"Thumb," I ordered, waiting for him to unlock it.

After a second of hesitation, he reached out, putting his thumb over the button, unlocking the screen.

"What does it say?" Jensen was right beside me, as anxious as I was for the information.

I read the short text before handing it off to Jensen.

Room 514.

"Who is this?" I asked Mack, not about to walk into a death trap.

"Go and find out," Mack spat out, trying to sit up through the pain. "It's in this hotel."

"Not good enough—"

Jensen cut me off. "Let's go. I'm done waiting."

My jaw dropped. "You can't be serious. We have no idea who it is."

"I have enough men with us to keep the upper hand," Jensen argued, his gaze turning deadly. "Mack hasn't talked to anyone besides that cop since you stabbed him. The Crows have no idea where he is. Stay here if you want; we're leaving."

He turned and strode out of the room with all his men following, except one. He stayed behind, keeping a gun on Mack. Jensen was acting irrational because all he could think about was Knox being alive. It was going to get us killed. But I couldn't let him go without me. Without another thought, I rushed to follow him. If there was a chance Vanessa was there, I didn't want Jensen getting ahold of her. Zak and Ryker were right behind me as we all headed to the stairs.

No one said a word as we climbed the one flight of stairs. As we pushed open the door to the fifth floor, we all pulled out our guns. Everyone was on high alert.

We were about two rooms away when the door of 514 opened slowly. Jensen gave the signal to stop, and a tense silence hung in the hall. Standing beside Jensen, I aimed my gun at the door as a man stepped out.

My gaze traveled from his jeans to his black shirt, already knowing who it was. The gun fell to my side as Jensen sucked in a breath. Mack had been telling the truth. I stared at the face of my brother with shock coursing through me. He had fading bruises all over his face, but his eyes were the same as I remembered from our childhood.

Sharp and cold.

Emotions I didn't know existed had me frozen in place. Relief from seeing my brother was there, burning in my chest. But something more sinister overtook it. Knox didn't look like a prisoner. His grin sure as hell didn't portray that of a tortured man.

"Son," Jensen whispered, falling to his knees. "I can't believe you're here."

"Dad," Knox greeted him casually as if he hadn't been gone seven years. "We have a lot to catch up on."

Still in disbelief, I took a step forward, freezing when Knox pulled someone out of the room. Vanessa stumbled out, staying on her feet only because of Knox's grip on her arm. The heaviness that had been weighing me down evaporated in an instant. A trace of guilt filtered through, realizing seeing my brother alive was nothing compared to laying eyes on my girl.

Then I met her gaze, and panic seized my gut before anger tore through me. She was staring at me with a look I'd never seen in her. *Defeat.* She stared back at me, broken. Her fight was nowhere to be seen. The fire that was always there was gone.

"What the fuck did you do?" I growled, shooting forward.

"Not so fast, little brother." Knox rested his gun against her ribs, making me halt a few feet from them. "Aren't you happy to see me alive?"

Vanessa didn't flinch. Not even acknowledging he had a gun on her. My chest heaved as I barely held on to my self-control. I tried meeting her eyes, but she refused to look at me. My glare focused on Knox.

"I swear if you did anything to her—"

Knox laughed. "Are you really threatening me? You're hurting my feelings, Ky. I thought you'd be happy to see me."

With the gun still pressed to her, his other hand left her arm and trailed up. My eyes stayed glued to his hand as I clenched my jaw. His fingers grazed her chest while she didn't move a muscle.

What the fuck was he doing?

He might have been alive this entire time, but as I watched his hand grip her throat, I wanted to put him in the ground myself. I would fucking kill him for hurting her. Whatever he'd done, it had broken her. And a piece of me was dying watching her fire being smothered.

"How fucking rude of me," Knox murmured, his eyes darkening with bloodthirsty excitement. "I never said why I came back. I'll explain it all. But first, did you know I saw Vanessa a few days ago?"

Vanessa finally showed a small piece of herself as pain flashed across her face. She met my stare for the first time with guilt swallowing her features. My eyes widened; Knox's words making sense. The secret she'd been keeping. This was it.

"Don't be mad at her," Knox said with a chuckle, wrongly thinking my silence meant I was angry at her. I wasn't. The only reason she wouldn't tell me was because she didn't have a choice.

"Let her go," I snarled, losing patience at seeing his hand still on her.

"I can't do that." Knox wrapped his arm around her, tugging her closer.

Rage pulled my muscles taut as apprehension coiled through my chest. Whatever the hell he was up to didn't have anything to do with me or the Kings. Like it used to be, it was only about him and how he could make his life better.

"It's time to celebrate," Knox announced with a wide grin, grabbing her wrist and lifting her hand up. "Show him, Vanessa."

She raised her hand and spread her fingers, showing everyone the back of her hand. The second I saw it, my heart fucking stopped. A scorching inferno invaded my bones, and I couldn't look away. The diamond caught the light as Knox's words drifted through my denial.

"Ky, why don't you welcome your new sister-in-law to the family?"

The End...Until Book Three

ABOUT THE AUTHOR

Kay Riley writes dark contemporary romance. She loves writing feisty, strong heroines, and keeps things interesting with unexpected twists. Kay grew up in the Midwest but has lived in some amazing places, including Japan.

When she's not writing, she is spending time with her husband and kids. She loves cats, coffee, reading, and her guilty pleasure is watching reality shows.

You can follow Kay on:
Website
Facebook
Tiktok
Twitter
Instagram
Amazon
Goodreads

AUTHOR'S NOTE

Thank you so much for continuing to read Vee and Ky's story! The revealed truths were shocking to say the least. I loved writing and showing Ky's point of view during this book. His love for Vanessa is undeniable through his actions and choices. Even though it seems the world is against them.

I know the cliffhanger was brutal, but don't worry. I'm already working on the third and final book for this series, and plan to release it as soon as I can! I hope you all are ready for the wild ending of their story. If you enjoyed reading Treacherous Truths, please consider leaving a review, it helps newbie authors like myself so much! Thank you again for taking the plunge into Suncrest Bay, and I hope you love reading Ky and Vee's story as much as I do.

ACKNOWLEDGMENTS

When I first started writing, I had no idea what I was doing or how I was going to publish. Then I found out there is an amazing writing and book community. I've been lucky enough to find people who became friends, and I appreciate them all more than I can even describe. They made the ride to publishing this book as fun and as easy as self-publishing can be.

I want to thank my friend Jo for letting me talk through some chapters I was nervous about writing. This was the first time someone read my book as I wrote it. The advice she gave was just what I needed to keep writing with confidence. She quickly became an amazing friend who I talk to every day. Thank you so much, Jo, for everything!

Alina, you've been on this journey with me since I thought about publishing Fateful Secrets. With Treacherous Truths, you chased my imposter syndrome away every time I had doubts. Your messages always make me laugh and lift my mood. Thank you for everything!

A huge thanks to my editor, Saxony, and my proofreader, Beth! With so much happening in my life, working on a timeline was nearly impossible. All I knew was I wanted to publish in October, and I never would have made my deadline if not for them working with me to make it possible. I appreciate you both so much!

And a huge thank you to everyone who has read both Fateful Secrets and Treacherous Truths. All the amazing messages and comments I receive make me want to keep writing. You are all the reason I write as often as I can to share my stories. Thank you so much for taking a chance on my books!